THE
CONSCIOUSNESS
PLAGUE

TOR BOOKS BY PAUL LEVINSON

The Silk Code
Borrowed Tides
The Consciousness Plague

TOR®

A TOM DOHERTY ASSOCIATES BOOK

NEW YORK

THE
CONSCIOUSNESS
PLAGUE

PAUL
LEVINSON

THE CONSCIOUSNESS PLAGUE

Edited by David G. Hartwell

A Tor Book
Published by Tom Doherty Associates, LLC
175 Fifth Avenue
New York, NY 10010

Tor® is a registered trademark of
Tom Doherty Associates, LLC.

ISBN 0-765-30098-2

Printed in the United States of America

TO NEW YORK CITY,

NOW AND FOREVER

ACKNOWLEDGMENTS

Thanks to my editor, David G. Hartwell, for his deft editing; my agent, Christopher Lotts of the Ralph Vicinanza Agency, for his savvy selling; Dr. Stanley Schmidt, editor of *Analog*, where Phil D'Amato (this novel's protagonist) first appeared in a series of novelettes in the 1990s; my wife, Tina, and our children, Simon and Molly, for their wonderful first readings of this manuscript; and the many readers of *The Silk Code*, my first Phil D'Amato novel, who said they wanted more. . . .

THE CONSCIOUSNESS PLAGUE

ONE

"Phil! Good to see you!"

Jack Dugan, one of the brass I usually worked with—recently promoted to the commissioner's right-hand man down at One Police Plaza—extended his hand. He pulled it back, to contain a wracking cough.

"You look terrible, Jack. What are you taking for that?"

"Nothing." He coughed again, then extended his hand again.

I took it and made a mental note to wash my hands as soon as I left the meeting.

"I guess I should get some antibiotics for this," Jack continued. "But I hate to use the stuff—they say so much of it is around that bacteria are building up resistance."

I sat down in the available chair across from his desk. It was cherrywood—big, battered around the edges, unevenly lacquered. Its rosy shine mirrored Jack's rheumy eyes. "Never knew you were so tuned in to public health," I said to him.

He gave me a pained smile. "Antibiotics give me the runs. I'd rather have the cough." He cleared his throat like a bulldozer.

"Yeah, well, antibiotics are like dumb cops, aren't they," I said. "They come on the scene and club everyone over the head—the good-guy germs in your system that help you digest your food, as well as the bad guys that make you sick."

He laughed, then coughed. His eyes teared. Finally he took

a deep breath, and let it out slowly. "Let me tell you why I asked you down here."

I nodded encouragement.

"You know, you and I have had some differences over the years about your penchant for bizarre cases—"

Yeah, tell me about it, I thought. He'd removed me from cases at least half a dozen times.

"—and, even though I've been a sceptic, I was talking to the commissioner the other day, and he thinks that there's no such thing as being over-prepared these days. He'd like you to head up a special strange-cases readiness task force—you know, just to be there, with some possible plans in the waiting, if something really wacky crops up." He bulldozed his throat again, then went into a coughing spasm. He pulled a bottle of Poland Spring water out of his desk and guzzled half of it down. "So, what do you think?" he finally managed to say.

JENNA SIPPED A glass of plum wine and smiled at me that evening. "I know, you hate committees," she said.

I leaned back on the sofa in our living room. "I've always accomplished more as a lone wolf," I replied. "I've seen loads of these task forces come and go. Usually all they do is mark time and eat up energy."

"But you told Dugan you'd think about it," Jenna said.

"Yeah. I suppose it could be good to finally have some people working under me. And some resources. . . . That would be an improvement on having to always go the Department on bended knee."

"You think there's some threat we don't know about that makes them want to do this right now?" Jenna asked. She patted her denim jeans.

I scowled. "They wouldn't recognize something bizarre if it smiled in their faces—they'd say it was a hoax, and do their best to bury the evidence."

Jenna coughed. "Well, this damned cold or pseudo-flu or whatever it is certainly seems to be getting out of hand. My sister told me everyone in San Francisco is out sick with it."

"Let's hope she didn't give it to you over the phone." I reached over and refilled her glass.

I CALLED DUGAN two days later to accept the offer.

"He's home sick with that bug," his secretary, Sheila, told me. "Both he *and* the commissioner," she added. "Got them both. Looks like the Department will be run by the secretaries for the next few days!" She chuckled.

"No different than usual," I responded in kind.

Now she laughed out loud. "Shhh, Dr. D'Amato. Don't you give away our secret, now!"

"It's safe with me, don't worry."

I WAS DOWN in Chinatown a few days later on a boring case. But it wasn't a total loss—I loved the crush of people and textures and fruit stands. I used the opportunity to replenish my supply of green tea and persimmons.

"Anything more?" the woman at the stand inquired, in a lilting voice. She was hardly more than a girl, with a very sweet face.

I shook my head no, and gave her a twenty.

She gave me two paper bags, my change, and started coughing her head off.

That reminded me to put in another call to Dugan.

"Good timing," Sheila's voice crackled through my cell phone. "He came back, fit as a fiddle, just this morning."

The sun was close to setting on this crisp March afternoon, and I was finished with my business in Chinatown, so I decided to hail a cab and go over to Dugan's office. It could be useful for me to see the expression on his face when I accepted his offer— see if there was any true pleasure there.

The traffic was worse than usual. I counted two water mains broken, and three potholes the size of basketballs.

Sheila was gone when I finally arrived. But Jack was still in his office.

"So, I see you're feeling better," I said, and took Jack's extended hand.

"I feel like a million bucks now," Jack said. "How you'd know . . . Oh, I guess Sheila told you I was sick?"

"Right—"

"I tell ya, this was a nasty one. I tried to fight it on my own as best I could—I hate taking antibiotics and those new flu medications—but it got to the point where I was up all night coughing. The commissioner was pretty sick, too—he picked it up from me, I picked it up from him, who knows?—but his doctor told him about some new antibiotic or something, ninety-five percent guaranteed not to upset the stomach. That stuff gives me the runs, you know—"

"Yeah—"

"So anyway." Dugan gestured to the available chair. "Have a seat, Phil. What brings you to this exalted office?"

"Well, I've decided to accept your offer," I replied.

"My offer?" Dugan looked puzzled.

"Yeah, you know, what you told me last week, about the task force."

Dugan looked at me as if I were putting him on, or confusing him with someone else. "I haven't the vaguest idea what you're talking about."

I HAD LUNCH the following week with a friend who was up from the Centers for Disease Control in Atlanta. "The thing is, I think Dugan was completely sincere about not remembering our conversation," I said, as I sipped the last of my tea.

I had told Andy Weinberg what had happened in Dugan's office. Andy was in New York for a conference about the flu or whatever it was that was making everybody cough. Jenna had it full-throttle now. I was beginning to feel a tickle in my own throat—but, who knows, maybe that was just the power of suggestion.

"You sure?" Andy responded. "You've been telling me for years how the Department supports you one day, acts like they have no faith in you the next—you sure this isn't just more of the same? Hell, I've been telling *you* for years that a forensic detective with your verve would be much happier down in Atlanta, haven't I?"

"Yeah, but I like New York, even this cold weather in March."

Andy shook his head in resignation. "Well, at least you seem to be holding your own against this new bug. Better than I can say—had me sick as a dog last month."

"Any chance it could cause some kind of memory loss?"

"Nah, not very likely," Andy answered. "It's some kind of flu—definitely nothing worse. We haven't quite figured out the exact strain. It's popping up all across the country—which means it's almost certainly a natural occurrence, not a biowarfare hit, thank God. But it can open the gate to bronchitis and pneumonia, like any flu—that's what we're concerned about. Of course, antibiotics can take care of the lung and bronchial infections—if they're bacterial, and the drugs are taken in time. But no, I've never heard of any flu-induced amnesia."

"Strange things, those flu bugs," I mused. "Killed millions in 1917, with no antibiotics for the complications. These days when you get it, you just *feel* like you're going to die. And not everybody gets it. Some people get it every year, some get it every two or three or four years, and some hardly ever at all. With no rhyme or reason to the pattern."

"Tell me about it," Andy said. "Even the worst epidemics knock out ten to twenty percent of the population at most. Very destructive to business and social life, obviously—and potentially deadly to old people, anyone with a compromised immune system—but still, how come the other eighty percent get a free pass? And meanwhile, the new meds are apparently effective in stopping or diminishing the flu for eighty to ninety percent of the cases treated. Damn it, I was in that noneffective percentage—I took the inhalant less than a day after I first felt the fever, right in the prescribed time range, and I was still out of commission for a good ten days."

"It didn't do much for Jenna, either," I said. "She took the pill, made her sick to her stomach, but here it is almost a week later and she's still laid up and coughing." I looked at my watch. "I better get home now and feed her a little chicken soup." I signaled our waiter for the check.

Andy looked at me with a twinkle in his eye. "Jenna? Who's she?"

I looked at him.

"Funny," I said. "But something strange did happen to Dugan's memory. I could see in his face that it was more than just run-of-the-mill forgetfulness."

JENNA WAS FEELING better by the end of the week. At first her cough had gotten worse. Her doc finally prescribed an antibiotic as a precaution, and, lo and behold, not only did she not contract bronchitis or pneumonia, but her cough had mostly subsided now, too. But if the cough was caused by the flu, and the flu by a virus, then the antibiotic shouldn't have had any effect—antibiotics snuffed bacteria, not viruses. Well, those kinds of things seemed to happen all the time. Maybe it was just coincidence—maybe the cough would have gone away anyway, regardless of the antibiotic. Or maybe it would have gone if all she had taken was a sugar pill. . . .

"You up for something a little more adventurous for dinner tonight?" I asked. I didn't have the heart to offer her another round of boiled chicken, even though my technique came straight from my late grandmother, the best cook in history.

Jenna's eyes lit up and she patted her stomach. "Absolutely! This Omnin was as good as advertised." She pointed to the sheet that had contained her antibiotic pills. One a day for five days; under five percent of patients report any stomach disorders, the indications form advised.

"Should we try that place in Riverdale?" she asked.

"Buena Vista?"

She nodded.

"You sure you can handle Italian?"

She nodded again.

The food at Buena Vista's was delicious. I had a mouthwatering concoction of clams, calamari, shrimp, and mussels over linguine, and Jenna had a marvelous *penne alla vodka.* Our dry wine hit the spot, too.

We walked slowly back to our car after dinner, and drove back to Manhattan with the windows rolled down. Spring had finally arrived in New York City, with evening temperatures in the low sixties.

"Let's take advantage of this heat wave and walk by the river," Jenna said.

We parked near West Ninety-sixth Street, and walked down to the Hudson. Hyacinths were already in bloom, purple and white in the moonlight, and their perfume was intoxicating. I kissed Jenna, with the waves of the river lapping against the shore as accompaniment. I couldn't recall the last time I'd kissed her like this in public.

"Let's go home," she whispered in my ear.

We were back in our bedroom in our brownstone on East Eighty-fifth Street in fifteen minutes. Jenna began unbuttoning my shirt, and I her blouse.

"You sure you're up for this?" I asked.

She responded by unbuttoning more. . . .

AFTERWARD, SHE LAY in my arms, eyes closed but not sleeping.

I kissed her gently, then said, "Let's get married—have some kids." We'd been living together for three years. It was time.

She opened her eyes, flecks of green on violet. "You sure you're up for this?" she asked, and smiled.

JENNA WAS SOUND asleep the next morning. I slipped out of bed, showered, dressed, and ate breakfast as quietly as I could. I poked my head back in the bedroom and considered waking her, but she looked so peaceful asleep.

I caught the clanking subway down to work. I realized that my throat had progressed from a tickle to an ache, but otherwise I felt great. I popped in a zinc lozenge, and hoped for the best.

Marriage is no small thing. Neither of us had been married before. I'd come close a few times but . . . no one had ever been like Jenna.

I had trouble concentrating at work. Looking at dead bodies, in pictures or the flesh, was never my favorite part of the job. But today they seemed especially out of synch with my mood. *You're a forensic detective,* some little voice inside my head chided. *Who cares about your mood? Live with it.*

I turned back to the pictures. Blonde, mid-twenties, strangled, stripped naked, found dead near Riverside Drive two days ago. Jeez, just a couple of blocks from where Jenna and I had been last night. Ed Monti, the new medical examiner, wanted me down in his office for a noontime meeting about this today.

I put on my coat and headed out. I tried Jenna on the cell phone. She had no reason to go across town to the Hudson today, as far as I knew, but I believed in being careful. No answer on the phone. Hmm . . . She was probably still sleeping. She'd likely have called to say hello before going out today.

The blonde was stretched out on the table in Ed's examining room. "You know, there's some tribe in Africa, I forget which, which has the same basic word for sleep and death," he said. "And they distinguish between the two by saying just 'sleep' for 'sleep,' and 'really really asleep' for 'death.' " Ed liked to wax philosophical. "But when you look at someone like this"—her name was Jillian Murphy—"there's really no similarity at all, is there?"

I'd had the same thought many times myself. I thought of Jenna sound asleep in bed this morning. . . .

Ed gave me the details of the Murphy case over lunch in his office. I left to tape a panel on *Crime in the New Millennium* over at Fox News on Sixth Avenue.

I finally got through to Jenna around four P.M.

"Hey," I said, grinning from ear to ear. "So how are you doing today?"

"I think I'm feeling better," she said. "But I'm maxed out on chicken soup. Should we take a chance and eat out tonight? I'd love some Italian—I feel like I've been cooped up inside for weeks."

"Well, sure. . . ."

I STARED AT my cell phone for a long time after we got off.

I knew Jenna wasn't kidding. Could she really have forgotten what had happened last night? I found it hard to believe.

I thought about taking her again to Buena Vista, to see if that might jog her memory. But on the chance that, who knows, maybe something she'd eaten there had triggered some kind of allergic amnesic reaction, I took her instead to Cafe Sambuca's on Seventy-second Street.

We lingered over veal scaloppine and salad. "I think I remember waking up yesterday, but I'm not completely sure it was yesterday," Jenna said, taking another shot at the issue we'd been discussing all evening. "I remember coughing like a lunatic, but I'd been doing that all week."

"Your cough was much better yesterday," I said, "almost gone. No way I'd say you were constantly coughing then."

"So you're saying, what?" Jenna's voice was hoarse. "I've lost a day out of my life—the very day that you said let's get married?"

"Could be a little more than a day," I replied. "The last thing we've established you remembering is the initial report on the eleven o'clock news about the Riverside Drive strangling, the day before yesterday. I was in the shower then, I didn't hear it, and it wasn't my case yet, so we wouldn't have talked about it afterward. You sure you remember that report—"

"Positive," Jenna said.

"So that's our current baseline for your last memory before the blackout," I said.

She shook her head slowly, still not completely accepting that a day's worth of memories—hers of yesterday—had apparently vanished. She finally managed a weak smile. "So how did I respond to your proposal?"

I smiled back.

"You still want to marry someone who shares this infuriating characteristic with Jack Dugan?" she asked.

"Well, I'm glad that you at least remember that."

JOKE ABOUT IT all you want—losing a day's recollection is no laughing matter. Something similar presumably had happened to Dugan.

"Scattered reports are beginning to come in," Andy told me on the phone from Atlanta the next morning, "but it's hard to track at this point. People are home sick, sleeping off a flu— they might not even realize they forgot a couple of hours when they were awake."

"Unless something important to that person happened in that time," I said.

"That's right," Andy said.

"Which has happened to me, now, twice," I said.

Andy sighed. "I hear you. But we can't rush this. Look, let's say there's nothing really going on here—"

"I think there is."

"Okay, let's say I agree with you," Andy said. "But what if we're wrong—what if there really is no memory loss—and we ask a randomly selected sample of physicians around the country to ask patients they've treated if they've suffered a memory loss? You know how that works—we're bound to get a few patients saying yes, just because of the halo effect."

"A percentage of subjects are always inclined to say whatever they perceive their questioner as wanting them to answer, if the questioner is considered an authority. Yes, I know that."

"So that's one problem," Andy said.

"Well, your survey should focus on patients who've been treated for this damn cough, anyway." I cleared my throat. It didn't help. "I bet you'll find that a lot more of them report memory gaps than whatever statistic usually results from the halo effect."

"That's what we're going to do," Andy said. "But until we're also able to get responses from a control group—if we can find a part of the country that was less wracked by the cough—we're not going to know much. That's another problem."

I frowned. Then cleared my throat again.

"We'll get to the bottom of this," Andy said. "But it's going to take a while. In the meantime, let me know about any other clear-cut cases of memory loss that you—"

My other phone line rang. I asked Andy to hold on.

It was Ed Monti. "Sorry to spring this on you last minute," he said. "But I was wondering if you had time to come down to the ADA's office right now for a meeting. It's about the Riverside case."

I WORK FOR the police department, not the medical examiner, so technically Ed Monti couldn't direct me to do anything. But I'd found over the years that it behooved me to be on the ME's good side.

I was in Elaine Rubin's small office in thirty minutes. She was assistant DA for the Riverside murder case. Ed was there, as were Claudia Gonzales—the foot cop who had been first on the crime scene—and Ron Greave, her partner. No one was smiling.

"Thanks for rushing down here, Phil," Elaine said. She was in her mid-thirties, short-cropped black hair, business suit, and a severe, angular face that Jack Dugan once described as a tomahawk. No nonsense, all business.

"Sure," I said, and tried to break the tension with a friendly air. I took the one empty chair.

"We're interviewing everyone who's had anything to do with the Riverside case, Phil. Could you tell us everything you know about it?" Elaine asked.

"Well, it's not really any more than I knew when I was called in on it—"

"That's okay. Please tell us what you know anyway. If it's okay with you, we'll record this," Elaine said.

I caught Claudia's eye for a second. She avoided my gaze. Greave was staring ahead, impassively. I looked at Ed. He nodded encouragement.

I shrugged. "No problem." I told her what I knew about Jillian Murphy, the victim. She was a Columbia University graduate student, going for her Ph.D. in English literature. She had been found naked, strangled to death, in the thread of park on Riverside Drive and 103rd Street, by a couple walking their dogs early in the morning. No sign of rape or foul play. There were rumors, so far unconfirmed, that she had had an intense relationship with a woman, also a graduate student at Columbia, about a year ago. The sexuality implied in her being stripped naked, combined with the lack of rape, and her rumored relationship, had led some people in the Department to speculate that maybe this was a murder arising out of a lesbian lovers' quarrel. "I'm sorry I haven't been able to do more on this," I concluded, "but I've been getting increasingly concerned about something else that—"

"That's okay." Elaine waved off my explanation. "No need to apologize. What you just told us is extremely helpful."

"There's been some inconsistency in the police reports about this case," Ed offered. "And we're just trying to get all accounts down on tape, so Elaine can build her case—so she can *have* a case—when an arrest is made—"

"I'm not being inconsistent," Claudia spoke up, agitated, aggravated. "I just don't *remember!*"

She suddenly had my complete attention.

"Officer Gonzales has no recollection now of first seeing the body," Elaine explained. "The couple who discovered the body went shouting for help, running with their dogs from Riverside Drive to Broadway. Gonzales was on her way to work, heard the commotion, and went with the couple to investigate. She arrived on the scene alone, without her partner. Her initial report gives very specific details on the state and position of the body—these could be crucial in our case—"

"I'm a good cop!" Claudia insisted.

Elaine looked at her.

"How the hell could I just forget a whole morning like that? I don't get it," Claudia said.

Her partner Greave reached from his seat and put a comforting hand on her shoulder. "With the stress of this job, it's not surprising," he said.

I opened my mouth to give a better explanation, but succumbed to a spasm of hacking coughs.

T W O

I dragged myself two evenings later to a lecture at Fordham University's Lincoln Center campus, a few blocks west of bustling Columbus Circle and Central Park. I was tired, coughing, on the edge of a fever. But the weather was kind, and this was a lecture I didn't want to miss.

Professor Robert McNair was a cognitive anthropologist. He studied the importance of thinking in the evolution of our species. His lecture tonight was on the significance of memory in human culture.

I looked around the audience—about a hundred students and maybe a dozen faculty. I saw no sign of Claudia. Perhaps she had forgotten that she had told me about this lecture, just this afternoon? Not likely. Claudia, Jenna, Dugan, and the handful of others I had learned had lost a piece of their memories had no trouble remembering from then on, once they had recovered. Still . . .

McNair took the stage. He was an impressive-looking man, in his late forties or early fifties, of mixed African-American and European ancestry. Appropriately, he spoke without notes. He had no paper to read. "I used to go through the pretense of carrying a batch of blank sheets up the podium," McNair began, "so the audience would feel I had prepared for the lecture. I hope you'll feel I prepared for this lecture even though it comes to you entirely from my mouth and my brain."

The audience chuckled. I sat in an aisle seat—always a good bet if you had a cough that might require a rapid exit. To my left was a priest, who looked to be in his early thirties. I didn't take this as a portent that I might die of the cough. Fordham was the leading Jesuit university in the United States.

"Memory makes the difference between humans and other organisms," McNair said. His voice was smooth and deep, like oatmeal. "As far as we know, we can look further into our past than any other species—and therefore further into our future. Most of our lives take place not in the immediate present, but the immediate past and the immediate future—we define ourselves based on where we've been and where we expect to be going. . . ."

I felt a cough coming on, and struggled to suppress it. I mostly won—it came out as a stifled thunderclap in my throat. I reached for my bottle of water, and guzzled.

". . . If memory makes us human, recorded memory makes us civilized," McNair continued. "The burning of the ancient library at Alexandria—which reputedly had a copy of every book ever written at that time—was a greater blow to human civilization than the sacking of Rome. Fortunately, later regimes in the Church and in Islam did what they could to preserve some of the ancient information. . . ."

Some in the audience were taking notes. I wondered what it would feel like to lose your memory of an evening like this, then come upon notes you had taken of this lecture. What would it feel like to read, in your own hand, notes you had no recollection of writing? Surely if people were suffering bouts of memory loss around the country, at least a few might have been taking notes in the affected time period? Then again, some of the people in this audience were taking notes on their laptops. Coming upon a file you had no recollection of writing would likely not be quite as disconcerting—it could be explained as some kind of glitch in a download, with an incorrect date-stamp, or whatever. . . .

". . . Poetry was likely initially invented as a memory-aid," McNair was saying. "Rhymes are Velcro of the mind. According to McLuhan, poetry became appreciated as an art form only after writing made oral memory unnecessary—the *Iliad* and the *Odyssey* shift in their roles from textbook histories to epic entertainment. Not everyone was happy about this in the ancient world. In the *Phaedrus*, Socrates worries that the written word will cause everyone's memory to atrophy. Fortunately—or unfortunately—for him, his pupil Plato troubled to write this wrong prediction down. . . ."

This guy was good.

Ah, there she was! I finally caught sight of Claudia in a quarter-profile of red-brown hair, in a row near the front and off to the side. She was seated next to a woman with a light green scarf. That would be Amy Berman, Claudia's friend and a graduate student here. She had told Claudia about McNair. . . .

THE THREE OF us waited for him after the lecture—Amy had taken a course with McNair at UCLA last year. "Shall we repair to O'Neal's for suitable libation?" McNair asked after the introductions were complete. I like the use of "repair" in that way.

"Yeah," I said, and we all repaired.

Alas, my cough seemed beyond repair this night, but I did my best to keep it in check with alternate sips of wine and water.

"So, Amy tells me you recently had a memory loss," McNair said to Claudia.

She nodded, and gave him the details. I offered my bit.

"Yes, I can see how that sort of thing could be distressing, especially to a police officer," he said, sympathetically. "But I never heard of a cough or a flu causing any sort of amnesia. It probably was psychological—I don't mean to make light of it,

I'm sure it was real to you—but that would be my guess, speaking as anthropologist and not a physician, of course."

"Is there any connection you can think of, in history, between illness and memory?" I pressed.

"Well, plagues, of course, can jeopardize institutional memory, if they're savage enough," McNair replied. "The Black Death killed as much as three-quarters of the population in some parts of the world in the fourteenth century—a century before the printing press. Must have wiped out at least some unrecorded advances in knowledge." He sipped his cognac.

"But that would be knowledge lost through the death of individuals," I said. "Like the solution Fermat claimed he had, but never published. Those things are fascinating to think about. But I'm really wondering, instead, about any epidemics on record that seemed to take away an evening, an hour, from those afflicted. Because—" I coughed several times, harshly, as if to underscore my question. "Excuse me." I took some water. "Because I'm concerned that might be happening now."

McNair regarded me. "Do you have any evidence of this? Beyond anecdotal testimony like Claudia's and your friend's? I'm not belittling what they experienced, but surely as a scientist you—"

"Of course—" I coughed again. "Of course you're right to want something more substantial. But so far it's all sub-rosa. Odd instances." I took some wine. "I have a friend in Atlanta who's looking into it."

"My daughter had an odd experience like that," Amy said. "She got an A on an anthropology test, and swore she had no memory of taking it."

"Really? You look too young to have a daughter taking an anthropology course!" I blurted out.

"Thank you." Amy smiled. "I'm thirty-four. Mindy is thirteen, and she's in a special gifted program."

"Well, I'm glad to see the program offers courses in anthropology!" McNair said, beaming.

"Did Mindy have the flu or a cough before that incident?" I asked, and of course started coughing again.

"Hard to say," Amy replied. "The kids have been in and out of the doctor's office ever since that heat wave in January. . . ."

I realized that I was feeling more feverish myself. I pushed back my chair and made to leave. The place smelled of fine spirits, but I needed fresh air. "I better get back home," I said. "To bed."

McNair cleared this throat, and nodded in commiseration. "I think I've got a little itch in here, too," he said.

We exchanged cards.

"Good to meet you—wonderful lecture," I said to him. "You too," I said to Amy. "Thanks for arranging this," I said to Claudia, and walked out of O'Neal's, coughing and eyes tearing. I took a few breaths and hailed a cab.

Jenna was on the phone when I got home. I looked at myself in the hall mirror—horrible.

I picked up a tape recorder sitting on a shelf, and carried it into our bedroom. I had heard a lot of interesting things tonight—ideas, theories, possibilities. I didn't want to forget. I rasped what I could remember into the tape recorder. Ridiculous way to live.

I AWOKE IN a sweat the next morning, with Jenna's cool hand upon my brow.

"You've got it full-blown," she said. "Here's some ginger ale, and I'm taking you to the doctor."

"Too bad they don't make house calls anymore." I lifted my head from my clammy, clingy pillow.

"Well, at least your long-term memory's intact," Jenna said. "Uncle Eli told me they haven't been doing that since the seventies."

"Marcus Welby was the last one," I said.

"Who?"

"TV doctor from the 1970s," I said. I swallowed a little ginger ale. It felt like broken glass going down—sad commentary on the state of my throat.

Jenna took me in a taxi to Dr. Steinbuck's, on East Seventy-eighth.

"Good thing the insurance is paying for this," I groused, and strove, in vain, to find a comfortable spot on the paisley-upholstered couch in the waiting room. "He'll charge a small fortune to say, 'Well, it's probably the flu, can't tell for sure, doesn't matter anyway, and here's a prescription for Omnin just to make sure pneumonia doesn't set in.' " I coughed, then shivered.

Jenna rubbed my shoulder.

"Dr. D'Amato?" Nan, the receptionist, called out after what felt like a month and a half. I often wondered how many patients had died in this, and other, waiting rooms, waiting to be seen. Well, maybe I didn't wonder about that too often, but the thought had occurred to me. At least some hapless schmuck had to have died that way. I could just see being called in as an investigator on that case. . . .

I took off my clothes, as told, and put on that pathetic piece of wrapping paper they give you in doctors' offices. I coughed and shivered some more.

Steinbuck finally came in, with a smile. "Phil, haven't seen you in a while. How are you doing?"

"Not good. Otherwise I wouldn't be here," I replied, and smiled back.

"Well, let's see what's going on," Steinbuck said, and gave me the full exam—cold part of the stethoscope on my chest, tapping my back, looking in my ears and eyes, the whole enchilada. "Well," he said at last, "it's probably the flu that's going around. We can't tell for sure, but it doesn't really matter. The important thing is that your lungs seem clear and your breathing's okay—means pneumonia hasn't set in. That's what we want to avoid."

I nodded.

"No point playing around with this, though," he continued. "You hear about our new secret-weapon antibiotic, Omnin? We'll put you right on that."

I nodded again. "Have you heard of any memory loss associated with this flu?"

Steinbuck looked up from his prescription pad. "No. Why? Have you been having any problems with your memory?"

I shook my head no. "So far, so good. And just to make sure, I took the trouble of reciting yesterday's recollections into a tape recorder before I went to sleep, and it jibed completely with what I remembered this morning."

He regarded me. "Good," he finally said. "But why were you worried about losing your memory in the first place?"

I told him about Jenna and Dugan and Claudia.

"Hmmm," Steinbeck mused. "Memory loss is usually brought on by undue stress, not enough sleep, too much work—that kind of thing. . . . Let me know if anything else develops, especially with Jenna." He turned to his pad, and produced his prescription with a flourish. "Omnin, once a day for five days, two doses to start. That should do it for any serious flu complications."

I glanced at the prescription, thanked him, and reached for my clothes—

"Just a second," I said. Steinbuck was half out the door.

"Yes?" He stuck his head back in.

"You dated this the twenty-sixth," I said, and pointed to the prescription. "Wasn't that yesterday?"

He looked a little confused, and shook his head. "No . . . Isn't today the twenty-sixth?"

"YORK AND EAST Eighty-fifth," Jenna told the cabbie, after she'd bundled me in and squeezed in herself. "We'll get you home first, then I'll go out and get your prescription," she said to me.

"He recovered pretty well," I said. Jenna and I had been talking about Steinbuck since we'd walked out of his office. "But I caught his expression when I first told him he had the wrong date—he definitely lost a day of memory." I coughed. It hurt.

"Come on," she said skeptically. "People make mistakes like that all the time. M.D.s are notorious for their absentmindedness, just like professors."

"This is something more," I insisted. "It's clearer to me than it is to you because you were one of its victims. I've had the pleasure of observing it all, in more than one person."

Jenna considered. "Well, I admit that the more days that go by, the less I'm clear about what exactly I forgot. . . . It's hard to distinguish between what I'm actually remembering and not remembering now, and what you say I should be remembering. . . ."

"Entirely natural," I said.

"Like waking up in the morning thinking you had a phone call in the middle of the night, but not being certain if you actually had that call, or you dreamt it," Jenna mused.

"My test for that is: Does the memory seem more or less firm as the day progresses? If it gets fuzzier, then likely it was a dream," I said.

Jenna nodded. "That's why I don't see how you're going to get to the bottom of this. We're dealing with very flimsy stuff here—memories. Let's say there *is* something going on—little lapses of recollection—and it happens all the time. How could you keep tabs on that? No one would really be aware of it."

"Some of the lapses haven't been so little—" I started coughing again. More aggravating than the pain was the sheer damned monotony of just about everything I uttered being punctuated by a cough.

Jenna took my hand. "The antibiotic should help that. I wish you weren't so stubborn about taking Robitussin."

"I don't like palliative medicine—I like keeping track of the symptoms. . . . Anyway, Steinbuck says he's been fine the last few weeks—he assured me he hasn't had this cough. If he's telling the truth, that means that something else is the cause of the memory loss." Our cab turned a corner sharply and I grimaced. Every muscle in my body ached.

"Let's just concentrate now on getting you better," Jenna said.

I FELT WORSE the next morning—head throbbing, throat burning—and I was sweating and shivering. And coughing.

"How about some Tylenol to bring down the fever—" Jenna began.

"No, it's not that high. I've had a lot worse than one-oh-one."

"But why suffer?"

I began to answer, but my throat hurt too much to keep talking.

"Okay, okay, I know—you want to see how this plays out, with a minimum of medication," Jenna answered for me.

I nodded, and put my head back on the pillow.

"The antibiotics should kick in later today or tomorrow," she said. "I'll console myself with that."

I DRIFTED IN and out of sleep. I heard some music playing out-side . . . some old rock 'n' roll, maybe earlier. . . . "I'm Gonna Sit Right Down and Write Myself a Letter" . . .

I started thinking about Socrates . . . he didn't like writ-ing, McNair had said. . . . Who invented writing? Maybe the ancient Phoenicians . . . No, they invented the alphabet. . . . There were hieroglyphics before the alphabet, but McNair said

Socrates didn't like the alphabet. . . . Why did the Phoenicians invent it?

I was soaked in sweat. . . . Maybe Jenna was right about the Tylenol. . . . I fell back asleep. . . .

The phone rang the next morning . . . or maybe I was dreaming. . . . McNair was talking again . . . about Lindisfarne, forgetfulness, Darius Morton, the alphabet, the sea peoples, the Phoenicians, Julian Jaynes, Marshall McLuhan . . . I was asking questions. . . . Maybe I should write this stuff down. But I fell back asleep . . . or maybe I was just dreaming that I fell back asleep. . . . Does dreaming of sleeping give you double the rest? I needed all I could get. . . .

I AWOKE AGAIN. It looked like late morning. "I feel a lot better," I called out to Jenna.

She came into the bedroom and smiled at me. "Right on schedule. Want some breakfast? It's past noon."

I nodded.

"Should I get you the phone for McNair? You said you had a few more questions for him, and I should remind you to call him back as soon as you felt up to it."

I put my arms through my polo shirt and looked at her. It felt good to move without a million nerves objecting, but—

"You don't remember McNair?" she asked, concerned.

"I remember him," I said. "I remember him. I just don't remember asking you to remind me to call him back. When did I do that?"

"Yesterday," she said. "Yesterday afternoon, after you got off the phone with him. You were still a little feverish, but you seemed to have a good talk with him—do you remember that?"

I shook my head no. "Damn it. I'll call him right now."

I finished dressing, and fished his card out of my wallet. Jenna brought me the phone.

I called the number on his card—looked like his office at UCLA. "Professor McNair's office," a woman answered.

"Hi, Phil D'Amato calling Professor McNair. I believe he and I talked on the phone yesterday afternoon—"

"I was out yesterday with a sick kid," she answered. "And Professor McNair's wife just called—he's laid up with that flu bug. Sounds like he'll be out the rest of the week."

THREE

I was on a plane to L.A. five days later—as soon as McNair was well enough to see me, and I was well enough to fly. The two dates fortunately coincided.

There wasn't much else that was lucky in this mess.

I was a total blank on the conversation that Jenna was sure I had had with McNair.

He said—when I had finally reached him by phone—that he more or less remembered it, but his bout with the flu had left him a bit fuzzy on just about everything he had done the few days before. Not an outright memory loss like Jenna's and Claudia's and mine. Just your garden-variety blurry memory that lots of folks have when they're sick or getting that way. Stuffed heads and watery eyes were never conducive to clear recollections. But given the endangered species that memories seemed to be these days, any loss was notable, especially one which might hold a clue to the cause of the bigger losses.

The plane arrived twenty minutes early, amazingly. I had the cabbie drop me off a flew blocks from McNair's home on Sunset Boulevard, on the edge of the UCLA campus. I used the found time to take in the scenery—around here a walk down the block was like going to the New York Botanical Gardens. I spotted a large, tropical insect feeding on an orange flower. I looked more closely at the vibrating form, suspended in breathtaking air just beyond the petals. It was actually a tiny hummingbird, splendid in blues and greens. I had never seen one before like this in the real world, outside of an aviary. . . .

Even the sign SUNSET BOULEVARD had a magic. Gloria Swanson, Carol Burnett, Harvey Korman, Erich von Stroheim . . . What was that line? *I'm ready for my close-up, Mr. DeMille!*

I knocked on McNair's door.

An attractive blonde, clad in loose canvas shorts and halter top, let me in with a big smile. "Phil D'Amato? I'm Rhonda, Robbie's wife—he's in the sunroom." She looked to be in her late twenties, about twenty years younger than McNair. She led me to the sunroom.

It was sunny indeed, bedecked with palms of varying size and foliage. McNair was reclining in a chair. He made to get up when I entered the room.

"No, please, sit," I said, and gestured for him to stay in the chair. "Thanks for letting me come see you." He didn't look very good—worse than I'd expected. He was still pretty sick.

He coughed and braved a smile. "It seems we have some common interests," he said.

Rhonda pointed me to a wicker chair with pillows. "Can I get you something to drink, Phil?"

"Uh, sure, thanks—orange juice."

"You bet," she said, and left.

I turned to McNair. "So I see you're still struggling with the bug—I can come back tomorrow."

"I think it's finally leveling off—five lousy days," he responded. "I look worse than I feel."

"What are you taking for it?" I asked.

"Not much," he replied. "Just a lot of vitamin C, zinc candy, garlic—I like the natural stuff."

"Nice if it works," I said. At least he didn't seem any worse than I'd been—if anything, a little better.

"So, you got your Department to fly you out here," he

asked, and cleared his throat. "Easier prying funds from police departments than university departments, I'd imagine." He laughed, coughed, and drank from a tall glass of iced tea. Condensation ran down its sides.

"The city doesn't want to get bit in the ass by some mystery epidemic," I said. "The scares we've had the past few years are enough."

McNair nodded, and sipped more tea.

I looked at him. "My problem is I don't quite know where to begin," I said. "Possibly you told me something important in that phone conversation that I can't remember."

McNair returned the gaze.

Rhonda came in with my orange juice. "Here you are, Phil."

"Thanks." I sipped. It was delicious.

She put her arm around McNair and kissed his cheek. They made a striking couple, sun and night.

"I guess I remember most of that conversation," McNair said. "It was mostly about the alphabet."

"Yes?" I encouraged.

Rhonda kissed him again, gave me a smile, and left the room.

"About its history, its origins," McNair continued.

"Why would I think that was important?"

"Ah, that's easy. Because most people think the alphabet was invented by the Phoenicians as a memory aid—a shorthand, slang improvement over hieroglyphics, to keep track of their maritime transactions."

"We're going a little too fast for me here—I don't get what you mean by slang hieroglyphics." I loved the way this guy talked and thought. It was almost poetry. But it was hard to pin down the meaning.

"Oh, sorry," McNair said, and took some more tea. "That's basic to media historians and anthropologists. The Egyptian hieroglyphic system ruled the world of writing then, you see. But it was a difficult system to learn and use—you had to master a separate little picture, or combination of pictures and little strokes, for every word you wished to write."

"Like Chinese writing today?"

"Precisely," McNair replied. "But the alphabet is much faster, slicker, cooler—twenty-six letters that look like nothing in themselves, and therefore you can make them mean anything you want them to. All you have to do is recombine them— like DNA, right? Looks nothing like the organisms it commands proteins into being. That's one of your specialties, isn't it?"

I smiled. "Usually for me it's DNA tagging death, not life."

McNair continued. "Anyway, the smart money says that the Phoenicians cooked it up—invented the alphabet—as a quick way of keeping track of all of their commercial wheelings and dealings."

"Fascinating," I said, though I still couldn't quite see what relevance it had to our current problem of memory loss. "How far did they, ah, wheel and deal? Did they encounter an illness somewhere which weakened their memory, and that's why they invented the alphabet?"

"Good question," McNair replied. "You asked me that on the phone last week. 'I don't know about that,' was my answer. I mean, I don't know if the Phoenicians suffered any plagues. I can look into that. But how far did they roam in their ships, buying and selling and trading? Well, the Mediterranean was their lake. And they traded for tin as far north as England. Some people think they even made it across the Atlantic, to the East Coast."

Rhonda entered again, with an apology. "Sorry to interrupt," she said. She turned to McNair. "Samantha's here with her master's thesis—she said you told her that you wanted to see her for a minute when she got here."

McNair nodded.

Rhonda turned to me. "He always makes a point of *personally* accepting his students' theses," she explained. "Samantha's one of his best students."

McNair started getting up, and I helped him.

"See? I told you I was better than I looked," he said to me, and walked out of the room. He was a bit wobbly but in no danger of falling, with Rhonda holding his arm.

I shook my head in admiration. Always good to meet another stubborn soul.

I looked at the near wall and two bookcases of handsome oak, chock-full of great titles.

I walked over and pulled one out: *The Origin of Consciousness in the Breakdown of the Bicameral Mind* by Julian Jaynes. Where had I heard that name before? The book had a striking cover—the title in black letters on a bright white background. What a title. . . .

"A real eye-opener, isn't it?"

I hadn't heard McNair come back in the room. My head must have been in the book for fifteen minutes.

"Yeah," I agreed.

"So what do you make of his theory that people in Homer's time were not really self-aware—didn't have the same sense of self that all of us now take for granted, as part of our humanity—and writing, the alphabet, somehow changed that?" McNair asked, setting himself carefully back in his chair.

"Pretty far-fetched," I said. "I can buy that at some point in our human past, we didn't have complete consciousness—we were more like, I don't know, chimps or apes. But I'd expect that state of mind—or lack of it—to have been a lot further back than Homer. And I don't see how just the process of reading could have changed that, and made us fully . . . self-aware."

"Jaynes thinks that reading and writing silenced the internal voices—the communication that went from one side of the brain to the other," McNair said. "And the result was our unified consciousness."

"Could writing have been *that* important?"

"Oh, I doubt it," McNair replied. "Not to mention that it's hard to fathom how writing—or the alphabet—could have been invented in the first place by people who lacked our level of self-awareness."

I nodded.

McNair went on. "But assuming that Jaynes might have been right about at least the first part of his theory—though maybe his dating was off—what would *your* favorite candidate be for breaking down the bicameral mind, and making us fully conscious?"

I considered. "Something physical, I don't know—some kind of powerful natural radiation, maybe a new type of food, maybe a virus. . . ."

"A virus," McNair repeated. "So you think illness somehow made us conscious, and now it's making us lose our memory?" He started coughing, then wheezing. Rhonda hurried in from the next room with an inhaler. I helped get it on McNair's face. He seemed OK. Then my cell phone rang.

It was Jenna. "They have a suspect in the Riverside case. There was an attempted assault in the park last night. The victim got away, and Dugan says they just picked someone up on her description. He says it's connected to the strangling. They want you on the red-eye back to New York—tonight."

ED MONTI WAS waiting for me at Kennedy. My mind was still focused on the memory loss, but I'd have to put at least a little of that aside now for the more prosaic puzzles of murder. Multitasking—the spirit of our age.

I shook Ed's hand. "So we can cross off the lesbian-lover angle now?" I asked.

"The lover, but maybe not the lesbian," Ed replied.

"The suspect's a woman?"

Ed nodded. "And the victim got a point-blank look at her."

He filled me in on the details in a cab back to One Police Plaza in Manhattan. Carol Michosky lived on West End Avenue, a block from Riverside Drive and the park and the scene of the Murphy murder. Michosky was twenty-three, blonde, and looked a lot like Murphy. Michosky was walking to her apartment building around seven P.M. last night, arms full with two packages of groceries she had just purchased on Broadway, a block over from West End, to the east. She had a feeling that someone was following her. We've found that often those feelings come from the victim's actually having caught a glimpse of the assailant. Michosky said that as she entered the courtyard of her building, the feeling that she was being followed grew stronger, overwhelming. She wheeled around and confronted a woman—who apologized for startling Michosky, and asked her how to get to a nearby theater. Relieved, Michosky gave the woman directions, turned to go into her building—then suddenly felt some rough garment around her neck, cutting off her air supply. She dropped her packages, struggled. She began to get dizzy, and sank to the ground. "She was sure she was about to die," Ed said. But with her vision hazy, she spotted a package of Reynold's aluminum wrap on the ground. She grabbed it, and jabbed it into what she thought was her attacker's midriff. The assailant cried out and released her. Michosky turned around and the assailant was gone.

"Is Michosky one hundred percent certain that the woman who startled her with the question about the theater was her assailant?" I asked.

"She says yes—she got a quick look at her would-be strangler in the struggle," Ed replied. "But that's obviously a weak link. She's certain that her assailant—the voice that cried out after the tinfoil jab—was a woman. And Michosky gave a detailed description of the woman who startled her—Michosky is an evening art student at the Fashion Institute of Technology—did I tell you that?—so she presumably has a pretty good eye for visual detail. A patrol car spotted a woman who fit the description, about two hours later. They took her in for questioning. She has no alibi. She admits that she was in the area, was thinking of going to a movie there, and may have asked one or two people for directions."

"She didn't actually go to any movie?" I asked. "She—"

Ed rapped on the glass partition to get the cabbie's attention. "Do you think that next time we pull up to an intersection with a yellow light, you could try going through it rather than stopping? We're in a little bit of a hurry here."

"Safety. More important than speed," the cabbie replied, in a Pak or Indian accent.

Ed turned to me, rolled his eyes. "The suspect says no about the movie—the weather was so nice, she decided instead to just keep walking around."

"It was nice here last night?" Couldn't have been as nice as in California, I thought.

"Oh yeah, a real lovely evening for this time of year—almost balmy," Ed said.

"Anyone examine her midriff for abrasions or black-and-blue marks?" I asked.

"Yeah, but she's clean there," Ed replied. "We don't know, of course, how hard Michosky jabbed her."

I nodded. "And whether there are any marks would also depend on what kind clothing she had on—how many layers, how loose-fitting. Though if it was warm, she likely wouldn't have been wearing anything too heavy."

Our cab pulled up to One Police Plaza. "They're bringing Michosky in for a lineup in about half an hour." Ed looked at his watch. "Dugan says you can use the bathroom off his office to freshen up."

"Okay," I said. "This seems more or less cut-and-dried—no worse than the usual complications in seeing if we have a true perp in hand. Why do you think they yanked me back here from California?"

"They were jealous?" Ed asked, with a laugh.

I looked at him.

"All right, here's a better answer: They're a little concerned with this memory business. You're the resident expert on that. They want to make sure it doesn't happen again and mess up this case—assuming that we can see it coming this time and can do something to prevent it."

THE LINEUP WAS ready ninety minutes later. It consisted of five women, in their mid- to late twenties. One was Claudia Gonzales. Three others were also policewomen. The fifth was the suspect—Sharalee Boland, a brunette, also in her late twenties. She had no record.

Dugan walked in, along with DA Tomahawk, and a few of the detectives who were investigating the case.

"Hello, Elaine." I smiled at her and Dugan.

Elaine nodded.

"Thanks for coming back on such short notice," Dugan told me. "The commissioner asked me to take a special interest in this case. No one likes college-girl assaults—they're bad for the city's reputation. We'll talk about what you learned in California later."

"Sure," I said.

"Are we ready to get started?" Elaine asked.

"We're waiting for Boland's attorney," Dugan began, just as a man about forty in a blue Armani suit walked through the door.

"Albert Everett, attorney for the defense," he said with his patented panache. Everett was one of the best defense attorneys in town.

"Good to see that Ms. Boland is so well represented," Elaine said drily. But she forced a smile to Everett.

"Her father is himself an eminent copyright attorney," Everett replied. "We've been friends for years."

"Didn't know that," Elaine said.

"But it hardly matters," Everett continued. "She didn't do it—the worst attorney in the world could get her off."

"Right," Elaine said. "Bring in Ms. Michosky," she said to one of the detectives.

Carol Michosky joined us a minute later. She did look a lot like Jillian Murphy—a disconcerting observation, because the only way I had ever seen Murphy was stretched out dead on Ed's autopsy table.

The detective painstakingly explained the lineup process to Michosky—she should take her time, be absolutely sure, just like they do it on television . . .

The curtain opened on the five women standing on the other side of the one-way–vision partition.

Michosky looked very carefully at the lineup.

"That's her!" she spoke up. "She tried to strangle me!"

At least one detective standing next to me hissed.

The finger on Michosky's outstretched hand was pointed at Claudia Gonzales.

"SHE LIKELY GOT a glimpse of Gonzales in the precinct last night," Elaine said. She, Ed, Dugan, and I were in Dugan's office for a postmortem of the dead-end lineup.

"Gonzales was there part of the evening," Dugan admitted, tiredly. "It's unclear if they actually met." He wiped a spot of something off his cherrywood desk with a tissue.

"All she'd need is a glimpse," I said. "If she was unclear or forgot the actual incident, Gonzales' face would be the only one that looked familiar." And Michosky had indeed become con-fused, now claiming that she remembered less and less of the attack, and couldn't be certain if she was remembering what had actually happened, or what people all around her were talking about.

All too familiar to me. . . .

"But she was crystal-clear last night," Dugan insisted. "What the hell happened, someone got to her?"

"Nah," I said. "This doesn't look to be a mob thing."

"Amnesia of various types can sometimes be brought on by this kind of trauma," Ed offered. "It's textbook, unfortunately."

"You think trauma from the attack caused this, or did the memory thing that you're investigating?" Dugan asked me. "Damn it, I had a feeling something like this was going to happen—that's why I called you back from California."

"I asked her if she'd been sick," I replied. "She says she's been under the weather a little lately, but nothing serious."

"So we catch Boland an hour after the attempted crime, on a pinpoint-accurate description given by the victim," Elaine finally said, having listened with growing impatience to our seminar on memory, "and she goddamn walks." She straightened her plain, beige suit jacket and shook her head.

AN ARTICLE IN the *Wall Street Journal* a few days later—DOCS SELF-MEDICATE WITH ANTIBIOTICS AS A PRECAUTION—got me thinking about the memory problem from a slightly different angle. Unidentified public-health officials quoted in the article worried that M.D.s who used antibiotics to keep themselves from getting sick might be exacerbating the danger of bacteria building up resistance to antibiotics via too much exposure in the population. "It starts for some in medical school," the article explained, but "there are no statistics on how many M.D.s continue to take powerful antibiotics prior to the appearance of any symptoms, as a precaution against falling ill."

I leaned back in my chair, put my feet up on my office desk, and wondered if Steinbuck, my doctor, was one of those who self-medicated. He apparently hadn't had the cough, but I was virtually certain that he'd suffered a memory loss. I could call and ask him, but who knew if he'd tell me the truth?

Okay, put Steinbuck aside, for the moment.

Dugan had had the cough, took medication, had the memory loss. Same with Jenna, Claudia, and me.

But McNair was sick as a dog, and so far had no memory loss. And he abhorred antibiotics.

What about Carol Michosky?

She hadn't been feeling well lately, she'd said. Could she have been a bit of a hypochondriac, and self-medicated with Omnin?

It wasn't too difficult to get a prescription from an obliging doc, or maybe a friend had been prescribed Omnin but didn't take it, or maybe someone in her family was a pharmacist . . . Lots of possible avenues.

I picked up the phone and called her.

"Oh no," she said. "I hate antibiotics—they make me break out in hives. I never take them unless I'm really at death's door with something."

Damn it. I believed her. Why would she lie about something like that?

I hung up, and fiddled with my papers and notes.

It looked like I might have been on to something—Omnin, the cure, not the illness, as somehow being the source of the memory loss.

But Carol had a memory problem, and hadn't taken Omnin. And I certainly had no proof about Steinbuck.

I sighed.

Cross the antibiotic off the list, or at least put a couple of more question marks after it. The people and their behavior and symptoms just didn't seem to add up on that one.

But what did, in this creeping amnesia that was now seriously undermining police work and who-knew-how-many personal relationships?

A lone shaft of late-afternoon sunlight illuminated the particles of dust suspended in the air between the window of my office and my desk. It fell just short of my face.

At this point, I was still mostly in the dark about what was going on.

FOUR

I drove up to Cape Cod on the weekend to see Andy Weinberg, who was at a conference at the Ocean Edge mansion in Brewster, on the bay. The conference was titled *Deadly Plagues in the New Millennium: How Likely?*

I couldn't think of a much more important topic. But I had my mind on slightly smaller things.

The sand was a bit too cold to be comfortable, but the sun was bright on this late-April day. I took my sneakers off anyway and rolled up my jeans and walked barefoot on the beach. Andy wasn't quite as adventurous—he kept his sneakers on. I did take the precaution of tying mine together in a knot and hanging them around my neck, just in case the soles of my feet got numb from the cold.

"The flu is receding with the winter, like it always does," Andy said, looking at the water, which like the winter was also in ebb tide.

"I almost wish it wouldn't," I said, "so we could have more time to study whatever it was that happened the past few months."

"Well, epidemics are like that," Andy said. "They tend to come and go on their own schedules."

"So you'd label the cough and flu as an epidemic this year?" I asked.

Andy shrugged. "It's just a name—all semantics. But the

number of victims—of people missing work—was pretty impressive. We're still not sure if it was one bug, or two, or more."

He stopped by a small patch of bright green sea grass. "Amazingly tolerant of different environments," Andy said, and touched one of the wet blades with his finger. I did the same. It felt slick, and sharp as a razor on the edge—like it could slice through your finger if you weren't careful. "I've been in love with this stuff since I was a kid," Andy continued. "Twice a day it's totally underwater, during high tide. Twice a day it's right out here in the open air, like it is now. And it does fine all the time."

I nodded. "But the patch is pretty small." It was a ragged square, about eight or nine feet long. I didn't see any others on the beach. I also didn't see what this had to do with the cough and the memory loss, but Andy sometimes had a way of approaching important points he wanted to make obliquely, from a seemingly unrelated angle. And this sea grass was beguiling in its quiet audacity, just growing out here, vivid green, in the middle of a half-drenched shore.

"There's a powerful network of roots underneath," Andy said. "Depending upon tidal patterns, storm activity that shifts sands, overall weather conditions, the roots send up more or fewer blades. Some years there's hardly any grass at all. Then the next year the grass comes back four times the area of this. On some parts of the coast it stretches for miles. But the roots are there, under the surface, all the time, unless conditions are so bad in a particular spot that they're totally wiped out. A lot like viruses vis-à-vis their human hosts—always there, always under the surface, some years they come out more than others."

Ah, so here perhaps was the relevance.

"Whatever caused the cough this season has likely been around for years," he went on, "maybe centuries, even millennia. The more we study these things, the more we realize they're nothing new."

"Yeah, but the symptoms are different," I said.

"Are they? That's what you've got to investigate. The CDC simply doesn't have the interest, officially—I think you'll find no government agency will."

"Why not?" I pressed.

"The symptoms are below the radar—they're not important enough, not disruptive enough," Andy responded.

"Hobbling a murder investigation isn't important?" I countered.

"Not when there are people actually dying of other illnesses," Andy said. "Show me a stone-cold murderer who actually got away because of this amnesia business—show me that ten, a hundred times—and then you'll get official national interest in this."

I sighed.

"I'm not saying *I'm* not interested," Andy said. "I am—even though I had the damn thing and haven't lost a second of memory, as far as I know."

"You didn't take Omnin." I had told him about my short-lived antibiotic theory.

"Turns out most people didn't," Andy said. "Actual prescriptions were much lower than initially projected."

"Maybe that's why we don't have more verified cases of memory loss," I said.

Andy laughed, and shook his head. "That's assuming the very point in dispute—that Omnin somehow caused the loss of memory. You know, the FDA put it through all the usual tests before allowing it out on the market. Not that those tests are infallible, but they certainly would have picked up any side effects as serious as amnesia. Anyway, it's not even clear at this point how many actual cases of memory loss we have."

I started to object that statistics and surveys weren't everything—

Andy interrupted. "Phil, I'm with you, personally—I agree that there's something more than a little peculiar going on. I've known you too long to think for a minute that you're just making all of this up. I'm just saying that, at this point, any investigation into what you think is happening will have to be done off the books, at least as far as my involvement in any official capacity is concerned. You've gone that route before."

I nodded. The story of my life.

"All right," Andy said. "So let's get back to your question about symptoms. Your hypothesis is that this memory loss is something new. Okay. That can be tested against history—have there been any times in the past in which any significant number of people reported losing their memories? A yes might be more valuable to us at this point than a no—if memory losses did occur in the past, we can see what else the two times, theirs and ours, have in common."

I took a deep breath of the salty air. "How far back do you want to go?"

WE WALKED ALONG the shore, past a cropping of glistening black stones, freshly uncovered by the still-receding tide. Gulls hovered above, dropping clams and mussels and other shelled creatures they had captured, so they fell and broke open on the rocks. Each shell made a loud *crack!* as it met its fate—like a finger-snapping scorecard of the seagulls' triumph. "That's a pretty old technology right there," I said admiringly, and pointed at the birds. "Human technology is supposed to have begun in equivalent ways—from what I've read—in opportunistic use of materials already present in the environment, like rocks."

Andy nodded. "You always had a yen for history. So I assume you've already done some digging into the history of epidemics and memory loss?"

I told him about McNair. "Not much that I can find—or anyone else seems to know—on that score. But McNair's work seems in some way relevant. What do you know about the Phoenicians?"

Andy opened his hands. "Not much. They thrived around the same time as the ancient Egyptians—or part of that time. They sailed around the Mediterranean. Their home base was where Lebanon is today. Didn't they found a colony in North Africa which later became Carthage?"

"Yeah," I said. "They apparently also invented our alphabet."

"Interesting," Andy said. "Does that have relevance to our problem?"

"Well, McNair looks at writing, the alphabet in particular, as a great memory aid," I replied. A seagull shrieked overhead. "Which of course it is."

"So you're thinking . . . that maybe the Phoenicians invented the alphabet because they were suffering from widespread memory loss?"

"The thought occurred to me, yes," I replied.

"Any proof—documents, whatever, from the time—to support this?" Andy asked.

"None that McNair knows of," I said. "It's all speculation as to why they invented it." We started walking the beach again. My feet were beginning to feel a little cold. "Did the Phoenicians suffer any plagues, epidemics?" I asked.

"I'm not sure about the Phoenicians," Andy replied. "I know the Carthaginians did—in Hannibal's time. I've seen it argued that Hannibal lost the second Punic war to the Romans because his men were too sick to fight—and the Romans were fine, because the battles were fought near their home ground, and they had immunity to whatever it was that got the Carthaginians sick."

"Hmmm . . . intriguing," I said. "I think I've seen that theory, too, now that you mention it. But Hannibal can't be very relevant to the invention of the alphabet—he crossed the Alps a good millennium later."

I DROVE BACK to the city that evening. The Cape had been beautiful. I could feel its pastels draining from my perception, and not just because it was dark outside.

I would have jumped in the bay—I love cold water—but my toes had insisted that it was too cold even for me. I made a mental note to return for a long swim in the summer with Jenna. Mental notes . . . Anything that smacked of memory left a sour taste in my mouth these days.

Too bad I had to leave the Cape right now, with or without the swim. There was no doubt I could learn more from Andy. But my cell phone had informed me about another Riverside attack—and this one was a murder, with no apparent witnesses at all.

I cursed under my breath as I drove towards Providence. The two big aggravations in my life these days—the memory loss and the Riverside assaults—had no deep connection I could fathom. Just two big pieces of bad news, unfolding at the same time. But our investigation of the murders was definitely being hamstrung by the amnesia. And every time something new happened in Riverside Park, a face leered out to taunt me that I hadn't made more progress on the amnesia. My face . . .

It was Dugan's face that was talking to me the next morning—Sunday—for a special briefing in his office. Just him and me. "Everyone else is already up-to-speed on this, so I figured I'd give them the day off," Dugan said. "Officer Gonzales is out of town—her mother had a stroke, in Philadelphia."

I felt bad for Claudia, but was glad for her that at least she wasn't in any way involved in the new murder. No one could have felt worse than she had, when Carol Michosky picked her out of the lineup. She'd been carrying around a load of guilt already for blacking out on the first Riverside crime.

Dugan was painting the context for me, which I well knew. "The mayor's livid about this," Dugan said, "this is not the kind of town we want—"

I'd heard this all before. I didn't need that kind of motivation—I'd help solve this, whatever the public relations. That was my job.

"—We have to get a better handle on these kinds of cases, much sooner," Dugan continued. "Maybe we should get cracking on that special unit I was talking to you about last month—"

"What did you say?"

"What? About the special unit? You seemed to think it was a good idea—"

"You remember that now?"

"Why shouldn't I?" Dugan looked at me like *I* was the one who was crazy.

"Because you haven't for more than a month."

Dugan continued to stare. "Look, Phil, whatever's going on in your head about the special task force, we can deal with it later. Let's get back to the murders—"

I held up a placating hand. "Just humor me for a few more minutes. What exactly do you remember about our conversation about the special task force, and its aftermath?"

Dugan made a disgruntled sound. "For God's sake, we talked about it right here in my office. You said you wanted to think about it. Then . . ."

I waited a few long seconds. "Yes?"

"Then . . . Well, with all this focus on the Riverside killings, I guess the special unit got lost in the shuffle." He cleared his throat. "That's why I brought it up again just now—I still think it's a good idea. . . ."

"You don't remember the aftermath, do you?" I said.

Dugan's cheeks flushed. "Goddamn it Phil, I'm not one of your witnesses on trial here!"

"I'm not a lawyer, I'm just trying to get to the bottom of this," I replied. "We're on all on the same side."

Dugan calmed down a bit, and reflected. "I guess I don't remember too clearly what happened right after I made the proposal," he admitted. "I was sick as a dog."

I nodded.

"So what exactly do you recall happening then?" he asked.

"I tried to tell you that I'd thought it over, and wanted to head up the special task force—"

Dugan looked at me, quizzically now.

"—and you had no recollection of making that offer in the first place."

I WENT BACK to my office. There was a peace in coming into your office on a Sunday, when most of the usual people with their usual problems weren't around.

This memory craziness was mutating into some kind of memory swapping, at least for Dugan, who now recalled what he had at first forgotten, and could not remember that he had forgotten it in the first place.

I called Jenna. She still had no recollection of my marriage proposal, but her piece of memory had been lost after Dugan's. Presumably it still had a few days to return, if that's what was going on here.

We got off the phone.

I tried to put some of the parts together—or, at least, identify them.

The key no doubt resided in the nature of memory. If I could know more about that, I would have a better chance of understanding what was disrupting it. I spent a few hours on the Internet.

From the reading I had been doing since all of this had

begun—and from what I already had acquired on the subject over the years—it was clear that no one had much knowledge of exactly how memory worked.

Engrams and all kinds of markers were proposed as the units of memory, and theories abounded as to how such units behaved and interacted. They were thought to be not additive but synergistic, so that a new memory transformed earlier memories, in the way that a pinch of orange powder dropped into a glass of water gave you not orange powder plus water, but water transformed into an orange liquid.

Most psychologists also agreed that the markers of memory were chained or linked together not only in before-and-after patterns, but in a densely packed web that radiated in all directions—an arrangement which would account not only for straightforward memory but creative leaps of imagination. Some researchers contended that memories of specific events were redundantly stored in several or lots of places in the network, or in a primary place with what amounted to backup.

That could explain what had happened to Dugan: His primary memory of talking to me about the task force had been short-circuited. Eventually his backup had kicked in—rebooted and replaced the damaged part of his system—so his lost memory returned. But the replacement also took out some of his newer memories, those that had accrued sometime between the initial damage and the rebooting. . . . There were indeed some reported cases of amnesia in which a series of memories rippled out and in, like so many markers going back and forth and back again in a game of mental poker.

Okay, so that at least offered an explanation for one aspect of Dugan's little odyssey.

But what caused it?

No one seemed to know what was responsible for the memory markers in the first place. All I could find were generalities about neurochemical networks—I guess this lack of specific knowledge was not surprising, since we didn't have much in the way of precise explanation of how the mind itself performed in the human brain. Some psychologists even denied that there was a mind, or anything beyond the sheer physical brain.

But what could the source of memory be, that it could be injured in the way it had been with Jenna and Claudia and me and Dugan, and now Dugan again with this memory swapping?

What kind of network gets knocked out by a flu or whatever, and then, in the case of Dugan, regenerates, recharges, but loses something in the process? If that's how some amnesias worked, what was it that those amnesias were attacking?

The shape of this problem and its possible solution came right from the realm of classic forensic science: You needed detailed knowledge of the victim, memory, in order to more specifically identify the assailant, amnesia.

Damn it, I still had a feeling that the assailant in this case wasn't the cough or the flu per se. I kept coming back to the Omnin. Dugan had taken it. And as of now, he had had the strangest memory symptoms.

Antibiotics. What were they? Anti-life, literally—they destroyed living organisms. They killed bacteria. But they had no effect on human brains, or memory, as far I knew. Still, Omnin was something new—available this year for the first time. Maybe it had some sort of new effect after all—one that the FDA had missed. Wouldn't be the first time, especially given something as slippery as memory. Everyone realized that the FDA wasn't omniscient.

But other people had lost pieces of their memory—Steinbuck, my doctor; Carol Michosky—and they hadn't taken Omnin. Or, at least, in Michosky's case, she had told me she never took antibiotics. And I really had no knowledge one way or the other about Steinbuck.

I pulled out some index cards. I still liked working with them, even though I also liked computers. Maybe I should start approaching this problem the old-fashioned way; investigate the network of memory not only with the network of computers, but with something more tangible than fleeting, invisible electricity—bring into play the paper perspective. I'd make a card for each person I knew who had any connection at all to the memory loss, and write down all pertinent information about them. Maybe the problem was that someone—deliberately or not—was leaving out some important detail. Maybe that's why this still didn't seem to add up. Maybe someone was lying.

But who?

It occurred to me that, in a case involving memory loss, there was no need to look for liars. Innocent loss of memory could account for information withheld. And the withholders were all the more difficult to identify, because they had no idea they were withholding. . . .

I shook my head. I'd find out more when other people's memories started coming back—including my own. . . . Assuming they did. And assuming that their recovery didn't erase another piece of the picture, as it had with Dugan.

Andy had suggested consulting history. That was a good place to start, too.

Yeah, history was also riddled with missing pieces, transformed recollections, winking in and out like a constellation of faulty neon lights across the ages. . . .

FIVE

Jenna's memory returned eight nights later.

"I love you," she said to me, about one o'clock in the morning. I was leaning over to turn out the light, my back to her, just as we were about to go to sleep. And I knew immediately from the tone of her voice that she remembered.

I turned to her, and she kissed me, full on the lips.

"I won't say I'm sorry I ever doubted you," she eventually said, "because I'm sure I didn't, and I don't remember if I did."

I had already told Jenna about Dugan and his memory recovery and new loss, so she was prepared for what might happen to her. I waited for my own missing memories to come back—I wanted every bit of my lost conversation with McNair, especially given his fuzzy rendition of what he later told me we had talked about.

I also worried about valuable subsequent insights I might lose. What should I do? Write down everything I knew or thought I knew about this memory puzzle? I had already been doing that. I had told Jenna exactly where my computer files and index cards were stored—three copies, in three different places, for safety's sake. But there were some threads of thought, parts of ideas, quick bits of insight that had half occurred to me when I was nowhere near a computer or an index card, and I never wrote them down. . . .

And what about new connections I was entertaining for the

first time in my head? What would happen to those live trains of thought if segments suddenly went missing? Would the trains be knocked completely off-track?

Well, they weren't exactly racing anywhere brilliant as yet, anyway, so maybe I shouldn't worry too much about their derailment.

And I had to give at least some thought to the damn Riverside homicides. Unlike murdered memories, murdered people never came back to life. They deserved my first attention.

ED MONTI, DUGAN, and I were in Dugan's office for the third meeting in a week. Since our procedure was a meeting per murder, the mood was worse than grim. Some of the media were now calling the killer "the Grandson of Sam." Others, aware of the distaff angle, were braying about "the Daughter of Sam." Two different takes on the Son of Sam—David Berkowitz, also known as "the .44-Caliber Killer"—who had held the city hostage with a series of lovers' lane–like murders in the summer of 1977, dramatized in Spike Lee's movie *Summer of Sam* in the 1990s. . . .

Count on the media to whip the city up into a new frenzy. Though I suppose it was good that people were scared to death of Riverside Park. Better being frightened than found dead there.

"It's good that Gonzales got her memory back." Ed grasped for a bright spot.

Dugan shifted uncomfortably. He preferred not talking about anyone's memory loss—or recovery—if he could help it. He forced himself. "Won't help much at this point," he said. "Enough people were witness to her memory lapse that anything she recalls now is suspect. And she didn't really see a lot in the first place. Rubin was just aggravated because losing her testimony about the conditions of that first murder—the position of the body, and all of that—seemed like a blow then, when there was just one murder. Not a good way to begin to gather evidence for a case. Little did we know . . ."

That that one homicide would turn into five now, with no suspects or leads at all, except that botched job with Carol Michosky—and the spring soon to turn into summer. . . . Dugan had a quarter of the detective force assigned to this now, carefully sifting through evidence, interviewing any witnesses they could find, and they hadn't come up with a single worthwhile lead.

"Phil, am I boring you with all of this?" Dugan asked, irritated.

"No, sorry," I replied. "I was just thinking that now that school is almost out, maybe we'll get a temporary pause, at least, in the killings." Ed's idea of accentuating the minutely positive seemed the best I could do in these circumstances.

"Wonderful," Dugan said. "And then what? They'll start up again in the middle of September?"

"Actually, most colleges begin at the end of August these days," Ed supplied. "My daughter hates it."

Not the news Dugan wanted to hear. He practically spat at us. "The mayor's furious about this—did I tell you that?"

"Don't take this the wrong way, Jack, but there's only so much Forensics can do here," Ed said. "You—we've—got a problem in *Detection*, if we can't come up with any suspects. I'm not trying to beg off, believe me, but—"

Dugan scowled. "We're on Detection's ass about this, every day, don't you worry. I'm not asking you guys for corroborative evidence—I know we have no suspects or even decent leads to corroborate. But anything you could give us to get us started, to point us in a direction, would be *very* appreciated at this point."

I nodded, sympathetically. Ed was technically right. We could examine corpses all we wanted, but unless our detectives gave us some leads and angles to play against, our evidence usually amounted to very little. We couldn't make things up that weren't there. Still, it wasn't in my nature to draw sharp lines between "your work" and "my work." The real world isn't like that. Life and death were stubbornly non-Euclidean.

"Well, the later murders support what we thought about the earlier ones," I said, "though we still have no real proof. The bodies are all naked, which suggests some kind of sexual motive, but they're not raped or even molested in any way that we can see. The strangulations are quick—no apparent struggle—which is another reason why the Michosky attack is the oddball. But the speed and efficiency suggest a surety of purpose—these aren't spur-of-the-moment crimes—and some physical strength in the murderer, and likely some knowledge of human anatomy."

"We were thinking maybe a nurse," Ed said.

Dugan nodded. This was old ground, but he appreciated the recitation. "A goddamn female Jack the Ripper. . . ."

"Well, at the very least, a strong, intelligent, driven woman," I said. "Assuming we're right about the attacker being a woman. Could be a gay man. Hell, the victims being undressed might have nothing to do with sex after all—which would mean the attacker could be anyone."

"But Michosky saw a woman," Dugan said.

"I wouldn't build a case on that," I said. "Lots of things don't add up in that episode."

Dugan sighed. "See, that's why I called you back for that one," he said to me. "I had a feeling this memory thing would rear its head again in this ugly case." He stopped, then laughed suddenly, briefly, without humor. "Who knows, maybe the murderer fell out with her lover because one of them forgot something important, personal, and that's what started this whole thing going."

"So you do, what, another canvass of lesbian bars to see if you can find any word of a shattered relationship?" Ed inter-

jected. "That was one of the first things you did, and it turned
up empty."

"So maybe we do it again," Dugan said. "I don't know. We
reexamine all the evidence, go over whatever few leads we have.
There's got to be something there—something that we over-
looked. Probably someone involved in this, one of the people
we talked to, was lying—that's usually the best place to start
again."

I agreed. Someone probably was lying. That, or forgetting.
Funny, but that was just the conclusion I had come to in my
memory investigation.

"LINDISFARNE" WAS THE first thing that came back to me—the
first piece of the missing conversation I had had on the phone
with McNair. It also came back to me how sick and feverish I
had felt then. I wondered if that would get in the way of my
remembering anything more.

I put a call in to McNair. I had tried to get in touch with
him a few times since my chat with Andy on Cape Cod, but
Rhonda had told me he was "on retreat," someplace up in the
mountains in Colorado.

I was glad to hear him answer the phone.

"What can you tell me about Lindisfarne?" I asked, after a
quick exchange of pleasantries.

"Lindisfarne?"

"Yeah," I replied. "I just recalled your saying something
about it in the conversation we had when I was sick."

He started coughing. I realized that he had been clearing
his throat and coughing on and off since he'd picked up the
phone.

"Still got that cough?" I added, unhelpfully.

"These things take time," he said, and coughed again.
"Anyway, Lindisfarne, yes, I may have mentioned that in our
conversation."

"Well, can you tell me its possible relevance to this memory problem I've been investigating?"

"Hmmm . . . tough one," McNair said. "Couldn't say, precisely. It was considered a holy island in the Dark Ages—a learned colony of monks and scribes lived there, and it was one of the cutting edges of Christianity on the British Isles at that time. Right off the coast of Northumberland, in northeast England. But I can't see exactly what that might have to with the amnesia you're . . . Oh wait, yes, yes . . ."

"Yes?"

"Well, you were raving on a bit about antibiotics when you were sick—I mean, totally understandable, I detest them myself, please don't take offense."

"Absolutely none taken," I assured him.

"Well, yes, I think I mentioned to you that the monks on Lindisfarne may have discovered antibiotics—there was a report a few years ago that they used them in their hospital—people went there to be cured in those days."

"Really. . . . What kind of antibiotics?" I asked.

"I'm not sure," McNair responded. "I gather they had some kind of mold farms, or something of the sort."

"Any reports of memory loss at Lindisfarne?" That would have been too good to be true.

"None that I ever heard of."

Okay, I'd have to settle for just what was true, then. "Do you think it's worth a trip to the island—could I find out more there?"

"I doubt it; there's not much going on there anymore. Just fishing, farming, and tourism. But there's a leading expert on the place—not that far away; he's located in Inverness, in the north of Scotland, if memory serves. You'll want to see him in person, if you can—he's notoriously monosyllabic on the phone."

———

I CAUGHT THE next morning's flight to London. I talked Dugan not only into letting me go, but covering it with NYPD money.

"You yourself said the memory losses and the Riverside murders might be connected," I told him.

"All right, see if you can book some sort of discount flight," he responded.

It was a measure of how desperate he was about the Riverside stranglings that he came through with the funds, even when I found it was impossible to get a discount flight on such short notice in June. Plus, Dugan was deeply troubled about the memory losses—not least of all his—in their own right. "Murders are ultimately commonplace," he had leveled with me one afternoon, when Ed had left. "Let's face it, they happen all the time. But I've never seen anything like this." And he pointed to his head, and shook it in a combination of self-reproach and confusion.

I arrived at Heathrow in time for dinner with my old friend Michael Mallory, my counterpart in New Scotland Yard.

"So, what is it this time, Phil?" he said affectionately, as we settled into a rack of lamb and Yorkshire pudding at the Serpentine in Hyde Park. The flight had been cramped and tiring. But I was keyed-up and wide-awake and hungry.

"Not to worry, no Neanderthals cropping up newly dead, as far as I know," I replied. The lamb was delicious.

"Well, that's a relief," Mallory said. "The lamb is savory, isn't it?"

I nodded, took another bite, and washed it down with a sip of red table wine.

"No secret messages popping up in someone's DNA?" Mallory asked.

"We seem okay on that front," I said.

"Well, spit it out then: What is it?"

"Something much more mundane—strange cases of people losing their memory. But the victims include Jenna and me, and, well, you know how I am about these things. . . ." I gave Mallory a thumbnail summary of the past months' events, including the Riverside killings (just to keep me kosher with the NYPD—though on some level I felt that they were related).

"No strange cases of amnesia here that I know of," Mallory volunteered when I was finished. "But I don't remember hearing anything about your new antibiotic Omnin over here, either."

"Possibly it's known here under a different name?"

"Possibly," Mallory replied. "I'll check into that for you. But I don't recall hearing about any new antibiotic under any other name, either. Been a pretty light flu season for us—nice, for a change."

"So England's another bit of evidence that Omnin may be the culprit."

"It would seem so, yes," Mallory agreed. "But don't forget that these sorts of things often act synergistically, with one factor working as a catalyst for the next. So even if your man is Omnin, he may not have been working alone. Is that too sexist for public parlance these days, or is it okay because I'm using the masculine to signify a negative?"

I TOOK THE Flying Scotsman the next day up to Edinburgh, and then switched for another train to Inverness. It was less colorfully named though equally comfortable, and the countryside out the window grew more colorful by the minute. Mauve swaths of thistle and rose-flowering heather were everywhere.

I went to meet Terry Briskman on the south bank of the Ness River, which flowed through Inverness—the same Ness as in the nearby Loch Ness, and its fraudulent monster. I hoped Briskman proved more substantial.

It was late in the day. Couples were cuddling on both sides of the river. Drunks were sleeping off their hangovers. Mothers were playing with their toddlers, who shouted with glee in delightful Scottish accents.

"Phil D'Amato!" A big man with a beard stood up and extended his hand as I approached our appointed meeting place, just to the side of the bridge. I had faxed him my photo from New York, and he'd directed me to his photo on his Web page.

"Thanks for meeting me, Terry," I said, and shook his hand. He looked just as he did in his photo. What I hadn't expected was his accent. "You're not from around here originally?" It was none of my business but I couldn't help asking.

Briskman grinned. "Huh—I'd have thought my original accent was better buried than that. But you got me: I was born and raised in the Bronx. Graduated the Bronx High School of Science. Went to City College for a while. Dropped out. I came over here to study with Karl Popper at the LSE—philosophy and history of science are equal passions with me. I fell in love with the British Isles and never went back."

"Amazing," I said. This was not the first time that I'd run into people in unlikely places who had grown up not far from me. "I'm from the Bronx, too—Christopher Columbus High School, hail the silver and the blue!"

Briskman laughed. "Yes, yes, I remember that song—I went out with a girl who went to Columbus—what a body! Didn't last too long, though—she was a bit of a snob. . . . But, yes, Columbus High School. Brings back all sorts of memories. Anne Bancroft—you know, the one who played the mother in *The Graduate*—she went to Columbus, didn't she?"

"Yes, she did. But that was before my time."

Briskman sighed, sat back down on the grass. "Have a seat," he said to me, and I did. I leaned back and looked at the river.

"So, what would you like to know about Lindisfarne?" Briskman asked, in almost hushed tones.

"I'd like to know about their holy antibiotics," I replied.

Briskman smiled. "The people on Lindisfarne thought everything they did was holy. They were, in many ways, followers of Francis Bacon and his philosophy that science and medicine and technology and rationality were all applications of the Divine Mind, expressed through humanity—except that Lindisfarne's beginnings in A.D. 635 predate Bacon by nearly a millennium. There's no way one can be a disciple of someone who won't be born yet for a thousand years, is there?" he asked, with a smile in his eye.

"Not that I've seen," I said.

"But of course some of the ancients had similar philosophies, so Bacon and Lindisfarne could well have been drawing on the same source—that's certainly possible, isn't it?"

"Yes, of course."

"And the ancients understood the antimicrobial effects of molds—though they couldn't see the microbes. But they understood those antibiotic properties—'Smite me with hyssops, and I shall be clean,' the Bible says. Molds grow well on decaying hyssop leaves."

"Yes, I've always found that fascinating—shows that modern high-tech science isn't the only path to wisdom. I came across the hyssop years ago in a biography of Alexander Fleming."

Briskman nodded. "Hell, I saw somewhere in *Nature* or *Science* that some *monkeys* use antibiotics in the wild. . . . So it goes *way* back. And didn't that fellow they found frozen in the Alps have herbs in his pouch? They could have been antimicrobial, and that's, what, about five thousand years ago? But back to the monks on Lindisfarne: It's not surprising that they knew about antibiotics—they inscribed the Old Testament in the Lindisfarne Gospels, after all. Beautiful, seventh-century illuminated manuscripts. . . . Hmmm, maybe the people who wrote the Bible got that knowledge from monkeys—ha, tell *that* to the Darwin-bashers. Not only are monkeys our fathers, they're our teachers! Monkey monks. Hey, isn't that the name of a rap group?"

"You're probably thinking of Marky Mark—he's an actor now." So Briskman evidently relished wordplay as well as wild ideas. Ordinarily I would have joined in, happily. But I had to keep this on track. "Does the Old Testament say anything about hyssop and forgetfulness?" I was pretty sure it did not, and I had no reason to think that Briskman was an expert on the Old Testament, still . . .

He shook his head. "Not as far as I know. That's the crux of what you want to know about Lindisfarne, right? Is there any evidence that their antibiotics caused lapses in memory?"

"Yeah. That's why I'm here."

"Then I'm afraid you've come here for nothing, on that score. I've read over their manuscripts quite carefully. No mention anywhere of memory losses."

I scowled.

"Of course, their antibiotics could have caused them to lose part of their memory, in ways of which they were not aware," Briskman continued. "That could account for why they didn't make note of it in their documents."

"Amnesia can be a tricky business," I agreed.

Briskman smiled. "So how do we decide which hypothesis is right—they forgot in a way that made them forget to record, or they didn't forget at all? Both are reasonable explanations for the evidence of no mention of memory loss in the Lindisfarne documents."

"Well, obviously the more reasonable explanation—the one that posits the least number of suppositions, and therefore wins on Occam's Razor—is that their records say nothing about memory loss because there was none," I said. "Not to mention, if their community was struck by amnesia, it likely wouldn't have afflicted everyone at the same time. And if it hit people at even slightly different times, then some would have been able to observe the amnesia in others, and make note of it before they were struck themselves."

"I see you're something of a philosopher of science yourself—and a not bad one. Where did you say you received your education?"

"I didn't say, beyond Columbus High School," I replied. "Lots of places, actually. New York University, John Jay, the New School for Social Research back when it was called that—"

"Well, they did a good job for you."

"Thank you."

"Look," Briskman said, "the actual use of antibiotics on Lindisfarne comes with the Benedictine restoration—we're talking twelfth century and after, our early Middle Ages. But I think the big story there happened much earlier—something far more important than antibiotics and amnesia, that everyone has missed about Lindisfarne."

"Yes?" Let people tell me the stories *they* wanted to tell. Sometimes these turned out to have surprising relevance to the story I wanted to hear.

"It's unclear, I admit," Briskman said. "But it's there in the manuscripts if you really understand their lingo."

I nodded encouragement for him to continue.

"You see, a lot of what they wrote down in the early times of Lindisfarne—in the seventh century—were not only the Gospels, but renditions of information passed down orally from centuries before, maybe even earlier than that."

I nodded again.

Briskman leaned closer, his face flushed with the zeal of stripping bare a hidden truth. I recognized the feeling. "The first monks on Lindisfarne say that the Phoenicians were really the ones who taught their ancestors to write," he said, "when they stopped in Ireland long ago on their way to the land across the great sea—that had to have been the Western Hemisphere. The Phoenicians taught those Celts to write on the way to

America. The Romans and their writing came to these isles much later."

IT WAS GETTING late, I was getting hungry, and this conversation was too good to cut short, so I asked Briskman if he would join me for a dinner at a restaurant of his choosing. He agreed, and suggested McTavitt's, a ten-minute walk.

The maître d' looked at me and frowned when we walked in. "Jacket required, sir," he said.

"Oh, sorry!" Briskman said. "I'd forgotten about their silly . . . this requirement."

I noticed that Briskman did have a jacket on—an ancient grey Harris Tweed.

I smiled at the maître d', and turned to leave.

"It's quite all right, Professor," he said to Briskman, without a trace of having taken offense. "We have an assortment of jackets from which your friend can select and wear while he is in our establishment. We keep them on hand just for these occasions."

"Sounds good to me," I said, still smiling. "Thank you."

I lost my smile then almost laughed out loud when I saw the jackets. I'm certainly no fashion plate. My shirt hangs out of my pants about as often as it's tucked in. But the jackets looked like they had been taken off of corpses in the 1930s.

"I think this one suits you, sir." The maître d' handed me some sort of black-and-white herringbone. It reminded me of test patterns on my grandmother's old black-and-white TV set.

"Thank you," I said, rubbed my eyes, and put it on. It was way too loose. But that was better than too tight. "This will be fine. Thanks," I said again.

I ordered a ginger ale when we were seated. I wanted as clear a head as possible for this conversation. Briskman ordered a lager.

"So let's get back to Ireland," I said, as the waiter left with our drink orders.

"Okay, here are some important early dates for Lindis-farne," Briskman replied. He pulled a piece of paper out of his jacket pocket, and scribbled a quick map. "The monks start a monastery at Clonard, in the middle of Ireland, in A.D. 520." He made a little X in the center of Ireland. "They send up a group and establish shop in Iona, on the northwest coast of Britain, in 563." He drew an upward arrow and made another X for Iona. "And Saint Aidan of Iona in turn begets Lindisfarne in 635." He drew an arrow across the top of Britain to the Holy Isle. "And while we're on significant dates, the Vikings attack the Northumbrian monastery on Lindisfarne in 793." He drew a westward arrow from Scandinavia in the east to Lindisfarne. "This may be significant, because the Vikings got to Greenland and then America in the next few centuries—that's established fact—and they may well have first heard of these new lands while on Lindisfarne. . . ."

WE STROLLED BY the Ness after dinner. The river moved like dark, inky diamonds in the moonlight.

"Oh!" Briskman looked at his watch. "You've missed the last train that can get you back to London tonight—we got too engrossed in our conversation."

"That's okay," I said. "I had a feeling I'd enjoy the conversation so much that I wouldn't want to leave—I've got a room booked at the inn."

"Well, you must cancel it, then! Maureen—my wife—and I would love to have you as our guest tonight. She's off with friends for the evening, but I'm sure she wouldn't mind."

"That's very generous, and I'd love to, but I'm already settled in at the inn. I'm sure I'd have to pay for the room at this point, anyway." And the truth was also that I liked some time on my own immediately after such significant interviews, to make any needed calls in private, collect my thoughts—

"All right, then," Briskman relented. "But next time—"

"Absolutely, I will," I replied.

"You do have a surprising appreciation of history, for a forensic detective," Briskman said. "Your field always struck me—speaking strictly as an outsider, of course—as a modern, high-tech playground par excellence. You use DNA evidence, and all of that, to look at just the immediate past. As you should: Last decade's crimes are usually last century's news."

"There's no statute of limitations on murder," I objected, with a smile. "Solutions to those kinds of crimes are always in demand."

"Yes, I'd imagine they would be," Briskman allowed.

"You're right that criminology is high-tech," I continued. "But death, as they say, is nothing new—it goes back a long way. So it's only natural that we have an affinity for history. You know the first forensic-science text appeared in 1248—*Hsi Duan Yu*, in China—'*The Washing Away of Wrongs.*' "

"Fine title!"

"Yeah, and it had some useful information, too—like how to tell the difference between corpses that drowned and corpses that were strangled and then dumped in the water."

"And how do you?" Briskman asked. "The drowned are more bloated with water?"

I nodded. "Water in the lungs for drownings, versus marks on the throat and broken neck cartilage for stranglings. So if you find a body in the water with damaged neck cartilage, chances are you've got more than an accidental drowning on your hands." *Chances are you've got murder by strangulation*, I thought, *as in the Riverside killings. . . .* I hadn't discussed them with Briskman.

"The year twelve forty-eight," he mused, "by then the Norse Greenland settlements were well in decline."

"Ironic that they died out entirely just before Columbus," I said, picking up on our dinner conversation.

"You see, Columbus had the card that counted," Briskman

said. "Reports of his voyage were published in pamphlets all over Europe—they became the best-sellers of the day. The printing press made that possible. All Leif Eriksson had going about his discovery was word of mouth."

"The unreliability of memory again," I observed, "even when it's working. What do you suppose would happen in a society that operated solely on memory, spotty as it is, and then it started crashing, en masse?"

"A reaction to your antibiotics?"

"For whatever reason."

"It would depend, I suppose, on how much of the society was wiped out by the memory crash—and how quickly, as we were saying before." Briskman considered. "If enough people were able to understand what was going on, and the danger it posed, they might be able to invent some substitutes for memory. . . ."

"Just what I was thinking," I said.

"I guess the printing press could be seen as a remedy for the memory loss created by the Black Plague," Briskman mused. "Or an inoculation for the collective mind of society, should the Plague strike again. . . ."

"And the alphabet? Was that a Phoenician response to some plague or crisis of memory they suffered?"

"None that I know of," Briskman replied. "But I'm only an expert on the Phoenicians insofar as they plied the waters of the North Atlantic. If you want to consult someone who knows everything about the Phoenicians and the alphabet, I'd recommend Darius Morton. He's also sure that they made it across the Atlantic."

"Who was that?" The name sounded familiar.

"Darius Morton—check out his book *Ahead of Columbus*, for starters. I'm pretty sure he's still at NYU—right in your backyard. And my old stomping ground, too. How is the Village these days? God, I remember it was a great place to pick up girls

with long blonde hair and short-short skirts when I was a kid—
the best place for that east of California."

I SLOWLY ATE a salad with prawns—mostly what they called
"shrimp" in the U.K.—on the Flying Scotsman back to London
the next afternoon. I put my index cards for the memory losses
out on the table.

Briskman had provided less than what I hoped to learn
about Lindisfarne, but much more about other things. If I
could take what he said seriously, along with what McNair had
told me in L.A., there was a Phoenician network afoot—at sea,
actually—around the time of Moses and slightly before, as
early as 1400–1300 B.C. The Mediterranean was a pond to
them, and the British Isles were in their sphere of commerce.
They were the maritime counterpower to Ancient Egypt and
its deeply entrenched land-based empire. Later, Phoenicia's
offspring, Carthage, would challenge Rome's ascent to power—
and lose. All of that was well-documented fact, not supposition.

Almost as certain was the Phoenician invention of the
alphabet—an improvement over Egyptian hieroglyphics. It was
borrowed by the Hebrews for the Ten Commandments, and by
the Greeks for their philosophy and science.

But Briskman also claimed that the Phoenicians had
reached the New World, sometime in the millennium between
Moses and Rome. He thought they had conveyed this knowledge and their alphabet to Lindisfarne—possibly as late as A.D.
500, via some remnant of Phoenician-Carthaginian culture that
reached Ireland, or likely via much earlier contact with the
Celtic-Irish ancestors of monks who eventually founded Lindisfarne. And just for good measure, Briskman thought the
Vikings had picked up this knowledge of the New World in
their attacks on Lindisfarne in the eighth century A.D., and

passed it on to Erik the Red and his son Leif. . . .

Quite a story . . . but how did it relate to the memory lapses that had just occurred in the New World—in the U.S.A., on my watch, in the past few months?

If I could find evidence of antibiotic use by the Phoenicians—something that might have triggered a memory loss, which acted as a stimulant for their invention of the alphabet—that would certainly help. So far, all I had on that was the reference to hyssops in the Bible—a slim reed indeed. Maybe Darius Morton could help with that. . . . I also needed to talk to Andy and find out more about the exact composition of Omnin. I never had thought to ask if it bore any resemblance to the mold spores on the undersides of decayed hyssop leaves.

Riverside Park had lots of leaves. . . . I thought again about the stranglings, about the bodies found under those leaves, and I felt guilty. They were never far from my mind, even here in England. I hadn't made any progress in finding their murderer, or murderers, at all. Well, at least my cell phone hadn't rung with news of another killing back home.

I took out my index cards on the stranglings. I had made up a set of them, too. I looked at the names and their connections to the case, and each other, a hundredth time. Jillian Murphy, Carol Michosky, and the rest . . . Nothing new. . . .

I looked at my amnesia cards. I'd just added Darius Morton, and half a dozen new notes about Briskman. I glanced at some of the others—Dugan, Andy, Jenna, McNair . . .

Hmmm . . . That would make an interesting third category of cards: names of people who figured in both the strangling and amnesia sets. Nothing earth-shattering, but something to keep in mind for future possible reference. I made out the handful of cards for the dual set.

I paid for my meal, collected my cards, and went back to

my seat for a catnap. The train would be at Victoria Station, London, in twenty minutes.

Instead of napping, I looked at the cards in all three sets once again.

SIX

At Victoria Station, a pretty girl was selling poppies from a tray. A picture right out of the Beatles' "Penny Lane." But as I made my way to the Underground, and its connection to Heathrow for my flight back home, the bright red poppies stirred another train of thought in my mind. . . .

Didn't the *Odyssey* have a section about the lotus poppy, and the forgetfulness it sowed in Odysseus' men? Another example of memory as a crucial concern of the Ancients. . . . Actually, the poppy and its forgetful effect seemed to pop up at all kinds of interesting junctures in what McNair called "cognitive history." For Coleridge in the nineteenth century, an opium dream was the source of the beautiful opening of Xanadu—sentenced to forever being a fragment by a knock on the door that had shattered the poet's dream. When he returned his attention to Xanadu, Coleridge couldn't recall what he had intended to write—the wispy inspiration of opium was too far dispatched to be retrieved. Better to be inspired by things that didn't play such games with your memory, I had always thought, about that episode. . . .

And didn't Joyce's *Ulysses*, the best novel of the twentieth century, have a chapter devoted to the many faces of the lotus?

I also recalled once reading somewhere—likely in Stuart Gilbert's work on *Ulysses*—that the *Odyssey* might have been based on a Phoenician journal of voyages in the Mediterranean.

Lots of the places encountered in the *Odyssey* had names that were Semitic in origin. "Scylla" was the Greek form of the Hebrew *s-k-l—skoula*—signifying "the rock." I wondered for a moment what the Semitic name for a land across a vast sea was, and if it somehow could have been alluded to in the *Odyssey*. . . .

I was accustomed to consulting biology, of course, even anthropology and archaeology and linguistics in my work. This was the first time I could remember poetry and literature having any relevance. . . . Well, if DNA was the language of life, and organisms its poetry, then why not work the other way, from literal poetry back to what it might say about the human organisms who created it?

THINGS BEGAN POPPING on a variety of fronts when I got back to New York.

Andy confirmed that part of the complex cocktail of antibiotics that was Omnin indeed bore a distant kinship to the mold that most commonly grew on decayed hyssop leaves.

Ed, who had reexamined the body of the last Riverside victim—Laryssa Qualter, twenty-three—inch by inch, for six careful hours, before its scheduled interment, found something that made him seek a temporary delay of the burial. It was a small hair on the inside of the victim's left thigh. Ed had missed it the first time, because it was the same reddish blond color as Laryssa's hair. But its DNA turned out to be someone else's—Laryssa's boyfriend, who had a reddish blond beard. When questioned the first time, he had claimed not to have seen Laryssa on the fateful night.

Confronted now with the new piece of evidence, he cracked pretty quickly. Jason Lumley thought—wrongly, it turned out—that Laryssa had been cheating on him (the relationship she had with her Columbia professor was strictly platonic, by everyone else's testimony). Jason had asked her about it after spending the evening with Laryssa in her apartment. He didn't buy her denial. He had heard about the Riverside stranglings on the news, and from a friend who was a rookie cop in a nearby precinct. Lying next to Laryssa in bed, he talked her into dressing and taking a late-night stroll along the Hudson River. They never got there. Her body was found in Riverside Park, strangled and stripped, the next morning. . . .

Jason had gotten some unpublicized details on the earlier stranglings from the rookie cop. This enabled Jason to make his murder look like the others. Dugan was at least pleased to be able to fire the blabbermouth rookie, and to have one murder solved. "We of course are no closer on the other stranglings than before," he told me on the phone.

"Well, maybe a little closer," I replied, "because now we can subtract everything about the Qualter murder—which would have given us wrong leads for the others."

"Yeah, you're right. I sent Ed a special letter letting him know what a good job he did on the Qualter case. You too—the Department's lucky to have you guys."

I thanked him, but knew I had done nothing on the Qualter and not much on the other Riversides, either.

"Let me know as soon as you come up with more," Jack said. He knew it, too.

We got off the phone. It rang about a second later.

"Nothing yet, Jack."

"Phil? Rhonda McNair! How are you are?"

"Oh, hi . . . I'm fine," I replied. But she sounded nervous, excited—I couldn't tell—about something. "Is everything okay with Robert?"

"Oh yes," she said, "that's why I'm calling! He wanted to remind you that he'll be coming to New York University next week for a summer lecture, in case you wanted to see him."

" 'Remind' me?"

———

I WALKED DOWN the hall to get an iced tea from the soda machine. It wouldn't take any of my dollar bills. I settled for reheated water over a stale teabag in a Styrofoam cup in the secretary's office.

So now it was my turn on the memory carousel.

I'd recovered my recollection of McNair's mention of Lindisfarne in our first phone conversation—the one we had had when I was sick. But according to Rhonda, McNair had later told me about his upcoming NYU lecture—right before I'd left his home in California. And I had no memory of that now. I wondered if I had *ever* remembered McNair telling me about his trip, *before* I recovered my recollection of Lindisfarne in the phone call. . . . If so, I'd regained an earlier memory at the expense of a later one, just like Dugan.

Jenna was the only one I might have spoken to at the time about McNair's new lecture in New York. I called her—she said it didn't ring a bell. But her memory was not exactly one hundred percent these days, either. . . .

I sighed, sipped my tea, looked out the window. I was beginning to see why Andy thought this whole business was almost impossible to investigate. A tapestry of pinpricks were enveloping me and my relationships. These were better than big gashes—major disruptions in social life due to memory loss—but they were all the more difficult to nail down.

But what if the effects proved to be worse in the long run—more pervasive in the population, more enduring?

What if the Phoenicians had discovered America twenty-five hundred years before Columbus, but forgot it in a memory plague? What if they had then invented the alphabet to act as a safeguard against later mass amnesias, but that invention had been too late to save the memory of their discovery of the New World? How would the course of our species have been changed if their discovery of America had made it onto the con-

tinuing map of civilization, rather than just into vague legends
of Atlantis, rumors and stories taken to be some sort of fantastic
fiction rather than fact?

What would happen to *our* world if we were ravaged by
such a plague? Would our massive libraries save us? Would the
Internet?

I was getting ahead of myself. I didn't even know that I
really believed that the Phoenicians had made it to the Western
Hemisphere. . . .

Which brought me back to Darius Morton.

"I'D IMAGINE HE'S been emeritus here for quite a while now,"
McNair said to me about Morton as we ate pizza on a park
bench on Washington Square, the afternoon before his talk.

"Yeah," I said, "but no one in the religion department
seems to know where he is right now."

McNair nodded sympathetically. "Skeleton summer staff.
But he's well worth your while to find—a brilliant man. You
know, I asked him to be on my doctoral committee, in the mid-
1970s."

"Really? I didn't know you got your doctorate at NYU. I
thought—"

"You thought right," McNair replied. "I'm a UCLA man, all
the way, from Ph.D. to professor. But they allow you to have one
outside reader on your doctoral dissertation committee from
another university, if you can make a case that such a reader's
expertise would be uniquely valuable to you."

"And that was Morton?"

McNair shook his head no, and coughed. "I made my
case—irrefutably, I would say. But the chair of my committee
thought otherwise. He thought Morton and his theories about
an ancient maritime civilization that colonized the world were
off-the-wall."

"You've still got that cough," I said. "I'm sorry, I don't mean to sound like your grandmother, and be such a noodge about this."

McNair laughed, then coughed some more. "You also sound like Rhonda, and just about everyone else who talks to me about the cough. But not to worry. I've been down this route before. Coughs untreated with antibiotics can hang on for months. But they usually go away in the end."

"Right," I said. "Usually. If they don't develop into pneumonia."

McNair shrugged. "I've got a good constitution. It's a chance I'm willing to take. I think the alternative is worse."

"Antibiotics? But you've said to me all along that you don't see the recent flu experience as responsible for the memory loss."

"We've actually discussed the cough more than the cure as the cause of the amnesia, but you're right, I have no knowledge of antibiotics causing losses of memory."

"Yet you do have a beef with antibiotics," I said.

"Oh yes," McNair said. "Look, their raison d'être is they destroy bacteria that hurt us. I suppose that's good—though some argue, and I tend to agree, that we're better off fighting those bugs with our own immune defenses—"

"Some deadly bacteria break right through our natural defenses, you know that," I objected. I had no love for antibiotics, either—but I couldn't deny their obvious benefits.

"Granted," McNair said. "My main concern is about something else anyway. The human organism is actually many organisms, living together in symbiotic relationships. What happens to our well-being when antibiotics attack bacteria that are our partners?"

"Omnin is supposed to go very easy on our stomach's inhabitants," I countered. "It was deliberately designed with that in mind."

"And what about its possible effects on inhabitants that we

do not know about? What about the things that those inhabitants do for us that we do not know about? Surely their assistance goes beyond just digestion. You know, bacteria, viruses, they're all a lot more . . . multifunctional than we give them credit for— Oh, that reminds me, I brought this clipping for you. Have you seen it? There've been a few articles on this over the years—this is just the most recent."

He coughed, and pulled a photocopy of an article out of his jacket pocket. It was from the *New York Times*—the *Science Times* section—from the week I had been in Britain. I had missed it.

BACTERIA SING; DRUGS AIM TO GET THEM OFF-KEY, the little headline said. The article explained that medical researchers were paying increasing attention to something called "quorum sensing"—a capacity of bacteria, discovered more than two decades ago, to apparently communicate among each other about how many of their kind were in the vicinity. The bacteria were thought to wait until they had sufficient numbers to overcome immune systems before releasing their toxins. New drugs were under development—"still a few years away"—to "jam" the bacterial signals, and thereby render the bugs harmless. . . .

I looked at McNair. "You think bacteria might be in our brains, singing our song? You think microorganisms might help us remember? How? They live in our head and work as conduits for our neural networks? And then what? Omnin gets past the blood-brain barrier, and kills those neural germs, or interferes with their communication?" It made some sense. . . .

But the cognitive historian slowly shook his head no. "That's going too far—or farther than I'd be willing to go at this point. We don't know enough about how memory actually works. You'd need to find out more about just how Omnin behaves in the body. All I'm saying is that there are lots of living and quasi-living things running around inside us—in symbiotic, parasitic, and probably mostly neutral relationships with us.

And these relationships—the symbiotic ones, especially—may well truly make us what we are as human beings. And part of that, in view of the bacterial gift of gab, could conceivably be helping our brains work, enabling us to think, remember—who knows? But in any case, taking antibiotics—any antibiotic, Omnin included—is like setting fire to those relationships . . . those we know about, those we do not."

I nodded my understanding. It was not complete agreement, because I could not imagine refusing antibiotics if I had a bacterial infection that could be deadly. Nor could I even entertain not doing everything in my power to give them to someone I loved who was similarly afflicted. McNair would likely say that I favored setting a fire to burn out vermin, even though the fire risked eliminating the whole forest. I needed to think more about that.

I also needed to think further about this bacterial theory of memory. I needed to find out more about Omnin. And I also needed to explain why Steinbuck and Michosky had had memory lapses even though I had no evidence that either had taken Omnin, and Michosky had explicitly denied it.

McNair coughed again, and smiled apologetically. "There's a lot of pollen in this park," he said. "I'm sure that's what this cough is about."

ANDY WAS UNREACHABLE on a schooner off of Maine. Who could blame him, given that it was hot and July? I decided to postpone my research into Omnin and bacteria for the two weeks that he would be out of touch, rather than bring someone new up to speed at the CDC. I did leave questions for Andy in various voice-mails.

But I also needed to devote more time to the Riverside murders.

So far, the summer armistice—at least on the part of the killer—had held. Indeed, with the last crime positively not by the hand of the earlier murders—Jason had excellent alibis for all the other stranglings, and no motive—we were well into our second month of what the *Daily News* had recently termed "the Riverside Respite."

That it was a respite, and not a permanent retirement, just about everyone involved in the case agreed. Killers, of course, were not invulnerable to being victims of murder themselves—many times they were, especially in the drug world and organized crime—nor were they immune to deadly illness or getting hit by drunk drivers. So one could always hope. But serial killers were usually not paid hitmen or drug muscle. They had a goddamn way of hanging around. . . .

So what, then, was the reason for this pause?

Ed and I had already raised the school's-out theory with Dugan, and I believed it could be a contributing factor. But something else was nibbling at me about this. . . .

Dugan had wondered—more ironically and desperately than seriously—if a memory lapse in the murderer had somehow ignited the grim reapings. If that were so, I wondered if the summer pause could in some way be due to the swapping of memory losses that Dugan, Jenna, and I had all experienced. Could the killer have remembered something that she forgot, which had removed the animus for the killings? or perhaps forgotten something else now, which had the same calming effect? If that were so, then what the hell would happen if she took Omnin again this coming fall or winter?

My phone rang.

"Claudia, how are you? Sorry to hear about your mother—hope she's doing okay." This was the first time we had spoken since before she had gone down to Philadelphia to attend to her mother after her stroke.

"Thanks for asking," Claudia said. "I guess she's holding her own. I'm grateful that at least she's still with us." Claudia sounded tired.

These things were never easy. My own mother was in her seventies and in pretty good health. My father had died suddenly of a massive heart attack almost ten years ago. Everyone had said it was a blessing that he went so fast, but it still hurt me every day, in a hole that never healed in my soul. . . .

"So, I was wondering if I could talk to you about something, regarding the Riverside case," Claudia asked diffidently.

"Of course."

"Well, it's the memory thing again," she said. "You know, first I gave a report about what I'd found on the scene. Then I couldn't remember any of that. Then it all came back to me—but the DA said it would all be suspect anyway, because there were lots of witnesses to my memory being unreliable—"

"Right."

"So I'm not sure what to do about these dreams I've been having," she said.

"Dreams?"

"Yeah. In the past few weeks, I've been having dreams about that morning in the park. The couple calling out for help . . . running with their dogs. . . . I run over to the park—I see Murphy's body. She's on her stomach, and the left side of her body from her ankle all the way up to her shoulder is visible through the brush. . . ."

"Okay, that makes sense—that's just what you said in your initial report."

"Yeah," Claudia said. "But now, in my dreams, I think I'm seeing something else—someone is looking at me, over my shoulder, as I'm looking at the crime scene. I can't see her, of course, but I know in my dream that she's there."

"Maybe it's an anxiety dream—you're feeling that someone is looking at you, over your shoulder, to make sure you're doing your job?" DA Rubin's face came into my mind. I shook it away—this wasn't the time to be playing Freud.

"No, I don't think so," Claudia said. "It feels like someone watching not only me but the victim—watching to see what becomes of Murphy. I see someone crouching in the bushes, standing up when my back is turned, peering out. She's tall, for a woman, with short blonde hair. I know it sounds crazy, and it can't be any kind of evidence. But I wanted to tell you. I think she's the murderer."

I HAD DINNER that evening with Jenna in an outdoor seafood restaurant on Columbus Avenue. "Claudia's recurring dream doesn't really fit with what we know—think we know—about how the memory loss works," I said. "If she had any kind of feeling that someone was in the bushes, watching her, when she was at the crime scene, then how come she didn't mention that in the first place, in the report she made before the amnesia struck?"

"Do you really know enough about the amnesia to rule out what she told you?" Jenna replied. "Maybe the mind rebounds after the memory loss—and the memory swap—and gets so sensitive that it recalls little things that went by too quickly, or were too subtle to be remembered, the first time around."

"I guess she might have caught a quick glimpse of someone in the bushes"—I drained my wineglass, held it up to the twilight, and considered—"and it registered subliminally. And then, somehow, in the aftermath of the amnesia episode, it penetrated her dreams. . . ."

Jenna nodded, and refilled our glasses.

"Anyway, I told her to write up what she told me, and fax it to Dugan. I've got a meeting with him tomorrow afternoon."

We finished our meal, forwent dessert, and walked slowly down the avenue towards Columbus Circle. The night was nicely cooling. Lots of stores were open late, lots of people were on the sidewalks. A beautiful New York evening. . . .

We started crossing from east to west on Seventieth Street. I noticed a cab on the southwest corner. A woman was flagging it.

She looked familiar. It was Amy Berman, I realized—McNair's student, who had told Claudia about his lecture that I had attended at Fordham University's Lincoln Center campus, just a few blocks from here, where I had met him for the first time. That I remembered perfectly.

Amy was in the cab before I had a chance to wave to her. But the passenger door was open, and I could see her waving to what looked to be a lingerie store on the corner.

A woman emerged from the store, carrying a package. She entered the cab and it sped away.

Jenna tugged on my arm. We had been standing in the middle of the street. The light had changed, and traffic was coming towards us.

We hustled to the far sidewalk. "You that interested in the lingerie store, the women in the cab, or both?" Jenna asked, smiling.

"I know one of them—she was at the lecture where I first saw McNair," I replied.

"Ah yes, I remember your telling me about that lecture— right before the flu got you," Jenna said.

I nodded.

"And the other? The leggy blonde with the short-cropped hair?" Jenna asked.

I looked at her.

"Oh my god!" Jenna exclaimed. "She looks like the one in Claudia's dream—the one we were just talking about—doesn't she?"

SEVEN

I called Claudia's precinct immediately on my cell phone. She wasn't on duty. I asked the desk sergeant to track her down, and have her call me right away.

I called 411 for Amy Berman's phone number and address. Nothing listed for that name.

Damn it. . . .

I called McNair. He was back in L.A. Amy was his former student. They certainly seemed friendly enough after the Fordham lecture. Maybe he had some idea where she lived—what part of town. . . .

Rhonda answered the phone. I got lucky.

"Let me check," she said. "I think she sent Bobby some e-mail a few weeks ago, and that might have her address and phone number—you know, in those little tag-lines they put at the end of the message?"

Rhonda checked and indeed it did. I thanked her. "How's Robert?" I asked her, quickly.

"Still coughing, but basically okay," she said.

I thanked her again and got off the phone.

I called Amy's number. No answer. Not even an answering machine.

"Let's grab a cab over to her address," I said to Jenna.

"You think she's in immediate danger?" she asked. A honking car almost drowned out the last of what she said.

"Probably not," I replied, and covered one ear, "but I'd rather be stupidly overreactive about this than sorry."

AMY LIVED IN a big apartment building on West End Avenue in the nineties. Our cab rushed us there in ten minutes. I had tried calling her several more times, but continued to get no answer.

We waited in front of her apartment about five minutes—it felt like five hours. I tried to look as casual and relaxed as possible, but I was sure I'd failed at that. Passersby looked us over; I was glad Jenna was with me. Someone likely would have called me in for loitering had I been alone.

"There she is!" Jenna spotted Amy, who had just turned the corner. She had a package of what looked like groceries in her arms.

I walked to her, smiling, with Jenna.

She looked, smiled back, and pointed at me. "Phil D'Amato! Claudia's friend. We met at Professor McNair's lecture, right? Small world to see you here!"

I explained to her that it wasn't that small—though I supposed it was tiny enough that I'd seen her on Columbus Avenue, and with a blonde who fit Claudia's dreamed description. . . .

"Leslie Roth?" Amy asked, amused, maybe a bit annoyed, not at all frightened. "She's no murderer—we've been friends since high school. She lives just a few blocks away."

I explained, as gently as I could, that most murderers had had friends in high school. I asked Amy if she could give me Leslie's address so I could go talk to her. Amy said yes, but only if she called her first, and only if she came along.

I got serious and official. I demanded that the she give me the address.

Amy refused.

I got more serious and official. I even mumbled something

about obstructing an investigation. I asked for the address again.

Amy glared daggers at me, and reluctantly complied.

I called the address into the precinct with a request that two detectives join me at Leslie's apartment. It was on Eighty-eighth and West End.

I also insisted that Amy accompany us—I didn't want her to call Leslie and tip her off.

I hailed another cab.

Amy squeezed in with Jenna and me, furious. Jenna tried to make small talk with her. It was ignored.

THE DETECTIVES BROUGHT Leslie in for questioning. Then they questioned her, with me watching and listening through the partition, for about fifteen minutes.

Dugan had been summoned from some ceremony at the Museum of the City of New York. He joined us. "So," he asked, "what do we have here?"

"She seems to have alibis for half the crimes, none for the others. The alibis are being checked out, of course. I don't know—her friend, Amy Berman, swears by her. We're putting Ms. Roth through a lot of aggravation just on the strength of Claudia's nightmares."

"We can't be too careful about this," Dugan said. "You were right to blow the whistle. Where is Claudia, anyway?"

She arrived about an hour later, disheveled. "I'm sorry," she said. "I was really exhausted—dead-ass unconscious. I didn't even hear the phone ring in my dreams." It had taken several loud knocks on her door to wake her. Fortunately, she lived in a one-room utility apartment.

Dugan directed her attention to Leslie, behind the parti-tions. One of Leslie's alibis had just checked out in a prelimi-nary interview over the phone.

"So," Dugan asked, "is she the girl of your dreams?"

Claudia looked carefully.

"No," she finally said. "I wish she was, but she isn't. I can see why you'd think she might be—she certainly fits the description I faxed you—but she's not the one. The face is different. Hers is sweeter, softer."

ED AND I were in Dugan's office the next afternoon. "I briefed the commissioner, who briefed the mayor, on last night's little fiasco," he told us. "Neither one is too happy, as you might imagine. The mayor cautioned that we have to be careful not to lash out at innocent citizens over this."

First time I had ever heard him raise a concern about that. Maybe the memory crash had gotten the mayor, too, and he'd forgotten how livid he'd been. . . .

"I know what you're thinking, Phil," Dugan said. "You're thinking: 'Here they go again, those brasshats and assholes. They have the attention span of a flea.' You're thinking: 'Here I am, working my heart out to get to the bottom of this mess, and they're going to pull the rug out from under me, just like they always do.' "

"Not exactly," I said. But I couldn't manage a smile.

"Well, here's something that might surprise you," Dugan continued. "I told them: 'No way.' You and Ed are doing a great job on this, and I want you to continue. I'm backing you with all of my weight, thin as I might be." He weighed about 160, and stood at about an inch under six feet.

"Thank you," I said, truthfully.

"All right, then," he said. "So tell me—what are your plans on this?"

Plans? Jeez, I felt lucky to have an odd hypothesis or two. . . .

Ed spoke up. "We're reexamining the autopsy evidence from the murder victims—a third time. Hey, I'll order exhumations for all of them, if need be."

Dugan nodded. "So maybe we'll get lucky if you keep at it and we'll find that yet another strangulation we thought was Riverside was really by someone else—that it?"

"You never know," Ed replied, deadpan, unsure if Dugan was baiting him or being genuinely supportive.

"Let me tell you, I'd gladly take it," Dugan said. He got up from behind his desk, walked over to Ed, and clapped him on the shoulder. "You bet I would."

Then he turned towards me.

I talked about memory lapses from the Phoenicians to the present, about antibiotics from hyssops to Omnin, about bacteria and quorum-sensing, and about how, if we could understand some of that a little better, we might have a key to a wild card in the Riverside murders.

The Dugan I knew would likely have lectured me to stay on point—pursue stone-cold killers, not half-baked hypotheses. But this version of Dugan took it all in. Then he clapped me on the back.

"And don't feel too bad about last night," he added. "You did the right thing. The Roth woman is friends with the Berman, right? Officer Gonzales and Berman are friends, right? Gonzales is having bad dreams, and she fills in an unclear face in the bushes with a face she's actually seen once or twice—that's the way dreams work, right?"

"I guess so," I said.

"Gonzales' dreams may still add up to something," Dugan continued. "Phil, you're the expert on this mental and memory business. Keep looking into it. What you told me so far makes a lot of sense—and it's helped me better comprehend my own little bout of amnesia."

It certainly had put him in a good disposition, of late. I had better make the most of it while it lasted.

———

BUT JENNA WOKE me the next morning with distressing news.

"Listen." She turned on the radio. It was the tail end of a report about a sea-squall in the North Atlantic, off the coast of Maine. Several yachts and schooners were missing. Coast Guard rescue teams were converging in the area.

"Goddamn *Perfect Storm*," I muttered. "I hated that movie anyway."

"Andy's on a boat off the coast of Maine, isn't he?" Jenna asked, though she knew the answer.

I nodded, and started making calls to newspapers, radio and TV stations, National Weather Service, Coast Guard, any-place I could find more information. I tried WINS all-news radio in New York, where I'd just heard the report. Their phone lines were crossed or down. "Some computer virus struck part of our switching operation, Dr. D'Amato," a supervisor with the phone company told me when I called and asked for an emer-gency connection to WINS. "I don't know when their service will be restored."

At the other places I called, unfortunately, either I had no contact in the organization—why the hell would I need to know anyone at the *Portland Tribune* in Maine?—or my contact was on vacation, or my contact knew nothing.

Jenna brought me orange juice and a pot of tea.

I finally was able to reach someone I didn't know—who was aware of the story—at the *Boston Globe*. "I can confirm that the Coast Guard fears that there's been some loss of life, but please don't quote me on that, Dr. D'Amato."

"Don't worry, I'm a forensic detective not a reporter," I snapped back. That was needlessly nasty, I knew, but I was aggravated.

"Then why are you calling in the first place?"

"Long story, close friend, never mind."

———

THE CALL CAME through in my office, on my direct line, later that day.

"Phil, I hear you've been looking for me."

"Andy, jeez, I'm glad you're okay," was all I could say.

"The initial reports were exaggerated," he said; "only three boats actually capsized—"

"Yeah, but five people—including two men your general age and description—are among the missing. Thank God you weren't one of them!"

"Thanks," Andy said sincerely. "You do have a melodramatic way of looking at the world, though. You're hot on the trail of some bizarre investigation, and someone with what could be important new information in the case is lost at sea before he communicates to you—"

"You have new information?" No need to go into the fact with Andy that, for reasons I've never been able to totally understand, my work often did seem like it came right out of the movies—though lately there seemed less and less distinction between nightmare movies and reality.

"Yes, I do," Andy replied. "From Australia—about Omnin and the brain—Damn, that's my other phone ringing, from Atlanta. Look, I'm taking a commuter plane day after tomorrow to La Guardia, to pick up a flight back home. How about we meet for lunch in Sbarro's or whatever at the airport, around two P.M.?"

"Okay, but I can also call you back now, in a few minutes, after you get off the other phone—"

"Hold on a second," Andy said to me, then started talking on the other phone.

He returned to our connection about thirty seconds later. "I've got a load of other calls to make," he told me, sounding harried. "Tell you what, I'll write down what I've learned about Omnin, and mail it to you before I get on the plane, if you're worried that it's going to vanish without a trace. It's nothing you need to know immediately. We on for lunch at two?"

"I'll be there."

TWO DAYS LATER I was in the Sbarro's closest to where Andy's commuter flight was supposed to arrive. I wasn't too happy. The clock on the wall said a few minutes past four.

I decided not to go the ticket counter a sixth time. Likely all I would be told again was that there was a lot of turbulence, the plane was small, so the pilot took a longer—but definitely safer—route. Why the hell couldn't Andy have taken a train? Either there wasn't one that ran straight from Maine to New York yet, or it was too slow. . . .

Three teas, a tuna sandwich with too much mayo, and a lot of heartburn later, Andy's plane came in. He looked tan, lean, fit. He grabbed a salad, and sat down at my table. "Have you already eaten?"

"I'm fine," I answered.

"Damn bumpy plane ride," he said. "Next time I'll take a train. Is there even a train line in Maine?"

"Beats me," I said. "There may be one that goes to the north of Boston."

Andy leaned back in his chair and appeared to relax. "Okay, here's what's happening. You know, I sent out feelers to my contacts all over the world, to see if they had any incidences of memory loss, the kinds of side effects you—we—suspect for Omnin—"

"Right, but so far, only the U.S. has been hit by the flu this year, and we seem to be the only place with any kind of mass use of Omnin."

"That's changed," Andy said.

I looked at him. "Australia."

He nodded. "Australia began getting whapped by the flu a few weeks ago—it's winter for them down there now."

"Right," I said.

"And as soon as I got reports of that, I got on the phone and started talking to people I know down there. See? I *do* take what you say very seriously, and my mind's always working on it." He smiled.

I returned it.

"And I got in touch with one guy in particular—Tom Stewart, works a job roughly parallel to mine, out of Sydney. Do you know Tom?"

I shook my head no.

"Well, fortunately, I was able to reach Tom just as he was coming down with the flu," Andy continued. "His doctor prescribed Omnin. I warned Tom about it. He decided to take it anyway, and be a guinea pig. His wife was in on it, too—she was thoroughly briefed, and told to take notes on everything that happened to Tom. And it played out just like you said—a memory loss of a few hours, just around the time that the Omnin was beginning to kick in."

"All right, that's good," I said. "It's good to have another confirmed case." But it didn't quite seem to justify the sense Andy was projecting that this was some kind of breakthrough. "So is the Australian government going to take any action—pull Omnin off the market?" I asked.

"Not clear, at this point," Andy said. "But there's more—about Tom Stewart. It's tragic, really. . . ." Andy's demeanor suddenly changed from joking, eager, to grim. It was an expression I couldn't remember ever seeing on him.

"What happened to Tom?"

"He was feeling much better, none really the worse for the memory loss—just like you—and he was driving on a curvy country road in the rain. He missed a turn, crashed into a tree. He was killed instantly."

"God, that's awful."

"But I took the bull by the horns," Andy said. "Nothing

could bring Tom back, but maybe his death could be of some help to us—make it meaningful rather than just a goddamn stupid waste. I spoke to the coroner down there, and of course Tom's wife. I told him what I wanted in the autopsy—I made sure Tom's brain was examined for any trace of Omnin."

I was hanging on Andy's every word.

"You wanted to know if Omnin crossed the blood-brain barrier. Well, turns out it was specifically concocted with that in mind. It comes packaged with a special agent—a bradykinin agonist called 'Neurolax'—which increases the permeability of the blood-brain barrier by activating B2 receptors on the endothelial cells of the brain's capillaries. Probably more than you needed to know."

"I want to know everything," I replied. "The endothelial cells on the brain's capillaries make the tight junctions that block diffusion of substances between cells, and the Neurolax relaxes these, opens them up?"

"Yes. For a brief period of time."

"Why?" I asked.

"Why what?" Andy responded.

"Why suddenly market an antibiotic that gets through the blood-brain barrier?"

"Because it's Omnin, remember?" Andy replied. "Good for all, everything. Including who knows what might be hanging out in the skull. Brain tumors are a nasty way to go. There are theories that some tumors might be caused by offbeat, low-profile bacteria. If Omnin can stop that . . ." Andy shrugged. "Well, you get the picture."

I nodded, and let what he was saying cross the barrier into my own brain—and, I hoped, my understanding. "So Omnin was found in Tom Stewart's brain?"

"Yeah. Traces were found in his corpus callosum—you know, the part of the brain through which the two hemispheres communicate. With that evidence in hand, I knew what to ask the FDA—and they readily admitted that Omnin is bundled with Neurolax. I got that confirmed just yesterday. They're not trying to keep it secret."

"I know the corpus callosum well," I said, mouth dry. "It's the part of the brain through which—if Julian Jaynes is at all right—the two hemispheres came together, began working as an integrated unit, giving rise to our sense of self and consciousness. This may have happened around the time the Phoenicians invented the alphabet."

"So, if that's right, Omnin attacks our consciousness in some way," Andy said. "Maybe by hindering that bacterial communication you were talking about in your voice-mail?"

"It's beginning to look as if Omnin's doing *something* to gum up the works," I replied. "But wouldn't the FDA have tested that out? Discovered that Omnin in the brain blots out memory?"

"I'm going to see if I can get an answer to that as soon as I'm back in Atlanta," Andy said. "They had to have tested Omnin pretty rigorously—no way it could have been released on the market otherwise. But, I don't know, maybe they rushed the Neurolax part of the tests—maybe they tested that part less thoroughly. That can happen with a compound drug, especially one put together under pressure of countering a possible flu epidemic. Don't worry, I'll find out."

I nodded.

"Don't worry, Phil," Andy repeated. "We'll get it off the market if need be."

"You know, I was just thinking," I replied.

"Yeah?"

"If we just remove Omnin, without really understanding why it knocks out part of our mind, how it does that, then maybe we're leaving ourselves open for even more devastating attacks from something similar."

EIGHT

I looked more closely into the corpus callosum.

I haunted half a dozen libraries, and fired up my Web browser into the wee hours of every morning. . . .

The brain operates in two hemispheres. In the 1960s, much was made of their apparently contrasting functions. People who received injuries to the left hemisphere had trouble with sequential tasks like reading and counting, but they could see images and recall music just fine. Folks with damage in the right hemisphere had difficulty recognizing faces, but could read and write as well as they ever could. The upshot was that the left hemisphere controlled the logical, linear parts of our lives, while the right directed our all-at-once tasks like encountering a picture or a sound.

The idea that left-handed people make up a disproportionately large part of the artistic population jibed with the brain-hemisphere analysis. The right side of the brain controls the left side of the body, and vice versa, so that left-handedness indicates that the right or artistic part of the brain is dominant.

Historically, left-handedness was sometimes also identified with underhandedness, deviousness—as in "a left-handed compliment." Presumably this was because a communication presented artistically or poetically was subject to more interpretation—and thus misinterpretation—than a straightforward, step-by-step declaration. I. A. Richards, a great literary critic of the twentieth century, had even defined the essence of art as ambiguity, or amenability to multiple interpretation. The more work a single word or phrase could do, the better.

Most people, of course—left- or right-handed—sport an intricate mesh of these characteristics. This makes sense, since the two hemispheres of the brain work together to control our mentality.

That's where the corpus callosum comes in.

It literally connects the two hemispheres—like the Bering Strait, before water overran the archipelago of islands and made it a strait. When the corpus callosum is overrun with injuries, or severed, victims find it difficult or impossible to coordinate tasks controlled by both hemispheres—like reading and listening to music at the same time.

All of that was known in the 1960s, when Jaynes proposed his theory. Since then, research had shown the hemispheres of the brain to be surprisingly adaptable—the left can learn to do right-hemisphere tasks, and right can learn left, under some circumstances.

I made sure these last few Web pages were stored with the hundreds of others I had read in the past week. Then I closed the pages and closed my eyes.

Jenna was already sound asleep. I left my work station, took off my clothes, and slipped into bed with her. But my mind was still racing along the corpus callosum.

Jaynes' theory had been extreme even in the 1960s, when the hemispheres seemed more distinct. He thought that in ancient times the hemispheres each housed a separate persona, and the two talked to each other through the corpus callosum telephone. Prophets hearing the voice of the deity were one manifestation of this—modern schizophrenia was a current, vestigial example. Jaynes thought all of that changed because of a variety of factors—ranging from natural disasters like floods and volcanos to artificial creations like the alphabet—melded the two minds into one.

Even McLuhan called that theory science fiction. Though, from what I'd read of McLuhan, that might have been a compliment. . . . Maybe a left-handed one.

What bothered me most about Jaynes' theory was not that he'd postulated two separate minds in people. For all I knew, that was possible, and his point about schizophrenia was well taken. But what I found hard to accept in Jaynes was what he thought had caused the two minds to merge into our current sense of self. The alphabet? Or some natural calamity causing people to lose faith in the old, "dual" way of thinking?

It had to be something more—something direct, something physical, that could act on the corpus callosum.

I now had the evidence from an autopsy in Australia that Omnin had been found in the corpus callosum of Tom Stewart, who had suffered a memory lapse after coming down with the flu and taking the antibiotic.

But what in the corpus callosum did Omnin impair?

I had also done some reading about quorum-sensing, communicative bacteria.

Were they or something like them the secret agents who had bridged Jaynes' "bicameral mind" to create our current form of consciousness?

Were we human, the way we are today, because of an infection of some rapster bacteria in our brain, an infection that shuttled information back and forth between the hemispheres—an infection that Omnin unknowingly reduced? And in so doing, threatened to reduce our humanity. . . .

But how to prove that? Try to get an analysis of every deceased person's corpus callosum from now on?

The presence of Omnin in itself would prove nothing.

I needed to find the gossiping little organism.

But like so many other times in my work, I seemed in pursuit of something which might well be below our current level of technological identification. If some strain of observable bacteria were inhabiting our brains, creating our sense of self, wouldn't we already have stumbled across them and taken notice of their presence? Even if we did not understand their function, wouldn't we have already seen them in some autopsy or other examination of brain tissue?

We had not.

Which meant that either the bacteria were camouflaged by yet some other agent, or the living organism was something other than bacteria, something a little less, a little more, a little different. But something which, unlike viruses, was hurt by antibiotics. . . .

Or maybe we had already noticed these pseudobacteria—or at least understood their effect upon our brains—sometime much earlier in history, before we even knew what bacteria were, before we could see them under a microscope.

I had to search for them not only here, not only now, but in the past. . . .

"Hey . . ." Jenna turned over, put her arm around my chest, and snuggled.

I kissed her gently on her eyelid.

"What time is it?" she asked groggily.

"Two in the morning," I replied.

"We're two in the morning," Jenna said, still half-asleep. "You and me."

"Yeah."

"Let's do it," she said.

Not that I minded at all—and Jenna looked especially good tonight, her skin milky in the moonlight—but she usually wasn't so blunt. "I should stretch out next to you more often, after burning the midnight Web about memory loss and bicameral minds," I said, and kissed her on the edge of her lips.

She laughed. "I meant, let's get married." She sounded more awake now.

"Ah, sure," I said. "When?"

"Well, if we're going to have a big ceremony, we need time to find a place, send out all the invitations. I think we should invite everyone you ever had an impact on in all of your cases, including the bad guys."

"Funny," I said.

"About having a big wedding, or inviting the perpetrators?"

"A big ceremony is fine by me," I said. "Better chance for getting at least some good presents."

She kissed me. . . .

"So how does next spring sound?" she said, a while later.

"Okay, I guess."

"What's the matter?" she asked.

"I just don't know what shape everyone will be in next spring, if people are taking Omnin en masse in the next flu season."

I CALLED ANDY the next morning, told him about what I had found about the corpus callosum, and further explained my idea of bacteria acting as catalysts for our consciousness.

"Sounds promising," he said.

"Look, we've got to do something to make sure that Omnin is off the market by the end of this year, or sooner," I said.

"I'm trying to build a case for that," Andy answered. "But I'm not getting much support for it down here. You know how it is—we've been over this. No one worries too much that a husband can't recall what he did on his boys' night out—wives are already very familiar with that kind of amnesia." He got more serious. "We need hard evidence, Phil. I've stirred a little interest here with the Tom Stewart autopsy, but we'll need more, much more. I'll get the word out on examination of brain tissue for suites of singing bacteria, but like you said, if they were there, we'd have seen them already."

"So they're some other micro- or submicroorganism with similar properties."

"Right," Andy said. "But no one's going to want to pull back a new drug that diminishes flu complications on the strength of an invisible, unknown organism that may help us remember—or because the Phoenicians may have reached America and then forgot it."

I knew he wasn't wrong. Speculation, theorization, was a far cry from proof. I needed facts—whether in the twenty-first century, or three millennia earlier, or anytime in between. Evidence. Even McNair had said I needed more of it, when he'd pointed me to the chatterbox bacteria. Just as Dugan had pleaded we needed for the Riverside investigation.

They all were saying the same thing: *Get me facts, Phil.*

I TRIED AGAIN to reach Darius Morton. To no avail. I'd have to consign myself to waiting at least until September to find him, when NYU was back in full session and staff.

His book *Ahead of Columbus* was riveting in its arguments that the Phoenicians had made it to the New World, but it presented no archaeological evidence. No remains that were indisputably Phoenician and carbon-dated at 1000 B.C. or any other time had been discovered in North or South America. Of course, before the Viking artifacts had been discovered in the 1970s at L'Anse aux Meadows in Newfoundland, and carbon-dated at A.D. 1000, Norse presence in North American had also been derided by many as myth. . . .

Maybe I ought to look into that Viking facet of this forgotten-America angle more closely. An artifact in the hand, after all, was worth far more than two in speculation. . . .

I knew someone with a special interest in the Vikings. I had sat next to Lloyd Halstad years ago in a course at the New School for Social Research, on the films of Kirk Douglas. I had taken the course because Douglas' *Spartacus* and *Lonely Are the Brave* were among my favorite movies. Halstad was there because he loved *The Vikings* with Douglas—and it was actually a pretty good film. We had stayed in touch off and on over the years.

I tried Halstad at his New York City number. The phone rang three times, and then segued into a slightly different sounding ring—call forwarding at work.

"Hello?" Lloyd picked up the phone. His parents had emigrated from Norway, and his voice had just the slightest touch of an accent.

"Lloyd? Phil D'Amato. How've you been?"

"Phil? It's been years! I just got out of the lake—we have a place up here in Red Hook—and I'm dripping wet, but fine!"

I offered to call back later.

"No, no," Lloyd insisted. "If you don't mind holding on a few seconds, I'll just get a towel and some dry clothes on."

"Thanks. Take your time." I held on, and when Lloyd returned I talked at some length about the reason for my call.

"Hmmm . . . Well, the explicit Lindisfarne-Phoenician connection is news to me," Lloyd observed, "but I certainly wouldn't rule it out. But you want to know if there is any evidence of a Phoenician influence in the Viking artifacts found in North America? Nothing like that in the Viking remains at L'Anse aux Meadows, as far as I know."

"How about at other sites?" I asked.

"Finding artifacts in North America that are indisputably Viking is controversial enough," Lloyd explained, "Lindisfarne or Phoenicia aside. But there are at least half a dozen likely places on the northeast coast of Canada—in addition to L'Anse aux Meadows—with physical remains, bits of weave, parts of tools, from Baffin Island to Ungava Bay on down. And then there are the genetic possibilities. . . . Would you like a fast crash course on all of this?"

I said I most definitely would.

Lloyd said that research into a Viking presence in North America had been going in and out of style for more than a century. "Earlier studies focused on physical artifacts and on Inuit reported to have European physiques and red beards," he continued. "The most ambitious theories had the Vikings sailing down the East Coast as far as South America and the Amazon, or west along the St. Lawrence or north up the Hudson, or sailing and hiking to the Northwest and Alaska, and then sailing down the West Coast to California. Or all three. Variants of these possibilities—far more convincing, I'd say—are that Vikings in Greenland and northeast Canada interbred with Inuit, and their progeny made the trip out West, reversing the path that conventional historians say the Thule people made from West to East. There's been scant evidence even of this, though, other than the odd report of a village of Inuit with European faces, which, alas, always seemed to succumb before it could be checked out scientifically. But gene-mapping kicked in about a decade ago, and could have some exciting results."

"But nothing conclusive as yet?" The possibilities were intoxicating to the historian in me—Vikings penetrating the extent of North America half a millennium prior to Columbus—but I still needed evidence.

"No," Lloyd replied. "The problem with gene-mapping is that even if we find Scandinavian genes in some isolated Inuit group in the Northwest, it's difficult to prove that the genes were introduced in, say, 1100, not A.D. 1700. And we have equivalent problems with fragmentary material remains. A Norse coin from the eleventh century was found in Maine—I've seen it, no doubt it's the real thing—but who can prove when it was left there? Could have been well after Columbus. Petroglyphs in

Canada with Viking faces are better—they date from the 1200s and there's no disputing the pictures were there then—but you know how it is with those faces in rock art. You squint at them one way and you see a Norseman, you squint at them another and you see your high school gym teacher."

I half laughed. "So L'Anse aux Meadows is the only really reliable site."

"Yeah," Lloyd said. "It was a whole settlement, dwellings and all. But even that has its frustrations. The Norse were apparently there for a very short time. The site has no midden piles, nothing to indicate any long-term habitation. It was in and out, a one-night stand as far as colonies go. That's likely why it had no impact on the world."

"The real problem is that we're dealing with two illiterate cultures here, Viking and Inuit," I said. "So there are no written records to put any of the sites, any of the findings, into clearer context." McNair would be proud of me.

"Exactly," Lloyd agreed. "And add to that the problem that the two cultures were not only illiterate but itinerate, constantly on the move, so you not only have no written records, but no stable populations to point at a stone and tell a story about it that their great-great-grandparents handed down."

"All right, one more question, then, Lloyd."

"Sure, I'm enjoying this," he said.

"If you had to pick one place in North America that the Vikings reached other than L'Anse aux Meadows, a place where perhaps they made an impact on a local, stable population, a place where—I know this is stretching it—maybe they talked about Lindisfarne and the Phoenicians, and perhaps did leave some lasting impression on the locals, in some form—where might that be?"

"Cape Cod," Lloyd replied instantly.

"Really?"

"Think about it," Lloyd said. "It juts way out into the North

Atlantic. It was the first land the Pilgrims saw. It had a relatively stable population of Indians. It's packed with little libraries full of moldy old documents. Yep, I'd put my money on the Cape."

"You wouldn't want to join me on a little research expedition there next week?" I asked.

"Love to, Phil, but I'm off next week for a year in Australia."

"You think the Vikings made it down there, too?" I jibed.

Lloyd chuckled. "Always possible. But, no. Actually, I'm going there to look at their rock art—it's become another one of my passions."

"Don't take any Omnin down under."

Lloyd laughed again. "Not to worry—I had the flu earlier this year, and I expect that makes me more or less immune to anything similar this year."

"Well, you take care of yourself anyway," I said.

I PACKED A suitcase for Jenna and me as soon as I got home. She had an adjunct teaching job at Princeton that started the last week in August. I was entitled to two weeks' vacation. That gave us plenty of time. I told Dugan I'd keep in touch with everyone on a daily basis about the Riverside case, and come back immediately if anything new came up.

"How does Cape Cod sound for the next two weeks?" I asked Jenna as she walked in the door. "I rented a little cottage for us off Ellis Landing Road, right near the place I met Andy in April."

"Sounds great!" She kissed me. "So will this be a real vacation or your kind of vacation?"

I smiled. "My kind, I'm afraid." By which we both understood: I'd be there to work. "But don't worry, we'll still have time for lots of long walks on the beach. . . ."

JENNA GOT TO take most of those walks alone.

I got to tour just about every library, historical society, and old and rare bookstore on the Cape. Any of these places could well have a one-of-a-kind handwritten document that even the New York Public Library on Forty-second Street did not know about. . . .

I hit paydirt twelve days later, in the Brewster Ladies Library, less than two miles from our cottage. I had skipped over the place at first, owing to its less-than-scholarly-sounding name. I wouldn't make that mistake again.

Right there on the open shelves of its tiny reference section were several local history books, published in the early 1800s. These held accounts of early sea-captains who had retired to their shorefront homes in Brewster. I would have found these engaging in any case. But a bound, handwritten manuscript written by an E. L. Costa in 1819 held special interest. . . .

The manuscript was ledger-sized, and contained about one hundred unnumbered pages written upon with what now looked to be a brown ink—the color of fall oak leaves after they had fallen. The ink was a bit faded, but it and the handwriting were legible. The title—*The Cape in Antiquity, Recent and Distant, with Considerations of the Provenance of Flora and Fauna and Prominent Families*—was enough to make me sit with it and read page by page, in a nearby, overstuffed chair by a big window.

Much of the writing was observation, charmingly accurate in an age before Darwin, of the ecological niches of the numerous species of birds that still thrived along the woods and shores of the Cape. "Each enjoys its own admixture of beach plum, wildberry, or other wilde seed or fruit. In so doing, each natural crop is attended by its own devoted winged Gardener. . . ."

But in the last third of the manuscript, I found this:

It has been claimed that the Cape was contacted by voyagers from the Olde World five centuries prior to Christopher Columbus. According to this history, pirates of Danish or

*Norwegian stock, seeking a safe haven for ill-gotten bounty, made several landings in the harbour of what is today known as Welle Fleet. Further, if this history is to be believed, the landing was the consequence of much planning. The pirates were said to be guided by a fallen priest from the Holy Island across the sea—*jeez, that would be Lindisfarne—*who himself was said to be guided by knowledge of North America by a civilization far more ancient than his. Legends say he left a written account of these voyages, which account was said to be consumed in fires commencing in the forests near the shore, which fires have been known since antiquity to sometimes beset this land, all due to the lightning storms which are at once the glory and bane of life on the Cape, as its many varieties of inhabitants including human beings have come to know.*

SO BRISKMAN'S STORY was confirmed.

"Though for all we know, Briskman may have read the very same account years ago," I said to Jenna as we finally got to stroll along the beach the next morning. "Maybe he visited Cape Cod as a kid with his family."

"No evidence is perfect," Jenna said. "There are always holes and soft spots. But I think your theory about a Viking-Phoenician connection to America is certainly stronger now than before we came up here."

I took her hand. The beach was especially beautiful today. Seagulls, sandpipers, even the colorful human gliders in the air were nice. A shack along the shore was broadcasting Beatles music to one and all. The shack seemed to vibrate with the best of the guitar licks, and the high notes Lennon hit, as if the cottage itself was one big AM radio, and the shimmering screen porch its speaker.

"This would be a nice place to retire to," I said.

Jenna smiled, perhaps a bit sadly. "You'll never retire."

"Is that okay?" I asked sincerely. I felt genuinely bad about

blowing most of our two weeks here in libraries, but what could
I do?

Jenna drew close to me. "If you don't look after the human
race, who will?"

I knew there was a touch of resignation, even unhappiness
there, as well as admiration.

We held each other for a few minutes.

"So, what's next?" Jenna asked.

"I checked in the phone book for 'Costa's this morning,"
I replied. "Pretty much of a hopeless case—it's a very common name here. A lot of the Portuguese sailors who settled
on the Cape centuries ago had that name. I'd say there's no
chance of locating any of E. L.'s heirs now. The ladies in the
Brewster library were no help with that, either, sweet as they
were."

"How about we drive to Wellfleet, and poke around there?"
Jenna suggested.

"Let's go for a swim first—the tide's coming in."

WELLFLEET WAS ABOUT thirty minutes east of Brewster, on Route
6A into Route 6. Parts of it were quaint and charming; other
parts were a bit too commercialized for my taste. I knew several
forensic psychologists in Wellfleet—I'd heard it said that every
psychologist in Boston vacationed here—but two didn't answer
their phones, and the third had none listed. They might have
provided some local leads. Well, the sky and the bay were pastel
consolation. . . .

I'd already checked all the book repositories I could find
on the Cape, earlier in the week. Jenna and I decided to devote
our time to the dozen or more antique shops in and around
town. These occasionally had a few old books.

We came up empty. It was past five already, and all we had
eaten all day was breakfast. Dinner seemed a good idea. There
were some inviting restaurants on Main Street.

We passed a very attractive couple on the street—both women.

"Got you thinking of the Riverside case again," Jenna commented, as we neared a little seafood restaurant.

"Yeah," I replied. I guess I hadn't been talking for the past few minutes.

"Large gay community in this part of the Cape," Jenna said, "especially Provincetown."

"Yeah," I said again. Provincetown was at the far eastern tip of the Cape. And I had indeed been thinking of the Riverside case—not only because we had walked past a lesbian couple, but because of the poster I had seen earlier on a wall, and forgotten, until I saw the couple.

The poster was from a gay women's group in Provincetown. It was devoted to countering antilesbian prejudice, and listed all the jobs that gay women held in society. None were really unusual, especially in this day and age.

But one stood out as suspect in the Riverside crimes.

NINE

 I woke up in my bed in New York the morning after next. Jenna was off with some friends for breakfast near Central Park.

It felt good to wake up in my bed. It was like day and night in comfort compared to the spongy spring that had passed for a mattress in our cottage on Cape Cod.

Other than that, nothing felt better about being back in New York. . . .

The dog days of August were nearly over. College kids would soon be back in class. I hoped that what I had said to Dugan about the Riverside murders being on hiatus for the summer was wrong—because the summer was soon to end.

My original notion about the summer was based on the idea that the murderer was specifically preying on Columbia University students, and she—possibly he—was a student there. That, of course, was still possible, maybe even likely. But there were other scenarios.

I needed to conduct more interviews—at least two more, at this point.

I showered, dressed, gobbled a bagel for breakfast, and got down to the office about an hour early.

I called Amy Berman—Claudia's friend—the one I thought had been in danger from Leslie Roth, the tall blonde with the short hair, who had turned out also to be Amy's friend, and no danger.

Amy hung up on me.

"Listen," I said on the second call.

She hung up again.

"Would you prefer I asked the police to detain you?" I managed to get out on the third call.

"On what charge?"

"As a material witness, possibly," I replied. "But look, I don't want to do that."

"So why are you bothering me?"

"I'm sorry for upsetting you and your friend Leslie—I overreacted, I admit it. I was trying to protect you. But there's still a killer out there—who seems to like women on the Upper West Side. Look, I don't mean to scare you, or upset you again, but I need your help. I just want to talk to you."

She sighed. "I'm already late for work. I can't talk to you now."

"How about later?"

She sighed again, more loudly. "I have an appointment with an adviser at Fordham at six P.M. I suppose I can get there fifteen minutes early. We can sit on the benches in front of the school—the southeast corner of the Lincoln Center campus. You know where that is?"

"Yes."

"I'm warning you, though. If you show up with cops in police cars with sirens, I'll sue all of you. For God's sake, you've got me sounding like a criminal myself already!"

I ARRIVED TEN minutes before our appointment, and Amy was already waiting for me. She was wearing a plum-colored blouse and a lavender skirt and looked very good. I realized that the only other times I had seen her, I hadn't been in any condition to notice. I had been on the verge of the flu the first time, and in pursuit of someone I thought might be on the verge of killing her, the second time.

She gave me a short, sour smile.

I took a seat and started talking. Better keep my preambles to a minimum, and get less-contrived responses.

"I know you don't have much time, and I very much appreciate your seeing me," I began. "Could you tell me about your relationship with Professor McNair—?"

"My relationship? I was his student at UCLA last year, as you well know. What exactly are you implying?"

"Nothing—I didn't mean to imply anything. I was just interested in how well you know him."

"Look, I may be divorced, but that doesn't mean I play around with my professors. I don't have the time, anyway. Between my daughter Mindy, my job, and school, I barely have time to breathe most days."

"I know," I said, "and you take very good care of her. She seems like a fine girl." Mindy had been at her grandmother's apartment on the night Jenna and I had shown up on Amy's doorstep. We had accompanied Amy to pick up Mindy after Leslie had been released—the least we could do was provide shuttle service for all concerned, after the aggravation of that evening. Amy had been so angry she'd wanted to refuse it—but she had only $2.43 in her purse.

"Thank you," she said softly, and appeared to calm down a little.

"I'm really just interested in your impressions of Professor McNair—I don't know how well you know him. But I mean, what kind of a teacher did you find him to be? Did you ever meet his wife Rhonda? Were you—and other students—ever to their home—?"

She looked at her watch. "I'll be late for my meeting. I don't really see the point of this." She stood up and walked away.

Well, at least I had got some of what I'd wanted in this interview.

I CALLED THE second woman on my list the next morning.

"Oh, hi, Dr. D'Amato," Carol Michosky replied. "What can I do for you?"

"Could we get together and talk today? Anytime would work for me—just for a few minutes."

"I'm packing to leave for a little vacation the day after tomorrow," she replied. "It's been a long hot summer for me, and I really need to get out of here."

"Our interview won't take long. I promise."

"But what do you want to talk to me about, anyway?" she protested. "I know I screwed up on that lineup. I tried my best. I was confused. . . ."

"I know," I said, trying to be as soothing as I could. "I'm not looking to hold you up on that. It's just . . . There are a few small points I'd like to go over with you."

"I'd rather not, really," she said. She had that tone like she was about to hang up.

"Look, I really must insist. This is police business."

Silence.

"Ms. Michosky? Tell you what: You don't need to come down to my office, if that's inconvenient. We can meet anywhere you like—even out in the park near your house, if you want." Public benches seemed to be my venues for interviews these days.

"Okay," she finally said. "There's a juice bar on Ninety-first and Broadway—I usually walk down there around eleven to get my daily fix of carrot and wheat."

"Been too long since I had a good glass of carrot juice myself," I said, truthfully. "Eleven it is."

I WAS IN a mood to walk, so I got off the subway at West Seventy-second Street, and grabbed a papaya juice from Gray's across the street. True, I was supposed to have a carrot juice with Michosky, but it had also been too long since I'd had a papaya, and besides, the carrot would make a good chaser.

I looked back at the Seventy-second Street station. It was late-Victorian in structure—maybe early-Edwardian; what was the difference?—and still looked great through its stains, at least to me.

I'd always felt a deep connection with the nineteenth, Victorian century. Maybe because it bore the origins of modern forensic science, with Fauld's letter to *Nature* in 1880, proposing the use of fingerprints to identify criminals. Or maybe because it was populated with the likes of Darwin, Mendel, Pasteur . . . I had respect akin to reverence for all of those biopioneers—not only for their discoveries, but for the way they exulted in, rather than apologized for, their belief in progress through science and rationality. Sure, the twentieth century had had its innings in the sciences of life—more than its innings, with Fleming and penicillin, Salk and polio vaccine, Crick and Watson and the alphabet of life. But walking here in the twenty-first, looking back at the nineteenth, I often felt as if I'd leapfrogged a large part of the twentieth century and its cynicism. Maybe the human genome and its wonders to behold would help rekindle the vision of scientific nobility that the atom bomb and other atrocities had almost extinguished.

Carol Michosky was standing nervously in front of the juice bar on Broadway and Ninety-first Street. She had the demeanor of a woman who smoked three packs of cigarettes a day, but had misplaced her third pack two hours ago. She ran her hand through caked dirty-blonde hair. It looked more dirty, less blonde, than I remembered it. She turned and greeted me.

"It's too hot in there," she said, and pointed to the juice bar. "I think the air conditioner is broken or something. I didn't feel like standing in line. Is it okay if we forget the juice and just walk?"

"Of course." I followed her lead and walked east with her on Ninety-first Street.

"Ordinarily I'd go towards Riverside, not Central Park," she said. "I used to feel safer going west—with all those wild-ings in Central Park and everything." She shuddered. "But now . . ."

I nodded sympathetically.

"It's like Scylla and Charybdis!" she said. "Hey, aren't I the poet!"

Now, where had I heard Scylla being talked about recently? No, not talked about—I'd been thinking about the theory that the *Odyssey* was taken from a Phoenician seafaring log, and the evidence that the Greek "Scylla" came from a semitic word meaning *rock*. What a tangled web I'd been caught up in lately. . . .

"I'm sorry I was so sharp with you on the phone," Michosky continued. "I really do need a vacation. I haven't been feeling well lately—can't seem to shake this summer cold. And I absolutely don't believe in antibiotics—I never take them."

"Never?"

"No," she replied. "Oh, right, you wanted to know if I had taken any Omnin. Absolutely not! The thought of that stuff running through my system makes me itch—I work too hard to build up all the acidophilus in my tummy!" She rubbed it and smiled.

"You don't know Professor Robert McNair by any chance?"

She looked at me, eyes open, innocent. "No. Should I?"

"He has views about antibiotics very similar to yours," I replied. But she was convincing about not knowing McNair. "Anyway . . . could we get back to the night of your attack for just a few minutes?" I proceeded, gently. "If it's not too painful."

"Yes, it's painful," she said. "But I figured that's what you wanted to talk to me about again, so I steeled myself for this, and I'm ready."

"Thank you," I said. "I was wondering if you could go over for me again why you think the woman who asked you about the movie theater and the woman who tried to strangle you were the same person—you were very insistent about that in your initial interviews."

"I don't know," Michosky said.

"You're not sure now?"

"I'm very fuzzy about that night now—that's why I made such an ass of myself at the police lineup. I'm not sure whose face I saw, now."

"So none of your memory has returned or gotten any clearer since the lineup. . . . It's the same or even worse now than it was then?"

She nodded and looked at me quizzically. "Do muddled memories sometimes get better in these kinds of cases?"

"Sometimes. It depends." So she likely was telling the truth about not taking Omnin—Dugan and Jenna and I had recovered some of our lost memories. Of course, she could have been lying—could be lying now—about her memory falling apart that night in the first place. I pressed her: "You told the police that you got a quick glimpse of your assailant, and saw the face of the woman who asked you about the movie theater a second earlier, right?"

"Yeah . . ."

I spoke more softly. "I don't mean to be cross-examining you here. I just want to try to . . . to understand this a little more. How exactly did you see your assailant for that brief moment?"

"Like, through my eyes?" Michosky answered in an exaggerated Valley-girl up-talk intonation. I wasn't sure if she was mocking me, or was just upset.

"I'm sorry," she said.

"It's okay," I said. "I know how tough this is for you. What I was getting at was, did you see the strangler face-to-face, or over your shoulder? What features struck you? Was the hair of your assailant the exact same as the moviegoer?"

Michosky let out a big sigh. "I know her hair was dark—that I'm sure of."

"Okay," I said. Sharalee Boland—the suspect in the lineup—did have black hair. And so did everyone else in the lineup, including Claudia Gonzales. "What else do you remember seeing in your assailant's face?"

"I guess I didn't see that much," Michosky admitted. She stopped in front of a nineteenth-century brownstone. We were already across the street from Central Park. "I just got a very quick look at her, over my shoulder, at a very painful angle. But I had a powerful feeling that she was the one who had just asked me about the movie house. That's what I told the police."

I thought for a moment. "You told the police you had a 'powerful feeling' the two were the same person? That doesn't sound quite the same as you had a quick glance and they *looked* the same. Believe me, I'm not trying to split hairs or grill you, but . . ."

Michosky looked at me, then ran her hands through her hair three times in rapid succession. "No, I see what you're getting at," she finally said. "Maybe my strong sense that the two were the same was not based on what I saw. But what, then?"

I encouraged her to speculate.

She closed her eyes. "They had the same smell," she said.

"The same smell?" I asked dumbly.

"Yeah, they had the same perfume on—they smelled the same. I got a whiff of what that bitch who attacked me was wearing. It was the same as the woman who was looking for the movie theater. But damn it, I really can't remember their faces at all anymore—just their smell. . . ."

So I had learned two things in this walk from Broadway to Central Park.

One, it was possible after all that the movie fan and the would-be strangler were two different women—who happened to look generally similar, but also happened to wear the same perfume.

And two, if I believed Michosky about not taking Omnin—which I still was inclined to—she had indeed suffered a memory loss for other reasons, maybe the trauma that DA Rubin had mentioned. That would explain her loss of visual memory. But olfactory memories can run much deeper, be less shakable, than visual recollections—maybe because the nose has a direct connection to the brain that bypasses the blood-brain barrier. I had learned that somewhere, maybe in one of my under-graduate classes in psychology and perception. And that would explain why Carol's "feeling" that her questioner and her assailant were the same person—based on their perfume—had endured.

"Any guess about the name of the perfume?" I ventured to Carol.

She shook her head no. "I just know it's not something I've ever worn. It didn't smell bizarre, or outlandish, though. It was maybe even familiar, in a way. I'll keep thinking about it."

"Okay. Can I give you a quick call tomorrow, so we can touch base one more time before your vacation?"

She nodded.

I thanked her—genuinely—and wished her a wonderful trip. I could negotiate getting a vacation number from her tomorrow, if need be.

In the meantime, I decided I'd better speak to Sharalee Boland again—she, at the very least, had asked Carol for direc-tions to the movie that night. And for that matter, I probably also needed to talk again to Leslie Roth. She had blonde hair, but brunette wigs were as common as chocolate kisses.

I was sure they'd be even less pleased to hear from me than Amy Berman and Carol Michosky.

But I had an important question to ask them.

What perfume did they wear?

ROTH WAS HIKING the White Mountains in New Hampshire, and would be out of range through Labor Day.

I had a bit more luck with Boland. She worked as a manager at a Starbucks on the East Side. I reached her by phone the next morning. She was nicer to me than I had expected.

"None of your fucking business," she replied to my query about what perfume she usually wore. And then she hung up.

Plan B for such occasions entailed my calling Laurie Feldman—not to find out what perfume *she* wore, but to enlist her aid in finding what Boland wore. Laurie was an undercover detective, with a knack for quickly making friends with women—at a checkout line in a department store, from a nearby table in a restaurant, wherever—and gaining their confidence.

She didn't disappoint.

"Shalimar," she told me on the phone that afternoon. "It's not cheap, not excessively expensive, moderately priced and moderately popular, I'd say. Most stores like Bloomingdale's have it—that's where I got lucky and made the connection with Boland today, right after lunch. Her friend at work told me that's where she'd be."

"Good work!" I said. "Do you think I could go down to Bloomingdale's, so I'd know what it actually smells like?"

"I'm one step ahead of you, Phil—I already bought a little vial, just for the occasion. Buy me a beer after work, and I'll give you a sniff."

I did as requested.

Later that evening, I sat down with Jenna for shrimp and corn on the cob at home. I told her about the Shalimar. "It smells like something I know," I said.

"That's probably because I wear it once in a while," she replied. "It's one of my favorites."

"So you're the one who tried to strangle Carol Michosky?"

"I can't recall."

"Nice."

I AWOKE THE next morning to the smell of Shalimar and the phone both ringing in my head. Jenna groaned and pulled the cover over her face. I reached over her and picked up the phone. She must have put a bit of Shalimar on before she went to sleep—I'd conked out early last night. The whiff pleased yet disturbed me, a good wine with a disconcerting undercurrent.

Dugan was on the phone. I didn't have to hear what he had to say to know it was bad news. He didn't call this early in the morning to tell me anything good.

"Meet me at Ninety-fourth and Riverside as soon as you can," he said.

I was there in under fifteen minutes—traffic was light at the beginning of the morning, at the end of summer, in the city. Dugan directed me to the body, stretched out facedown, unclothed, near a tree. One of the cops said something half under his breath about her having a nice ass, and cupped his hand as if to caress it. Dugan glared him away before I had a chance to shove him.

I pictured Carol Michosky's face, the last time I had seen it, just yesterday. It had borne a general resemblance even then to Jillian Murphy's face—delicate, tragic, somehow still pretty even in death on Ed Monti's table. Now Carol's face, in quarter-profile on the ground, was more complete in its resemblance to Jillian's. They were twins in a trait that was the last word in resemblances.

And I also knew with gnawing certainty that I was in part responsible. Murders don't usually happen by accident. Something in my flurry of interviews the past few days had called forth a killer for Carol.

TEN

"Nothing especially unusual here." Dugan gave me a printout of a hastily compiled log of Carol's recent phone activity, at a hastily arranged afternoon meeting of just him and me in his office. The log included calls from her cell phone as well as her apartment in New York City.

"There's a call from her home to my office number at five-twelve P.M. yesterday," I noted.

"Yeah, I saw that. What did she say to you?"

"I wasn't in." The call had come in right around the time I was buying Laurie a beer and finding out the secrets of Shalimar.

"Did she leave a message?" Dugan inquired.

"Nothing on my voice-mail when I came in this morning," I replied.

"Did she talk to someone else in your office?"

"I'll check when I get back there." I shook my head. "Unconsummated calls like that always lead to no good." And this no good was about as bad as it got.

"Well, here's something else to get you aggravated," Dugan said, and slid another printout to me across the table.

It was a breakdown of crimes and convictions during the past six months. "As you'll see, violent crimes are up and convictions are down. Just the kind of diverging lines the commissioner hates."

"What prompted the special six-month summary?" I asked. Usually they were weekly, monthly, yearly. "They worked it up this morning after Carol's murder?"

"As likely a reason as any," Dugan replied. "Look, on the one hand, by all means send this along to your friend Andy at the CDC—maybe it's more evidence of the memory bug's impact. The drop in convictions might be due to law-enforcement amnesia. On the other hand—get me the Riverside strangler already. We damn well better not forget about that."

JENNA GOT ME on the cell phone just before I got back to my office. "I've been trying to reach you for an hour," she said. I usually turned my phone off before meetings with Dugan—he didn't like interruptions and I didn't blame him. I had just turned it back on. "Take a look at the obituary page in today's *New York Times*."

I walked into my office and picked up the copy of today's paper that had been sitting on my desk, unread past the first page, since the morning. "Jeez," I said to Jenna when I turned to the obits.

ROBERT MCNAIR, UCLA PROFESSOR OF COGNITIVE ANTHROPOLOGY, DEAD AT 47, the headline on the quarter-page obituary read. There was a picture of him, looking good, likely from at least a decade ago. I scanned the text. "Natural causes . . . pneumonia suspected but not yet confirmed . . . had been in ill health for years . . . funeral in his hometown of Chicago tomorrow at noon . . ."

"I'm not really surprised," I said sadly. "He put too much faith in those homeopathic remedies. Still . . ."

"I know," Jenna said.

"I had no idea his hometown was Chicago," I said.

"It says he lived there the first eighteen years of his life."

"Why the hell didn't someone call me when he was sick? Rhonda, his wife, someone . . ."

"You don't really know them that well," Jenna replied softly. "You know how that is. He's important in your world, in a case you're working on, so you naturally think you're important in his."

"I'm going to call her now anyway," I said.

"Okay," Jenna said.

I tried, but there was no answer.

I got Jenna back on the phone. "I'm going to Chicago for the funeral."

"You spoke to Rhonda?"

"No," I replied. "But I'm going anyway. The obit doesn't say anything about it being private or just for family."

Jenna didn't completely approve, but knew better than to argue with me. "I'll get you on a plane—you want to leave today or tomorrow morning?"

"Let's try for a flight that gets in around nine in the morning tomorrow," I said. "I've still got lots more work to do today on Carol's murder."

Jenna called me back twenty minutes later. "Bad news," she said. "Thunderstorms around Chicago, security problems on two airlines—flights are being canceled left and right. I can't get you anything to Chicago tomorrow or today."

"Goddamn." I thought for a second. "I'll drive it."

"No," Jenna said sharply. "I'm not going to let you. You're already tired, emotionally drained. You're not going to do this case or the memory problem or anything any good by winding up crushed behind a tree!"

"I'm going anyway."

"You're not," Jenna insisted.

"I've got to get to that funeral—it may be the only chance I'll have to pick up something valuable from Rhonda, or from who knows who else will be there. . . ."

Jenna sighed. "Let's think if there's another way. Do trains run from here to Chicago?"

"I don't know," I said. I looked at my watch—it was 3:37. "I don't think our trains move fast enough, even if they go to Chicago. We're not like France or Japan."

"Let me at least check," Jenna said. "If the trains won't do it, then I can at least come with you in the car, and we can share the driving."

"I thought you had a crucial committee meeting tomorrow at Princeton."

"I do," Jenna said. "But . . . we're wasting time. Let me check the trains."

She got back me to me five minutes later. "You're booked on the Lake Shore Limited, leaving Penn Station at four thirty-five this afternoon. You better get moving. They said you can pick up your tickets on the train—I told them it was police business. Just show them your photo-ID."

"What time does the train get to Chicago?"

"Eleven-fifteen tomorrow morning. The funeral's at noon. It's not more than twenty minutes by cab from Union Station—I checked it out. So you should be there just in time."

I looked again at my watch—it was now 3:43 P.M. Penn Station shouldn't be more than a half an hour, at most forty-minute, ride from my office at this time of day. I took a quick glance at myself in the small corroded mirror that hung on one of my walls. I had on a dull corduroy jacket, pants that needed pressing, and no tie. Wait a minute—I was sure I could buy a quick tie at Penn Station.

I threw Jenna a kiss. "Thanks, baby. I'll call when I'm situated on the train."

I DASHED INTO the train at 4:31, with four minutes to spare and a cheap seven-dollar tie around my collar. I had actually done the cab ride in under forty minutes, but the tie store I had ducked into in Penn Station seemed devoid of cashiers. I was on the verge of counting out seven dollars and leaving the cash on the counter, when someone finally appeared, to take my money. And then I had trouble locating the track with the Lake Shore Limited. But I had made it.

"Take a seat by the window on the left-hand side if you can find it," a conductor advised me, after processing my tickets, "it has the best view of the Hudson on the way up."

I did as suggested, and plopped into a very comfortable seat with plenty of legroom. This would have to do for the next eighteen hours—all of the private sleeping compartments had been reserved days ago, Amtrak had told Jenna.

But I didn't really mind. First, I doubted if the city would have covered the $400 for the round-trip sleeper. Second, I wasn't sure if I would have been willing to put out that money myself. Third, I was looking forward to mingling with some of the other passengers—total strangers could sometimes be sources of odd insights and valuable bits of information.

The train slid quietly out of its berth. This was one of the things I had always liked about trains—the way they started their journey almost imperceptibly, atom by atom, unlike the roar and boom of an airplane. It was 4:44—nine minutes late already— but the train would have plenty of time to make this up along the way. I reclined the seat and stretched out my legs and looked at the first view of the Hudson and New Jersey beyond.

"This seat taken?" A tall man with a two-day stubble on a ruddy complexion was standing over me. He looked genial enough, though—and besides, I couldn't just lie to him.

"Be my guest," I said, and gestured to the empty aisle seat beside me.

"Thanks." He threw a heavy, clanking bag into the over-head luggage rack, sat down, and took off his shoes. He wasn't wearing any socks. His toenails looked like they had last been clipped in the Pleistocene.

I shifted slightly in my seat. "Beautiful view," I offered, looking out of the big window.

"Oh yeah," my companion said, "maybe the best in the whole railroad system. Except maybe the Pacific route."

"You ride the trains a lot?"

"Oh yeah," he said, a second time. "You get to feel like you're really part of the country that way. Not like popping in and out of the city like an impostor from on high, like you do in an airplane."

Looking at him, I had trouble believing he could even afford to travel by plane. But his words rang true.

"We've forgotten what it's like," he continued. "What it feels like to be connected to people and places in *real time*—everything's airplanes and—what do you call it?—cyberspace today. Yeah, everything's computers—but lots of the system ain't up yet—hey, set the alarm clock earlier! Time to get up, Computer! The system's sleeping. We've forgotten what it's like to live without computers, but the system ain't up yet."

I looked at him carefully. He would have had my attention even if he hadn't uttered "forgotten" twice—a word that was sure to compel my interest these days. "What have we forgotten about railroads?" I asked.

"Are you kidding? They paved them over into bike paths, for God's sake! How far can you get on a bicycle? How many people can it carry? A bicycle built for two? And they missed the boat on those fast trains, too."

"You mean the Acela? The one that goes from New York to Boston in three hours?"

"The very one," he said, nodding. "Why do you think it took so long to get them going? Why do you think you're still on this slowpoke to Chicago—you're going to Chicago, right?"

I nodded.

My seatmate continued. "I'll tell you why the fast train took so long to get moving: Because the people who were working on it forgot what they were doing! And you know why they forgot?"

"No. Tell me."

"Computers! Half the time they're not up yet, see? They're down! And people rely on them, instead of their memories, and they lose information. . . ."

Well, it would be too much to believe if he had blamed the forgetting on Omnin. But his point about computers and memory loss was reminiscent of what McNair had said the first time I'd met him, when he was talking about Socrates and his critique of writing—the philosopher's fear that writing would cause our memories to atrophy. That was a great lecture. . . . Poor McNair. Hard to believe he was dead—though I, of all people, knew death was all too easy to believe.

The conductor made the first call for dinner in the dining car. My stomach was grumbling. I asked my companion if he'd care to join me, my treat.

"Oh no. Thank you, but no," he said. "I'll be just fine with this." He pulled a greasy paper bag out from under the seat. I didn't want to hang around to see what was in it.

He stood up in the aisle, so I could get out. It wasn't really necessary—there was more than enough room for me to pass. "You sure about dinner?" I tried one more time. "It would really be my pleasure."

"I'm fine, really," he replied. "But thank you again for the offer."

DINNER REALLY WAS a pleasure—not so much because of the food, which was okay, but the view. Light from the setting sun bounced off the Hudson outside my window, and seemed to reach my face in golden packets that accompanied every bite I took. An elderly gentleman sat across the table. He was on his way to Chicago, too. The wash of light, the gentleman, the motion of the train against the river, made me feel like I was traveling a long time ago. . . . The Lake Shore Limited, with service to Buffalo, Cleveland, Chicago, and the last two centuries. . . .

The gentleman excused himself as I finished my cup of tea. It suddenly occurred to me that my friend with the paper bag and the poetic edge might be gone when I returned to my seat. I paid hurriedly, and made my way back.

He was still there, mumbling to himself about something. His face lit up when he saw me. "So, was your dinner good?" he asked.

"Wonderful," I replied.

"Yeah, they always are, this time of day, this particular place. Hey—I saved your seat for you! I had to go to the bathroom. When I got back, some kid was in your seat! I told him it was taken. He said sorry, he hadn't realized. I told him no problem, that's why they put erasers on pencils. To correct mistakes. Our brains work that way, too—nothing has to be permanent in there. Our brains can erase mistakes, and then write the correct stuff in—though that could be wrong, too. But that could be erased too. Wouldn't you agree?"

"Yes, I would."

We continued conversing like this until we got to Albany. "I'm off in Schenectady, next stop," he said, as he put on his shoes and stood up. "I'm going to stretch my legs a little." He smiled, and walked down the aisle. His gait was a little shaky, but he didn't seem in any danger of falling.

We had a forty-five-minute wait in Albany, and were told we could walk outside if we wanted. I decided instead to lean back and close my eyes, for at least a few minutes. . . .

Just about everything that guy had said had relevance to the memory case—Amtrak taking so long with the Acela because people had forgotten some of the details of their work; the brain erasing and rewriting. . . .

Visions of bacteria in the shape of little pink erasers and tiny points of lead filled my head. . . .

Was this guy talking like this because he had some connection to the memory events, or was he just some guy talking, and I was so primed about this that I saw relevance in even a casual, offbeat conversation on a train?

I opened my eyes, and realized that I hadn't been in touch with Jenna since I'd boarded the train. She no doubt knew from Amtrak that I was aboard, but I had promised to call her once I was under way. I wondered why she hadn't called me.

I took out my cell phone—it was still on, and seemed to be okay. I called Jenna. Some kind of "circuits busy" announcement greeted me. Typical for this time of day, I guessed—just past the evening rush hour—but annoying; these phones had a habit of losing service just when you most needed them. Well, at least this wasn't any kind of emergency.

I looked at my watch. The train still had twenty minutes in Albany. I decided to walk outside.

There was no sign of my friend, but a blonde woman around thirty, in tight, worn bluejeans, walked by and caught my eye. Made me think about Carol, and those stranglings. . . .

Damn it, I thought I had an inkling of who the killer might be, from what had popped into my head that last day on Cape Cod, in Wellfleet. I could see a face behind the hands that had strangled the life out of Carol Michosky, Jillian Murphy, and the others. But I had to know more before I moved—before I risked destroying someone's life on no real evidence, just a bunch of possible connections. I needed to know how my conversations with Amy Berman and Carol Michosky and anyone else on that day had somehow lured the killer into action. I needed to know at least that, before I moved—

"All aboard," a conductor announced over a loudspeaker. "We'll be moving in a few minutes."

MY FRIEND WAS at his seat, napping, feet unshod, when I returned. He opened up an eye. "Glad to see you made it back," he said.

"I was tempted to wait until the train started moving, and then run alongside and jump on, but I thought the better of it," I said, and smiled.

He rewarded me with a belly laugh. "Plenty of times I did that, as a kid."

"Somehow I knew you'd say that," I replied.

The train slowly left the Albany-Rensselaer station behind with the sunshine. I looked out at the darkening landscape, then back at my companion.

"What kind of work do you do?" I asked.

"Carpenter, freelance, retired," he answered. "I love working on private homes—you get a chance to make people's dreams come true."

"That's a worthy rarity, isn't it? All too often we step on them."

He nodded. "What's your line of work, if you don't mind my asking?"

"Of course not," I said. "I just asked you yours. I'm a forensic scientist."

"Like Quincy!"

"Sort of." Quincy, of 1970s television fame, had actually been a coroner—a medical examiner—Ed Monti's job. But it was close enough to mine for purposes like this.

"So how come you're taking the train rather than flying?"

"Bad weather around Chicago, lots of flights canceled—this was the only way I could make sure I'd be in Chicago tomorrow morning," I replied. "But if I'd known how much I'd enjoy the views and the conversation, I'd have gone this way even if they had a flight that picked me up at my door."

He chuckled appreciatively. "Like I was saying before, this is the only way to travel. Well, this, and the water—the lakes and rivers and oceans. We don't realize these days how far people got in those old days. And they saw much more, too."

I nodded. "You know anything about the Vikings?"

"The football team?"

"No, the real Vikings, from Norway," I replied.

"I know," he said. "I was just pulling your leg."

I smiled. "So, you think the Vikings may have made it here, to America?" That I was even asking him this was a measure of how far I was stretching in the memory investigation—trying to get information, confirmation, whatever, from a stranger on the train.

He shrugged. "Don't know. . . ." His eyes gleamed with another thought. "Quincy!" he said. "How about that? I was sitting next to Quincy on the train—wait until I tell the wife about that! The first thing she'll ask me is what kind of murders you're working on. Would it be okay if we talked about your work?"

"Believe it or not, we already have," I answered.

He laughed. "Oh, I get it. Now you're pulling *my* leg. Fair is fair. I'm game. So you're working on a Viking murder case? They did go in for a lot of rape and pillaging, didn't they? You mulling over some old bones?" He laughed again.

"Sort of. . . ."

The conductor announced that we would soon be in Schenectady.

"Well, that's my cue," my friend said. He put on his shoes, stood up and grabbed his clanking bag from the overhead, then offered a big, bony hand to me—all in a single, disjointed move. "Quincy!" he said again. "The wife's not gonna believe it!"

I shook his hand. "It was fun riding with you."

"Same here," he said, and lumbered away, down the aisle, to one of the exits.

The train stopped very briefly in Schenectady, and then

slipped slowly out. It was now almost completely dark outside. I leaned back in my seat and closed my eyes.

I saw the bacteria in my brain again. This time they weren't pencil points and eraser heads. They were little cells—little cell phones—sending out streams of molecules to one another. I had read about some molecular form of bacterial signaling on the Web. Is that what Omnin jammed? Of course it did, or something similar! I should have been more definite about that with Andy. I'd known all along that Omnin was a different, new kind of antibiotic. "Ninety-five percent guaranteed not to upset the stomach"—that was the first thing I had heard about Omnin, from Dugan. How it could be so close to certain of not killing acidophilus and other helpful bacteria in our digestive systems? Well, the traditional way was to target specific, pathological bacteria—antibiotics that only went after dangerous, illness-causing germs. But Omnin's very name said its strategy was otherwise—it was designed to knock out the widest possible range of bacteria. How could it do that without killing good bacteria?

By interfering with bacterial communication, that's how. The result would keep all bacteria from overly multiplying. Good bacteria could continue, maybe a little tongue-tied, maybe a little hard of hearing, at their normal levels in our body. Acidophilus strains would continue helping us digest our food. But bad bacteria would go nowhere after getting a foothold in an initial infection. They'd be deaf and dumb after invading us—blind strangers in a strange land. Unable to build up a quorum for full-scale invasion. All good results for us, the human host.

Except in one place, our brains. For if bacteria or something like them in our heads enabled us to think and remember via their communications, then what we needed was not just their staying alive, but their continued communication—

My cell phone rang. It was Jenna.

"I've been trying to reach you for hours," she said.

"I was probably in some sort of pocket with broken coverage."

"You're not going to believe this," she said.

"Try me." Hadn't my clanking friend just said that about his wife?

"Darius Morton's secretary called here about an hour after you boarded the train in New York—he's finally returned from his summer residence."

"Excellent! We can set up a meeting when I get back."

"You'll likely see him before that," Jenna said. "He's on your train!"

"What?"

"He's going to McNair's funeral. His secretary ran into the same flight problems we did. There's only one comfortable way to get to Chicago if you can't fly, especially if you're Morton's age. The Three Rivers train leaves New York for Chicago at twelve forty-five in the afternoon—Morton couldn't make that one. So he's on your Lake Shore Limited. It's the only other train from here to there."

I took it all in. "You wouldn't happen to know the last time Morton cut his toenails?" I asked. But that couldn't be right. My loquacious companion had detrained in Schenectady, not Chicago.

Which meant that Darius Morton—who of course was an old friend of McNair's, a mentor, and likely the main source of McNair's and Briskman's knowledge of the Vikings in America, and who knew what else, maybe insights into plagues and people in history—was still on this train.

ELEVEN

What did Darius Morton look like?

I wracked my brain.

I had seen a picture of him on the back cover of one of his books. It was a picture of a man in his fifties, with a full shock of dark hair. But that was at least three decades old.

I tried to picture my copy of *Ahead of Columbus*. Damn, that book didn't have a picture at all. That's what I got for purchasing it in a used bookshop—a copy with no dust jacket.

I really had little if any idea of what Morton looked like.

And Jenna had said he was on this train.

I could speak to a conductor, and see if Morton could be located. I got out of my seat, and walked towards the cafe car.

I found a conductor about halfway there. I pulled out my NYPD ID, and explained my need.

The train lurched a little, and I reached up to an overhead compartment for balance.

The conductor shook her head. "Only way we'd know where he was for sure is if he was in a sleeping compartment," she replied in a Jamaican accent.

"Well, could you check that for me, then? It's very important."

She agreed, and asked me to wait a few minutes. She called the request in to another conductor.

The crackling walkie-talkie response came back pretty

quickly. I made out enough of it to understand that Morton was not in a sleeper. Jenna had already told me that Morton's reservation on this train had been as last-minute as mine, and mine had been too late to get a sleeper, but I figured it couldn't hurt to check.

"We have no Darius Morton in any sleeper," my conductor repeated the message to me.

"Okay. Thanks for checking. Is there any other way we can locate people on the train? Don't the tickets you collect have names on them?" I had paid for mine on the train, and my name had been written in.

"Oh, of course," she said. "But that wouldn't tell us where on the train he is." She looked around the train car, dark now except for the dim, overhead evening panels and a few personal reading lights. "I could make an announcement—but it's pretty late for that. We don't even announce stations on the loudspeaker past this hour. Too many passengers are sleeping."

I looked at my watch. It was a few minutes after nine.

"But if it's an emergency, I suppose I could make an announcement. Let me ask the other conductors what they think," she said.

"Let's see what you can come up with first, with the tickets," I said. I didn't feel good about waking the whole train up—including Darius Morton. I wanted a cooperative subject, not someone who would be justifiably annoyed about being woken by a booming announcement on my account. "Meanwhile, I'll just a walk around a bit and see if anyone looks familiar," I added.

"Okay," she said. "Meet me in the cafe car in about thirty minutes. We should have a good idea by then if your Mr. Morton gave us a ticket on this train."

THE CAFE CAR was two ahead of my coach car, towards the front of the train, which featured the dining, lounge, and sleeper cars. I decided to walk the other way first.

A few of the coach cars in the rear had come from Boston and had hooked up to our train in Albany. Morton was not likely to be in one of them, since he had boarded in New York, but I might as well eyeball their passengers as best I could anyway. Maybe Morton had changed his seat.

The gentle rocking of the train to and fro as it moved along—what had Arlo Guthrie called it in that song, "the rhythm of the rails"?—was a tonic to most of the passengers, who were in various states of sleep. I tried to look at the faces as quickly as possible. I felt a little like a Peeping Tom, looking at so many sleeping people. At least their eyes were closed, so they couldn't see me scanning for a trace of what I recalled of Morton.

I barely looked at the women at all—a reversal of my usual watching habits—or anyone who appeared young or even middle-aged. I saw four legs in jeans protruding from an undulating blanket. . . . I smiled. More power to them.

I entered the last car, and nearly tripped over someone sprawled on the floor between the first seat and the front of the car. It was a girl, who looked to be about eighteen or nineteen, with her shirt ridden up and her jeans slung low so the small of her back and a little below was exposed. I almost reached down to carefully turn her over and look for a wound or a mark where a blow had been received, but stopped myself just in time. She was just sleeping—soundly—but just sleeping, on a train. Not, thank goodness, stretched out dead in Riverside Park. . . .

I reached the end of the last car, and tried to picture Morton's face. I didn't have a photographic memory—not to mention the other problems with my memory, of late—and the more I tried to clarify that blurry image from his book in my mind, the more diffuse that face became. Still, I had a feeling that I had seen someone who looked like Morton somewhere on this train. Maybe I was confusing hope with recollection.

I walked slowly back towards the cafe car, and carefully stepped over Sleeping Beauty. She had turned over on her side, had a slight smile on her face, and looked contented. God, this was the way people with their eyes closed were supposed to look. I'd seen enough girls and boys with eyes closed for the other reason—murder—to last a lifetime. Every murder victim was really a girl or a boy, whatever their age. When murder takes your life, it's a certainty you died too soon. . . .

I realized that most of the passengers on this train were either in their late teens or early twenties—likely college kids, graduate students, going back to school—or well over middle age. But most of the elderly, especially the oldest, were couples.

Did Morton have a wife? I didn't know.

Would he take her on a train to McNair's funeral in Chicago? Maybe.

I guess it depended on how close both had been to McNair, whether Morton was too frail to travel alone, other factors. From what Jenna had said, my impression was that Morton was traveling alone—"he's on your Lake Shore Limited," Jenna had said—but that wasn't conclusive.

I got back to my car, and proceeded on to the cafe. I looked at my watch. It was past nine-thirty, and more than half an hour since I had talked with the conductor. There seemed to be a few more lights outside. If I remembered the schedule correctly, we'd be arriving soon in Utica, New York.

THE CAFE CAR was filled with people drinking coffee, tea, beer, and stronger stuff. One of the tables featured a poker game. Another had what looked like gin rummy. A third had four guys and two women loudly singing some Coasters song from the 1950s, totally off-key but in great spirit. My conductor was sitting at the end of the car, sipping a cup of coffee, staring off into space. A big sheaf of tickets were on the table in front of her.

"Dr. D'Amato!" she said, and gave me a big smile as I approached. "I was ready to send out a search party for you! Any luck finding Mr. Morton?"

I shook my head no.

"Well, he's on this train," she said. "Here's your proof." She put the top ticket in my hand. It said DARIUS MORTON. And there was a shaky signature with that name on the top left corner.

"So where is he?" I asked.

"Did you check the bathrooms?"

"No," I said. "What I am supposed to do? Knock on every closed bathroom door?"

She laughed.

I did, too. "Most of the bathroom doors were open, anyway," I added.

"The toilets are a long shot," she said. "He's more likely asleep in his seat with a blanket or a scarf or a hat pulled over his face, if you didn't spot him. How urgent is it that you speak to him right now?"

I considered. "I guess not urgent enough for me to break into bathrooms or pull blankets off sleeping passengers," I said.

She nodded agreement. "Our first breakfast announcement will be a little after eight in the morning, right before we pull into Bryan, Ohio. I can ask him to come to the cafe car then. Can you wait that long?"

"I guess so," I responded. "Let's say he gets off before then?"

"His ticket says Chicago," she said.

"Yes, of course, I knew that." I was getting tired. I yawned.

"But let's see," she continued. "We'll be in Utica in a few minutes. Then Syracuse, Rochester, Buffalo in New York; Erie, Pennsylvania; then Cleveland, Elyria, Sandusky, and Toledo, Ohio; before Bryan—"

"Great name, Elyria," I said. "I don't think I've ever been there."

"Sounds like 'delirious'—it's just a small little place," she said.

The train started slowing down. The car swayed. I touched the top of the seat for support.

"Why don't you join me? Take a load off," she said, and pointed to the seat across her table.

"Good idea," I said. "Maybe I'll also get a cup of tea. It'll keep me up for a few hours, but maybe I'll come up with some bright ideas. Can I get you more coffee?"

"Love some," she said. "And, look, I'll tell the other conductors to ask any senior gents who leave the train at any stop before Bryan if they happen to be named Darius Morton, just in case."

"Thanks," I said, and went to get the caffeine.

FOOD AND DRINKS were dispensed in a narrow, bustling area just beyond the seating in the cafe car. The line was long but good-natured. Three near-misses of Coke, beer, and a pizza on the chests of innocent bystanders elicited nothing but smiles of understanding. The jostling of the train seemed to agree with most of the customers. It certainly did with me. Maybe because it brought back days in the bumper cars of Rye Playland, Coney Island, and Palisades Park.

I eventually returned to the conductor's table with paper cups of tea and coffee. She smiled at me.

"I don't know your name," I said, and passed the coffee her way.

"Regina," she replied.

"So you work the first part of this route, and then a new crew takes over in Pennsylvania or Ohio?" I asked.

"Oh no, we work the entire route—all eighteen hours. We spell each other for breaks, but we all work the full shift."

"Isn't that exhausting?"

"Sure," Regina said. "But we get used to it. And we get time off on either side, in Chicago and New York. A sociologist once told me—a professor traveling with us from Chicago to New York—that we're a self-contained community. We come into existence just for this trip, and then a new one for the trip back. Like a big family, in a way. I guess ships that used to sail across the ocean were like that."

I nodded. "And maybe spaceships will be like that, too—eighteen hours at faster-than-light to the next star." Something about the lights in the small cities outside the window made me think of that. They reminded me of an old French movie, Godard's *Alphaville*, in which travel to another star was filmed along a dark highway with the lamplights on the sides shining like stars. I looked out the window now. The lights of Utica were already receding. Next star system would be Syracuse.

"You've got quite an imagination, Dr. D'Amato. I like that," Regina said.

"Comes in handy in my business," I said. "Call me Phil."

We chatted about trains and stars and cities for a long time. Boats of old could have been part of the discussion, too—we were traveling almost right alongside the Erie Canal, in some parts—but I preferred not thinking about Phoenicians and amnesia and murder in the quiet of this moment. They could all keep until morning.

"Well, time to go on my rounds again," Regina said. "I start with the sleeper cars. Good talking with you, and thanks for the coffee."

I told her the pleasure was mine.

She promised again that she and the other conductors would keep an eye out at all the stops for old men who answered to the name of Darius Morton. "And listen for my announcement a little after eight A.M. that Morton is wanted in the cafe car."

I smiled thanks, then made my way slowly back to my train

car. Almost everyone was asleep now. I still couldn't see a single face that looked like what I recalled of Morton's.

I kept walking, and realized that I had gone beyond where I had been sitting.

I turned around and walked even more slowly.

Hmmm . . . This car did not look like the one I had been in, now that I was focusing on this. Why would I overshoot my seat so badly? Had I forgotten where I was sitting? I was more tired than I thought.

The next car looked more familiar. I walked to the end, and turned around. . . .

I finally spotted my seat about halfway back, and realized why I had missed it the first two times. Thank God it wasn't my memory.

When I had left my seat, the one next to it had been empty.

Now it was occupied. I made my way over.

She looked to be in her mid-twenties, with a clingy sweater and a short knit skirt. She was sound asleep, her head lolling slightly from her aisle seat over to mine.

I looked around to see if there were empty seats. There were none. More people must have boarded the train than left in Utica—

"I'm sorry. Did I take your seat?" she opened her eyes and asked groggily.

"No, no," I said. "That's okay."

She looked embarrassed. She had big brown eyes.

"Um, mine is by the window," I said, and moved carefully around her.

"Sure," she said. "I'm sorry I was hogging your seat." She pulled herself entirely over to her side. "I'm just so sleepy."

"Believe me, I understand," I said reassuringly. "It's okay." I settled back into my seat, and closed my eyes.

Something about her seemed familiar. . . . *Here we go again,* a part of me thought.

No, we're not, another part said. *Time for some sleep.*

I drifted off and started dreaming of Shalimar. *That's what seems familiar about her,* I said to myself in my dream. *It's that perfume again.*

I SLEPT FITFULLY, opening my eyes at a few stops, catching sight of the Cleveland skyline. I saw the first light of morning over Sandusky Bay in Ohio. Kira—I could see her name now on the overnight bag at her feet—moaned softly and shifted in her seat. Her backside pressed against my thigh. I drifted back into daydreams and sleep. . . .

I awoke to some kind of announcement. It was about breakfast soon being served in the dining car. I could smell Kira's perfume more clearly. She had shifted again—or maybe I had—and her head was touching my shoulder.

I looked at my watch—it said two minutes after eight. I rose carefully, so as not to disturb Kira, and made my way to the cafe car.

"Mr. Darius Morton, Mr. Darius Morton . . ." an announcement said. I recognized Regina's voice. "Please come to the cafe car for an important message." Her announcement was repeated twice.

Regina was at the same place she had been last evening. She greeted me with a smile.

"You look none the worse for a hard night's work," I said.

"You do," she joked, "and you weren't even working."

I laughed. Jenna always said she thought my mind never stopped working. "Thank you for making that announcement," I said. "Much appreciated."

"Well, your man should be here soon," she said, and eyed a man about sixty in a pale blue polyester jacket who had just entered the car.

"Nah, too young," I said.

She nodded. "I checked with all the conductors, and no one over forty or fifty left us at any of the stops after Utica, except one elderly couple, and their name was Jenson or Jenkins, not Morton."

"Okay, thanks." I yawned and took a deep breath and tried to wake up fully. "I'm going to get some tea," I said. "Coffee for you?"

"I'll pass this time," Regina replied. "My stomach's complaining already. But you get your tea, and I predict Mr. Morton will be here when you come back."

I did.

He wasn't.

"You were gone almost fifteen minutes," Regina said. "Must've been a long line."

I nodded.

"Maybe he was on it, and wanted to get his food first? I'll make the announcement again," Regina offered.

"Thanks."

The second announcement yielded the same no show.

"What could have happened to him?" I asked. "Maybe he didn't actually get on the train."

"We have his signed ticket, and your information was that he was on the train. I'd say he was with us."

"So what's going on?"

"Only one of two possibilities," Regina said. "Either he's still with us, and for some reason doesn't want to present himself, or he left the train at some stop before Syracuse—maybe Utica, Schenectady, Albany."

"But his ticket is for Chicago, like you said last night. Why would he get off earlier?"

"Happens once in a while. Maybe he wasn't feeling well. Maybe he got a call on his cell phone from a friend who wanted to meet him in Albany—it's a whole new world out there with those cell phones, let me tell you."

I sighed. "What about the first possibility—that he's on the train right now but doesn't want to come forward?"

"I guess that would be his prerogative. We like passengers to come forward when we ask them, but I don't know that there's any law, not if they haven't done anything wrong. But you're the expert on that. Do you want me to walk seat by seat, and ask every man who looks the age if he's Darius Morton?"

I considered. "No. I just want to talk to him. He's not a suspect or anything like that. I guess he's entitled to keep to himself if that's what he wants. I'll try to catch up to him in Chicago."

I thanked Regina again. She told me to look for her— "Don't forget, Doc, I owe you a coffee"—the next time I was on the Lake Shore Limited. I did have a return ticket. But I knew I might need to take a plane instead, if a flight was available.

I left the cafe and stepped between cars for a breath of air. It was nearly nine o'clock already. The train was still in eastern time. I set my watch back an hour in anticipation of Chicago time. I could probably catch Jenna if I called right now, before she left for Princeton.

"Hello?" She sounded as if she'd been fast asleep.

"Hiya, sorry I woke you. I thought you had a meeting."

"Yeah—I did. . . . But the secretary called yesterday afternoon. . . . Didn't I tell you that last night? I guess I forgot, with everything going on about Morton. . . . Anyway, Hanley—the department chair—completely forgot about the meeting—he was still on some river in California yesterday. . . . So my meeting was rescheduled for next week. Sometimes forgetting can be good—it let me sleep late today."

"Until I called."

Jenna laughed. "No, I'm glad you did. You all right? You make it through the night okay on that train?" She seemed more awake now.

"I'm fine." I filled her in about Morton, and made a tiny request.

"You want me to call his secretary, and have me cross-examine her about whether he got off the train?" Jenna asked.

"I could call her myself. But I don't want to risk antagonizing her and Morton with a call from the police, and you seem to have a relationship with her."

"I do?"

"Well, better than mine," I replied. "Plus, my phone battery looks like it's running low." Which it was.

"All right," Jenna relented. "I'll get back to you as soon as I speak to her."

"Have something to eat first." I threw her a kiss and went back to the cafe to get a ham-and-egg sandwich, myself.

I sat down at a table, plugged my phone recharger into a socket on the side, and my cell phone into the recharger. A teenaged couple joined me. They were replaced by a mother with two towheaded boys, who were in turn supplanted by an elderly woman. An entire life cycle, in twenty rolling minutes. . . .

My phone was recharged. It rang just as I was starting to walk back to my seat.

"Here's the story," Jenna said. "You were right. Morton left the train in Albany. According to his secretary—Mrs. Dayson, if you need to know—he got a call on his cell phone just before the train was about to pull out of the Albany-Rensselaer station. It was from an old friend in the area—one of Morton's students, who was also close friends with McNair. Morton had put a call in to him, telling him about McNair's death, asking if he was going to attend the funeral. The guy has a pilot's license and a small plane. He talked Morton in getting off the train in Albany and flying with him to Chicago. Morton didn't need too much convincing. His secretary said he wasn't too happy about traveling all night scrunched up in a coach seat."

"I hope he does better than Buddy Holly." A stupid line at a time like this. Buddy Holly, Ritchie Valens, and the Big Bopper had all died when a small plane they were taking from Mason City, Iowa, to Moorhead, Minnesota, crashed after their Clear Lake, Iowa, concert, at two A.M. on February 3, 1959. They had taken the plane to avoid traveling in a cramped, jumpy bus. For no important reason, I knew all the exact details—I'd memorized them as a little kid; maybe because even then some part of my brain was stuck on forensic science. I even went over them with Jenna once, after "Maybe Baby" had been playing on the radio. . . .

"Not to worry, he's already in Chicago," she said. "You should be there in a little over two hours yourself. How was *your* coach seat, by the way? Did you get any sleep? I was up until about one in the morning last night, but didn't want to chance waking you with a call."

"The seat wasn't bad at all," I said. "Not as good as a bed, but pretty comfortable. I had some interesting traveling companions, too. One was wearing Shalimar. I'll you about it when I get home."

I returned to my seat. The train was pulling out of Elkhart, Indiana—another town with a nice name that I'd never heard of. "South Bend, Indiana, will be our next stop, in about twenty-five minutes," a conductor's voice said, not Regina's. South Bend I had heard of.

Chicago was two more stops.

Kira was awake and getting her bags together.

She smiled at me. "I'm getting off at South Bend," she said.

"Chicago," I said. "Good luck at school." I could see the angles of textbooks poking through the side of one of her canvas bags.

"Thanks," she said. "Have a safe journey."

She walked away.

She was a complete stranger. But between her perfume and her backside against my leg and my daydream, I felt as if I knew her.

And I was glad she was going to school in South Bend, not New York right now.

I looked out the window, and tried to turn my attention to Chicago.

TWELVE

The announcement came as we were pulling out of Hammond, Indiana: We would be arriving thirty minutes late at Union Station in Chicago. We had been waiting as an endless freight train passed by us in Hammond, the last stop before Chicago. "Conrail owns the tracks," someone behind me grumbled. "Merchandise has the right-of-way over people." The black oil-cars on the freight train had been great to look at—a Lionel train set come to life—but I would have all I could do to get to the funeral home in Chicago before the eulogies started.

Fortunately I was traveling light—just the jacket on my back, a wallet and a cell phone in either pocket. I washed up as best I could in the bathroom on the train. FORGET YOUR TOOTH-BRUSH? AMTRAK HAS SMALL QUANTITIES OF THESE AND OTHER AMENITIES AVAILABLE TO MAKE YOUR TRIP COMFORTABLE, the sign on the mirror said. I flagged down a conductor and took them up on aftershave as well as toothpaste and brush. Not my brand, but beggars can't be choosers. I straightened my Penn Station tie, walked out of the bathroom, and stood by the door at the end of my car, ready to rush out and through the station.

The train arrived forty minutes late.

I was the first one out of my car, but passengers were pouring out of all the cars in front of me. I ran the field like I was playing quarterback at Columbus High School back in the Bronx, which I had never played in the first place except in my imagination. The passageway was long; I came razor-close to bumping into two elderly women, a man who looked to be even older (but he was not Morton—he was Asian), and a little boy sprinting away from his mother. I apologized to everyone, especially the man. Morton's secretary had said he had gotten off in Albany, but I looked the man over carefully enough to make sure he wasn't Morton anyway.

I ran through two more lengthy corridors and a big flight of stairs that looked familiar—maybe it was the one in Brian DePalma's *The Untouchables*—and I was a few feet from the taxi stand. I was short of breath, but the escalators that ran along the last flight of stairs had been too filled with people for me to chance.

I hopped into a cab. "Johnson's Funeral Home on North Avenue," I told the driver. "I'm really in a hurry today."

"Just two miles," he replied in what sounded like a Slavic accent. "No problem!"

I leaned back and breathed slowly. "Thanks. You're from Central Europe?"

"Montenegro!" he responded. "Actually, I lived in New York. I came here for a friend's wedding last year, and didn't leave!"

"You like Chicago better than New York?"

"Sure I do. It's more quiet than New York. Chicago sleeps sometimes. New York never."

"Some folks consider that a plus," I said.

I had no idea what traffic was usually like at midday in downtown Chicago, but mercifully it was moving today—certainly better than in New York at noon. We pulled up to Johnson's at eighteen minutes after twelve.

I gave the driver a five-dollar tip on a five-dollar fare—he had gotten me here pretty fast. Besides, the smallest bill I had was a ten, and I didn't want to wait while he made change. "I bet Chicagoans don't tip that well," I told him.

I left the cab and walked up to Johnson's front door. This had better be the right place. It had to be. It was mentioned in the *New York Times* obituary for McNair—well, that was no guarantee—but Jenna had called Johnson's to confirm the time of the funeral before booking my Amtrak ride in New York.

A man about thirty with a suitably lugubrious expression opened the door to the funeral home. I recalled what an old undertaker I used to know on the Lower East Side in Manhattan always told me about how he talked to his customers. "Never tell 'em how sorry you are about their loss. Hell, you're not sorry, and they know it. You're happy, because their loved one's passing has just put some income in your pocket."

I asked the gentleman at the door where I could find the McNair funeral.

He pointed to the right, without a flicker of change in his expression. He didn't tell me how sorry he was for my loss.

McNair's chapel was packed. I slipped in and took one of the few empty seats in the back. I looked around and tried to see if anyone looked familiar. It was impossible to tell. All I could see were the backs of people's heads. They numbered in the low hundreds, at least.

A man who announced himself as Reverend Taylor took the podium. "Robert McNair was known around the world for his work in cognitive anthropology," he said in rich, ringing tones, "but he never forgot his roots here in the city of Chicago." The reverend talked about the Baptist faith, McNair's faith, and about the marriage of faith and reason in McNair's work. "A man needs both," Taylor went on. "Faith without reason is blind, and reason without faith has no meaning. A great philosopher by the name of Immanuel Kant once said something like that, and Robert McNair took it to heart, as words to live by. His reason took him to places that were unpopular in his chosen profession, his faith told him that did not matter. Popularity is a perishable commodity, a tissue of minutes and days. Faith is a rock of the ages. . . ."

Reverend Taylor talked like this for fifteen minutes. The audience loved it, offering verbal affirmation—repeating phrases that Taylor had uttered, saying, "That's right"—in the black Baptist tradition.

I loved it too. I kept looking around the audience. I thought I could see Rhonda in the front row, most of her blonde hair hidden in a kerchief.

Taylor said that several of McNair's colleagues would now be coming up to the podium to speak. The first was "Professor Kelvin Williams, a longtime colleague of Robert McNair, now at the University of Michigan."

Williams spoke eloquently of McNair's work, and the connection it had to his own life's calling as a scholar, who investigated the importance of bodily fluids in human history. "They laughed at Robert McNair and they laugh at me. But truth has a nasty habit of washing away ridicule. . . ."

Two women and a second man walked up to speak about Robert McNair. I had an urge to do so myself, though as Jenna had pointed out the day before, I hardly knew him.

Reverend Taylor was at the microphone again. "Every serious student of humanity has a mentor," he said. "Alexander had Aristotle, Aristotle had Plato, and Plato had Socrates. And Robert McNair had his mentor, too. It is heartbreaking for the mentor to see the student die, just as it is for the parent to see the child not survive. It goes against the natural grain of things. But at the same time, the world is fortunate, we are fortunate, that the mentor of Robert McNair still walks with us on this Earth. Professor Darius Morton. . . ."

A figure rose from one of the front rows, on the extreme left side. He was tall, dignified. He looked as if he might have needed a cane, but his strength of purpose was sufficient support. I could somehow see all of that as he walked to the podium, in half-profile to me.

He turned to face the audience, and pulled up the microphone to reach his mouth.

God, he did look very familiar. But not so much because of that photo on the book jacket, which the face before me only vaguely resembled.

No, I realized in a rush. Darius Morton looked familiar because I had sat across a dinner table from him just last evening, as the sun set through the window on the train near Albany.

THE SERVICE ENDED forty minutes and five speakers later. I knew there were two people I needed to speak to before the audience dissolved through the doors: Rhonda McNair, whom I had come here to see in the first place, and Darius Morton, the object of my valiant, fruitless pursuit on the Lake Shore Limited.

About two-thirds of the crowd was already surging past me and out the exits. The other third was either milling or slowly converging towards the front in an attempt to express personal condolences to Rhonda and family, shake hands with Reverend Taylor, or deposit a phrase or two of discourse in the ear of one of the speakers.

Morton seemed to be a bit closer to me than Rhonda, so I approached him first, while keeping an eye on Rhonda. I couldn't let either leave without making contact.

"Phil D'Amato," I said as I came within handshaking range of Morton. "I'm a great admirer of your work."

That was a mistake. He turned and looked at me, as if I were some kind of superannuated graduate student. "That's not my name," he said, and turned away.

"I've been trying to reach you for weeks," I continued. "I'm with the New York City Police Department."

That was a mistake, too. Now not only Morton, but about twenty other people who had come to pay their respects turned to look at me, with expressions ranging from distaste to distrust.

"Please, I just need to talk to you—you're not under investigation. We were on the Lake Shore Limited together."

That seemed to be the magic phrase. Morton regarded me with dawning but incomplete recognition. The rest of the crowd started turning back to their business, as if not to intrude on our personal conversation. I extended my hand to cinch the deal.

Morton took it, tentatively. "I wasn't on that train very long," he said.

"I know," I said. "We had dinner together near Albany yesterday. The sunset was magical."

He smiled. A thousand tiny lines appeared on his face. "That it was. I remember. How come you didn't introduce yourself and talk to me then?"

"I didn't know you were Darius Morton then," I replied. "Look, do you think we could sit down and talk someplace for a few minutes? I just need to express my condolences to Rhonda McNair over there, and I'll be right back." I could see that the crowd around Rhonda was beginning to thin, and she was starting to make her way out. My idea was to work out a time I could talk to her later in the day, if possible, and then get right back to Morton here.

"I'm actually pretty hungry," he said, "apropos that dinner in Albany. Perhaps we could get a bite to eat."

"Sounds good to me," I said. "You're not going to the cemetery, then?" That had been my original plan—to accompany the mourners to the cemetery—but I had to be flexible.

Morton shook his head. "My doctors would kill me. Not in this humidity!"

"Okay. I'll just be a minute, and then we'll pick a nice restaurant." I turned and walked towards Rhonda.

She had already donned sunglasses. With that and her kerchief and blonde hair, she looked for all the world like Lana Turner or some 1940s starlet attending the funeral of a close friend.

A middle-aged woman approached her. "He was such a wonderful man, wonderful man," the woman said, in high-pitched grief. "Do you have any idea how wonderful he was?"

Rhonda lifted her sunglasses and looked at her. "No. I was only his wife." She turned and caught sight of me.

"Phil? Phil!" she shouted, and came towards me and flung her arms around me.

"Rhonda, I'm so sorry—"

"I shouldn't have been so sarcastic with that woman," she said. "It's just so painful. . . ."

"I know, I'm sorry," I said. The woman was already sharing her good opinion of McNair with someone else.

Rhonda put her face close to mine. I could smell as well as see her tears.

"Robbie thought so highly of you," she said. "I'm so glad you were able to come. I was afraid that some of the announcements wouldn't reach back East in time."

I just nodded. No point in telling her in these circumstances that my announcement apparently was one which hadn't made it back East.

"I want to talk to you," she said, very seriously, very quietly, very clearly. She pulled back and looked me in the eye. "Will you be staying in Chicago? Are you coming with us to the cemetery?"

"Well—"

"No, we wouldn't be able to talk there anyway. And you look so tired. You have to take care of your health. That's what I always told Robbie. . . ." Her red eyes watered. She composed herself. "Today's shot," she said. "How about tomorrow? How about breakfast? Is nine o'clock too early for you? I'm still confused about the time—I'm still on West Coast hours."

"Sure, nine o'clock breakfast tomorrow would be great. Where will you be staying?"

"No, no," she said. "Let me come to you—we can talk more freely that way." She looked around. I followed her gaze. A group of about fifteen remaining people were courteously giving us space to talk. They were trying very hard not to overhear. I also glanced at the back of the room for Morton, and saw he was still there, leaning against a bench. "I'll be staying with Robbie's sister," Rhonda said, even more quietly. "It's better we talk alone. Where's your hotel?"

I thought frantically. I had no hotel. I had heard someone talking about staying at some nice hotel as I was running through Union Station. What was the name of it?

"The Hyatt Regency," I said.

"The Hyatt Regency?"

"Yeah." I hoped I had not just conjured up that name in my fatigued recollection.

"The one on East Wacker Drive? It's beautiful."

"Yeah," I said hopefully.

"So I'll meet you there tomorrow at nine o'clock in the lobby, for breakfast." She hugged me again, and pressed her face against mine. She left with a flourish. The others slowly followed. I let the residue of her tears evaporate on my face.

She walked out the door, and barely looked at Morton. Maybe she didn't see him.

I walked slowly up to Morton. Rhonda was right about my being tired. Funerals were always tiring, and this one was after nearly nineteen hours on a train.

"So, where should we eat?" Morton asked, and stood up straight.

"How about the Hyatt Regency?" I replied. "It must have a decent restaurant."

"Good choice!" he said. "It's not more than ten minutes from here by taxi."

LUNCH AT THE Hyatt was in a skylit atrium. For the second time in under twenty-four hours, I sat across a table from Darius Morton. The view this time was not as good—lily pads in the water that bordered and crisscrossed the dining area—but it was still quite nice for an indoor arrangement. And the conversation promised to be a lot better.

I presented my story, my theories, as best I could to Morton . . . about an antibiotic that jumped the blood-brain barrier and attacked some unknown bacteria or bacteria-like microorganisms in the corpus callosum that helped enable our consciousness . . . about memory loss being the current result . . . about how I needed some evidence, any evidence, that this might have happened in history . . . about the Phoenicians and the alphabet and what they and the world might have forgotten about their presence in North America . . . about how Morton was the expert in this history, and I needed his help, any help, that he could provide, lest Omnin be gobbled up like popcorn this fall with who knew what consequences. . . . I even told him a little bit about the Riverside stranglings, just in case he had any ideas about their possible connection to Omnin and the memory loss.

He took it all in, with his Caesar salad and his iced tea. He nodded. "I believe it all," he said when I was finished. "It's happened to me."

"You've had memory lapses?"

"Oh, of course," Morton replied. "I attributed them to my advanced age—ninety-two, you know."

"But you took Omnin?"

"Of course I did," he said. "And I would again. At my age, I can afford to lose a little memory—I have plenty to spare in this old head." He touched his temple, and chuckled. "But I can't afford to get too sick, or even stay a little sick for too long. You see what happened to McNair."

"But it makes sense to you that the Omnin might have caused your memory loss?" I could see again, right across the table, the problem that Andy had been wrestling with since this whole memory mess had begun. There were too many other reasons for memory loss. They were more plausible than Omnin as the culprit. In Morton's case, it was just old-fashioned old age.

"Yes, what you're saying makes sense," he said. "The Phoenicians were ravaged by disease. All people in those days were. That's why life expectancy back then was so short. But they probably built up a bit of resistance to some diseases—traveling to so many different areas, being exposed to a bit of this here, a bit of that there, like a series of booster shots. Probably earlier peoples went through this as well—any wide-ranging nomadic existence would do it. So yes, such civilizations on the move, such bands of roaming people, might have had just a little more time to come up with cures, antidotes, anything that might work against those illnesses. They might well have used what we would today call antibiotics. They could have developed them on their own, or picked them up at some learned port of call."

"Are there any written records of that?"

Morton shook his head no. "That's the great irony, at least for the Phoenicians, you see. They invented the alphabet. But as far as I can tell, they used it mostly to keep track of their customers, for records of transactions. Memory was always in short supply. First, because people didn't live that long—so there weren't many people around with long memories. And you might well be right that antibiotics made it worse. Let's examine your scenario: Humans achieve consciousness because bacteria trade information back and forth between the two hemispheres of the brain, just like the Phoenicians sailed back and forth between the Old World and the New. Antibiotic substances—whatever they were in those days—are taken to fight illness, but one penetrates the blood-brain barrier and also compromises consciousness. The Phoenicians perhaps realize at least part of what is happening. So they create the alphabet, as a desperate attempt to preserve information lost to faltering memory. But so much information is already lost that, by the time the dust settles, the Phoenicians have an alphabet, all right, but no recollection of why they originally invented it. Yes," he nodded more to himself than to me, "I believe that is possible."

"How come it hasn't happened again, until now?"

"Maybe it did, and we don't know," Morton replied. "You ever wonder why great civilizations—the Incas, the Aztecs, the Romans, hell, even the British—suddenly went down the tubes? Maybe because a crucial part of their population lost a crucial amount of memory at a crucial time, because of some medication that censored the bacteria that keep our minds perking, if you are right. Or, if that didn't happen, maybe you're still right, and antibiotics that cross the blood-brain barrier—get through those constricted capillaries in the brain—are very rare, and so that's why we have no definite, confirmed cases of memory loss until now. Certainly molds and their antibacterial effects seem more common than microvessel relaxants."

I could see why this man was so beloved by his students. He had a way of making the wildest ideas seem reasonable. He was really telling me no more than what I had pretty much hypothesized already, and yet coming from his mouth, it all seemed so possible, so real. "Could you write some of this down in a letter?" was all I could manage.

"Why? You afraid I'm going to die soon, and won't be around to explain all of this?" He smiled, and chuckled again. I half expected him to cough, and was glad that he did not.

"No," I said. "It's just that a letter from you, in the right hands—"

"—won't do you any good." He finished my thought, not in the way I wanted. "You know enough about me to know I'm not taken seriously by very many people. Hell, I've got *hard* evidence that the Phoenicians were here in America—carvings of their alphabet on rocks—and that's pooh-poohed by the 'experts.' No one's going to pay any attention to a letter from me about a bacterium in the brain that no one can see."

"You're content to just stand by and let us go the way of the Phoenicians?" I countered.

"Not likely," he replied. "That we'll go that way, I mean. We've got too many other surrogate memories working for us now—the Web, television, video stores, even the old printing press and the books it churns out are far more than the poor Phoenicians ever had. Hard to imagine amnesia sweeping all of that away."

"You taught McNair, Briskman, Jaynes, McLuhan, all pretty well," I said. I could see the source of many of their insights into our media and consciousness and cognition in Darius Morton.

"Well, McLuhan and Jaynes got a lot of it on their own," he said modestly, but still pleased. "And if you ask me, Jaynes got a lot of it wrong, too. I think consciousness arose much earlier than Jaynes says—maybe even the Neanderthals had it. After all, bacteria have been on this planet a lot longer than people. If their concertos in our brains are what got us thinking, there's no reason to assume that they waited until just three or four thousand years ago to start the overture."

I just smiled at him.

"All right, I'll write your letter," he said. "Tell me where to send it."

I gave him Andy's address in Atlanta. I had it memorized.

"Okay," Morton said. "I'll write it and send it as soon as I get back home." He looked at his watch.

"Where's that? I mean, if I need to contact you?"

"You'll have to do with NYU," he replied. "I like you. I like the way your mind works. But almost no one knows where to reach me. That's the only way I can continue doing any useful work at my age. I do the reaching, when I have the time."

"I understand," I said.

"I have to get back to my hotel," Morton said. "My friend's flying me back to New York. He's very rich, you know. One of my few students who did very well in the material world. Most seem to confine their accomplishments to the ideational."

"He was at the funeral?"

"Oh yes, but standing in the very back," Morton said. "He had to slip out early for some business meeting or some such."

I nodded, and tried to recall if anyone left early. I had been sitting in the next-to-last row, so I guess I wouldn't have noticed anyone leaving who had been standing by the door.

Morton pulled his chair back, and started to rise. "Oh, the bill," he said, and reached for his wallet.

"I've got it, I insist," I said, and walked around the table to gave him a hand.

"Thank you," he said to me. "And I think you're right about the memory loss tying in to your murder investigation, too. Subtract even a small piece of memory from people's lives and it does strange things—puts their realities at variance with everyone else's, because their common thread is frayed. But I won't put that in my letter. It'll be controversial enough as is!" He winked, clapped me on the shoulder, and walked slowly towards the escalator.

I SAT BACK, looked at the lily pads, toyed with the bill.

"Will you be charging that to your room, sir?"

"Ah, no," I told the waiter. "I haven't checked in yet." I gave him my credit card.

I had to face realities. Morton's support felt good, like it could save the day, like water for a goldfish that had leapt too high. But I was still more likely to smash against the side of a rock than swim to triumph on this one. Morton was right about how his letter would be received. No one would take it as more than the musings of a crackpot unless it happened to land in the hands of someone who already believed in Morton and his ideas. Another example of Plato's Meno paradox in action: You had to already possess some relevant knowledge in order to recognize new knowledge. Nothing impresses those who know nothing. Amazing how often that reality reared its infuriating head in my work.

Well, at least Andy had the requisite knowledge. But whom would Andy show Morton's letter to? Whose mind would be open enough, prepared enough, to take it seriously?

I couldn't worry about that now. I just had to make sure that Morton wrote the letter and sent it to Andy, for whatever good it might do. Before Morton forgot. Before he died. What an awful situation—I felt lousy even having to think that last thought.

I sighed. I had no reliable way to even stay in touch with Morton. The letter was completely in his hands.

The waiter returned with my credit-card slip. I signed it and went to the front desk to get a room for the night. I felt like I could sleep for a week.

I CALLED JENNA when I got to my room. I hadn't talked to her since I'd been on the train. I was looking forward to hearing her voice and talking to her on a clear, non–cell phone connection, in private.

"I've been trying to call you all morning," she said. "Your cell-phone battery must be low again or something."

I looked at my cell phone. I had turned it off before I had reached Johnson's—nothing ruder than a cell phone ringing during a funeral—and had forgotten to turn it back on.

"Sorry," I said. "It was turned off. What's the problem now?"

That came out harsher than I had intended, which was not to be harsh at all. "Sorry," I said again. "I'm just bone tired."

"I know," she said soothingly. "I just wanted to tell you that Dugan called—"

"Don't tell me there's been another murder—"

"No," she assured me. "It's just . . . He was getting back to me about about your travel to Chicago, and he's getting a bit antsy about it."

"About what?"

"You know," she said. "He says his superiors are starting to get on his case. He believes in what you're doing for the memory problem, he supports you on that, but he just wants you more in the office and less on the road."

"I can't come back tonight," I said. "I've got a meeting with Rhonda McNair for breakfast tomorrow." Goddamn predictable about Dugan. My grandmother used to have an expression: The cow was good and good, filled up the whole bucket of milk—and then it kicked it over.

"I thought you might not be able to make the Lake Shore Limited at seven tonight, so I checked with a whole bunch of airlines, and I've got you on a flight back to New York that leaves O'Hare at eleven forty-five tomorrow morning. Would that work?"

"Yeah."

"So I'll cancel the train reservation?" Jenna asked. "It costs only thirty dollars for a cancellation. You can mail in your ticket and get the balance."

"Yeah," I said again.

"Get some sleep," she said, and blew a kiss.

"I will," I said, and kissed her back. "Sorry for being so grumpy."

I stretched out and slept like a log.

A CRUELLY RINGING telephone woke me up.

I fumbled with it, put it to my face, and cleared my throat. I said something like hello and squinted at the time on the clock radio. It was 7:35 P.M.

"Phil?" a familiar voice said.

"Yeah?"

"Phil? It's Rhonda. Hope I didn't wake you."

"Oh no," I lied. "I was just relaxing, reading the paper." Why is it that no one ever wants to admit being woken up by a phone call? You'd think the act of sleeping was akin to robbing a bank or stealing groceries from someone on crutches.

"Okay. Good," she said. "Look, do you think we could meet right now, in your hotel, and not wait until tomorrow morning?"

"Well . . . sure," I replied.

"I'm not interrupting anything . . . you sure? I'd . . . I'd think I'd feel better if I could see you now rather than waiting."

"Absolutely," I said. "Let's do it now."

"Okay," she said. "So I'll meet you in the lobby of the Hyatt in about half an hour."

WE MET AS planned, and took the escalator one flight up to the restaurant.

I ordered a light dinner—grilled-chicken salad. Complemented the grilled-shrimp salad I'd had for lunch here just a few hours ago. Rhonda ordered a margarita.

"Thanks for seeing me," she said, for at least the third time since she'd arrived. "I want to tell you something—I wanted to get it off my chest—something Robbie wanted me to tell you." I looked at her carefully. She hadn't said that before.

"It's okay," I said, and took her hand. She had come without kerchief or sunglasses. Her face looked puffy, cried out, vulnerable.

"Robbie knew that you were suspicious of that new antibiotic . . ."

"Omnin."

"Omnin—thanks . . . that you thought it might be hurting

bacteria in our brains that help us think. And he talked to you about his not taking any antibiotics, and you told him you were concerned about his health, that maybe sometimes it did make sense to take antibiotics, even with their bad side effects."

I nodded.

"Well, Robbie wanted you to know . . . He wanted you to know that he definitely didn't die from that flu thing that was going around, not from its complications, either." She started to cry.

I patted her hand.

"Robbie died from cancer," she said through tears. "Lung cancer—that's why he was always coughing. Lymph cancer. Liver cancer. It spread *everywhere* in the end."

"I see. . . . I'm so sorry," I said, my voice thick with emotion, too.

"Robbie wanted you to know that antibiotics wouldn't have done him any good. He didn't die from any infection. He wanted you to know that. He said your instincts were good. He said you were right to distrust antibiotics. He said you should keep that up."

"I will."

"He was so sick," she said, crying again. "Everything hurt. He was a brave man, but he didn't want to go on anymore. I couldn't talk to you about this in front of his family. He asked me to help . . . to help ease the pain. . . . He didn't want to leave, but he couldn't take the pain. What was the point in his suffering, if I could do something to help it?"

I squeezed her hand. "You don't have to say anything more." I could see where this was going. I had to forget what she had just been trying to tell me. I thought: *Here I am struggling with a memory problem, and I have to forget this part of our conversation.* I was part of law enforcement. I had a moral and legal obligation to bring even the best-intentioned euthanasiasts to the attention of the authorities. But this one I had to let pass.

"That's why I didn't invite you," she said. "I lied to you about sending an invitation—I'm sorry. But I wasn't sure how I would react when I tried to tell you about how Robbie died. I didn't want to make a spectacle in front of the family."

"It's all right," I said.

"I'd better get back now," she said, and gave me a weak smile. "Thank you, I feel much better now." She got up to leave. "Oh, here, let me pay for my drink." She opened her purse.

"Not necessary, I've got it covered," I replied.

"No, please, I insist." She dug into her purse and—

Our waiter scooted up right behind her, carrying my food and her drink. For some reason, he was looking at me, not Rhonda.

"Here you are, sir," he said, and smashed right into her arm.

The drink and the contents of her purse went flying. The grilled-chicken salad shook on the plate, but survived. Our waiter put my food down on our table.

"I'm sorry, sorry," he said. "I'll get you another drink."

"No need," I said, "really. Let's just help the lady with her purse."

Rhonda's, like every other woman's purse I had ever known, seemed to have contained a galaxy of lipsticks, cough drops, pencils, pens, rouge, little soap bars, paper pads, pieces of paper, packs of tissues . . .

The three of us spent a few minutes hunting everything up.

"I think that's about it," Rhonda said shakily.

"I'm sorry, sorry," the waiter repeated.

"It's okay," we both told him.

"I'll be right back," I added to the waiter, and gestured to the table. "Don't take the chicken away."

"No, no, of course not," the waiter said.

I walked Rhonda down the escalator flight, and got her

into a cab. "No need to talk to anyone else about this," I said. "You just concentrate on your family now, and getting back on an even keel."

She hugged me through the open taxi door. I closed it, and the cab sped away.

I walked back upstairs to my grilled chicken, and sat down.

"Uh, mister?" A boy, about eight or nine, came over to my table.

My first fork of grilled chicken was half an inch from my mouth. I put it back on my plate, and smiled at the boy. "Hi."

"Um, I found this on the floor—I think it was from that lady's purse. My parents said I should give it to you." He pointed to a couple, beaming, three or four tables away.

"Well, thank you very much," I said, and shook his hand. "Tell your parents they have a very good son."

He smiled and loped back to his table, nearly knocking into my waiter, who now was carrying a trayful of food to another table. The waiter cursed softly in some sort of subcontinental tongue.

I smiled, and looked at what the boy had given me.

It was a piece of paper.

It had three names written on it, with phone numbers.

Claudia Gonzales, Amy Berman, Carol Michosky.

A line was drawn through the last.

THIRTEEN

I put in a call to Rhonda the next morning as I paced around the American Airlines boarding area of O'Hare.

I didn't have her number in Chicago, so I called her at home, intending to leave a message for her to call me. Her voice-mail greeting wasn't encouraging.

"You probably know what happened to Robbie," she said in a quavering voice, "and if you don't, it's none of your business. I need some time alone now. Lots of time, I think. Please don't leave your number, because I won't return your call. I don't care about your damn credit-card and house-loan offers. If you're a burglar and want to steal from me while I'm away, be my guest and take your best shot. I've already lost the best thing in my life. And my neighbors just got a really vicious guard dog—Gary—and he'll rip your lungs out if you take one step onto my property." And then it beeped. I needed to talk to her, ask her questions about the names on the piece of paper—why they were there, what that meant—but decided this was not the time to leave a message on Rhonda's machine.

I called Claudia. She was at a special sex-crimes training conference in the Catskills. I called Amy Berman. A surly woman who professed to be her mother told me that Amy was on vacation for the week. I didn't contest the point. If Amy was not in New York, that likely meant she was safe for the time being.

I called Jenna. No answer there, either. One of those days. No one and her grandmother were home. Just Amy's mother.

A muffled boarding announcement blared forth. I was able to comprehend enough to know it was for my plane to New York.

I was in my seat about ten minutes later. The plane took off about two hours after that. I took the paper with the three names out of my pocket, and looked at it for what must have been the fiftieth time since I had boarded the plane.

The list could have signified a lot of things, none clear to me. McNair, of course, knew Amy—she was his student—and he had met Claudia at the Fordham University lecture. But why was Carol's name there, crossed out? Well, the crossed-out part had to be because she was dead. But why was her name there at all? Carol had told me she didn't know McNair. Yet here was her name on his widow's list—in a manner, moreover, that suggested that Rhonda knew that Carol had been killed.

There were three possible explanations that I could see: *(a)* Carol had for some reason lied to me about not knowing McNair; *(b)* Carol indeed did not know McNair, but knew Rhonda (in some context which did not identify Rhonda as McNair's wife); *(c)* Carol's name was known by Rhonda—as a victim of the Riverside stranglings—even though Carol did not know the McNairs. Well, I suppose there was also a fourth possibility: *(d)* The writer of the list was not Rhonda McNair. But then what was it doing in the depths of her pocketbook? It was probably best to put that hypothesis aside, until I knew more about Rhonda.

I still carried a gut feeling from my final meeting with Carol that she was telling the truth, so I was inclined to rule out *(a)* as well. That left *(b)* and *(c)*, both of which pointed to Rhonda playing some role in the past few months other than her being McNair's wife. But if *(b)* were the case, what was the likelihood that Carol coincidentally knew Rhonda at the same time I was pursuing Rhonda's husband for his knowledge of the alphabet and its history and its pertinence to the memory loss? Or, if *(c)* were the explanation, the same question followed: Why would McNair's wife be keeping track of the Riverside murders? Was she a serial-murder buff in her spare time?

So *(b)* and *(c)* looked to be in the same boat as *(d)*—all grounded pending more knowledge of Rhonda.

I still had trouble thinking of Rhonda as anything more complex than the "Rhonda" of the Beach Boys song. But the last two days and the piece of paper in my hand and even the tone of her voice-mail greeting said otherwise. And if years of work in forensic detection had taught me anything, it was that looks—blonde surfer-girl or otherwise—could be perilously deceiving.

But who was in peril here?

I looked again at the list of three names on the paper.

I wished the answer was as easy as *A-B-C*.

But I was still mostly preliterate when it came to this.

IT WAS NEARLY five P.M. New York time when my plane landed at La Guardia. The late start and then circling around La Guardia had nearly trebled the two-and-a-half-hour flight time. And no one as interesting as the carpenter with the uncut toenails had been seated next to me.

I took a taxi straight to One Police Plaza. If I could get there by six, there was a fifty-fifty chance that Dugan would be still be in. I tried Jenna on the cell phone. Still no answer.

The traffic was obliging, and I was in the building by 5:55. I rushed up to Dugan's office. Sheila, his secretary, was already gone, but Dugan's door was open. I peeked in—

"Phil, the world traveler, returneth!"

"Well, Chicago's hardly 'the world,'" I replied.

Dugan smiled and pointed me to a seat. "You know, I was talking to Jenna—" he began.

"I know," I interrupted, "and I don't blame you. But it turns out that I found something apparently very relevant to the Riverside stranglings in Chicago. Unfortunately, I'm not quite sure what it means." I gave him the piece of paper with the three names, and told him how I had come to acquire it.

Dugan studied it. "So you think this is a hit list?"

"Always a possibility when the line's through a victim's name," I replied.

Dugan looked at me. "Have you notified Officer Gonzales and the Berman woman?"

I told him about my unsuccessful attempts to reach them.

He resumed his scrutiny of the list. "Tell me what you know about this Rhonda McNair."

I told him everything I knew, with the exception of her talk about helping to end McNair's pain.

"So you don't know where she is now?"

"No," I said. "And her voice-mail in L.A. is no help."

"Should we call up our friends in the LAPD, and see what, if anything, they know about Mrs. McNair?"

"Yeah. I guess so." I hated to bring her into this as a potential suspect, but we had no choice.

"I don't like those goddamn cowboys out there—they make it worse for the rest of us." Dugan picked up the phone and called his counterpart in Los Angeles. He then asked him, sweet as could be, if he could do a quick search for anything relevant about Rhonda McNair.

There were a couple of calls that I needed to make about Rhonda McNair as well.

DUGAN HAD AN event to attend uptown, and offered me a ride home.

Jenna opened the door as I was putting in the key.

She flung her arms around me. I kissed her.

It was a measure of how on edge I was about everything

that I was not only glad to be holding her, I was even happier that she was all right.

"I feel like I've been gone a year," I said softly, into her ear.

"You're safe and sound now," she said, and hugged me.

I wanted to stay just like this, but there was someone I wanted to reach in California, while he—I thought it was a he, but maybe not—was still in his office. It was now a little past seven, New York time, which meant it was a little past four in the afternoon in Los Angeles.

"Do you still have a copy of the *Times* obituary for McNair?" I asked Jenna.

"Uhm, I think so. . . ." She pulled away, and went to our kitchen table, the usual repository of recent newspapers. "That was just . . . let's see . . . day before yesterday, right?"

"Yeah."

"Feels to me like you've been gone a year, too," Jenna said. "Okay, here it is: ROBERT MCNAIR, UCLA PROFESSOR OF COGNITIVE ANTHROPOLOGY, DEAD AT 47." I joined her in the kitchen and read through the obituary carefully. "Natural causes . . . pneumonia suspected but not yet confirmed . . . had been in ill health for years . . ." The article went on to say he had been diagnosed with lung cancer nine years ago, had fought it off at first, but his wife and doctor said he'd been losing the battle of late. "Pneumonia came on in his weakened condition. . . ."

I was looking for his doctor's name.

It was near the bottom of the obit. "Professor McNair died at his home, near the UCLA campus, with his wife and his doctor at his side. According to Dr. Carlos Santucci . . ."

I put down the paper and went for the phone. Jenna rubbed my aching back.

"Yes," I said to the Directory Assistance computer voice—I always felt like an idiot responding to that voice—"I'm looking for Dr. Carlos Santucci, Los Angeles."

"Checking . . ." a live voice now informed me. "We have three listings for Dr. Carlos Santucci in the Greater Los Angeles Area. Our new cross–area code directory lists—"

"I'll take all three," I interjected.

"Thank you," the operator replied, and he gave me all three numbers.

I dialed the first.

"Doctor's office," a cheery female voice informed me.

"Is Dr. Santucci in?"

"Who shall I say is calling?"

"Dr. Phil D'Amato, from the New York City Police Department. It's about Professor Robert McNair."

"Hold on."

Maybe I'd gotten lucky. . . . I turned my head and smiled up at Jenna, over my shoulder.

"Dr. Santucci here," a smooth, deep male voice said.

Amazing. First person I'd reached by phone on the first try in the last few days.

I explained who I was and what I wanted.

"Robert McNair did die of pneumonia," Santucci responded, "as I indicated on the death certificate and as I believe was reported in the papers."

"Yes, I understand. But what I wanted to know about was the state of his underlying cancer. I understand he was pretty far gone, and that's what set him up in the end for the fatal pneumonia." Maybe I wasn't so lucky after all—I thought I had just clearly explained that question to Santucci.

His reply was now silence.

"Dr. Santucci?"

"I'm afraid I really can't divulge that kind of information, Doctor . . ."

"D'Amato. Phil."

"Dr. D'Amato. Yes, sorry. You're not an M.D., is that right?"

"Yes, that's right. I have a Ph.D. in forensic science—"

"Well, then, it would be doubly wrong for me to divulge any more information about Robert McNair's death. You're not a consulting physician or a colleague. You're with the police. I really shouldn't be talking to you about this at all—doctor-patient privilege. I'm sure you understand."

Actually, I didn't. Or if I did, it was that Santucci felt that he had something to hide. Why else make such a big deal about a relatively innocuous question? But there was no point in getting confrontational with him on this.

I tried a softer tack. "I understand, of course," I said, as reassuringly as I could. "I'm just a friend of the family—and a great admirer of the professor's work. I'm just trying to get a better idea of why he died, so I can deal with it better. His death was a great shock to all of us."

"Then I suggest you ask his family," Santucci replied coldly. "Look, Dr. D'Amato, I have a patient to see in about five minutes. I need to look over her file. I'm sure you understand."

"Okay," I relented. "I appreciate your even talking to me to the extent that you did." I could see I wasn't going to get anywhere with Santucci today, likely not tomorrow or the day after, either.

I hung up, turned to Jenna, and shook my head.

"What's he trying to keep secret?" she asked.

I told her what Rhonda had implied about helping to take McNair's life. Jenna was the one person in the world I could trust with that kind of information.

"So you think Santucci's some kind of Kevorkian, and Rhonda assisted?" Jenna asked.

"Euthanasia's a lot more common these days than Kevorkian," I replied, "especially when it comes to advanced, painful cancer." I exhaled slowly. "That's why I want to find out more about McNair's condition."

"So who can you call to find out about that, other than Santucci?"

I rubbed my eyes with my fingertips. "Can't think of any-body right now. I'm too tired, and hungry, and missing you."

Jenna smiled, and stroked my head. "Well, I can do some-thing about the second and third, even though it might work against the first."

We had dinner in the pretty good Italian restaurant around the corner, then went to bed, then to sleep about two hours later.

Actually, only Jenna went to sleep, head against my chest, snores soft as a whisper.

I ran my hands gently through her hair, and tried to think of who else I could call about McNair's condition before he died.

I was half asleep when a name popped into my brain. Samantha, that student of McNair's who had delivered a paper to his home, while I waited, looking at Julian Jaynes' book, in McNair's sunroom.

I also thought of Amy Berman. But she was out of town, and I wasn't sure how close she had been with McNair the past few months.

I didn't even know Samantha's last name. But she was the only person I could think of right now who might know some-thing about what I needed to learn about McNair.

SANTUCCI WAS EASIER to reach than Samantha.

It took me most of the next day just to convince the appro-priate person in Records at UCLA to give me the phone num-bers of all women named Samantha who were pursuing a master's degree in Anthropology. There were three. Lots of parents must have been watching reruns of *Bewitched* twenty years ago.

I managed to reach just one Samantha that evening. She was the wrong one.

I reached another the next day. She wasn't the right Samantha, either.

Only one more Samantha was left. I realized that I had no idea what the voice of McNair's student sounded like. One of the wrong Samanthas conceivably could have been lying.

But why?

Another possibility was that my Samantha was not an anthropology student after all. She had written a master's thesis for McNair, who taught in the anthropology department. But for all I knew, she could have been a psych or sociology or even a communications student. According to Jenna, a lot of cross-disciplinary study was going on at universities these days.

I shook my head and put another call in to Rhonda, just in case she had come home. I wasn't surprised to get the same message I had heard at O'Hare.

I called the last Samantha.

"Hello," a high-pitched voice answered.

"Hi," I said. "I'm Dr. Phil D'Amato, a friend of Professor Robert McNair. Were you his student?"

"I gave the statistics to Dr. Felgus," she said defensively. "He said that would be okay."

"Oh yes, I'm sure it is okay," I said. Bull's-eye! Maybe. "So you were Professor McNair's student?"

"Yes?" she half answered, half asked, still suspicious.

"Well, this probably sounds crazy," I said. "But I don't know if you remember, a couple of months ago, when you delivered your thesis directly to Professor McNair's house? I was in the next room, and I was very impressed with your conscientious-ness—that you would deliver your thesis right to his home." Actually, I was more impressed that McNair would be willing to *accept* a document like that, with his being ill and all, but why split hairs? "And McNair—the professor—spoke very highly of you." That was true. Or, if McNair hadn't, Rhonda had.

"That was my thesis," Samantha said proudly. "I hope to have it published as a book someday."

"I hope you do."

"And you said your name was . . . Al D'Amato?"

"Phil."

"You know, I do remember Professor McNair saying he had very important company in the next room. . . ."

Great, now she was snowing *me*.

". . . and would I like to go in and meet him? But I had plans to drive down to La Jolla. . . ."

"Well, that was me," I said.

"Good to meet you—finally," she said, and laughed.

This was likely as comfortable as she was going to get. "Listen, I have a question. You know, Professor McNair's death came as such sudden blow to all his friends. And it would help if we knew a little more about it."

"I don't know very much," Samantha said, tightening up again.

"I know," I said. "But I was wondering, you know, he was suffering from cancer for such a long time . . ."

"Yeah, but that's not what killed him. He'd beaten that."

"Really? I thought it had metastasized all over near the end. Those kinds of things can be awful—"

"No way!" Samantha insisted. "I mean, he might still have had cancer inside him somewhere, and he had that lousy cough for months, but that wasn't cancer. Professor McNair said it was a hangover from that flu bug."

"How do you know he . . . was telling the truth?" I pressed, as delicately as possible.

"Because he had plenty of energy," she replied. "I mean, sometimes he was tired, like everyone. But he walked two miles with me, and was barely out of breath, about ten days before he . . . died." Her voice caught on the last word.

"You sure?" Cancers could move devastatingly fast. I knew that. But ten days . . .

"Yes," she said, with a bit of indignation. "Of course I'm sure."

"So when did the pneumonia come on?" I asked.

"I'm not sure. I didn't see him again after that last walk. I think—I don't know, I talked to him on the phone less than a week before he died, and he sounded okay then, too. So I guess it came on after that."

I BROUGHT SUSHI home. Jenna and I ate in that night.

"I really need to fly out to California and conduct a proper investigation," I said. "It's hard for me to assess how truthful Samantha was—I couldn't see her face, her lips, her eyes."

"Dugan won't go for it," Jenna said. "Don't even call and ask him. I'm not too thrilled about you taking another trip now, either."

"I know," I said, and poured a little white wine for both of us.

"If Samantha is telling the truth, what does that mean?" Jenna asked. "Why would Rhonda lie like that?"

"I don't know. Rhonda lying to cover up a mercy killing makes sense, but if we believe Samantha, that McNair wasn't that sick—"

"I know what you're going to say, and it's crazy," Jenna said.

"Is it? I think it's been pressing against a nerve in the back of my mind since Chicago, but . . . Look, if Samantha is right that McNair did not have metastasized cancer, and maybe not even pneumonia less than a week before he died, then what the hell killed him?"

"Rhonda, but . . ."

"Right, Rhonda. But if he didn't have cancer, and didn't have pneumonia, then where the hell was the mercy in her killing him? What was he being saved from? If the answer is 'nothing'—no mercy, no mortal illness—then the killing wasn't mercy at all. It was just plain, goddamned murder!"

"You better call Dugan tomorrow."

I DIDN'T HAVE to.

He called me first. Very early in the morning. At home. The ever-accurate bell-ringing harbinger of bad things gone worse.

"Hello," Jenna answered, sleep-slurred. "Sure, he's here." She passed the phone to me.

"You're not gonna like this, Phil."

"I know." I'd heard that salutation too many times not to know.

"It's Amy Berman this time."

"Oh God. She was out of town."

"Well she's out of town now for good."

"What happened?"

"The report came in shortly after midnight. It's a little different, this time. She apparently got back to the city yesterday. Her body was strangled, all right, but it was found just inside the southwest corner of Central Park—you know, right near the fancy subway entrance for the A and D trains by Trump Tower."

"Yeah," I said, sick to my stomach. "Near Fordham University's Lincoln Center campus. She was a student there."

"That's probably why she was in the area," Dugan agreed. "You want to come down and look at the body?"

"Okay," I said.

"Okay. See you in thirty minutes. I'll get a tea for you—"

"Did you contact Claudia Gonzales?" I asked.

"What? No, not yet," Dugan replied. "I think she just got back from her training session. You want me to talk to her about this?"

"I want you to arrest her."

FOURTEEN

Dugan didn't say anything for a long time.

He hadn't hung up. That wasn't his style.

I could hear the live electricity in the silent connection.

Jenna groaned and turned over, under the covers.

"Phil," Dugan finally spoke. "Haven't we gone through this already?" He said the words very carefully, almost tenderly, as if he was very concerned—about me.

"What do you mean?"

"I mean, your wild idea that Officer Gonzales is somehow involved in this as . . . maybe more than an investigating officer."

"I don't know what you're talking about—honestly," I responded. "You're saying I already told you my suspicions about Claudia?" I had no recollection of that at all. What the hell was this? Another chapter in my memory-loss book? Did the losses come in some sort of diminishing ripples? The stone of Omnin hits the bacteria center in your brain, and memories depart like ripples on a pond?

Or was Dugan so resistant to the idea of Gonzales as the Riverside killer that he would lie, saying I had already told him about Gonzales, just to throw me off? That didn't make sense, either.

"Yeah," Dugan replied. "You told me sometime after the Michosky foul-up—I mean, the one in which she picked Gonzales out of the lineup. You told me that the thought had first occurred to you on Cape Cod, when you saw a poster that talked about gay women as cops. She was the first one on the scene of the first murder—so, you thought, who knows what she was able to cover up, or change around to look like someone else did it. You said maybe she was using the memory bug as an excuse not to remember, so she could be deliberately vague and discourage the DA. And then, in classic D'Amato fashion, you came up with the best twist of all: Maybe Michosky picked Gonzales out of the lineup because it was in fact Gonzales who attacked her!"

"I told you all of this?" In fact, I had indeed been thinking about all of this—and more about Gonzales and the murders—for a long time. I had been agonizing, or so I had thought, about whether I should go to Dugan with this. I didn't want to jeopardize the career of someone who could be a fine officer, until I had more evidence, until more of the pieces fit. "I have no memory at all of saying anything about this to you before this phone call," I said.

"Yeah, well, you did. And we also talked about Gonzales' being in Philadelphia with her mother at the time of the murder that occured after the Michosky attack. Do you remember that?"

"I remember that she said she was. I remember our discussing it at the time. I don't recall talking to you about it in a conversation in which I made allegations about Claudia as the strangler, no."

"Well, you did," Dugan said.

"And what did you do about all of that?"

"I made discreet inquiries."

"And?"

"And we found nothing substantive, Phil. Nothing. She was there at the scene of the first murder. So what? She's a police officer—that's what we're supposed to do. And that Michosky woman—God rest her soul—was a flake. And I had Claudia's mother tracked down and I called her myself. She seems to be recovering well after her stroke. She confirms that Claudia was with her in Philadelphia at the time of that second Riverside murder."

"Does Claudia have alibis for the other murders?"

"No," Dugan admitted. "But I'm sure a quarter of the cops on the force don't, either. Phil, most of the murders were done in the middle of the night."

"If you won't arrest her, at least let me question her."

"In a box? I won't have that."

"Anywhere you like. Just make sure that she can't leave, in case she confesses or gives herself away. You can watch the questioning yourself. You can do that for me, can't you?"

Dugan breathed heavily into the phone. "All right, Phil. I'll do as you ask." He breathed heavily again.

"Thank you."

"Phil, I'm concerned about you."

"I know. So am I. But bring in Gonzales. Please."

I PUT THE phone down and looked at Jenna. She was wide-awake now.

"I have no recollection of your ever talking to me about Claudia as the killer, either, for what for it's worth," she said. "Score one for you—though my memory is hardly sacrosanct these days, either."

I shook my head. "These damn memory outages are tricky, especially if they're taking out slivers of time rather than whole days or evenings. I hate to say it, but it's easy to see how I could have a lost a conversation with Dugan."

"But with me too? What's the likelihood of my losing a whole conversation as well, on the very same subject?"

"Not very high," I allowed, "which suggests I never told you my suspicions about Claudia." I tried to recall. I pressed my memory. It felt like a tired muscle. . . . How the hell were you supposed to remember something you *didn't* say?

"Remember our little outing to Wellfleet?" I continued. "I saw something on a poster there that made me think of Claudia. It was some sort of flyer from a lesbian antidefamation group, with a list of successful careers that lesbians pursued. One was something like 'beat cop in major metropolitan cities.' "

"I remember Wellfleet—great little town. But you never said anything about a poster."

"All right," I said. "I guess score one for me, then, after all. My impression is that I thought about that in Wellfleet, but didn't say anything to you or Dugan about it at the time. Still doesn't completely prove that I didn't talk to Dugan later about Claudia, though. But why on Earth would he make something up about that?"

"I don't know," Jenna said. She thought a bit. "You think Claudia's gay?"

"That's been the favored theory all along—that the killer was a gay woman," I replied, relieved to be talking about anything other than my memory. "A string of violent crimes with sexual elements—the victims are stripped naked—but no penile penetration. A lesbian killer is certainly logical."

"And a gay policewoman would have the physical strength— all that exercise."

"Exactly," I said.

"So does Claudia wear Shalimar?"

"A good question," I said. "One of many still outstanding."

I WENT DOWNTOWN to my office. I felt worn, and it was only nine o'clock in the morning.

There was a loose end I needed to track down. I had dropped it in all the hustle and angst about McNair. I hadn't given it a thought since my return from Chicago. But it was bothering me now. It might have relevance.

I asked around the office. Had anyone taken a call from Carol Michosky the night of her death, a few minutes after five? The phone log indicated that she had called my number. Depending upon how I had set my phone that day—and I couldn't remember that, either, but I guess there was nothing pathological about that—her call might have been automatically routed to the receptionist's number, or perhaps someone else in the office. I did know that there was no message from Michosky in my voice-mail when I came in the next morning.

No one knew a thing. No one remembered getting a call from Carol Michosky that or any other day.

"But wait a minute," Libby, our receptionist, said, as I was walking away, scowling. "Wasn't I on vacation then?"

I turned around and looked at her, hopefully.

"Oh yeah. I was," she said.

"So that means . . ."

"Well, there would've been a temp in here for me that day," she replied. "But wouldn't you remember that?"

I shook my head no. "I was too wrapped up in other things." That would have been me doping out the goods on Shalimar with Officer Laurie Feldman. Not to mention my quicksand recollection, which was the last thing I wanted to get into now. "Can we find out her name? I mean, assuming the temp was a she."

"Sure," Libby replied. "Anything's possible, with time."

Libby got back to me well after lunch.

"Sorry this took so long." She came into my office with a piece of paper, on which was a name and two phone numbers. "Cezanne Beck was the temp."

"Nice name," I said.

Libby nodded.

"The first number is the Hot Temps headquarters that

hires her out. The second is where she should be right now—Bloom, Oringer, and Rosep—a law firm."

"Thanks," I said gratefully. "I appreciate your going the extra step and getting the number of where she is now."

"No problem," Libby said, smiled, and left.

I called the law firm.

"Bloom, Oringer, and Rosep," a female voice answered.

"Hi. Is this Cezanne Beck?"

"Oh, you mean the temp today?"

"Yeah."

"I think she stepped out for a minute. Can I take a message for her?"

I considered leaving my name and number. But I didn't want to scare her off. "No thanks—I'll call back."

I called back about fifteen minutes later.

A different female voice answered this time.

"Hi," I said. "Is this Cezanne Beck?"

No reply. This was like pulling teeth—

"Yes," she answered. "Are you the party who called before?"

"Yes, I'm the party." I told her who I was, and the purpose of my call. *It's my party, and I'll cry if I want to.*

"I think I did get a call from Carol Michosky. She was the poor girl who was found strangled the next day? I remember talking to my friends about that. Poor girl. It really creeped me out."

"Murders can do that," I said. "What exactly did she say to you? Did she leave a message?"

"No, I asked if she wanted to leave a message, and she said no, she'd prefer talking to you on the phone about it tomorrow—the next day. Poor girl. I definitely would have left a message for you if she had left one."

"Of course. I know you would. Did she give you any idea about what the 'it' was?"

"The 'it'?"

"Yeah. You know, the thing she said she would rather talk to me about the next day," I said.

"Oh, that."

"Right."

"Sure," Cezanne said. "She said she remembered the perfume she was talking to you about. Shalimar."

"I see," I said. "Tell me, did anyone overhear your conversation?"

"Overhear?"

"I mean, was anyone standing next to you when you received this call?"

"I don't think so," Cezanne replied.

"Hmmm . . . Well, this might sound like a strange question. But did you talk to anyone about Carol and the Shalimar? Anyone around the office?"

"Well, now that you mention it, not in the office, but in the street—you know, in front of your police precinct."

"Can you tell me about it?" I prompted. "Whatever details you remember."

"Well, I walked out of the building, and a gust of wind blew some dust or something in my eye, and I had take out my contact lens—"

"Right, and the Shalimar?"

"Well, a group of policewomen passed me by, and whew, did I get a whiff of Shalimar! And you know, I hate that stuff— my boyfriend's old girlfriend wore it and he loves it and I hate it—and I blurted out something like, 'Wow, today's a day for cops and Shalimar.' And one of the policewomen looked at me, and asked me what I meant, and I figured I'd better cooperate, so I told her I'd been temping in your office, and a call came in for you about Shalimar."

"Did you mention Carol's name?"

"Yeah . . . I think so. I was pretty nervous. Was that wrong? It was a policewoman who was asking."

I felt like screaming: *Was that* wrong? *It just cost Carol Michosky her life, that's all!* But Cezanne had no way of knowing. "What happened next?" I said, as unemotionally as I could.

"Well, the policewoman said thanks for talking to her, and not to worry about the Shalimar crack—I was concerned that I had offended her, because she was the one wearing the stupid perfume, and I guess it showed on my face—and then she walked away with the other policewomen."

"Do you think you would recognize her?"

"No, my vision was very teary and blurry. I had dust in my eye—"

"Right—"

"I could see she had dark hair," Cezanne offered, "and I think dark eyes, but I didn't really see anything very clearly. Why, did she do something wrong?"

I didn't answer.

"Did I do something wrong? Was I wrong to mention Carol Michosky's name?"

I still couldn't answer.

All I could think was, *I'd bet any amount of money that that policewoman was Claudia Gonzales.*

And it looked like I still couldn't prove it.

"No, you're not to blame," I said.

I WENT TO wash my face in the bathroom. I splashed lots of cold water on my face, and wiped it with a paper towel. I didn't like what I saw in the mirror: bags under bloodshot eyes.

I walked back to my office.

Standing in front of it was Dugan—and Claudia.

"Phil," Dugan said. "I told Officer Gonzales you wanted to talk to her about a few things. She came right over."

I smiled at both of them. I caught a whiff of Claudia's perfume as I opened the door and invited them in. Whatever it was, I knew it wasn't Shalimar. Of course not—she had no doubt stopped wearing it the night she strangled Carol Michosky.

"Okay if I sit in?" Dugan asked.

"By all means," I said, and showed Claudia and him to the two comfortable chairs in front of my desk. I thought about all the suspects, all the sleazes, who had sat in these chairs over the years. And now one was a goddamned police officer. . . .

"Thanks for coming in to see me," I said to Claudia.

She nodded. I could tell from her demeanor—unless she was a Meryl Streep–class actress—that she had no idea what this would be about. Good for Dugan.

"I'd like to talk to you a little more about your relationship with Carol Michosky." I might as well begin with my best shot.

"My relationship? I didn't know her. She picked me out of the lineup, as you know." She rolled her eyes as if to say, *Another screwball witness.* "And I heard that she was strangled. And I feel terrible about that, because I still feel guilty about muffing that first crime scene with Jillian Murphy, although I don't know that we would have actually caught anyone even if I had been totally *compos mentis*—that's the phrase, isn't it?"

I tried to look sympathetic. "It is. I understand." She was good, which presented a classic dilemma: Either she was good because she was innocent, or because she was a clever killer. And the better she was, the more that supported *both* contradictory propositions. But I was sure I had the goods on her. "Do you recall what you were doing the evening of Carol's murder?"

She laughed. "Sleeping, if I wasn't working." She stole a look at Dugan. Good, she was beginning to see where this conversation was going. Now we'd see how long she held up. Dugan's face was impassive.

"Well were you working or sleeping?" I pressed.

"Sleeping, I guess."

She had no choice but to say that, of course. If she had

been on the job that night, there would be records of that all over.

"And I assume you were sleeping alone?"

"Oh yeah, and in the nude, with a bottle of scotch on the dresser, all ready in case you or the commissioner wanted to drop by for a quickie. What the hell is this about?" Now she turned, completely and demandingly, towards Dugan.

"Apparently it's about alibis, Officer," he replied.

"Or lack of," I added.

"But let's talk this through—there's no sense getting upset at this point." Dugan extended his hand, to calm the ruffled air.

Claudia snorted. She wasn't calmed. Good.

"Let's talk about the late afternoon," I said.

"Which one?" she parried.

"The late afternoon before the evening in which Michosky was murdered and you were sleeping," I replied.

She struggled to keep her composure. "I honestly don't remember."

"Back to that again?" I needled.

"Hey, it's happened to lots of people—including you, from what I've heard. But I'm not saying that was the memory thing, anyway. I just don't particularly remember what I was doing late that afternoon. Do you remember, on the spur of the moment, what you were doing some afternoon, weeks ago?"

"So you think you might remember if you had more time?"

"This is bullshit!" she said, and shifted in her chair as if she were making to leave.

Dugan discouraged her with a stare.

"Should I call my PBA representative, my lawyer?" Claudia's question was both sarcastic and real.

"No one is charging you with anything now. We're just having a conversation," Dugan replied.

"Maybe I can help jar your memory a little about that afternoon," I said. "Were you in front of this building?"

She looked at me. She was beginning to realize what I had on her. What she couldn't realize, of course, was that I had nothing that would stand up in court, or likely even to Dugan. Any law student could poke holes through Cezanne's spotty vision. But those were the cards I had to work with. The key was showing just enough of them to Claudia—I had a witness, but not a witness with dust in her eyes.

Plus I had to play the excruciating joker, not revealing too much else of Cezanne's identity lest she end up on Claudia's hit list, in the event that Dugan let Gonzales walk out of here.

I glanced at Dugan. He was back to his poker face.

"Suppose that I was in front of your precinct," she said slowly. "What of it? Was someone strangled there that I don't know about?"

"No, but you might have picked up information there that convinced you Carol Michosky was better dead than alive."

I could see Dugan, in the periphery of my vision, leaning in with interest.

"Picked up information like that from whom?" Claudia asked.

I shrugged, smiled. She knew who—Cezanne. I prayed that Claudia didn't know her name—it was a hard one to forget. Even if not, Cezanne wouldn't be safe for long. I had tracked her down in just a few hours. Her life now could well depend upon my capacity to bluff enough of a confession out of Claudia to get Dugan to take her badge and gun and let her leave this room only under arrest.

"Maybe you overheard me talking," I offered.

"Oh, were you outside then?" she retorted.

"Good question, Phil," Dugan said.

"Yeah, I was out of the building"—technically true, but on my way to meet Laurie Feldman, not standing in front talking to her or anyone. But I had no choice about making this play now. I had to scare Claudia into some kind of admission, some kind of guilty response that would give Dugan enough to take her off the street. I looked steadily at her dark eyes.

"He's lying," she said, vehemently.

"How do you know that?" Dugan asked mildly.

"It's obvious," she replied.

"Yes, obvious to you because you were there, right?" I demanded. "How else could you be so sure that I wasn't?"

"So you *are* lying," Dugan remarked to me. "You weren't there."

"I'm leaving," Claudia declared, and now she did stand up. "I've had enough of this shit."

"Sit down," Dugan said, with the full authority of his office. "Please," he added, more kindly.

Claudia hesitated, then sat, reluctantly.

"You have anything more, Phil?" he asked. "At this point, it's not much better than 'he said/she said.' "

"Yeah, I do," I replied. "Tell us about last night," I asked Claudia.

I thought I saw Dugan wince.

"Last night?" Claudia responded.

"Yeah, last night, around the time Amy Berman was murdered." I resisted adding, *And don't tell me you have trouble remembering that?*

She laughed.

But it wasn't hysterical, hopeless laughter.

"I was off-duty, in a bar on the West Side, getting good and drunk with at least five other officers. We started about seven-thirty in the evening, and were there till closing. Would you like their names?"

Amy had been murdered between nine and ten in the evening. Could Claudia get five cops to lie for her? What about the other people in the bar? I cleared my throat and started to reply—

"It checks out, Phil," Dugan said first, in a pained voice. "I made some calls earlier. It checks out."

Claudia smiled triumphantly.

Dugan shook his head sadly. "You can go now," he said to Claudia. He looked at me. "If that's all you have, Phil."

"Put her under arrest," I pleaded to Dugan. "You're jeopardizing—"

"You can go now," he said again to Claudia.

She walked out the door, still smiling.

FIFTEEN

Dugan regarded me, appraisingly.

"Jack, I—" I began.

He held his hand up for me to stop. His expression said he didn't want his thought process interrupted.

I talked anyway. "The temp who worked here the day Michosky was murdered is now on Claudia's radar—the temp was the one who told Claudia that we were on to her perfume, and Claudia knows that I know that."

Dugan made a face as if he didn't fully comprehend what I was saying but was not concerned.

"Claudia's probably ferreting out the temp's name right now," I continued. I felt better not saying the name Cezanne myself, though I knew of course that Dugan was not the threat to her.

"We've got a tail on Officer Gonzales, Phil," he said at last. "We've got the bases covered. We're not stupid."

"Good." I was delighted to hear that. I picked up the phone and called Libby's extension. If we were lucky, she might well be the only person in my office who was fully aware of Cezanne Beck—her name, and the name of her company.

"Hi Libby, Phil here, quick question: Did Officer Gonzales talk to you or anyone in the office on her way out?"

"She didn't talk to me, but I didn't see her leave," Libby replied. "I was in the ladies' room."

"Okay, thanks. Listen. Please do not tell Officer Gonzales or anyone anything about Cezanne Beck—unless I tell you first that it's all right."

"You mean the temp we were talking about before?"

"Right. The temp. Please don't talk to anyone about her."

"No problem," Libby said.

I put down the phone and turned, somewhat relieved, to Dugan. "That should shut off Claudia's most likely pipeline of information . . . I guess, if she has any brains, which she obviously does, that the last thing she'd do right now is kill the temp, when she knows we're on to her."

"Right," Dugan said, "so you needn't be so hyper about this."

"No, we need to be hyper," I responded. "We can't be too careful."

"Of course it's always good to be careful," Dugan said. "But that also means being careful not to overreact. I wouldn't say we're 'on' to Officer Gonzales. I'd say we're trying to cover all possibilities, however remote. A more likely reason for her not going after the temp is that she's not your perp."

I started to object.

"Phil, I'm concerned about you. You've been over-the-top on this case for months now."

I looked at him. I could understand his being upset about what had just happened—about my indictment of Claudia, followed by her damned alibi for last night—but "over-the-top for months"?

"I thought you said you supported what I've been doing on this case," I finally said, quietly.

Dugan looked surprised, then shook his head, as if this were more evidence that there was something wrong with me. "When exactly did I say that?" he asked.

I DIDN'T KNOW whether to laugh or scream.

I took a breath and my time.

I answered as calmly as I could. "You're saying you have no recollection of telling me that you appreciated what I had been doing on this case? And, although you were of course unhappy that we hadn't yet nabbed the killer, that you thought the memory bug might well have relevance, and you approved of my exploring possible links between the amnesia and the Riverside stranglings?"

Dugan looked confused. He was struggling to make sense of all of this, too. He was basically a good person, and a good top-level cop. I rarely had much doubt about that.

"I . . . I may have *felt* that way, Phil. I did feel that way. And a part of me still does. But no, I don't remember explicitly telling you that I supported you on this."

I smiled sadly. "You see our problem, then," I said softly.

Dugan nodded. "You don't recall speaking to me a while ago about Claudia. I don't recall telling you a while ago that I approved of your approach. We're each missing little pieces. Hard to have a meeting of the minds with such jagged edges."

"Yeah."

"How do we decide who's right?" Dugan asked.

"I'm willing to accept that we both are—we're both victims of this memory lapse," I said.

"I thought it was over," Dugan said.

"Obviously not," I replied.

Dugan sighed. "Phil, I spoke to the commissioner about you this morning. I had no choice—he called me."

"Why?"

"Claudia's no dope," Dugan said. "I invited her down to this interview. Soon as we got off the phone, she called her PBA representative. He got right through to the commissioner—the two get along pretty well. So, the commissioner calls me to find out what's going on."

"Claudia called her PBA rep because she's guilty," I said.

"Don't let the ACLU hear you."

"What did you say to the commissioner?" I asked. I wasn't usually so pushy with Dugan about his conversations with top brass, but he had certainly opened the door on this one.

"I had to be honest with him," Dugan said. "I told him my concerns about you. He knew about your running off to Chicago—"

"How?" I asked.

"I don't know," Dugan said. "I didn't ask. But I told him I didn't necessarily think that was the best way to spend your time on this—that's part of what I mean when I said you've been over-the-top—"

I started to disagree—

"But I also told him I have a lot of confidence in you," Dugan continued. "And I do. And I also think that Claudia did behave oddly in our interview—certainly with more hostility than if she were totally innocent. But we've got to keep our minds open for other suspects in the Berman homicide. I even checked out Leslie Roth this morning—the woman you saw walking with Berman, who you thought looked like the suspect in Claudia's dream—but she has an airtight out-of-town alibi." He smiled, pensively. "You had a theory about Claudia's dream, too—you thought she made it all up just to throw us off track."

I frowned. "I remember thinking that. I can't remember telling you."

"It was all in the same conversation we had about Claudia," Dugan said.

"She's been acting strangely in this throughout, Jack."

He considered. "I don't know . . . maybe she's covering something up. Or maybe it's just the guilt she feels for losing her memory of the Murphy site."

"It's more than that. Much more."

"But she does have an alibi for last night. That's a fact," Dugan said, gravely. "And she was in Philadelphia for the second Riverside strangling. So, if you still want her for the other murders, you've got to see last night as a copycat."

"Or maybe she has an accomplice."

"Who?" Dugan asked.

I shook my head. "I don't know," I said.

"Maybe it's someone we don't know at all," Dugan said.

"Let's pray not."

I LEANED BACK in my chair after Dugan left, and closed my eyes.

I had seen this kind of progression many times, in crises in my life as well as my cases. It always seemed to start the same way. You bang your head against the wall. Everything's opaque, occluded, clogged like a fatted artery. Nothing gets through that blood-brain barrier. And then there's a quickening. A few things begin to make sense. But this very stirring also seems to unravel your sources of support. Friends pull back, antagonists are emboldened. . . .

I could see all the signs. Dugan and the commissioner were concerned about me? I wouldn't put it past Dugan, much as I liked him, to be putting a goddamn tail right now on me as well as Claudia. That was his job. It wouldn't surprise me to learn I had already been tailed for weeks. Whatever was happening, I knew I didn't have much time. I had to get some conclusive evidence, on all fronts.

I called Andy Weinberg. We hadn't talked in a while. Maybe he'd have something I could use.

"Phil. I was just going to call you." His tone was mixed, but on the whole not very positive.

"Well, that's encouraging," I replied. The optimist doubts nothing, except his own pessimism. I needed to be optimistic.

"I just received a long letter from Darius Morton this morning."

"Wonderful! What's it say?" That *was* encouraging.

"It's very eloquent—inspiring, really," Andy said. "Not

much about the Phoenicians in America. He says he's taking the longest long-range view of the historian—looking at the history of humans and life on this planet. He says he met you in Chicago at McNair's funeral, and you told him your concerns, and all of that got him thinking about life and death on the grand scale.

"Here, I'll read you the best part: 'Mitochondrial material from bacteria may have been in our cells for millions of years. Many anthropologists accept this now. It may have helped make us human. Why not bacteria or something similar in our brains? We don't yet know the physical substrate of thought. We do know that bacteria are inherently colonists, which means they're in the business of communication. Is it so far-fetched to consider, as they go about their business in our brains, if that business enables processes we know as thought, consciousness, memory? Perhaps they infected us long ago, and that plague turned prehominids into thinking beings. If there is even a chance that such is the case, as Dr. D'Amato suspects, is it wise to risk it all on just a new type of penicillin? Isn't it better to come up with a different new kind of penicillin instead, or market this one in a form that respects the blood-brain barrier?'

"I'll fax you the whole letter," Andy concluded. "It's really something."

So Morton had come through. I breathed out slowly. "Please do fax it to me," I told Andy. "What's the bad news?"

"Well, I heard from the FDA yesterday," he said. "They're not inclined to put a brake on Omnin at this point."

"But that was before Morton's letter."

"Yeah, but judging from the reasons they gave me, I don't think his letter will change their minds," Andy said. "I mean, it's possible, and I'll certainly keep pushing, but they feel the deaths from pneumonia and other bacterial complications of the flu that Omnin can avert, well, the FDA feels they far outweigh losses in memory, however aggravating. Look, you were

right, Omnin was specifically designed to target bacterial communication, to stop the song so the singers can't multiply, but
leave them alive, and the FDA is *proud* of that—one of their guys
told me that makes Omnin 'ecologically sound.' I'm not sure
what if anything we can get from them at this point . . . maybe
some kind of label warning—"

"Like what? 'The most common side effect of this drug is
that it may make you lose your mind?' Or maybe, 'Not to be
taken by anyone who values his or her memory'?"

"I know, Phil, I know."

"Would it help if I told you I just had another memory-loss
experience, and so did Jack Dugan? And that it's beginning to
get so much in the way of our Riverside strangling case that I'm
worried we may never get the killers?"

"You think there's more than one now?"

"It's a possibility I'm considering—assuming I remember it
tomorrow. I feel more and more like that guy in *Memento*."

"Phil, I've collected solid reports of memory losses in the
hundreds. I'm completely with you on this. But a few more
examples—especially from you—are not likely to change anyone's mind in Washington. The losses are just . . . too minor.
And that memory-carousel effect—where the lost memories
come back and new ones are lost—just makes it worse. No one
is even clear about what exactly they forgot. I think even you
have to admit that, if you're honest with yourself."

"How long do we have before they go into production for
the fall batch of flu-season Omnin?" I asked, rather than admit-
ting anything.

"They've already started," Andy said.

"Jeez—"

"But until it's actually shipped and put into hospitals and
pharmacies, we still have a chance," Andy said. "If we could just
come up with a major, dramatic example of memory loss caused
by Omnin, that might convince the FDA, with or without the

germs-in-the-brain theory. No one's found any bugs in the brain yet, either, and I've received a bunch of reports on that already too." He sighed. "It's tough, Phil, it's tough. . . . Maybe it would help if we brought Morton down to Washington to testify. I have a few friends who have connections on Capitol Hill, maybe we can get some sort of hearing going."

"Better act quickly if you want to get Darius Morton down there," I said darkly. "He's no youngster."

I WAS BEYOND tired. I'd been working constantly since before the crack of dawn. But I had to stay on top of this—especially the murders. If I stopped pursuing Claudia for even an hour, she and the stranglings could slip away from me. They might never be within reach again.

She had an alibi for the Berman murder. Okay. She wanted that alibi to make us believe that someone else had strangled not only Berman but all the other women. Whatever had really happened with Berman, I had to figure out a way of disproving what Claudia wanted us to think.

I called Ed Monti. I got his voice-mail. What was going on these days? Was I the only person who ever answered the phone?

I left a message. "Hi, Ed. Phil D'Amato here. I don't know if you've done the Berman autopsy yet, but if you haven't, I'd like you to look for something for me. And if you have, and you could go back and take another look, I'd really appreciate it. I need to know if you see anything that would lead you to think that Berman's killer was someone other than the Riverside strangler. I have nothing specific. But I'd like anything you might find—any difference in the strangling MO, any unusual marks on the body, any kind of sexual molestation, I know the others were clean in that area—anything at all. Thanks."

I put down the phone. Who else could I call? I picked up the phone.

"Is Laurie Feldman there?" I asked after dialing her number.

"Hold on, sure," a male voice said. "Who's calling?"

"Phil D'Amato."

"Okay, hold on."

"Phil!" Laurie said cheerfully. "You got another request for me? I loved that beer the last time!"

"Just a question, for now," I said. "When you talked to Boland—and coaxed her to reveal her perfume—did she by any chance talk about who else she might have seen in the area the night that Carol Michosky was attacked?"

"The night Michosky picked Claudia Gonzales out of the lineup?" she asked. She knew nothing of my suspicion of Claudia.

"Yeah, that night."

"Hmmm . . . You know, Phil, I hate to say this, but my memory of my conversation with Boland is a little fuzzy. I know we talked about the perfume—because I told you about that, right? But I can't recall what else we discussed. I should have taken notes, but, you know, this was a favor to you, not an official investigation. . . ."

"Of course. Don't feel bad about it. I'm really glad you were able to help with the perfume ID," I said.

"I'm sorry," Laurie said. "I do feel bad. I hate to let you down. I really should start taking notes all the time—my memory just isn't what it used to be."

Welcome to the club, I thought. "Did you have the flu or a cough earlier this year?" I asked.

"Why?" Laurie responded. "Does that have a bad effect on people's memory?"

"Not completely clear, as yet," I said. "Did you take anything for it?"

"Yeah. My doc prescribed that new antibiotic, Omnin. He said I'd be good as new in a week."

"It may have made you too new."

"Huh?"

I told her I would call her back when I had a chance and explain the dangers of Omnin, and she should ask her doctor to call Andy Weinberg at the CDC in Atlanta if he wanted to prescribe Omnin again.

"Okay," Laurie said.

We hung up. Maybe it was good that the more I dug into the Riverside case, the more I hit against Omnin. Maybe that way I'd figure out how to come up a winner in both cases.

But not today.

I packed it in, and went home about ten minutes early.

I WAS TOO exhausted to fully enjoy the lasagna and salad that Jenna had made, but I did my best. The wine was good.

"Let's go to sleep early," I said.

We did just that. . . .

And somewhere in deep sleep I dreamed that Dugan called again, early in the morning again, to tell me about another body discovered in the park—

Then the phone did ring.

I had just been dreaming that the phone had rung, but it was really ringing now.

I opened my eyes. It was barely dawn. Jenna was holding the phone. "Hold on a second, Jack, he's right here."

She handed me the phone.

"Yeah," I said groggily, for at least the second day in a row, in this goddamn unending nightmare that was all real.

"Phil, you're not gonna believe this," Dugan said.

"Jack, I'm too tired for *Twenty Questions* or *Millionaire* or whatever the hell they call those game shows now."

"They found someone else in the park," he said.

"Cezanne Beck!" I shouted, furious. "I knew it! What the fuck happened to that asshole tail you said you had on Claudia?"

"Who's Cezanne Beck?"

I started to answer, loudly.

"Phil," Dugan interrupted. "The tail's son had an appendicitis attack—he was on the phone with the hospital, took his eyes off Claudia just a minute—"

"And gave her time to slip away and kill Cezanne. I told you—"

"No, no! Phil, listen to me: Claudia was the victim!"

"What?"

"Yes, Claudia was the victim—they found her in Riverside Park about an hour ago. Stripped naked."

I was speechless.

"But Phil, she's alive."

SIXTEEN

 I walked into Dugan's office about ninety minutes later. I was coming in so early so often I might as well as put a bed in the hall.

He started talking.

I did too.

Two unshaven, exhausted disputants, with more bile than orange juice or coffee for breakfast.

"Doesn't mean she's not the killer, Jack." I jabbed with my finger for emphasis. "Nothing's really changed."

He looked at me. "She was bare-assed, unconscious, stretched out in the park, and you want to tell me she faked it?"

"It's September not December, nighttime temperatures are in the sixties—that's a little chilly for just skin, sure, but not fatal. And she's alive," I insisted. "You think that's just coincidence?"

Dugan considered. I couldn't tell which lines of his face were wrinkles or the harsh imprint of morning through uneven window blinds.

"We can't lose sight of the things that still point to Claudia," I continued, "even with her alibi for Berman and now this. Where is she now, by the way?"

"Beth Israel, for observation," Dugan replied. "My problem with your theory is that I didn't see those things in the first place the way you do. Even Claudia for the Michosky murder is still a big question—we haven't received a statement yet from that temp."

"I know." I had been standing since I had come into Dugan's office, giving a lecture. Now I sat down for more careful discussion. "Who found Claudia this morning?"

"An eighteen-year-old Columbia University student," Dugan replied. "I interviewed him about an hour ago. He was out jogging. He says he saw Claudia lying on her side in the grass near the path. At first he thought she was dead, but then he saw she was breathing. He tried to rouse her—he says he said 'miss, miss' a few times, and touched her shoulder. But she didn't move or respond. So he ran down a block to the nearest phone and called 911."

"Do you believe him? If by some chance Claudia isn't lying, do you like him for the attack, maybe the other stranglings?" No point in not at least considering every possibility.

"He seemed very nervous, embarrassed," Dugan said. "Understandable, given the circumstances. It may be he's fibbing about where he touched her—maybe not just on her shoulder. Always possible in these cases. But we checked his record and he's had no problems of any kind with the law before. I believe him on this. As for the murders, he's a freshman at Columbia, and was in high school in New Orleans last spring. He just got here two weeks ago. So there's no way he could have strangled anyone in New York other than Amy Berman and maybe Carol Michosky. I'll check on the exact date he came to New York, and his whereabouts on those two evenings. But I think he'll come out clean on those, too."

I nodded agreement. "Okay, so, he called EMS. What happened when they got to the park? Was Claudia still out cold?"

"Martha Willis and James Towson took the call—two very experienced people," Dugan said. "They said she started to wake when they put the blanket around her."

"So as soon as medical people arrive—people who could tell pretty quickly if she was playing possum—she opens her eyes."

"She had abrasions around her neck," Dugan countered.

"Those could have been self-inflicted," I shot back.

"I still find it hard to believe that she would just stretch out naked like that in the park," Dugan said. "It's taking quite a damn risk. She might have been raped by just your average sick slob wandering by. Even killed."

"She was desperate. She had to be, after our meeting yesterday—however much she was smiling when she walked out of my office. Desperate people do desperate things. What did she say she was doing in the park then, anyway? Or is she claiming the attack took place somewhere else?"

"I talked to her briefly by phone in the hospital," Dugan said. "She said she was feeling very bad again yesterday, after our interview, about her loss of memory in the Murphy case. She couldn't sleep. So she decided to go back to the scene, to see if it could shake loose some memories, and was on her way there when she was attacked from behind. She said she didn't see her assailant. All she recalls are very powerful hands around her neck, and losing consciousness very quickly."

"If her 'assailant' was her accomplice, then Claudia's plan might have been to get choked just enough to lose consciousness, to make her ploy really convincing. That's another possibility," I said. "But, then, of course—Oh God! Jeez!"

"What?"

"You said haven't received a statement yet from Cezanne Beck—the temp who was in my office the day that Michosky was killed—about Cezanne's conversation with a female cop who I am sure is Claudia."

"Right . . . ?" Dugan half said, half questioned what I was talking about.

"Where's the new tail on Claudia?" I asked.

"I assume at the hospital," Dugan replied. "Why? You expect her to go kill the temp now?" he asked sarcastically.

"No," I answered in kind. "But Claudia's accomplice could be in the process of hunting or killing Cezanne right now—"

"Goddamn it Phil! We don't even know that there *is* an accomplice!"

"Oh, I see. We don't even know. So, you're comfortable with just sitting back and risking another woman stripped and strangled?"

Dugan stood up. His face was rouge with anger. His fist was clenched. I could see him struggling with whether to throw me out of his office, put me into some kind of mandatory psychological counseling, or give any more consideration to what I was saying.

His better part won out. He slowly sat down. He was basically a reasonable man.

"Is this where you think your temp is currently employed?" he asked evenly. He passed a piece of paper to me, with Cezanne's name, her temp company's name, and its address.

"How'd you get that?"

"You told me her name when I woke you up, remember? It wasn't that hard to track down the rest of it," Dugan replied.

I nodded. I remembered. I looked again at the paper. "Yeah, it's all correct." I looked at my watch—it was a few minutes before nine. "No guarantee she'll be at Hot Temps now, though—she may already be at her assignment. Hell, she may be home."

"Understood," Dugan said. He called in a two-person protection unit, and directed them to Cezanne's office. "They should be there in ten minutes. They'll find out where she is, if she's not on the premises, and they'll get to her, don't worry."

"Thanks," I said genuinely, and tried to relax a bit. I couldn't.

I stood up. "I'm going over to Hot Temps myself," I said and walked toward the door.

"Phil," Dugan called after me.

I turned around.

"Phil, you're going to run yourself ragged on this. You've got to take it easy, at least a little."

"I don't recall how to do that anymore." The truth was, I never did.

TRAFFIC LOOKED THICK, so I took the subway to Hot Temps headquarters on Eighth Avenue and Fifteenth Street. I wanted to make sure that Cezanne's superiors were crystal-clear about not revealing anything about her to anyone—including other cops—except the protection unit.

The area was a little seedy, but the building had an art-deco elegance. I thought I saw someone familiar standing near a bunch of people in the middle of the lobby, but the group dissolved as I approached, leaving just a delivery man, an elderly woman dressed like it was Easter Sunday, and a younger woman in blue-jean shorts who looked good but not familiar at all. My nerves and imagination both were going from bad to worse.

I took a gold-leafed elevator to the Hot Temps offices on the ninth floor. A tall, well-built man in a reasonably priced suit was sitting in the reception area. I didn't know him, but figured him immediately to be half of our protection unit.

I showed him my identification and extended my hand. "Phil D'Amato," I said.

He looked surprised. "Dennis Molloy," he said, and showed his badge. "Is everything okay with Ms. Beck? We just got here. My partner's inside, talking to her boss."

"As far as I know," I said, and sat down next to Molloy. "I just wanted to come by and give you and your partner a little more background on this."

"Sure," Molloy said genially. "The more we know, the better we can do our job and protect her."

A redhead in a sharp, pinstriped business suit came out of the inner office and smiled first at Molloy, then me.

Molloy got to his feet. "Allison Barnes, my partner—Dr. Phil D'Amato, Forensics," Molloy made the introductions.

She extended her hand and crisply shook mine. If looks and demeanor were any indication, Dugan had assigned a top unit to this job.

"I briefed the supervisor and three of her colleagues," Barnes said. "They're certain they hadn't talked to anyone before me about Ms. Beck. I think we can count on them not to talk to anyone else. Meanwhile, Ms. Beck is temping today at an insurance brokerage firm on Sixth Avenue—across the street from Rockefeller Center. I spoke to her briefly on the phone. She's not too happy with our involvement—she's understandably concerned that her bosses, where she's temping, might not like us looking over their shoulders—but I think she understands the danger. I told her we could be up there in about twenty minutes, and she said she thought she could take a little break then and talk to us."

Now I was impressed with the job Barnes was doing, as well.

"Dr. D'Amato wants to give us a little background briefing on this," Molloy said. "How about I take the briefing and you go up to see Ms. Beck?"

We walked out the front doors of Hot Temps. Barnes pressed the elevator button.

"I'd be happy to ride with you to Rockefeller Center, and brief you on the way," I said.

Molloy and Barnes looked at each other. "Sure," Barnes said. "That way we both get to hear what you're saying directly."

I nodded. Right, that. And I also wanted to tag along on the very remote possibility that Barnes, Molloy, or both were in league with Claudia. My good impressions of these two went only so far. Files were full of murderers who were elegant, intelligent, and efficient.

WE ARRVIED AT the offices of Welch and Clendon, Incorporated, about twenty minutes later, just as Allison Barnes had estimated. The decor was 1970s stucco-fluorescent—a maze of open, partitioned offices, with walls that didn't reach the ceiling, relieved by the occasional cactus in a big clay pot and glimpses of the city through distant picture windows on the outside walls. Presumably, the executives had private offices with floor-to-ceiling views made entirely of those picture windows. But semipublic cubbyholes were all that we, and very likely Cezanne, got to see.

Barnes announced our presence to the outer receptionist, and Cezanne came out to see us about five minutes later. She seemed younger than I had expected—not much more than her late teens—but I wasn't sure on what I had based my assumption of her age in the first place. Maybe her name. She looked upset. That, I thoroughly expected—and felt very bad about.

Barnes introduced us.

"We talked on the phone, right?" Cezanne asked me.

"Yes," I said. "And your information was very helpful."

"And that's why I'm in danger now?"

"Well—"

"Is it okay for you if we talk here," Barnes interjected, "or would you prefer someplace more private?"

Cezanne looked around. We were in the open reception area—a very big room—with the receptionist on the far side and well out of earshot. "Here's fine," Cezanne said. "I don't have too long for my break now, so I'd rather not use up time looking for someplace else."

"Good." Barnes said, and gave Cezanne a friendly smile. "The truth is, you may not really be in any danger at all now. We want you to live your life as you always have. But we just want to be safe. The important thing is, Detective Molloy and I—and sometimes other detectives we will introduce to you—will always be close by. We won't get in your way, I promise. Most of the time, you won't even know where we are. But we'll be there for you. After we finish this conversation, you'll just go back to work. I'll talk to your boss here, and smooth everything out."

"Okay," she said, without much conviction. "Thank you. But . . . I wish I'd never gotten involved in this in the first place." She laughed nervously. "I don't even know what it is that I'm involved in." She looked at me.

Barnes answered before I could. "It's better that you don't know. Honestly, we're not even sure ourselves. We're just being careful."

Cezanne nodded.

"One other thing," Molloy added. "Don't assume that just anyone who shows you a badge or has a uniform is your friend. Only the people that Detective Barnes and I introduce to you."

"Okay," Cezanne said.

She looked even more upset than before, but Molloy was completely right to emphasize this point. It couldn't be repeated enough, given my suspicions about Claudia having some sort of accomplice.

"Is this some kind of police-corruption thing?" Cezanne asked.

"Maybe, in a way," Barnes answered. "But we're not really sure."

"All right," Cezanne said, and looked at her watch. "I guess I better get back to work."

"Good idea," Barnes said.

Cezanne smiled quickly at all three of us, and left.

"You two seem right on top of this," I said.

"Thank you," Barnes said. "We better go talk to her boss now. You want to come along?"

I thought about it for a second. "Thanks—but you seem to have this well in hand."

The two turned to walk towards the receptionist.

"One other thing, though," I said.

The pair turned around.

"If you have the names of the detectives on your night team, I'd appreciate getting that," I said. "Just so I know who I'm talking to, in case I call."

Molloy looked at Barnes, who nodded.

He wrote on a small piece of paper, and gave it me. "Four names," he said. "Two other teams of two, in addition to Detective Barnes and me."

"Thanks," I said. In addition to knowing everyone's names for the purposes of conversation, it wouldn't hurt for me to check them all out.

"Off to see the boss here, then," Barnes said, and the two turned back towards the receptionist.

This will probably wind up getting Cezanne fired, I thought unhappily, *as good as Barnes and Molloy seem to be.*

But better to lose your job than your life.

I WALKED OUT into the rich September sunshine. It seemed to coat the city with a fragrant heat. I didn't feel very warmed by it right now, though. I felt hungry. Likely because a cup of tea and a swig of orange juice had been all I'd consumed today, hours earlier.

I treated myself to a hot dog from a cart. I knew it wasn't the best thing for my stomach. Not the best for any part of my body, with all its nitrates and nitrites. But the resonance with ball games at Yankee Stadium was more important to me at this point than good nutrition. Victories were always so much easier there, so clear-cut. A crack of the bat, a ball out of the park. It had been too long since I'd heard that. I hadn't been to the stadium all season. These days I measured success in how many innocent lives I managed not to lose. . . .

I hoisted myself up to sit on one of the stone ledges on the perimeter of a plaza with fountains on Sixth Avenue. The sound of falling water was a comfort. I tapped out some beat with my heels against the ledge, and looked out at the passersby—

Damn it. I caught a glimpse in the distance of a face that looked familiar. I couldn't relax even here like a normal human being and enjoy my frankfurter without my mind acting up on me.

I looked again. . . .

He approached me slowly, with a smile.

I returned it and got off the ledge.

"Phil D'Amato!" he said, and shook my hand. "Let me introduce myself properly to you this time."

It was the toenail man from my trip to Chicago on the Lake Shore Limited.

WE DECIDED TO go to a nearby Japanese ramen place for noodles and green tea. I was still pretty hungry. I figured the noodles and hot dog were not likely to fight too much in my stomach. And green tea was a good mediator.

"I don't recall telling you my name on the train," I said, as we reached the restaurant.

"You didn't," the toe-man replied. "I learned your name from another source—my superiors in the Department. I'm Jerry Divone." He pulled out his badge—NYPD detective. "I've been investigating you."

The maître d' seated us.

I wasn't really shocked. That's how the damn Department worked: Trust no one. "You're working for Jack Dugan?" I asked.

Divone shook his head no. "Higher. I'm reporting straight

to the commissioner. In fact, Dugan is a bit under a cloud himself."

"I'm happy to hear that," I said, and smiled thinly. "Not that Dugan's under suspicion, but at least he's not the goddamn one who's knifing me in the back."

A waiter who had approached to take our order looked a little concerned at the word "knifing," which I had said pretty loudly. "We were just talking about hibachi cooking," I said. "It's nice the way they cut up your food for you right at your table."

"Yes," the waiter replied, and bowed slightly. "Hibachi chefs are good with knives!"

We gave him our order and he left.

"The commissioner thinks Dugan's mind may be going— he's concerned about Dugan's lapses of memory," Divone said.

I laughed without mirth. "And the commissioner's sure, of course, that his own memory has been fine?"

Divone didn't answer.

"Why are you telling me all of this?" I asked. "Is this the culmination of your investigation?" Meaning the next step would be I was off the case for sure—maybe even out of a job?

"In a way, it is the end of the investigation, but not the way you think," Divone replied.

"Oh?"

"I very much enjoyed our conversation on the train," he said.

"So did I," I said.

"And, frankly, I found nothing wrong with you then, nothing the Department should be worried about." He rubbed the stubble on his chin. He still had a little of the derelict about him. That part of his costume was apparently real. But he also seemed more substantial, more focused, than on the train.

"But you've changed your mind about me since?" I prodded.

"Actually, the opposite," Divone said. "I've done a lot of

research into your history, your past cases. And into this case. And something else happened that made me see what you're trying to do in a different light."

Our food arrived.

"You were saying?" I coaxed, and dug into my green buckwheat noodles. They were delicious.

"My daughter had the flu last spring. She took Omnin. She's twenty-four—a very bright young lady. Much brighter than her old man. She's finishing up a doctoral program at Hofstra."

"You must be very proud of her."

"Thanks. I am. You have any kids?"

"No. Not yet."

"Well, I highly recommend them," Divone said. "They're miracles. Not that they don't drive you nuts. They do. But it's worth it. The wife and I have just two—the twenty-four-year-old, Gabrielle, and her kid sister, Jocelyn, eighteen."

I nodded.

"Gabrielle's completing her Ph.D. at Hofstra, like I said," Divone continued. "And as part of that process, she has to go through something called a final oral defense. She told me that five professors would grill her on what she wrote in her doctoral dissertation, and she'd be lucky if any one of them read it in its entirety—if any two of them read the damn thing at all."

"I know the process well—something like it happens with a lot of the reports I hand in to the Department," I said.

Divone laughed, briefly. "Yeah. Anyway, the day of Gabrielle's final oral defense was last Thursday. The date was set six weeks in advance—"

I could see exactly what was coming—

"—and she blows it! Five professors sitting like stooges around the conference table, picking their noses, looking at Gabby's empty seat! And she can't even say she was sick—she's having a bite to eat in a coffee shop, right on campus. Some other old-fart professor spotted her there!"

"It wasn't her fault," I said.

"I know it."

"One of the first memory losses I heard about in this case was someone's daughter—Amy Berman's—totally forgetting she got an A on an important exam."

Divone nodded. "That's why I'm here—I read that in one of your reports. See, I'm better than the brass—at least I read those things."

I smiled.

"I still don't understand it, though. What kind of amnesia comes on months after the trauma—if Omnin was the cause—and makes someone go blank on an appointment she's had for weeks?" Divone asked. "Gabrielle's a serious girl. She's broken up about this."

I shook my head sympathetically. "I don't understand all of it yet, either. She probably had some memory losses earlier, but didn't pay them much attention, because they didn't take out anything crucial. Likely she woke up on the day of her oral exam—knew that she had an exam coming up, because she'd been thinking about it for weeks—but the memory scythe came in and lopped off her specific knowledge that the oral exam was that very day. She probably also suddenly recalled something then that she had forgotten previously—I think of this as the 'memory swap' or 'carousel'. It can make you crazy."

"I believe you," Divone said intently, and leaned over the table towards me. "I talked to the wife about this last night. From this moment on, I want to work *with* you on this case. I want to be on the inside with you, not spy on you from the outside. I want to help you figure out whatever the hell's going on here. My girl comes first. I choose her and you over the commissioner any day."

I put down the noodles I had wrapped around my chop-sticks. "You know, of course, that that's precisely what you would be saying to me if you were actually continuing the investigation on the commissioner's behalf, and wanted to get closer to me, on the inside. You lied to me on the train. Everything you just told me could be the same."

"I didn't lie to you so much on the train," Divone said. "I *am* a carpenter, in my spare time."

"You didn't tell me you were a detective," I countered. "That's still a big lie of omission."

"I'm not lying to you about my daughter," Divone main-tained vehemently.

I don't even know that you have a daughter, I thought. *But I guess that could be checked.* I sighed. Once again I was in a situa-tion in which a big splash of evidence—Divone coming over and talking to me like this—could support two rival hypotheses about him: He was still investigating me; or he really wanted to help me with this mess, from the inside, like he said.

"So your plan would be to keep feeding the commissioner whatever line of bullshit about me to keep him satisfied that you were still working for him, but you actually would do whatever I asked that might help with this case?"

"Whatever you wanted—I would do whatever you asked," Divone said. "I'd be your de facto partner."

I considered. If I said no to Divone, and he was really still working for the commissioner, someone else would be assigned to take over his investigation of me. I would be no better off than I was now, except for the confirmation that the commis-sioner was after me, which I already knew anyway, more or less, from Dugan. But if I took Divone in with me, and he was work-ing for the commissioner, I could be careful about what infor-mation I gave Divone. Hadn't Vito or Michael Corleone talked about the advantage of keeping your possible enemies close to you? Great, I was so far gone I was taking advice from a mafioso, and a character in a movie at that.

Of course, the best outcome would be if I let Divone in, and he was telling the truth about his daughter and his wanting to be a partner. God, I could use a partner. I felt constantly on the verge of going out of control, doing so much of this alone.

I extended my hand across the table. "Okay, let's give it a shot and see what happens."

I needed the help. It might not be help I could thoroughly trust, but I was in no position to shop around.

SEVENTEEN

Three voice-mails were waiting for me in my office after lunch—from Ed Monti, Andy Weinberg, and Jack Dugan. *I should stay away from my office more often,* I thought. I seemed to get better results on the phone that way.

The voice-mails contained no detailed messages, just requests to return the calls.

Andy's was the first I returned. I didn't specifically decide to do that. My fingers just did the walking, as they used to say in that old ad about the Yellow Pages, though fingers these days tended to leap across keys rather than meander around rotary dials.

"Phil, I've got some great news."

"I'm in short supply—tell me," I said.

Andy laughed. "We've got a hearing with three FDA staff in two weeks. Someone there was impressed enough with Morton's letter to ask if he could come down and talk to them about his germ theory of consciousness, and how Omnin might endanger that."

"Spectacular!" I said, delighted. "How'd you do it?"

"One of their top people missed a congressional meeting—not because he was sick—he just missed it. He was sipping bourbon in a bar at the time. And he claims he had no recollection whatsoever of the appointment. Apparently some secretary messed up as well—she sent just one notice about the meeting, with no follow-up. The guy who missed the meeting is very well respected. He's been one of their big guns for years. And his friends at the FDA are inclined to believe what he's saying about his memory loss. My package with Morton's letter arrived at the right time. We got lucky. We're not home free by a long shot, but at least we've got a game now."

Unbelievable, I thought. This was the second time today that these damn memory outages were beginning to work in our favor. Then something else occurred to me. "Two weeks is pretty tight," I said.

"What?"

"Not much time before Morton's appearance," I replied.

"I don't get you—I thought you wanted to get moving on this as quickly as possible, before Omnin was out en masse on the market again."

"I do," I said. "But we don't know how to get in touch with Morton."

"What are you talking about?" Andy asked, incredulous. "Wasn't there a return address on his letter? Just contact him there."

"Take a look at it," I said. "No return address. I doubt there was one on the envelope, either. He was very clear to me in Chicago that he never gives out his home address."

"Didn't you tell me he's professor emeritus at New York University?"

"Yeah, but it sometimes takes weeks for the secretary there to hear from him or get through to him. I went through that this summer."

"Phil, you've got to reach him, somehow, and get him down here for this meeting. Everything depends on that. We won't get a second chance."

"I know." I congratulated Andy again and hung up the phone and considered. He was one hundred percent right that the FDA interview in two weeks would be our best chance, very likely our only chance, to get the FDA to put a stop to Omnin. And without Morton there, we were dead. The bourbon drinker and his loss of memory wouldn't be enough—when push came to shove, his missing the congressional meeting would be ascribed to bourbon before Omnin. That's the way the world worked—and thought.

I pushed back my chair and grabbed my jacket. I needed to get over to NYU and Morton's secretary as quickly as possible.

But Ed Monti's and Jack Dugan's names were still sitting on my desk, on my list of unreturned calls.

I sat back down and pulled a card out of my pocket.

I picked up my phone and called my new partner, Jerry Divone.

I heard the subway running in the background through his cell phone. "Phil D'Amato here. Where are you?" I asked.

"Ah, Phil," Jerry replied, over the *clackety-clack* of the subway. "On my way down to Fourteenth Street, and then over to Beth Israel Hospital to see what I can pick up about Officer Gonzales, as we discussed."

"Well, see if you can take that train down to West Fourth Street, and NYU, instead," I said, and explained our urgent need to obtain Morton's address or phone or some contact information from his department's secretary—if she had it.

"Extracting information from secretaries is one of my specialties," Divone replied. "Comes with my working-class solidarity."

"I believe it," I said.

"But you sure you want to take me off the Gonzales beat for this?—seeing how it concerns the ongoing series of homicides and all," Divone asked. "I thought you said you wanted her behind bars before you could devote full attention to—"

"I'm not sure," I replied. "But in the long run, more lives

could be hurt or even lost if this memory drain gets worse."

"No argument from me there," Divone said. "I'll get back to you as soon as I have something on Morton."

I got off the phone. I felt good about having someone I could work with in this way. . . . Assuming that he was being honest with me.

Of course, there were worse things Divone could be than an undercover cop who was lying to me about his disloyalty to the commissioner, just to get me off guard. For all I knew, Divone could be Claudia's accomplice—whom no one else apparently believed existed anyway. But that thought had occurred to me. And if it were true, I had just pointed a killer in Darius Morton's direction. . . .

I shook my head. I had to trust someone in this, or I was bound to fail. Divone made the cut, shaky as it was.

I picked up the phone again and thought about my next return call.

I dialed.

Dugan answered. "Phil, we uncovered a connection between Officer Gonzales and the fourth murder victim," he said. "I wanted you to know. You may be right about her after all."

"My lucky day," I said, only partially sarcastically. "And the fourth victim was . . ."

"Eileen Sheflin," Dugan supplied. "The Cooper Union grad student visiting her friends up at Columbia. I know—after a while they all blur together. That's the way it is with these damn serial murders."

I suspected my problem ran a little deeper than that blurring effect—I had no recollection at all of an Eileen being strangled in the past few months—but there was no need to get into that right now. "What did you find out about her connection to Gonzales?" I asked.

"They both went to the same high school. According to

other people we were able to track down and interview who were in the school at that time, Gonzales and Eileen both had the same boyfriend—at the same time."

"Who got to keep the boyfriend?"

"Eileen—she went on to marry him, though they later got divorced."

"Pretty thin motive for murder—what would it be, ten years later?"

"Fourteen," Dugan replied.

"But even if Claudia killed Eileen for personal reasons, how would that explain her motive for the other killings? Surely the victims didn't all steal her boyfriends. So that leaves us . . . with what—Claudia strangled the others, before and after Eileen, as a smoke screen? To make us think we had a serial killer on our hands, when in fact we had a clever lady who was still stewing about her teenage rival?"

"It's been known to happen," Dugan said.

"I suppose . . . but it's got to be more complicated than that."

"At least it's progress," Dugan said. "It's the first sense that we've been able to make of this at all. You should be happy. It gets you maybe a little off the hook for your wild theorizing. It tells me perhaps you weren't so wild."

"Oh, I'm happier," I said, truly. "Just not satisfied. Do you really think Claudia is the serial strangler now, on the basis of the high-school connection to Eileen?"

"I don't know," Dugan conceded. "I'm saying maybe it's a little more likely than it was before."

"What are you doing about Claudia in light of this? Will you put her under arrest now—at least take away her badge and gun?"

"I just sent surveillance back to her hospital," Dugan said.

"I didn't know they'd left."

"She was in the hospital, for God's sake. Found nude in the park. Under a doctor's care. I can't have surveillance everywhere," Dugan retorted.

I stopped myself from saying, *Well, she's in the hospital right now, presumably still under a doctor's care, and yet you're sending in surveillance.* "I don't mean to be giving you a hard time, Jack. I'm just tired. I owe Ed Monti a call, and then let's talk some more about Claudia."

I DIDN'T CALL Ed Monti right away. Something else demanded my attention—something that been bothering me below the surface almost all day.

This memory loss—mine, everyone's—was getting worse. Or, it had been getting worse all along, but I hadn't fully noticed it. In the past few hours alone, I had heard about Divone's daughter's memory lapse, the FDA bureaucrat's memory lapse, and the commissioner's concern about Dugan's memory lapses—which may or may not have been the same as the Dugan lapses I knew about. Plus, now there was my own latest memory loss, about the Eileen Sheflin murder. For all I knew, maybe there were other lapses I'd heard about or even experienced myself today, but they, too, were gone in yet another blackout in my brain. . . .

The very fact that I could even seriously entertain that—and I was—showed how bad the situation had become. If it kept up much longer, I didn't see how we could bring Claudia Gonzales to justice even if we had all the goods on her.

What jury would convict anyone on the testimony of witnesses who were demonstrably forgetful? If the trial took any length of time, some members of the jury themselves might start forgetting testimony. The effect that Omnin apparently had on the bacteria in our brain—if that in fact was what was going on—was insidious.

Andy was right about the time pressure. We had to stop Omnin now. We—everyone—might not be mentally competent enough next year to do the job.

Morton, McNair, Briskman—jeez, I couldn't remember who now—had said something to me about declines and falls of empires. Had the Incas, the Carthaginians, who knew who else, succumbed not to plagues of bacteria, but natural antibiotic agents—like mold spores—that silenced the bacterial voices that helped make us human? If that was even remotely the case, what was in store for us?

I tried to think about who had said that to me. I really couldn't recall. But maybe I shouldn't be so hard on myself— didn't people, hadn't people, always had little problems with memory from time to time, especially in high-stress conditions? Or maybe I couldn't remember who had told me about the decline of the Incas because it was my idea in the first place. . . .

I thought again about calling Ed Monti. I picked up the phone. Our conversation would have to be easier than this self-interrogation—anything would be.

He answered. My "luck" today was still holding out.

"Phil, sorry I took so long on that second look at the Berman case. My best assistant liked San Francisco so much on her vacation that she decided to get a job there and stay, and I've been buried in bodies the past two weeks."

"I wouldn't mind a few weeks off in San Francisco myself," I said. "Come to think of it, I wouldn't mind a few weeks off any-where." Had I even taken a vacation this summer? That working trip to Cape Cod was the closest.

"Tell me about it," Ed commiserated. "Anyway, I had a care-ful look again at the results of the Berman autopsy—we had just completed it when I got your voice-mail—and I also examined the body again. And I compared all of that with our findings from three of the other Riverside stranglings—I figured that would be the fastest way of uncovering any differences. And I found two interesting differences. I'm not sure what they'll mean to you. . . ."

"You've got my rapt attention."

"Well, first, the strangulation print—the damage to the neck—is positioned at a slightly different angle on Amy Berman. More upward-to-downward, as if the killer were reaching from higher above than on the other victims."

"A man strangled her—in contrast to a woman who strangled the others?" I asked.

"Well, it certainly suggests that Berman's strangler was taller than the hypothetical other killer—that would account for the difference in angle. But Amy was also a few inches shorter than the other victims, who were tall, leggy blondes. That complicates any possible conclusion about the height of her killer."

I considered. "Yeah, Amy is the odd one out in several ways. But you don't like the male-versus-female as her strangler?"

"I don't necessarily see it," Ed answered. "At least, not on the basis of the neck damage. It's not substantially worse than for the others—no wider area of damage, no deeper damage, nothing that suggests greater strength in the strangler."

"All right, fair enough," I said. "And the second distinction between Amy and the others?"

"Also not much to go on. I found some different pollens on Berman's clothes."

"Amy was killed at the foot of Central Park, and the others in Riverside Park—that could account for that difference, right?"

"Probably," Ed replied. "But I'm seeing if I can get a more precise idea of just where the pollen on Amy might have come from."

"It would be nice if it came from some plant that only polli-nates in the dead of summer in the middle of Alaska, and we had a suspect who'd been to Alaska just last month, wouldn't it?"

Ed laughed. "Yeah."

"Okay," I said. "Thanks. Oh, one more question: The three other autopsies you looked at again—other than Berman's—was one of them Eileen Sheflin?"

"The Cooper Union girl?"

"Right."

"No. You want me to take a second look at her file, too?"

"Could you? And while you're at it, the woman who was strangled when Claudia Gonzales was in Philadelphia—"

"Chloe Josephson? She wasn't one of the three I looked at again, either."

"Could you go over again what you have on her, too?" I asked. "Hell, I know you're swamped, but if you could check them all, one more time, that would be the best thing."

"Sure . . . and what exactly am I looking for? Just differ-ences?" Ed inquired.

"Yeah, differences," I replied.

I PUT THE phone back in its cradle, and walked down the hall to get a bottle of iced tea from the glittering new dispensing machine. This one took my money just fine. I drank down the cool, sweet tea and thought things over as I made my way back to my office.

Actually, what I wanted from Ed were not only differences but similarities. If the Josephson and Berman murders—the ones committed when Claudia seemed to have strong alibis—were not only different from the rest but similar to each other, then that would suggest both were the work of the same person. It was of course possible that this person was not Claudia's accomplice—these two stranglings, if they were the handiwork of one person, could have been copycat killings. That was

Dugan's suggestion about the Berman murder. If Josephson proved out to have been dispatched by the same hands, well, a copycat could just as easily copy twice as once. Jeez, any number of times—a goddamn xerox killer.

But I didn't think so. I didn't buy copies—twice or once—for the killings in this case. I put my money on someone in league with Claudia.

But who? In league for murder was serious business. It went beyond friendship, partnership, even family most of the time. Who would be willing to take one, two lives on behalf of another? Claudia's partner Ron Greave had occurred to me. I'd been on such a treadmill the last couple of days that I hadn't had a chance to ask Dugan to check him out. I suppose it was possible that Greave and Claudia were lovers, that Greave had no alibis for the Josephson and Berman murders. But my gut said otherwise. And Ed's findings suggested that Berman's strangler was not a man.

But a smart male accomplice who wanted to throw us off—wanted us to think that the murders were all done by the same person, a woman who was not Claudia—could have deliberately strangled Josephson and Berman with tender hands, in a way that inflicted damage sufficient to kill but not announce itself as a man's job. I suppose some sicko copycat male killer could have done the same. But stranglings so precise would require detailed anatomical knowledge, not just any smarts. . . .

I plopped back into the chair in my office, and swigged the last of my iced tea. No . . . I still thought the accomplice was a woman. But I would ask Dugan to look into Greave anyway, just to be sure.

Dugan thought that, if there was an accomplice, we might not know her—or him—at all. That was the worst scenario, for it would mean that we were still missing a very substantial part of what was going on.

So who, then, was this damn phantom accomplice? What

was I missing? There was a time when I at least could have relied on my memory as I tried to untangle events. . . .

I shook my head in self-disgust, looked at my empty iced-tea bottle, and tossed it halfway across my office to the waste-paper basket.

It made a smooth, dead-center landing.

The phone rang at the same time.

"Phil." It was Dugan. "Don't worry, I'm not calling you about another homicide." But he still didn't sound too happy.

"Of course not," I replied. "It's not five-thirty in the morning."

He barely laughed. "I, uh, I wanted you to know that Officer Gonzales seems to be no longer in the hospital."

"What do you mean? I thought you had surveillance on her again. God damn—"

"I did. I mean, I wanted to . . ." Dugan sounded upset, confused. Christ, was his memory just from an hour ago going now too?

"Surveillance got to the hospital," he said. "The nurses, the doctors, the physicians' aids there all thought that Claudia was in her room. And then when she wasn't there, they thought maybe in the bathroom, or maybe she walked downstairs to the cafeteria. But she wasn't anywhere—she was gone."

I cursed some more.

"She wasn't under arrest, Phil! She was entitled to leave whenever she wanted. Hospitals aren't lockups. But we . . . I just didn't expect this."

"She'll go after Cezanne Beck," I said.

"We've got her very well protected," Dugan said. "You saw some of the people we have on that—they're the best. Beck is safe. And Claudia would be crazy to go after her now, anyway."

"I think she's crazy."

"So far, the killer's acted pretty damn carefully," Dugan insisted. "If Claudia's the one, she's likely lying low until she can figure out a way to get out of New York. But I sent out the usual advisories to the airports, trains, buses, and bridge and tunnel authorities anyway."

"All right, that's good," I allowed. "But let's at least focus on who else might be in her sights now, right here in town—assuming she resists the impulse to kill the temp."

Dugan cleared his throat. "Well, if we want to be comprehensive about it, Phil, there's you."

"Me?"

"If she's guilty, and suspects you know she's guilty, and may be close to proving it, then, sure, it's a possibility," Dugan said.

I said nothing. This was the part of the job I liked least.

"But she'd be even crazier to go after you than the temp woman, Phil."

EIGHTEEN

Dinner that evening with Jenna was no pleasure.

Two officers had driven me home and escorted me upstairs. Jenna had seen them at the door as they were saying good night; I had to explain their presence. I would have anyway—I didn't keep things like that from her.

We maintained an uncomfortable silence through salad and dinner, which consisted of succulent pan-seared tuna and rice. She let me have it over dessert. It may not have been thoroughly just, but it was deserved.

"What's going to happen when we have kids?" she demanded, taking the spoon of banana flambé she had lifted and slamming it down on the table.

"I'd go with ice cream instead at that point," I said. "These kinds of desserts are too rich for kids."

"I'm not in the mood for your stupid sense of humor now," she flared. "It won't protect our kids when some maniac you stir up comes after them!"

I put my hand over hers. It was quivering. Maybe mine was too.

She started crying. "It won't protect *you*."

"Claudia's not some superwoman," I responded softly. "She likely has no idea where we live."

"She knows where you work," Jenna retorted. "She's a cop.

She has a gun." The desperation in Jenna's face was undiminished.

"It's my job," I said.

"No. It's your life. That's what's at risk here. That's the most important thing. It's our lives together."

"What do you want me to do? Walk away from the NYPD and get a job somewhere as a professor? Lecturing students and grading papers?"

"I don't know," Jenna said. She wiped her eyes. "I just don't know anymore."

I looked at the dessert and pushed it away.

"You know what's ironic about this?" Jenna continued. "The weird thing you're investigating—that bacteria may help us remember, and antibiotics that hurt those bacteria may be causing us to forget—well, that's not what's threatening our lives now. It may be dangerous, it's certainly fascinating, but it certainly isn't strangling anybody in Riverside Park or pointing a gun at you. No, you're the target now of just another commonplace asshole murderer. She may be ingenious, she may have a badge, but when it comes right down to it, human knowledge won't be furthered one damn bit when that bitch is brought to justice!"

I shook my head back and forth, slowly. "I can't investigate the fascinating stuff without the authority of my office. The only reason I'm taken seriously—those times that I am—is because I'm a forensic scientist in a big-city police department. It's the price I have to pay. And besides, I'm sure these two cases are related—"

"Maybe you need to think of another way," Jenna said, and walked out the room.

I WOKE UP in bed the next morning, and squinted at the alarm clock. The red numerals glowed 7:51. . . . Good. A day that I was able to wake up without a call from Dugan was a fine day, regardless of what else was going on.

Jenna walked into the bedroom, wearing just a dark, short T-shirt that rode slightly above her waist.

"I'm sorry about last night," I said. We had both gone to bed shortly after our dinner conversation, and promptly fallen asleep.

She looked at me. She still didn't seem very happy.

"You know, we talked about this a little on Cape Cod," I went on. "You seemed to understand then."

I sat up in bed. Jenna strode towards me. I felt like doing something other than talking—

"What do you mean we talked about this on Cape Cod?" she asked harshly.

"When you were saying that you knew I would never change about getting involved this way in all of these cases, but that was okay?"

She snorted. "Here we go again. Either you're dreaming or I'm not remembering, or both. Didn't we have this discussion already? Didn't I or you or someone say, 'Here we go again'? Maybe I'm dreaming that, too, or not remembering, or who the hell knows anymore!" She turned and walked to her dresser. She pulled out a pair of panties and jeans and put them on.

Suddenly the day wasn't so fine anymore, even absent Dugan's voice.

I had to face the possibility that even if Andy and Morton were able to stop the FDA from opening the floodgates to Omnin, it already might have done permanent damage to everyone who had consumed it. That, in a way, was part of Andy's point about memory lapses being hard to document— maybe they'd been happening already for centuries, for millennia, because of brief unknowing encounters with antibiotics that beat the blood-brain barrier—

"I'm meeting a friend for breakfast at Grand Central Station," Jenna said. "Will I have the pleasure of an NYPD escort?"

"There should be a patrol car across the street," I replied. "I assume it's been there all night. Tell them I said they should drive you down to Grand Central, and keep an eye on you. They know how to be discreet—you won't even know they're there. By the way, who's your friend?"

Jenna scowled at the intrusion of the question. Had she not been angry at me, she would have told me in the first place. "Joel Napoli. He was a student with me at MIT. He lives in Denver now with his wife and kids. We try to get together whenever he's in town—once every year or two."

I smiled. I remembered his name. At least the Omnin didn't seem to affect long-term memory. "Have a good time," I said sincerely.

She nodded. Her face relaxed a little. "What about you?"

"Oh, I'm pretty flexible. I have a good time with just about any breakfast companion, including myself."

"Ha ha," Jenna said. "I meant, who is going to be watching out for you if I take the patrol car downtown?"

"Don't worry, I'll be fine."

"I'm worried anyway," Jenna responded. "How about we call another patrol car for you?"

"I doubt the Department can spare it," I said truthfully. "Who knows what strings Dugan had to pull to arrange for the one outside. Nobody's taken a shot at me, or even voiced a hostile intention."

Jenna shook her head in frustration. "All right, how about this, then: The patrol car drives us both downtown. One of the officers gets off with me at Grand Central station, and does his discreet act in the background. The other drives you down to your office. Do you think the NYPD can handle those logistics?"

JERRY DIVONE WAS waiting for me at my office.

"No luck with Dr. Morton so far," he told me. He declined the chair I offered him, and commenced pacing in front of my desk. "The secretary's a tough old bird. She seems immune to cajoling as well as implied threats that she could get in trouble with the law if she doesn't help us."

"What do you suggest?"

He scratched his head. "If the need wasn't so urgent, I'd recommend waiting until she takes a day off to visit the grand-kids. I'd likely have better luck with anyone else."

"The need's urgent," I replied.

"Yep."

"Who sits at her desk during lunch break?"

"No one, apparently. The religion department is very small—they don't even have a student assistant. The secretary just closes up shop for an hour."

"There must be other lines of attack."

"None that are swift and legal," Divone replied. He stopped pacing. "Look, I can break into her office at night, and pull a Watergate. Or I can hack into the university's computer at night, and pull a cyber-Watergate."

"Unbelievable—just to get a professor's goddamn phone number?"

"Now you know how the poor students feel." Divone chuckled at his own observation.

I pondered.

"There's a lot riding on that phone number," Divone coaxed. "All that you told me depends on it—getting Morton to testify in Washington."

"I know," I said. I thought some more. "All right. We've still got eleven days before the FDA meeting. How long would it take you to make preparations for a . . . physical break-in?" Wonderful . . . between Divone's characterizations and the reality of what we were discussing, I was beginning to feel like I was Richard Nixon playing me in some third-rate made-for-TV movie about my life.

"I could hack the computer faster," Divone said.

"Maybe. But from what I've heard, these universities have pretty powerful firewalls around faculty personal information—they don't want those phone numbers scribbled on bathroom stalls."

Divone popped a piece of candy into his mouth and considered. "I could arrange an after-hours physical inspection of the premises in two, three days at most."

"Good," I said. "That means we still have a little time. Let's give your friendly legal persuasions another day or two. See if there's anyone other than the secretary down there who might know Morton's whereabouts. Talk to students. Chat up the waitresses in the diner. You know the routine better than I do."

"I probably do," Divone replied. "But you're talking the fine art of eliciting information. Picasso can take a lot more time than crime in that line of work."

"Let's try it the artistic way—for at least today, maybe tomorrow." I knew there was no way we could get a judge to move fast enough—if at all—to make a break-in legal with a court order. And I didn't want to risk Dugan's finding out about an illegal break-in—and then suspending Divone and me, maybe even placing us under arrest—unless I absolutely had no other choice.

Divone bowed. "You're the boss. I'm on my way."

THE PHONE RANG about ten minutes later.

It was Dugan. "We've got more on the Sheflin-Gonzales connection, Phil."

"Yes?"

"Apparently Gonzales got pregnant in high school," Dugan said. "And the father was the boyfriend who dumped her for Sheflin. Gonzales had an abortion. Her friends say she was eaten up with guilt about it. She became withdrawn, stopped dating, focused completely on her schoolwork. So, to the outside world, she became a model student. She went on to college and the police academy. But inside . . . who knows, maybe she becomes a psycho."

"But why go after Sheflin and not the boyfriend?" I asked, playing defense attorney.

"The boyfriend's been in Australia since the divorce from Sheflin."

"Okay, makes sense." I had the mixed sensation of feeling good to be finally proven right about something in this case, and upset that I hadn't uncovered this myself, and much sooner. Maybe I would have, if Eileen Sheflin hadn't dropped off my screen in some memory wipe. "And why now? Why go after Sheflin a decade later?"

"We're still working on that, Phil. Maybe it was just a chance encounter—Gonzales passes Sheflin on the street, they run into each other at Fairway—if Gonzales is as unstable as we're theorizing, any small thing could have set her off."

"Where is she now?" I asked. "You taking her in?"

"Not quite yet," Dugan replied. "It's a very serious thing to put an officer under arrest. Given the conflicting evidence and alibis in this case, we need to be very sure. I'm only telling you about the abortion motive because I wanted you to know we are making some progress—"

"And you don't know where Claudia is now, so you couldn't place her under arrest anyway, right?"

"We don't know where she is," Dugan conceded. "She didn't go home, she didn't come into work. No one's seen her since she left the hospital. I've got people out looking for her, but I can't yet justify putting out an all-points bulletin on Officer Claudia Gonzales."

I sighed. "She's probably lurking behind a tree somewhere, waiting to strangle Cezanne Beck."

"We've got that part covered, Phil. Beck's at home today. I

just heard from Molloy. He says she's surfing the Web or whatever they do on her computer."

"All right."

"The worst that can happen to you on the Web is you catch
a computer virus—it can kill your computer but not you, right?"
Dugan concluded, pleased with his wit. Ordinarily, I might have
enjoyed it too.

"Yeah."

"Phil, you don't seem very upbeat."

"I'll be upbeat when we have Gonzales behind bars and
we've tied together a few more of these frazzled ends." *Not to
mention we stop Omnin and figure out how far and deep went its damage to memory.*

I GOT OFF the phone and worried more about missing memories. How could we ever bring the Riverside case to a satisfactory
resolution—which protected lives and brought the guilty to
justice—if we were still losing bits and pieces of our recollection?
How could we know what we no longer knew? God, it felt like I
had been wrestling with this painful paradox for centuries.

One of the keys was whether the loss was still continuing,
unabated. My sense was that the recent lost pieces were mostly
from a while ago. I had realized just yesterday that I had lost recollection of the Sheflin murder, and that realization was certainly aggravating me right now. But the actual memory was lost
months ago.

I logged on to the Internet with the computer on my desk.
What was needed was some sort of national Web site, where
people could post about their memory losses. That would give
everyone a better idea of the proportion of the problem. But it
wouldn't come in time for Morton's meeting—if he could be
located—with the FDA in a week and a half. And even if we had
more time, posts on the Web weren't exactly reliable sources of
evidence. All kinds of nutcases had access to computers.

Well, maybe everyone should at least start getting into the habit of writing down a summary of their experiences every day, and posting them in some private place online. The Web as diary. I really had intended to start doing that myself, but had been too busy, and too tired at the end of the day.

I typed "memory loss" into my search engine—I did this a few times a week now—to see if I could find anything new. The same long list of Web pages came up. I started reading them anyway. "The hippocampus is the computer directory or card catalog of memory," one page said. "Amnesia can result when the directory is corrupted or the catalog is trashed, because that puts the memories beyond retrieval. But the memories themselves are not destroyed, as evidenced by memories that can return, when the amnesia abates, and the card catalog is operational again. . . ." Well, nothing new there—that page, of course, explained why some of Dugan's and Jenna's and my memories had returned. But there was nothing anywhere about spirochetes turning the digital switches of the memory directory, or bacilli delivering singing telegrams from the hippocampal catalog. . . .

I noticed the time on the computer screen about forty-five minutes later. This no doubt had set some sort of record for me for the past few days, for time elapsed without a jolting phone call—

And the phone rang, as if it had been reading my mind.

"Phil!" It was Jerry.

"You got some good news about Morton?" I asked hopefully.

"Sorry, not yet," he replied. "But I just picked something up on the police band. I couldn't make it out completely. It sounded like another murder, of the Riverside persuasion."

"In broad daylight?"

"Well, it wasn't clear when the murder took place. But it sounded like they just found a body," Jerry said.

"Where?"

"Bryant Park—in back of the New York Public Library," Jerry said.

"That's way off the usual track," I contended, as if I could argue him out of just having heard about a murder that rang Riverside.

"Well, yeah," Jerry responded, "but the murders did move south to Columbus Circle last time."

"True," I agreed. "You didn't make out the name of the victim?" *Please don't say Cezanne Beck*, I thought—though any murder victim was a tragedy.

"No, I don't think they know who she is yet."

"But they know it's a woman?" I asked.

"They referred to the victim as 'she,' " Jerry said.

"Okay, thanks, I'll get right over there," I said.

"Need any help there?"

"No," I said. "Better you keep combing the NYU campus for Morton's address."

OFFICER PEREZ—WHO had driven me to work—had been sitting in the reception area all morning, watching over my office. I was glad to see him there, considering what I had just learned.

"You up for giving me a lift to the New York Public Library?" I asked him.

"At your disposal, Doc. Which one?"

"Fifth Avenue and Forty-second Street," I replied.

He nodded. "The one with the lions."

"The very same."

We bypassed the elevator and ran down the stairs. Perez put on his siren and lights and cut as best he could through late-morning traffic.

Dugan called me on the cell phone. He started telling me about the strangled body just found in back of the library, but our conversation rapidly dissolved into a mush of static. I heard nothing from him that I hadn't just heard from Jerry.

Perez screeched into a blatantly illegal spot on Fortieth Street, between Fifth and Sixth Avenues. He called something in on the radio, smiled at me, and said, "Let's go."

"Good job," I said gratefully, and clapped him on the back.

We pushed our way through the crowd to the blue police barricade.

"Oh God," I said. I could see Dennis Molloy—one of Cezanne's "protectors"—on the other side.

Perez and I showed our badges and walked through the splintery wooden barricade.

I confronted Molloy. "How the hell did this happen?" I demanded. "Why'd you let her come here?"

"She got some e-mail from an old friend while she was on her computer," Molloy answered, a lot less smoothly than the day before. "The friend wanted to meet her for lunch. We advised against it, but she's not a prisoner. We figured we could protect her. But—"

I couldn't bear to hear anymore. I walked past Molloy, towards the knot of cops gathered by a tree about ten feet from the back of the library building. Dugan was there. So was Allison Barnes, the other half of Cezanne's bodyguard team.

Allison had her arm around another woman, who was bending over something on the ground. Allison looked like she was trying to escort her away. . . .

The woman turned towards me. Jeez . . . It was Cezanne Beck!

"Phil!" Dugan called out. "Glad you made it—I wasn't sure how much got through on that lousy cell phone."

"Who's the victim?" I motioned to the body, now covered with a police blanket.

"See for yourself," Dugan replied. His voice had a very strange tone.

I approached. One of the medical examiner's assistants—Ed didn't seem to be here—pulled back the blanket.

Totally nude, mid-twenties, and I could see instantly that she wasn't play-acting this time.

Claudia Gonzales was stretched out in front of me, dead.

NINETEEN

I spent the rest of the day huddled with Dugan in his office. Personnel, phone calls, faxes sped in and out. The place felt like a command center—which it was. Claudia's killing had jolted the whole Department into a state of crisis. Any murder of a cop will do that. And Claudia's was more.

"I'm still not clear why Cezanne went to the park," I said to Molloy, shortly after we had set up shop in Dugan's office. "Why was Claudia there? Did she and Cezanne both get the same e-mail invitation to lunch?"

"Barnes is checking out Beck's computer right as we speak," Molloy replied. His partner had taken Cezanne home, after Dugan had quickly questioned her in the park. Cezanne was too shocked to say much. "Barnes is a whiz with the Internet," Molloy continued. "We should hear from her soon."

We did. Molloy shook his head and relayed her findings. "Cezanne has a Web page. Barnes says she posts highlights there of her most interesting temp experiences. Her day in your office is right up there, for the whole wide world to see."

I shook my head too, in disbelief. "After all we did to try to keep her identity from prying eyes. After all we told her to be careful."

"Well, Barnes says Cezanne posted that before anyone told her to be careful," Molloy responded. "She must have forgotten about it in all the excitement. But there it was, in all it's glory—Barnes says the page comes up anytime you do a search on 'temp' and 'NYPD.' "

"Goddamn Internet," Dugan joined in, and put down the phone from another call. "We were better off with IBM Selectric typewriters, weren't we. At least people could write about themselves and have some privacy then."

He had a point. Though of course no one forced Cezanne to put her writing online. "So how did her Web page wind up getting her to Bryant Park?" I prodded Molloy for more. "The 'friend' who contacted her was an online impostor?"

Molly nodded. "Her friend's e-mail was bogus. Barnes checked out the sender. She's an old friend of Cezanne's, all right, and her name and e-mail are listed on Cezanne's Web page, but she swears she hasn't sent Cezanne e-mail in weeks."

"So someone forges an e-mail to make it look like a message from an old friend, and lures the Beck woman to lunch behind the library," Dugan said.

"Right. Trivially easy," I said.

Molloy agreed. "The friend's name is Leslie Sullivan. Her e-mail address is LSullivan@cymail.com—her impostor set up an address under LESullivan@cymail.com—Cezanne didn't notice the extra *E*. No reason she would."

" 'Death by Extra *E*,' " Dugan muttered, and smiled tiredly. "Has an Agatha Christie flavor."

"More like Sue Grafton," I replied. "So who was the ersatz Sullivan?"

"You think it was Claudia, I know," Dugan said. "But that wouldn't explain who killed *her*." He was no longer smiling.

"I don't think she was just an innocent victim in this, no." I stood my ground.

"You're a stubborn man," Dugan told me.

"You know her background better than I do at this point," I said. There was no sense in keeping anything from Molloy now.

"You think she just happened to be strolling on a fine September morning on Forty-second Street?"

"No, I don't think that," Dugan allowed.

"Good. I'll tell you what *I* think, then: Claudia and her accomplice set the Bryant Park appointment in motion to kill Cezanne. And then at some point the accomplice decided to get rid of Claudia instead. Maybe it was a last-minute reaction to something; maybe it was the plan all along—"

Dugan's phone rang. His door opened. Ron Greave, Claudia's partner, stormed in.

"You goddamned son of a bitch, you happy now?" he shouted, and lunged at me.

Molloy was on him in an instant.

"You didn't believe her," Greave was still shouting at me over Molloy's shoulder, though he was pretty much permitting himself to be restrained. "She said you were a no-good prick, and she was right. You were out to get her. I'm gonna bring charges against you now." He turned to Dugan. "Bring him up on charges." He pointed to me. "I'll be the first to testify. He was persecuting my partner. He wouldn't leave her alone. That's not right."

Dugan put down the phone and coolly regarded Greaves. "That was Sheila, my secretary, calling to tell me you had just arrived and you wanted to see me and would it be okay. It's okay. You have my permission. See how easy it is? There's no need to shout, Officer."

Greave started to reply, loudly, and my cell phone rang.

"Excuse me," I said, and took the call. "Uh-huh. Okay. Good work—that could be *very* helpful. Great. All right. Thanks."

I turned to Dugan and interrupted whatever Greave was saying. "That was Ed Monti. He thinks whoever killed Claudia killed Berman and Josephson. He found the same out-of-state pollen on all three."

"What kind of pollen?" Dugan asked.

"*Dietes bicolor*," I replied. "A kind of iris—native to South Africa but it's grown here. It can't survive more than the lightest frost, so it's mostly in Southern states where the temperature's warm all year long."

"I see," Dugan said, and took it in. "Not conclusive, but suggestive. . . ." He looked at Greave. "You been to Florida recently, Officer?"

"I . . ." Greave began.

"You have family there, don't you?"

"What of it?"

"Why don't you have a seat, Officer—join us for lunch," Dugan asked.

Greave started to refuse, but Molloy put a heavy hand on his shoulder.

"Pizza okay?" Dugan inquired.

"Sure," I said.

"Fine," Molloy said.

Greave glowered.

Dugan phoned out for pizza and Cokes, then made a few other calls—facing away from us, voice muffled, so no one else could make out what he was saying. At least one call was to get some detectives positioned outside his office, I suspected, in case Greave declined his hospitality and tried to leave. Another was no doubt to initiate a check on Greave's whereabouts this morning.

"Actually, I'd prefer a ginger ale," I said, after the round of sotto voce calls was completed.

"Me too," Molloy chimed in.

Dugan frowned and picked up the phone. "Anything different for you?" he asked Greave.

"I don't give a shit what you order," Greave replied, defiant from the seat he had taken in the corner. Molloy continued to stand over him.

"Fair enough," Dugan said, and called back the pizza place

to correct the order. "You want me to call in your PBA rep, or an attorney?" Dugan asked Greave.

"I don't need an attorney," Greave spat back. "I have nothing to hide."

"Good," Dugan said. "Tell us about your trips to Florida, then."

"I go down there five, six times a year. My sister lives there. She has a big family. The kids love me. I love them. I'm their favorite uncle."

"Does she have lots of flowers planted around her home? Irises?" I asked.

Greave shrugged. "Sure—about the flowers. Everyone does down there. I don't know about the irises. What do they look like?"

"Very pretty," Dugan replied, very seriously. "Just like those dead girls."

"You're all crazy," Greave said, agitated. He started to rise. Molloy got him to sit.

"Humor us, then," Dugan said. "Tell us about your relationship with Officer Gonzales."

"More specifically, tell us what you know about Claudia and Eileen Sheflin," I said. "You know, just to narrow this down a bit." I looked at Dugan. It was presumptuous for me to refine a superior's question—let alone Dugan's—but I wanted to get to the nitty-gritty. Dugan slowly nodded his assent.

I looked back at Greave. He looked embarrassed.

"You're concerned about Officer Gonzales' privacy, I know," Dugan said. "And that's commendable. But we've got some very explosive issues here—issues that could destroy your career, Officer Greave. Maybe worse. So take my advice, think of your future. It's got to be more important to you now than any commitment you made to Officer Gonzales not to talk to us about her. There's nothing you can do to help her now. You've got to help yourself."

Greave turned from Dugan to me, and then to Molloy for good measure. He turned back and addressed Dugan.

"You know what happened to her in high school?" he asked hoarsely. "To Officer Gonzales, my partner?"

"Why don't you tell us," Dugan said.

"Some foreign kid, some creep from Australia, got her pregnant," Greave said. "Claudia—Officer Gonzales—she wasn't like that. She comes from a very strict family. He probably got her drunk and took advantage. . . ."

Dugan tried to look sympathetic. "How does that tie in with Eileen Sheflin?" he coaxed.

Greave swallowed hard, shook his head. "She was sleeping around with the same Australian kid—his name was Mark. Claudia just slept with him once—one night. She refused to see him again. But Eileen Sheflin, she was much more accommodating. So of course this Mark walked out on on Claudia. She had the abortion all on her own." His voice was thick with emotion.

"You cared for her," Dugan said, "I understand."

"No, there was nothing between us," Greave insisted, in a tone that proclaimed otherwise.

"That's okay," Dugan said. "Bring us up-to-date on the Sheflin girl."

"Claudia never got over that," Greave responded. "I used to wonder a lot about what she was like before those two destroyed her world. She carried everything around inside. She held it in, but I could see it. She put on a good show, but I knew it was there, hurting her, all the time. And one day she came into work, hopping mad. She'd run into Sheflin on some line in an A&P on the Upper West Side." He snorted. "Life's full of coincidences like that, ain't it? Claudia's finishing up, helping out on someone else's case, and she walks into a supermarket in a neighborhood she's never been in before. And she turns around, and standing right in back of her is Eileen Sheflin— who says, 'Hey, how're you doing?' And Claudia thinks, 'Not too bad, considering you fucked up my life.' But Claudia doesn't say that."

"But she unloads on you the next day," Dugan prompted.

"She was furious! What'd you expect?" Greave replied. Dugan nodded.

Greave continued. "Eileen says to Claudia on the super-market line, 'You remember Mark? He was sweet, but I got tired of him, so I sent him packing back to Oz. Hey, didn't you and Mark go out a little, too? We got a lot in common! We should be friends! Let's get together for a drink sometime. Whaddaya say?' Just like that. Matter-of-fact. Claudia was seething."

Dugan nodded again. "And what did she say to Sheflin's offer?" he asked. I had to admire his interviewing technique.

"Claudia said yes," Greave said. "I didn't know what she was thinking, and I told her. I said, 'Forget this woman. What do you hope to gain by meeting with her?' "

"But she didn't take your advice?" Dugan asked.

"No."

"And were you concerned that, with all that anger that you've been describing, that maybe something wrong might happen as a result of those meetings?" Dugan prompted. "I don't mean that *you* did anything wrong in not blowing a whis-tle at that point. I mean, in retrospect, can you see now that maybe Claudia meeting Sheflin, so furious and all, was going down a path that was not the best?"

Greave leaned forward in his seat. "You see, that's the thing of all this," he said earnestly. "I was worried at first. I wasn't sure what to do. Claudia met with Sheflin three or four times. I didn't know where it was going, and I was concerned. But then one morning, all of a sudden, Claudia came up to me and she said she and Sheflin had worked it all out. She said she and Sheflin had had a really long heart-to-heart the night before, and it had come to Claudia that maybe Sheflin was a human being just like Claudia—they both had been vulnerable girls—and both had been victimized in their own ways by this same Australian jerk. And Claudia really seemed at peace with herself that morning. I've never seen her happier."

"Do you think she was telling you the truth?" Dugan asked.

"Yes," Greave insisted. "That's what makes this all so nuts."

Dugan looked a little confused. I felt the same.

"So, Claudia and Sheflin became . . . friends after that?" Dugan asked.

"No, no," Greave said, and shook his head repeatedly. He looked a little confused now as well. "About two weeks later, Claudia starts going on again about what a bitch Sheflin was, and how people like that should not be allowed on this Earth—"

"The two met again, then, and it didn't work out?" Dugan asked.

Greave shook his head no. "Claudia caught the flu then. She was laid up."

I had a sick feeling in the depths of my stomach that I knew the rest of this story. "What time of year was this?" I asked quietly.

"Late February," Greave said. "Yeah, she came back to work right after Presidents' Day—sometime that week. And the first thing she does is she starts in again about Sheflin. She said just thinking about her, and what she did, had made Claudia sicker, longer. I said to her, 'I thought the two of you worked it out, had a meeting of the minds.' And Claudia just looked at me like I was crazy—like I was making all of that up. I figured, 'She's done some soul-searching while she was laid up, and changed her mind again about Sheflin.' And she's looking at me like I'm out of my head for trying to remind her that she ever felt otherwise. She was so angry— I guess I should have confronted her on it, but I didn't want to stir it up even more."

"She didn't change her mind, she lost it—or, at least, that part of her mind that contained her memory of her rapprochement with Eileen Sheflin," I said. And I thought, *Goddamn Omnin again. Too bad we can't bring that pill up on charges of homicide.* It ruined bacteria and—via the memory loss it had caused in Claudia—people. My instincts had been right about the antibiotic all along. It equaled anti-life in this case indeed.

But Claudia was no innocent, either. She was not only a victim of Omnin, but a manipulator of its amnesia for her own murderous purposes.

The pizza arrived—smelling great—with three cans of Coke. Dugan sighed and called Sheila. "Is the delivery guy still there? I changed the order to one Coke and two ginger ales, but we got three Cokes anyway. . . . All right. Never mind."

"Maybe they forgot the order." Molloy offered his attempt at a joke.

This was the first one I'd heard from him, but I couldn't bring myself to laugh. Neither could Dugan or Greave.

"I think we can chalk the Coke up to perennial inefficiency," I said. "I can use the caffeine anyway."

Dugan handed a can to me, and looked at Molloy.

"No thanks," he said.

"I'll have it, if no one else wants it." Greave spoke up.

"Sure," Dugan said, and lobbed the can to him.

Greave caught it, opened it, took a long drink. "How much do I owe you for this?" He put the can down and reached for his wallet.

"On the Department," Dugan said. "But let's get back to the homicides. Tell me about the first one."

"Jillian Murphy?"

"Yeah. Anything strike you as strange about that, or about how Claudia acted—you know, since she was acting a little crazy about Sheflin?"

Greave took another drink and shook his head. "No—why

should it? There was no connection. What did Murphy have to do with Sheflin? I do remember thinking, 'Well, maybe Claudia should see a doctor, because she seems to be forgetting a lot of things lately.' She was stressed about Sheflin, maybe that affected her memory and how she performed in the Murphy case, I don't know. I felt terrible for her after that meeting in the DA's office. You were there," he said to me.

I nodded. "Did you ever actually tell her to go see a doctor?"

"Yeah, more than once."

"And did she take your advice?"

"I don't think so."

"But you believed her when she said she'd forgotten the initial details of the Murphy murder site?" Dugan asked.

"We back to that again? Hell, yeah, I believed her. I don't get you guys. You've got the whole Department running around in circles over this memory shit—but for Claudia, you believe that she was lying about losing her memory in the Murphy investigation? Why would she do that? Oh yeah." His tone turned from sincere to sarcastic. "I get it. Claudia told me. You think she faked her amnesia to cover up that *she* was the one who killed Murphy? And then the others? She was the cop, for crissakes, not some sort of criminal genius!"

I had to admit that Claudia never struck me as a genius, either. But, who knows, that could have been part of her genius. Contradictory conclusions from the same evidence, again. . . .

"But surely you were concerned when Eileen Sheflin turned up strangled, Officer Greave—with all that you knew about her relationship with Officer Gonzales," Dugan pressed.

"Yeah, I was concerned. I was surprised. But I thought it was just a lousy coincidence. In fact, I figured that the other murders—the ones before Sheflin—pretty much let Claudia off the hook for the Sheflin. I mean, we were dealing with a serial killer here, right, not a grudge homicide."

"Maybe that's just what she wanted everyone to think," I said.

Greave shook his head. "You're out of your mind. You're obviously suffering memory damage, too. Claudia was out of town with her mother for one of the murders before Eileen Sheflin. How do you explain that?"

"We think maybe she had an accomplice," Dugan answered. "That's one of the reasons we're talking to you right now."

"I'll say *you're* off your rocker, too, then," Greave said hotly. "I don't care what your rank is. I didn't kill anyone. When was the exact date of that murder? I'll be glad to tell you what I was doing then."

Dugan wiped his mouth and hands with a napkin and reached for a folder on his desk. He took out three sheets, and passed one each to Greave, Molloy, and me. "Names and dates," he said. "I can get you the times too, if you like."

I looked at the list—a rundown on the Riverside victims:

```
Jillian Murphy, March 21
Carol Michosky (assault, not homicide),
  April 5
Chloe Josephson, April 13
Tara Calisi, April 26
Eileen Sheflin, April 29
Michelle Deets, May 2
Carol Michosky (homicide), August 28
Amy Berman, September 7
```

My first reaction was: Who were Calisi and Deets? I knew that there had been seven stranglings, but the two names were news to me. Which of course was impossible. I no doubt knew them last week as well as I knew Murphy and Berman. I felt myself sweating. I had to stop that. Their names weren't important at this specific juncture. I had to stay calm. I looked at Dugan—fortunately, his eyes were on Greave.

"Claudia's name should be added to the list," Greave said.

"Yeah," Dugan agreed.

"So you'd like to know what I was doing on April thirteenth, when Josephson was strangled and Claudia was in Philly," Greave said.

"That's right," Dugan said. "And September seventh—Claudia had an alibi for Berman's murder, too. And also this morning."

"I took today off—I was looking for Claudia."

"Anybody see you—anywhere away from Bryant Park?" Dugan asked.

"I don't know."

Dugan looked at him a long time. "Officer Greave, I'm going to have to ask you to turn over your badge and gun to Detective Molloy. And then I'm going to have to place you under arrest. You have the right to remain silent—"

"You think I killed those two women and then I turned on Claudia and killed her?" Greave yelled, and got to his feet. Molloy pushed him back in his seat.

"Please, don't make this any more difficult," Dugan said. He pressed a button on his phone. The door opened and two detectives walked into the office.

"You're arresting me for murder?" Greave said, unbelieving.

"Please, turn over your badge and gun to Detective Molloy, now."

Greave took a deep breath, and slowly did as told.

"Thank you," Dugan said. "At this point, the charges are accessory. I think you realized, somewhere along the line, what Claudia was up to, and either you helped her outright or said nothing—which, for someone in your position, was acting as an accessory. Please do get legal representation as soon as possible. I want your rights to be fully respected. We'll see about the murder charges when we know a bit more."

Greave stood up, shaken. One of the detectives put handcuffs on him, and they took him away.

"You don't seriously think that Greave is the accomplice," I said to Dugan, after the door had closed.

He leaned back in his chair and rubbed his eyes. My eyes could have used a rubbing too, or whatever it took to make them see more clearly. I was getting close, I knew that, but I still wasn't getting everything.

"He has the trips to Florida which give him access to the pollen," Dugan responded, "he has no alibi for this morning, and God only knows the relationship Greave had with Gonzales—but no, I don't think he's the accomplice. He doesn't feel like a murderer. I took him out of circulation mainly to give us one less complication on the loose to worry about."

"So you agree that there's an accomplice?" I asked. Our situation was still too grave for me to feel triumphant.

"Well, somebody killed Claudia," Dugan replied.

"Yeah, but you've been holding out for one killer for everyone, and that killer not being Claudia," I said. "Not that I blame you."

Now Dugan closed his eyes and massaged his temples, for a long while. "Don't worry," he said. "I'm not suffering another memory loss. I remember being resistant to Claudia as the killer. But with that same southern pollen on Josephson, Berman, and now Claudia . . . well, it certainly suggests two killers. And what Greave said about Claudia certainly gives her enough motive to be one of them."

"Ed didn't exactly say the pollen was southern," I said, and tried to recall precisely what he had said. "His point was that the variety of iris was mostly likely to be found in warm climates— like the South—that have at most just light frost."

"I'm not sure I see the distinction," Dugan said. He opened his eyes and regarded me.

Molloy spoke up. "Maybe the killer is from the New York area, and came into contact with the iris growing in a pot on a windowsill with a warm southern exposure." He walked over to the pizza box and the last slice. He looked at Dugan and me for our assent.

We gave it—for the slice.

"Certainly doesn't work that way for my outdoor gardens," Dugan responded to Molloy about the iris. "Anything that needs warm weather all year around won't bloom up here until late summer—if it blooms at all. My wife is really into that stuff," he said proudly.

"Chloe Josephson was killed April thirteenth," I said. "And the past winter was cold here."

"So that rules out the iris outdoors in New York," Dugan said. "I suppose it could have been forced—grown—in a pot indoors. . . . I don't know, I'd have to check to see whether that variety of iris can be grown that way."

I nodded . . . and shifted into shaking my head no. "That's still not it—I don't think this turns on the accomplice brushing against a plant in a flowerpot in New York."

"Where, then?" Dugan asked.

"I don't know." I felt like the answer was right in front of me. But I just couldn't see it.

"So *your* memory is acting up again now?" Dugan asked in all seriousness.

I continued shaking my head. "All I know is that until we plug this memory drain—or at least understand it better than we do now—we're banging our heads against the bottom of the sink—"

My cell phone rang.

It was Jerry.

"I've got Professor Morton here," Jerry said. "He wants to talk to you."

TWENTY

"Darius! How are you?"

"I'm fine, Phil. I understand from your friend Mr. Divone that my letter did some good?"

"Oh yes, it did," I replied into my cell phone. "Can you join us in Washington next week? Did Jerry tell you about the special hearing? I think your being there would do even more good."

"Yes, yes," Morton replied. "In fact, I have some ideas about other people we could bring along for this meeting. You know, nothing impresses the government like numbers, including numbers of experts. I know several folks who could be very helpful. One's a biologist from Pittsburgh. She's very charming—quite cute, too. And she has a real head on her shoulders."

"That's sound like a great idea," I said. "Look . . . where are you? Could we get together and talk about this?"

I became aware of Dugan and Molloy looking at me, questioningly. "Is this about the pollen?" Dugan half mouthed and asked.

I shook my head no, and held up my hand to indicate I would explain to him in a minute.

"—right off Washington Square," Morton was saying. "Right around the corner from NYU. Sometimes right under everyone's nose is the best cover."

I smiled. "You would have made a great detective."

"I already am," Morton replied. "All historians are, if they're any good."

"Absolutely true," I said. "So when can we get together?"

"How about right now—or as soon as you can get over here. The Waverly Tea Pot is quite good. It's on the northwest corner—"

"Sounds perfect," I said. "I know just where it is. Could you put Jerry back on the phone for a second?"

"Good work," I said to Jerry. "You can tell me later how you found him. For now, don't let your eyes off him."

I FILLED IN Dugan and Molloy.

"All right," Dugan acceded to my meeting with Morton. "But don't stray too far—we're finally getting to the endgame here with the Riverside stranglings."

" 'The memory stranglings' would be just as good a name for this case," I replied as I left. "Omnin's as much an accomplice as the hands that strangled Chloe, Amy, and Claudia."

Just to be safe, I had Officer Perez drive me to Waverly Tea. Claudia's pollinated comrade was still at large, and could conceivably sting not only me but Morton if I was followed.

Our car pulled up to Waverly Place. Perez got out, looked around, and signaled that it was okay for me to follow.

A couple were kissing on the corner—always nice to see. Otherwise, people moved in various states of speed, dress, and conversation on the sidewalk. Most appeared to be students. Nothing out of the ordinary. Like corpuscles in a bloodstream, but with no knowledge that the body they traversed was fighting a crippling infection.

Perez opened the door to the tea shop, and peered in. "Looks okay, Doc," he said. "I'll wait outside and keep an eye on what's happening on the street."

I nodded and entered. Jerry and Morton were seated at a nearby table. Both waved me over.

"Good to see you, Darius!" I shook his extended hand. It was much firmer than the first time I had shaken it, at McNair's funeral in Chicago. What a difference a death made—or, in this case, Morton's evident excitement about being able to do something to perhaps prevent rather than just mourn another calamity.

"So, I see our ace bloodhound here was able to track you down," I said to Morton, and smiled at Jerry. I pulled out a mahogany chair and sat. It was surprisingly comfortable.

"It always pays to look at pictures," Jerry said.

"The iconic is more fundamental than the scriptic," Morton agreed, in his own way.

"NYU's bookstore is fortunately very well stocked with the professor's books," Jerry continued. "First thing I did was scope out the photos on the inside covers—I had a good amalgam in my head of what he looked like."

I recalled that old photo of Morton on the cover of *Ahead of Columbus.* It barely looked like the face in front of me. Good thing Jerry had had other photos in the mix—or maybe he was just better than I was with pictures.

"So, I was just standing on the corner, drinking a cup of *coffee*," Jerry said, with a special whisper of "coffee," presumably because we were in a tea shop, "and Professor Morton just strolls on by. Sometimes you get lucky," he concluded with a big, toothy grin.

I agreed enthusiastically, and called over the waitress. "Do you have Monk's blend?" I asked. It was a dark tea with vanilla and grenadine—a nice celebratory tea.

"Of course," she replied.

"I'll have a cup," I said. I turned to Morton. "Let's talk about Washington. Your presence at this meeting could make all the difference."

"I'm ready," Morton said. "I've been working on this ever since I got back from Chicago. You really got me thinking about this bacterial notion of consciousness, and what antibiotics could do to it. You know, there are lots of examples in history that could apply. People eating moldy bread in the Middle Ages and hallucinating about witches—well, what's attributed to hallucinogens could really be the work of antibiotics causing memory loss, or maybe both at the same time. Someone dreams or hallucinates someone else is a witch. Then realizes this is just fantasy, not reality. Then forgets this realization, and truly believes the other person is a witch. You see, the two could work hand in hand."

I nodded. "But I think we'll need more than witches to convince the FDA," I said gently.

"Absolutely," Morton said. "That's why I was telling you on the phone that we have to assemble a team. I already have several people in mind. We go down there, to Washington, and we touch all the bases—biology, neurophysiology, psychology of mind, epidemiology, all of them—as a team. Much more than I could do alone."

"Sounds like a good strategy," I said. "And you think you can assemble this team by next week? You were telling me on the phone about the biologist from Pittsburgh?"

Morton nodded. But he looked distressed. "I wish we could have McNair with us," he said sadly. "Brilliant man. I was telling Rhonda just yesterday—"

Something went off in my head. "What did you say?"

Morton looked at me. "About McNair? He was brilliant, and I miss him."

I shook my head. "No. I meant his wife."

The tea arrived. My brain and stomach seemed to merge. I felt like a computer looking for something on a disk which wasn't in the drive—

"You okay?" Jerry asked me through the buzz.

I nodded and sipped some tea. "Yeah."

"Rhonda? You mean Rhonda McNair?" Morton responded.

I nodded again. I had been on the verge of thinking something about her, a few days ago. . . . But with all the focus on the Riverside case, on Claudia's killing, that piece of thought about Rhonda had just gone from my mind. Was that due, too, to the wounded bacteria in my brain?

But now it was beginning to come back. Much faster than any previous memory loss. Maybe my bacterial colony, or whatever the hell it was, was healing itself, building its strength back up, making music again. "Yeah," I said to Morton. "Rhonda." I sipped some more tea, like I hadn't consumed a thing in weeks.

"I just saw her yesterday," Morton said.

I DON'T THINK I said anything for a long time. Several years ago, my ears had become very clogged after a bad cold. One day they opened up, like magic, and the clear sounds of the world began pouring back in. That's the way I felt now about what I had realized about Rhonda a day or two ago, and forgotten, until this minute. . . .

"Do you think she should join us in Washington, be part of the team?" Morton was asking. "I'm not sure how much she knows about her husband's work, but she's highly intelligent, I can tell you that."

"She was here in New York, yesterday?" was all I could say.

"Yes, yes," Morton replied impatiently. "I'm cutting down on unnecessary travel—I got very tired this summer."

"What's going on, Phil?" Jerry asked, concerned.

"Can you excuse us for a second?" I asked Morton. "I just need to talk to Jerry about an urgent police matter. We'll be back in a few seconds."

I got up from the table, as did Jerry.

"Is Rhonda in danger?" Morton asked.

"No," I answered truthfully. *At least, not from any killer*, I thought.

Jerry and I walked out of Morton's earshot. I kept an eye on him—I didn't want him slipping out of the restaurant and into the vast unknown again.

"I saw her in Chicago," I hurriedly explained to Jerry, as quietly as possible. "She dropped a piece of paper, with a list of three names—Gonzales, Berman, and Michosky. There was a line drawn through Michosky's name. She was the only one dead at the time."

"And now we have all three on their way to their Maker," Jerry said. "You think this McNair woman killed them? But you were looking at Gonzales, for at least Michosky and some of the others. You think Ms. McNair took care of Gonzales?" Jerry scratched his head.

"Maybe Berman, too," I replied. "Claudia had an alibi for Berman. I began to wonder about Rhonda when someone told me that her husband—Robert McNair—didn't really have cancer—"

"Whoa! You're going too fast for me," Jerry said. "What does Mr. McNair have to do with this?"

"I'm not sure," I said. It was all coming back to me, but the "all" still had some gaping holes. I told Jerry about what Rhonda had told me about McNair's galloping cancer and her mercy killing, but how McNair's close student Samantha had been certain that he had nothing of the sort.

"Okay," Jerry said. "But let's face it, his student could be wrong. Why trust the student over the wife? Or, maybe the wife did murder the husband, but that's still a long way from the stranglings in New York."

"There are other things," I said. I told him about the warm-climate pollen. "And there's still that damn list. And now we find out she's here in the city."

Jerry scrunched his face and considered. "Fair enough," he finally said. "But what's the connection between Rhonda and the Riversides? What's her motive?"

I shook my head. "That, I don't know as yet."

Jerry nodded. "Okay. I'd say she's worth our attention. What do you suggest we do?"

I looked over at Morton. He was fidgeting with his teacup, and looking irritated.

"First thing is we make sure Morton and his people are in Washington next week," I replied. "Another first thing is we keep him away from Rhonda McNair. And another first thing is we find her."

WE RETURNED TO the table. I soothed Morton, and asked him what he could tell me about his meeting the day before with Rhonda. McNair had been one of the few who had Morton's home number—the two had been very close. Morton said he had received a call out of the blue from Rhonda. They met for lunch. "Truthfully, I was surprised—she never gave me the time of day when Robert was alive."

"What did you discuss?" I asked.

"Mainly my memories of Robert," Morton replied. "She wanted to know if I recalled the last thing Robert and I had talked about—she's thinking of putting up a Web page about him, and wants to have a section called 'Last Quotes.' I was very touched by that."

I nodded. "And did you remember what you and Robert had talked about?"

"Unfortunately, no," Morton said. "And not because of this memory sieve. The last time Robert and I talked—it was maybe more than a year ago. We had that kind of relationship. Very close, very deep. But sometimes years would go by between contact. Yet when we did talk, it was a real as it ever was. . . ." He sighed, softly. It was clear how much this relationship had meant to him—how much he missed it now. "The roots are still there, still deep," he continued, "only now there can never be new flowers. He had called me the last few times he was in New York—left messages on my machine. But I was too busy—with unimportant things." He waved his hand in disgust. "Most things we do are unimportant, aren't they?"

I put my hand over his. It felt frail now, withered skin and bones. Morton hadn't seemed so shaken by McNair's death in Chicago. Some people were like that—put up a good show, for yourself and everyone, at the funeral, and then you get home and the black pain pools to the surface.

"So you didn't know about McNair's cancer?" I asked gently.

Morton shook his head slowly. "No. Just what Rhonda told me."

I smiled as reassuringly as I could. "Okay." I encouraged Morton to cast his net as far as he could for our Washington panel of experts. "Jerry will be here to help you, and let's keep in touch on a daily basis now."

IT WAS PAST five when I got back into the car with Perez.

"Let's head home," I told him.

"You got it."

I realized, as I had several times already, that I was putting a lot of faith in Jerry. I would like to have been one hundred percent confident that Morton was in good hands. But I had learned that one hundred percent confidence was unavailable in this life—at least, not in my life and this line of work.

Still . . . anything I could do to raise that percentage made sense.

I pondered. . . . I couldn't call Dugan and ask him to check up on Jerry, because that would likely blow his cover. I didn't want the commissioner or Dugan figuring out that Jerry was working for me.

"Laurie? Glad I reached you." I called my Shalimar undercover friend on the cell phone. "I need you to do a last-minute, no-questions-asked computer intersection check on two people: Jerry Divone—D, I, V, O, N, E, and Jerry with a *J*—and Claudia Gonzales. Both are on the job—or, in Claudia's case, was.

I just need to know if they ever worked on a case together, that sort of thing."

"No problem," Laurie said cheerfully. "You got time for a beer?"

"Not tonight," I said. "Maybe later next week." If I made it through the FDA meeting, I'd have time for lots of beers.

"Okay," Laurie said, regretfully. "I'll be back to you tomorrow morning with anything I find on Divone and Gonzales."

"Thanks." Of course, this meant that I was trusting Laurie Feldman. But she was presumably less in a position to do damage than Jerry. . . .

Perez drove me up to my brownstone. "I'll stay out here until my replacement gets here—should be by six," he said.

I thanked him and climbed the outside flight of stairs. There was no sign of Jenna or her police protection.

I picked up our mail—just a few phone bills, one for each of our cell phones and home phone, and the typical annoying assortment of junk advertising. I hiked up the additional stairs to our apartment. No sign of Jenna there, either.

There was a message from her on our voice-mail. She had tried to reach me a couple of times on the cell phone, she said, to no avail. She was having dinner in the Village with a friend—at a restaurant just half a block away from where I had left Morton and Jerry, I realized. The best part of her message came at the end: "I'm sorry for biting your head off this morning—it'll be okay, don't worry," she said. I felt that way, too, at least about Jenna and me.

I sat down on the couch, and put my feet up on the coffee table. What a day. . . . Rhonda McNair popping back into my mind and everything else without warning. . . . I had to find out more about her, and her possible connection to Claudia.

Who could tell me more about Rhonda?

It was still afternoon in California—lots of time to track people down there. . . .

No, that was the wrong direction. All of Morton's talk about assembling a team for our FDA hearing gave me an idea about someone else who might know something about Rhonda. Someone in Scotland.

It was nearly eleven in the evening there, but I tracked down my Rolodex of phone numbers, and looked up Terry Briskman.

"Hullo?" a groggy voice answered.

"Terry? Phil D'Amato here. Sorry to call so late—I hope I didn't wake you."

"I was sleeping."

Great, not only was he roused from his sleep, he was the one person in the world to admit it. "I'm sorry," I said. "It's about something really important. Would it be better if I called back tomorrow?"

"No."

Jeez, he was really angry. Though . . . I seemed to recall McNair saying something about Briskman being terrible on the phone. I hoped it was that—

"I'm off to New York at dawn," Briskman said.

"Great!" I was thankful for the news, as well as the longer sentence.

"Morton's invitation," Briskman continued.

"He's asked you to be on his team—come down to Washington with us and testify about Omnin and history?"

"Right."

I debated about whether to press my luck any further and ask about Rhonda.

"Just one quick question," I said. I couldn't afford to wait. "What was your impression of Rhonda and Robert McNair—were they happy together?"

"Never liked her," Briskman replied.

"Why not?"

"She didn't like me."

"And?" I prodded.

"Let's talk in New York—I'm at the Empire." The last word was garbled in feedback.

"I'm sorry—did you say 'Empire'?"

More echoing garble.

"Terry?"

I finally heard him say, "Yeah."

"The Empire Hotel? Near Lincoln Center?" I asked.

"Yeah."

"All right, thanks," I said. "I'll call you there tomorrow."

I got off the phone. These long distance calls were still prone to static and feedback sometimes. . . .

I guess I could rely on Briskman's memory staying intact until tomorrow. The British Isles had been spared most of the flu and Omnin this year.

But could I rely on mine? What if I forgot this conversation?

I wrote myself a note and attached it with a magnet to the door of our refrigerator.

Actually, my recollection seemed to be repairing . . . at least since my meeting with Morton this afternoon. I chuckled sadly—that had been among the first words McNair had ever said to me—"Shall we repair somewhere for a drink?" . . . My memory *was* getting better. . . . I could picture McNair saying that to me, with Amy and Claudia at his side. . . .

But the three were dead now—all at the hands of the same killer? I could see scenarios in which Rhonda killed all three; all revolved around her having some sort of relationship with Claudia, something which perhaps McNair had uncovered and tried to stop, something which Amy had witnessed or otherwise knew about, something which had later gone sour with Claudia. . . . But what? And why?

I still needed more information to piece this together. Memory wasn't enough. I pictured chains of dancing bacteria in my brain, joining to form bigger chains, fixing broken chains, parting to make new chains and links. . . . On the other hand, who knew if these reeling packets of consciousness or memory or whatever they were even looked like bacteria?

I rubbed my eyes. I was really tired. I was also hungry. There was leftover tuna and rice in the fridge. . . . But I decided instead to walk over to my easy chair and take a little nap.

As I dozed off, I recalled a case study I had come across in lots of my readings about memory loss. Some poor guy had sustained an injury to the brain when he was young. The effect had been fascinating, horrible, devastating. He woke up every morning, as he lived his life, still thinking he was the age he had been when his brain had been damaged. The longer he lived, the worse each new day became for him. He would wake up some mornings and look at himself in the mirror, before anyone had a chance to talk to him, and he would cry, because he saw a lined face with shocks of white hair. *What the hell happened to me?* he would demand of the mirror, of himself. *I went to sleep a young man. Where has my life gone?*

I thought there were tears in my own eyes, as I fell asleep, but I couldn't be sure because my eyes were closed. . . .

The phone awoke me later.

Probably Jenna.

I looked at my reflection in the mirror as I walked quickly to the phone. Thank God. Same image, same age. . . .

I picked up the phone. "Hey . . ."

"Phil?" a woman's voice said. It wasn't Jenna's.

"Yes?"

"Rhonda McNair!"

TWENTY-ONE

I awoke the next morning.

"Jenna?"

I got out of bed, pulled on a pair of jeans, and walked barefoot to the kitchen.

Jenna was prying out half of a poppyseed bagel from the toaster. She turned around and smiled at me. "Why don't they make these wider?"

I sat down at the table. One toasted piece of poppyseed and two toasted pieces of sesame bagel were already on a plate. Jenna joined me with the pried-out piece and two glasses of orange juice.

"So have you decided?" she asked.

"Yeah, I'll take the poppy."

The teakettle whistled. "I'll get it," she said, and kissed me.

But I hadn't yet finally decided on what lay ahead this morning, I thought. And everything depended on it—or at least half of everything I had been grappling with for the past half-year.

All of that, and maybe more, would be decided today.

PEREZ WAS WAITING for me downstairs. Seeing him surprised me at first. Yesterday felt like a long time ago. I had him give me a lift to the subway, and told him I would be in touch by phone. He wasn't happy about leaving me, but I gave him no choice.

I took the train downtown, and switched at Forty-second Street for crosstown and then uptown trains, in a direction away from my office. There was nothing my office could give me today. I had my cell phone for calls.

I got off at Ninety-sixth Street and Broadway, and made my way to Riverside Drive. It was breezy, clear, and in the low sixties. Much like that night in which Jenna and I had strolled by the river, hyacinths in bloom. Except now the hyacinths had long since shriveled, and we knew that Jillian Murphy had been murdered that spring evening before, about seven streets up . . . and then seven other women including Claudia. . . .

Today was much like that hyacinth evening, except now I was contemplating a different kind of pollen, and we were on the fall side of the curve. I recalled that in some cultures the fall, not spring, was celebrated as the confirmation of life, because you had the harvest in hand. I hoped that proved true today.

I ran my hand over rusty, wrought-iron rails as I walked slowly up to 103rd Street, then down near the river and the piece of the park where Jillian Murphy had been found. You couldn't tell that she had lain there, naked and insensate, dead to the universe yet crying out to tell her story, all those months ago. Summer had smoothed all imprint of her body from the brush, just as time and Omnin had muffled her cry. But perhaps not completely.

I sat on a bench, not far from her final bower, and looked out for a while at the roiling Hudson.

A good place to die? No—no place was good to die. There were only good places to live.

A good place to remember? Oh yes—forgetting was a form of death.

I took out my cell phone and made some calls.

"PHIL! YOU LOOK like you're contemplating the end of the world!"

I had been gazing northwest, towards the George Washington Bridge and the Palisades. Rhonda approached me from the south. I stood up and smiled.

"You picked out a nice spot," she said, and joined me on the bench. "Robbie always loved New York. I can see why."

I nodded. "But you have it pretty nice in California, too."

She sighed. "Always in bloom, like a Disney movie. I don't know if I can ever go back there."

I regarded her.

"Like I was saying to you last night," she continued, "I miss Robbie too much. Everything in L.A. reminds me of him. But that's not what you want to talk to me about."

"Well, actually, I do—a little about Robert, anyway. Would that be okay?"

She looked at me. Her eyes were skies without clouds. No doubts at all. "Sure."

"How well did you know Amy Berman?"

Her expression saddened. "She was one of Robbie's favorites. I'll never forgive what Briskman did to her." She shook her head. "And now she's gone."

"Briskman? As in Professor Terry?"

Rhonda nodded. "I'm sorry—I didn't mean to just blurt that out. Robbie didn't like to talk about it. But that man screwed her—pardon my French—both ways."

"Meaning . . ."

"He seduced her—bedded her—on the promise that he would get her into his program in Scotland. And then the committee turned her down."

"As a graduate student?"

"Yeah. Ph.D. She was crushed. Robbie was so upset. He took the well-being of his students very much to heart."

"Yet Robert spoke highly of Briskman—he suggested that I see him in Scotland."

"Oh, as a scholar Briskman is brilliant," Rhonda said. "Robbie kept that separate from his opinion of Briskman as a human being. Look . . . let me be honest with you. One of the reasons I wanted to meet with you now is I'm worried about Briskman. Darius Morton told me yesterday that Briskman was coming to New York—to attend that hearing all of you are organizing in Washington."

"Even if Briskman is a bastard, what's there to be worried about?"

"I think he's worse than a bastard," Rhonda replied, very quietly. "I think he murdered Amy."

That stopped me for a few seconds.

"All the way from Inverness?" I finally asked.

"So he hired someone in New York to do the job—that happens all the time, doesn't it? Wouldn't be the first time for Briskman."

"He was involved in a killing before?"

Rhonda shook her head yes. "Why do you think he ran off to Scotland? How many New Yorkers do you know who love the Highlands that much? You would be bored out of your mind if you had to spend more than a year or two there."

"Tell me about the murder," I said.

"It was at UCLA, years ago, right after Robbie got promoted to full professor. I was just a kid in third grade, in La Jolla, but Robbie told me about it. Briskman was visiting then, as junior faculty. He was sleeping with any female student he could get his hands on, as per usual. One of them got upset, threatened to make trouble. She was found dead in her dorm of a heroin overdose. Robbie was sure she'd been off the stuff at least six months and—"

I heard the crunch of footsteps on the path leading to our bench. I stood up and shook the hand of the man who had joined us.

"Your ears must be burning," I said to Terry Briskman. "Rhonda was just filling me in on your distinguished career."

RHONDA RETAINED HER composure, mostly.

"You two have been in touch," she observed.

"I spoke to both of you in the past hour. I thought I'd invite both of you here, and see whose story held up best," I replied.

Briskman was a bit out of breath, having just hiked up from the Hudson. He grunted. "Hercule Poirot rides again, with *Death on the Riverside.*"

"Have a seat." I pointed to where I had been sitting. Briskman sat with a thud and another grunt. Rhonda moved away from him, to the edge of the bench. I stood between and in front of them, like a conductor leading an orchestra of two.

"So, Rhonda tells me you had Amy Berman murdered," I began, and looked at Briskman.

He snorted. "Only intellectually. What kind of monster do you take me for?"

"So you admit that you undermined her admission to your graduate program in Scotland?" I asked.

Briskman shrugged. "The truth is she wasn't that good— her mouth worked best in the sack, not the classroom. There were better candidates that year. I could have exerted some pressure to have her admitted, sure, but I declined." He shrugged again. "It's embarrassing having former lovers around as your students."

"Amazing you have any women students at all, then," Rhonda said.

Briskman smiled, and looked as if he took that as a compliment. "You had a far better reason to kill Amy Berman than I did," he said to Rhonda.

"What would that be?" I asked.

"Robert McNair and I had the same taste in students," Briskman replied. "We had a friendly rivalry going on for years."

"You're saying he slept with Amy?" I cut to the chase.

"Ridiculous," Rhonda said. "Robbie was too sick to sleep with anyone."

"Maybe this year, maybe the last few months of his life," Briskman allowed. "Maybe not."

"All right, then. Let's talk about Claudia Gonzales," I said.

"Never heard of her," Briskman said.

"She was Amy's friend, wasn't she?" Rhonda said.

"Yes, she was," I said. "And we think she murdered most of the Riverside victims, and we think we know why. But not Amy."

"Didn't I read in the paper that she was a policewoman, and was just murdered herself?" Rhonda asked.

"Yes, I'm sure you did—it's been all over the media," I replied. "And you say you never met Claudia?"

"No, I didn't say that," Rhonda replied. "I think I may have met her once, a year or so ago, when Robbie and I came to New York. We went out to dinner with Amy and a few of her friends, and I'm pretty sure Claudia was there. But who cares whether I ever met Claudia? You yourself just said that she killed most of the girls in your Riverside case. And I'm telling you *he* killed Amy Berman." She grimaced in Briskman's direction, then looked back at me. "What more do you need?"

"An explanation of how I could have killed someone in New York when I was in Scotland?" Briskman asked sarcastically.

"She thinks you hired a hit man," I said.

"What's *your* explanation?" Rhonda asked me. She was now more than a little ruffled.

"I think whoever killed Amy also killed Claudia," I replied. "And you've been in New York since right after Robert's funeral in Chicago, right?"

"What of it?" Rhonda asked, indignant. "You can't think *I* had anything to do with the deaths of those two? Why on Earth would I want to hurt them?"

"If your husband was sleeping with Amy, that would be

motive enough for you to kill her," I replied. "As for Claudia, how does this theory strike you: You somehow found out, maybe through Amy, that Claudia was strangling women in New York. It dawned on you that if you could kill Amy in the same way, the police would think she had fallen victim to the same killer. So you approached Claudia with a proposition—you would give her an alibi, murder some random victim yourself, when Claudia was away in Philadelphia. That was back in April. In return, Claudia agreed to do nothing when you later killed Amy, under cover of her Riverside stranglings. That was an easy decision for her, because it gave her the benefit of an alibi for a second strangling. Meanwhile, Robert found out what was going on, so you got him into the hospital for his cough—which probably wasn't as serious as it seemed—and you 'mercy-killed' him before the doctors realized what was actually happening. Autopsies when mercy killings are involved rarely dig too deep. And with all the memory loss, you gambled that any nurse or doctor who had seen that Robert was not in such bad shape might well forget that the next day. Or be foggy about what they had seen."

"You're the one who's a sick man," she hissed at me.

"We can have Robert's body exhumed and prove that he wasn't that ill," I said. "Oh, and back to Claudia: Just to tie up any loose ends, you killed her, too."

"I was in California all through March and April," Rhonda protested. "I can prove it."

"Maybe you can," I conceded. "But whoever strangled Chloe Josephson in April had some some pollen on her hands—from an iris or some similar bulb that usually grows in warm climates, like southern California. So maybe you hired someone to do the job—maybe that's why you're so keen on the the hired-killer idea for Professor Briskman here—and you sealed the deal in your garden, with your irises in bloom, shedding pollen on your table linen and your hair and your hands. Nature's gift to the solving of this case."

"Stupid old-lady flowers—they were Robert's favorite."

"Under the circumstances, I can well understand why you would dislike them now," I said.

She got up from the bench.

"Don't," I said. "There's nowhere to go."

She pulled a gun from her jacket. The drawback of meeting here in the park. But she never would have agreed to come to my office. I was wearing a bulletproof vest. But of course, that wouldn't protect my head. It ran through my mind that no memories or life—mine or bacterial—would likely survive bullets in the brain.

She pointed the weapon at Briskman. I had arranged for him to be fitted with a vest as well. But I couldn't be sure that he actually had his on. And there was also his unprotected head—

"Tell him," she screamed at Briskman. "Tell him about all of your talk about 'you and me and the heather forever.' " She turned to me. "This was all his plan. 'Get rid of Amy, get rid of Robbie, come live with me in Scotland' . . ." She turned back to Briskman, and shoved the gun in his stomach. "Tell him!—"

I couldn't wait any longer. I gave the signal.

Perez and three other officers came out of the bushes.

"Drop it!" Perez shouted to Rhonda. "Drop it!"

She wavered for a second.

"Please," I pleaded. "Put the gun down."

Her eyes darkened.

Her arm shook.

She put down the gun.

Perez cuffed her, read her rights to her, and took her away.

BRISKMAN EXHALED LOUDLY, leaned back on the bench, and slapped his stomach. I could tell from the sound that his vest was on. "Good idea, this vest," he confirmed, and slapped his stomach again.

"Yeah," I said, and patted my own midsection.

"You took your time calling in the cavalry, though—you told me they'd be just a few feet away for the whole interview with Rhonda."

"They were," I replied. "But I wanted to let the discussion go on as long as possible. Lots of truth can emerge in those last high-tension moments."

Briskman looked at me. "You put on a pretty good show. Almost had me convinced that you thought I *was* a suspect." He laughed.

"I'm convinced that if I had a daughter who was interested in Lindisfarne, the last place I would send her to study would be with you," I said.

Briskman guffawed. "You're really something, Phil."

I smiled thinly. "Let's talk about your testimony in Washington next week. In the long run, what happens then will be much more important than the Riverside stranglings."

TWENTY-TWO

We all took the train down to Washington the following week for our hearing with the FDA. It was Morton's preferred mode of travel. It was becoming mine. Jerry Divone loved it, of course. Briskman grumbled that our trains still were not as comfortable as BritRail's, but he agreed that they beat planes and cars, especially when the trip was New York to Washington.

Laurie Feldman's quiet investigation had made me thoroughly comfortable with Jerry: There was no record whatsoever of any connection between him and Claudia. Meanwhile, our colleagues in California had confirmed the worst about McNair; his mercy killing apparently had no mercy.

His exhumed body had shown no evidence of lung cancer on the verge of ending his life. Rhonda had now completely progressed from protesting her innocence to claiming Briskman had put her up to killing McNair in L.A., and Chloe, Amy, and Claudia in New York. She said she'd worked around Santucci, McNair's physician, and had paid off some orderly to administer the fatal dose. LAPD was looking for the orderly. Santucci was out of town, and due for questioning when he returned.

But there were no phone records, e-mails, or any other kind of evidence that demonstrated a relationship between Rhonda and Briskman during the past six months. Rhonda said

Briskman had insisted that she contact him only by plunking quarters into public phones, so there would be no record of their communications. We called the phone company in California, but they said it could take weeks or longer to track down those kinds of calls—if they could be tracked down at all.

Our train glided into Union Station in Washington about ten minutes early—a fleet two hours and twenty minutes from New York. Andy met us on the front steps, and ushered us into a waiting cab. "Mayflower Hotel," he told the driver.

We had gone over the details in half a dozen recent conference calls. Jessica Samotin—the "cute," brilliant microbiologist from Pittsburgh—would be joining Andy and the four of us from New York at the meeting. In the end, she was the only outsider we—mainly Darius—had been able to rally. Two others had begged off at the last minute, pleading family emergencies and poor health. We understood these to mean understandable fear of being publicly involved in "flake" science.

"They often hold public meetings in Washington hotels," Andy explained about the FDA's choice of venue, "because their offices in Rockville are a bit out of town." This recap was mostly for Jerry, who had missed some of the conference calls.

"But our meeting's private," Jerry said.

"Right," Andy said. "And that worries me—a little. They said they had no room in Rockville for such a last-minute hearing."

"But you don't believe them?" Jerry prompted.

Andy shook his head. "I don't know. Maybe they want as few people as possible from the FDA to know about our meeting, in case they want to minimize its importance—or pretend it never happened."

"Can they really do that?" I asked.

"I don't think so," Andy replied. "I've never heard of anything like that. But then again, if they ever pulled that kind of thing, I wouldn't know about it, would I?"

Briskman chuckled. "This memory-lapse business has got us all a little jumpy, hasn't it?"

"It's nothing new to history," Darius advised. "We're always struggling to find evidence of things of which there are no surviving records. The silver lining, when you're dealing with deliberate attempts to conceal or obliterate, is that there are usually records of the obliteration, if you know where to look."

Our cab arrived at the Mayflower.

"I got it," I said, and reached for my wallet, though the Washington practice of charging extra per passenger made the fare seem high even by New York standards. Didn't matter—the NYPD was paying for all of this. Apprehending Rhonda had given me a honeymoon with the Department and a vacation from its usual penny-pinching. And Dugan still had an interest in getting to the bottom of the memory loss—or at least doing something to prevent its resurgence and spread.

Jessica was waiting for us in the lobby. "Darius!" she said joyfully, and flung her arms around him.

He took in every bit of it, and then made introductions.

She was attractive indeed—long dark hair, slightly almond eyes, and a captivating smile. I hoped Darius was also right about her mastery of the field and her persuasiveness as a scientist. Judging by Andy's anxiety, we would need every drop of her talent and mind at our meeting. She had been good on the phone, but sitting across a table from a tribunal of government doctors could be intimidating.

We were about forty minutes early for the hearing. We sat in a corner of the hotel cafe and ordered coffees, teas, and sodas.

"We'll be meeting right down the hall," Andy said, "in a room on the far left side of the corridor."

"Do you know yet exactly who will be there?" I asked.

"Cal Jenkins, for sure," Andy replied. "He's the one who

suffered the memory loss. He's a toxicologist, Ph.D. That means at least one of the others, maybe both, will be M.D.s. The FDA usually tries to balance Ph.D.s and M.D.s at these kinds of hearings. At least one will also be an epidemiologist."

"I thought they usually field ten to fifteen of their people at these meetings," Darius spoke up.

"My information is there'll just be three—this isn't their normal kind of meeting," Andy replied. "It's . . . I don't know, half fact-finding, half emergency, half just courtesy to Jenkins, as I've explained to Phil. But I think we have a real chance."

"Too bad about that third half," Jessica observed.

"Like three hands clapping, eh?" Briskman said.

"That's a lot better than nothing," I said.

Jerry nodded. "And look at the bright side. At least we won't be outnumbered by the fifteen."

Andy agreed. "And the FDA has some good people— they're by no means all likely to be hostile to our agenda."

The caffeines and ginger ale arrived.

"Milk?" Briskman asked Jessica about her tea.

"Yes please, thank you," she replied.

He made a show of slowly pouring a large drop in her cup.

Andy reached into his old-fashioned cowhide briefcase, and pulled out large sheaves for each of us. "The FDA already has these," he explained. "They're summaries of all the memory losses that seem bona fide, and not just 'The dog ate my homework.' "

"Has that been a problem with this?" Darius asked. "People using Omnin as an excuse for not getting things done?" He sipped his ginger ale. "Too many stimulants at my age are no good," he added, confidentially, to no one in particular.

"Human nature," Andy replied about the bogus reports. "People are always forgetting to do things—easy to blame it on an antibiotic that makes you lose your memory."

"I showed up for a signing of one of my books last week,

and the bookstore had no books!" Jessica said. "The store manager flat-out forgot to place the order!"

"Oh, you have to call at least two weeks in advance, and
always check with these bookstores," Darius said. "That kind of
foolishness has been around since the invention of the bookstore, I'm sure!"

"What's the name of your book?" Briskman asked.

"*Common Colds and Destiny,*" Jessica replied. "It's in the tradition of *Disease and History, Plagues and Peoples,* that sort of
thing. Except rather than arguing how deadly epidemics crip-
pled whole armies and wiped out civilizations, I focus on how
minor incapacities caused by colds—headaches, tiredness, not
being your best in interpersonal encounters—can make a deci-
sive difference in the lives of individuals. You know, a child not
doing well on an important exam, someone striking out at a big
interview, even a candidate for political office looking bad in a
televised debate."

"Fascinating," Briskman and I both said at the same time.

"Thank you."

"It's good you're here," I said.

She smiled.

"Maybe the clerk at the bookstore had a cold, and that's why
he—or she—forgot to place your order," Jerry said, also smiling.

"Proves both points," Andy said. "Head colds likely do
cause a little forgetting. And they also make great excuses."

I leafed through the stapled pages. "It's an impressive col-
lection, even limited to just the bona fide cases," I said.

"Yes and no," Andy replied. "We've got some good examples in there, all right, but other than indirect situations like the
role of memory loss in your Riverside stranglings, not enough
deaths."

The story of my life—or at least my professional life, I
thought. Only in my line of work could "not enough deaths" be
a problem, not enough of the best kind of evidence. . . .

Briskman stroked his teacup, then lifted it in a toast. "Here's to more deaths, then—or whatever it takes to lick this memory bug." And he laughed.

WE TROOPED DOWN the corridor to the room on the far left side about thirty minutes later.

"They'll be inside already," Andy advised. Presumably, the three FDA staff had crept in on little cat's feet through a back entrance somewhere. There certainly had been no sign of them in the Mayflower cafe.

Jerry opened the door.

The first thing we noticed was that five people, not three, were seated on one side of a long wooden table.

Then: "I don't see Cal," Andy said in my ear.

Jerry heard. "Maybe he forgot about the meeting," he cracked.

Briskman heard, too. "Are you sure we're in the right room?"

"Andy Weinberg?" A man in the center of the five stood up, walked around the table, and ushered us to seats opposite the the four still seated. "I'm Jim Rush. Why don't we go around the table and briefly introduce ourselves?"

"What happened to Cal Jenkins?" Andy asked.

"He's been ill the past few days," Rush replied. "Everyone agreed that he would do best to take the rest of the week off. Bad timing for this meeting, I know, but sometimes it happens."

Andy nodded, not happily.

"So," Rush continued. "I'm Jim Rush, as I said. I'm an M.D., with a specialty in narcotics, and I'll be chairing this meeting in Dr. Jenkins' stead."

"I'm Karen Quintano," the woman to Rush's left said, "also an M.D., and Dr. Rush's assistant." She was about half his age. Rush looked about fifty.

"Gregory Pelan," the big, bearded man to Quintano's left

offered, in a basso profundo voice. "I'm a Ph.D.—late of Vanderbilt University and its psychology department. I was professor and chair of the department there, but I decided to go where the action is." He smiled. "My specialty's memory. I was known as 'Dr. Memory' at Vanderbilt—wasn't there a deejay by that name?"

"I think so, yes," I said. I wasn't really sure of that, but I said yes anyway. *Do what you can to get them on your side. . . .*

"Ralph Lefcourt," the smaller man on Rush's right said. "Ph.D. and M.D. Epidemiology."

"Catherine Shayes," the woman to his right said. She was the only person on the FDA side of the table in a suit. "I'm staff with the House Committee on Science, Space, and Technology."

"We hope it's okay with you that Dr. Shayes is here," Rush said. "We work closely with quite a few congressional committees."

"Sure it's okay," Andy said. "Part of the reason for this meeting is to get the word out on Omnin."

"I'm just here as an observer," Shayes said. "I won't be making any decisions."

"Well, none of us will really be making any decisions," Rush said. "This is strictly a fact-finding meeting, and our task will be advisory."

I nodded. Andy had gone over this part of the process with me in detail. Rush was downplaying his importance. Others in the FDA might well be part of any decision, but the advice that came out of this meeting would likely be the single most significant factor.

"Okay," Rush said to us, and cleared his throat. "Why don't you briefly introduce yourselves, for the record, and we can get started."

Andy began the bio briefs. I took it as a good thing that I was the least qualified of our group to be here, with the exception of Jerry. And he had come along for another reason.

"Thank you," Rush graciously said, when our side had concluded. "Well, we've looked through the case histories you provided, and I must say they do look impressive." Copies of Andy's report were now on top of everyone's pile of papers. "Anything more you would care to add?"

"Not much more in terms of case histories," Andy replied, "but we do have some important broader—societal—concerns we'd like to call to your attention."

"Could we stick with case histories for now?" Rush asked.

Andy nodded slowly. "Okay."

Rush continued: "As I said, they're impressive—one hundred seventeen people with odd memory losses, some leading to serious personal embarrassment, others to significant business setbacks, all apparently happening in the aftermath of ingestion of Omnin. We all take that very seriously."

Everyone on his side assented.

"And we think it not unreasonable to suspect, therefore, that Omnin was the cause."

"That's good," Andy said, warily.

"But we have to weigh the setbacks suffered by one hundred seventeen people against the enormous benefits of Omnin to millions," Rush said.

Ah, here it was.

"But surely you recognize that if we have one hundred seventeen cases compiled at this point, that means there are many, many more out there," Andy objected.

"How many more?" Rush asked. "Ten times? A hundred times? Still doesn't compare to the millions who are helped by Omnin."

"You're saying millions of people have already taken Omnin?" Andy asked. "Our understanding was that the numbers are much lower."

"I'm saying millions will benefit when Omnin is mass-marketed this fall," Rush replied.

"That's exactly the problem—that's exactly what we want to stop," I said.

"We understand that, Dr. D'Amato," Rush said. "But you can surely understand that we must take the health interests of all Americans into account. As Dr. Weinberg I'm sure will confirm, the numbers of people who die of pneumonia and other complications from influenza are unfortunately far greater than ten or even a hundred times one hundred seventeen— even in this day and age, they're still knocking on a hundred thousand a year."

"These are still early days for Omnin and its ill effects," I said.

"Cal Jenkins thought this was worth looking into," Andy added. "Perhaps because he experienced the effects of Omnin firsthand. Dr. D'Amato has, as well. Sometimes you've got to go beyond statistics, and look carefully at personal testimony on a case-by-case basis."

"That's why we're here," Rush said. "And I already explained about Dr. Jenkins."

Something was odd about the way Rush reacted to the mention of Jenkins. I would have expected Rush to bristle at Andy's calling him on Jenkins, but this was something else. . . .

"Can we talk a little more about Dr. Jenkins' absence?" I asked. "Forgive me if this is private information, but could you describe for us more specifically the nature of Dr. Jenkins' illness?"

"That's not really relevant and, yes, it is private—" Karen Quintano, Rush's assistant, began. He stopped her with a gentle hand on her shoulder.

Rush looked around at his group, some of whom nodded.

"Cal—Dr. Jenkins—is suffering from Alzheimer's," Rush said quietly. "He apparently has been for almost a year now. He would show up to a meeting a week after it took place—a meeting which he had chaired—and have no recollection that it took place the first time. We're not sure how long he'll be able to continue working. I apologize for not telling you the whole story upfront, but we wanted to protect his privacy as much as possible. I'm sure you understand. It's a tragedy for everyone. It's very sad."

"Yes, it is," I said truthfully. It was sad indeed—not just for Jenkins, but for what it did to our bid to stop Omnin.

"So you attribute his memory loss that instigated this meeting, not to Omnin but Alzheimer's?" Andy voiced what I had been thinking.

"Yes, that would be the reasonable conclusion," Rush replied.

"But that doesn't mean Omnin wasn't responsible for all of our other cases," Andy said. I wasn't sure if anyone else at the table noticed, but there was a tone of pleading in his voice.

"No, of course not," Rush assured. "But it does show the alternative explanations we have to look at in all of these claims about Omnin. At least a few were likely due to early Alzheimer's—it's a veritable epidemic in this country."

Our side grew silent.

Gregory Pelan—"Dr. Memory"—tried to break the freeze. "Would it be appropriate now to talk about some of the larger, societal concerns that Dr. Weinberg alluded to before?"

"Yes, of course it would," Rush said encouragingly. "Please do."

Andy looked to Morton and Briskman, who were sitting to his left. I and then Jessica were on his right.

Briskman began. "Shall I offer a little historical context?" His accent sounded twice as British as it had in the cafe.

"Please," Rush said.

"My specialty's Lindisfarne, and Phoenicia, and a few other ancient and medieval realms, as you know," Briskman said. "And my study of them convinces me that many civilizations and societies have been plagued by memory loss—some to their eventual extinction."

"Could you elaborate?" Rush requested.

"The discovery of America—the New World—was clearly the most significant event in the history of Europe until then. It changed Europe. It changed the world. And yet we know now that Columbus was not the first European to get here. Certainly the Vikings were here in A.D. 1000—we have carbon-dated Norse artifacts in Newfoundland to prove this. And we're pretty sure other cultures got here as well—the Irish, very likely, and Professor Morton can tell you about the Phoenicians. And yet the world has no record of these, no memory. For that matter, there may well have also been contact from the other side—voyages to America from the Far East. But again, no records, no memory. In other words: We have the greatest case of memory loss right here under our noses, but we're unaware of it, precisely because no one from the affected times remembered or wrote it down."

"Or maybe it just didn't happen," Rush's assistant said.

"But we know it did happen—carbon-corroborated—with the Vikings and Leif Eriksson," Briskman countered. "It's the same Atlantic Ocean—stretches the same distance from Europe—for as long as there have been people living in Europe. And the seafaring prowess needed to make the trip was achieved by more than one civilization. How many made the trip and forgot? That's what's at stake here. A similar amnesia could happen to us."

"But what could Omnin possibly have had to do with ancient and medieval amnesias?" Pelan asked. "Assuming, just for the sake of this argument, that some did occur."

"Not Omnin, but other antibiotics," Briskman replied. "The monks had them at Lindisfarne—we know this for a fact, from their manuscripts. The antibiotic property of decayed hyssop leaves—which translates into molds—was known in the ancient world. It's in the Old Testament. And we have plenty growing all over America—especially on the East and West Coasts. California's crazy with mushrooms and molds and spores. Westchester County, especially along the Hudson, is one of the mold capitals of the world. I'm saying these ancient voyagers breathed in those spores, which wiped cleaned their memories. Or at the very least impaired them."

I had heard most of this from Briskman before, but was impressed by the sweep and passion of his argument.

Alas, I was among the already converted.

"Yes, yes, but that's hardly proof, Professor Briskman," Pelan responded. "As Dr. Rush was saying, surely we can't call back an antibiotic that could save hundreds of thousands of lives, save millions more from some of the discomforting complications of influenza, just on the basis of historical speculation—however exciting and even plausible."

"As I said, I believe our whole civilization could be compromised, or worse." Briskman stood his ground. "You gentlemen—and ladies—really want to risk that?"

"The truth is, we're not empowered or even permitted to speak for civilizations," Rush said, in a peculiarly resigned tone of voice. "Civilization is a bit beyond our mandate."

"What isn't, then?" I couldn't help asking, with more derision than intended.

"People, Dr. D'Amato," Rush answered. "Individual people, populations. Americans first, others by extension. Our mandate is their health; in a way, just as their safety is with you, Dr. D'Amato—you work to protect people, not civilization, am I right?"

I started to reply that it was more complicated than that—you can't draw a neat line between people and civilization—but Ralph Lefcourt started to speak. His voice was thin, almost quavering. Something about it made me want to hear what he had to say.

"You know, one of my professors once told me that it's helpful sometimes to assume a position or a theory you're examining is correct—accept its premises—and try to understand it on that basis," he said. "Could we do that with this?"

"Of course, fine with us," Andy said, without much enthusiasm.

Rush's side of the table looked with courteous attentiveness at Lefcourt. "Well, let's assume, then, that Omnin is really having this effect," he said. "I'd like to comprehend a little more about what you think is going on in the brain beforehand, that Omnin could have this impact upon it. Are you saying bacteria are the source of our consciousness—what religious people call 'souls'—and Omnin going through the blood-brain barrier is killing them?"

Jessica and I started responding. I deferred to Jessica.

"No, not really," she said. "Our hypothesis differs from what you described on several significant points."

"Could you tell us which ones?" Lefcourt invited.

"Well, first, no one really thinks that we're dealing with literal bacteria in the brain—" Jessica began.

" 'Literal' bacteria?" Rush's assistant, Karen Quintano, asked.

"I think Dr. Samotin is saying that whatever her team hypothesizes is giving rise to our consciousness, it's some organism in the brain, but not necessarily bacteria, is that right?" Lefcourt attempted to clarify.

"Right—I'm not even sure I would call it an organism, but certainly not a bacterium," Jessica replied. "Or not bacteria as they are currently known."

"Not bacteria," Lefcourt repeated. "Because, if what you were talking about was a bacterium, we would have spotted it in any number of autopsied brains already—such as the unfortunate fellow's brain in Australia, mentioned in Dr. Weinberg's report."

"Correct," Jessica said.

"But then, doesn't this pose a problem for your Omnin hypothesis?" Lefcourt asked. "As far we know, antibiotics kill bacteria—not other organisms. Omnin was designed to short-circuit the communication of a wide range of bacteria—as you know—not information that might be conveyed among other microorganisms. Certainly not viruses."

"Yes, we know that antibiotics hurt bacteria, not viruses," Jessica acknowledged. "But we don't know anything about the effect of antibiotics on other possible forms—quasi-organisms, proto-organisms, semiautonomous parts of organisms that could be in our brain, and enable us to think. One of those could be sending out streams of molecules, signals to the hippocampus, that help us remember."

"But why would Omnin, an antibacterial agent, have any effect on that?" Quintano interjected.

"There's of lot of redundancy in nature," I answered. "A submicrobial form might well use a communications system similar to the bacterial modes targeted by Omnin."

Jessica nodded and looked at Lefcourt. "You yourself just described Omnin as 'wide-range' in its attack. All we're suggesting you consider is the possibility that the range includes some quasi-organism that communicates on a molecular level in a manner similar to conventional bacteria."

Well, Darius was certainly right about her intelligence, too, I thought.

" 'Quasi-,' 'proto-,' 'semiautonomous'? Those are very interesting words, Dr. Samotin, with all kinds of implications, and Dr. Quintano is now, no doubt, about to ask you what they mean," Lefcourt said with a smile. "So let me beat her to it."

One side of the table laughed, not ours.

"The current thinking about mad-cow disease is that it is caused by some kind of peculiar protein in the brain," Jessica replied. "It's not a virus—not even semialive in the sense that viruses may be. But it seems to disrupt the proper operation of other proteins, and it reproduces to the point where it begins to outnumber healthy proteins."

"You're talking about prions," Lefcourt said.

"Yes," Jessica said. "They're definitely not bacteria. And they don't reproduce the way viruses do—they don't co-opt the machinery of other cells. But they have some way of . . . well, processing information, maybe other than through genetic structures. And the result of this apparently hurts the brain, in some cases."

"But we've identified prions, and they do seem to scramble, not help, brain activity in mad-cow disease, as you said," Lefcourt observed. "Are you saying prions also give us consciousness, and are impaired in their function by Omnin?"

"No, I'm using prions as an analogy," Jessica replied. "I'm suggesting that just as prions were unknown until just a few years ago, so could there also be other prionlike quasi-organisms—I think I like that word best—in the brain, that we don't know about, which enable us to think. But let me be more clear about that: I'm not saying these symbiotic, beneficial prions are conscious in themselves. I'm not saying some quasi-organism colonized our brains eons ago, and what we take to be *our* thoughts, *our* self-awareness, is really theirs. I'm suggesting, instead, that perhaps they transmit information back and forth, in some way—just like quorum-sensing bacteria—and these transmissions form an underlying network—a grid, even an Internet of the brain, within the brain, if you will—and our consciousness, including memory, exists on top of that matrix. In other words, the existence of this neural-molecular grid, created by the quasi-organisms, makes our consciousness possible."

"Pretty tall order," Lefcourt observed, "but I suppose we couldn't rule it out completely. Would neuropsychologists agree with you?"

Darius spoke for the first time. "Neuropsychologists don't really understand the physical substrate of thought. No one does—we all know that. We understand something about the concentrations of neurons in the brain, we can see how they're connected, but we don't know how we get from there to the sense of self we have—how those neurons add up, combine, augment one another, to make us human. What we are proposing is that maybe there's some quasi-living other tiny thing running around our brain. A 'symbiont,' to provide a word for what Jessica just described. We help it to live, or exist. And it runs back and forth, to and fro, from neuron to neuron, carrying infinitesimal packets of information, a million or a billion or whatever times a minute—and that's what enables us to think, to be who were are."

Lefcourt and his colleagues took that in.

"If I may make a suggestion . . ." Darius took advantage of the silence. "It seems to me that all we really need to do here is prevent Omnin from getting through the blood-brain barrier. The problem is not the effect that this superpotent antibiotic has on the rest of the body, just the brain. So why not repackage Omnin without the . . ."

"Neurolax," Jessica supplied.

"Without the Neurolax, thanks," Darius continued. "Without the component that gets it to the brain?"

"That would leave all the people afflicted with bacterial meningitis out to dry," Rush observed.

"I understand," Darius said. "But is it too hard-hearted of me to nonetheless note that the number of people afflicted with bacterial meningitis—let us expand that to include all Americans with bacterial illnesses of the brain—are surely far fewer than the millions you cited before as benefiting from

Omnin, and not as many as the numbers you cited as succumb-
ing to pneumonia?"

"Bacterial meningitis has become extremely rare in this
country," Lefcourt agreed. "The vaccines are very effective."

"That would be true, yes," Rush conceded. "But—"

"But you're still concerned about even one definite death
from bacterial meningitis which could be prevented by Omnin
with Neurolax, and rightly so," Darius interrupted. "But you
have to admit that's not the only consideration. Dr. D'Amato
can tell you at great length about how a murder investigation
was impeded, almost stymied, by the ill effects of Omnin on the
mind—that's a murder case, and surely the lives involved in that
sort of thing must count, too."

I had intended to talk about this myself, but the words
sounded better from Darius. Only someone his age could have
cut off and lectured Rush with no apparent offense.

"Well, that's what we'll need to carefully consider, Dr. Morton," Rush said mildly.

"You need to consider what the human brain gives rise to,"
Darius pressed, "because that's what Omnin endangers. All that
we hold dear and crucial to our humanity comes from our
brain. We can transplant a heart, live without a lung, survive via
dialysis with impaired kidneys. You all know that far better than
I. But the brain is unique—if it's tampered with, adjusted, compromised in the slightest, we're in peril. We can't be fully
human with anything different. What have the brains of chimps
and great apes given rise to? What works of art, literature,
poetry, what discoveries in physics? All that we are, all that we
will be, stems from healthy human brains. Now, if there's even a
small chance that Professor Samotin is right—if there is some
kind of half-living cluster of molecules running around our
brain that makes it work, makes us human—do you dare risk
hobbling that with a dose of Omnin?"

"What he's saying," Briskman added, with barely a trace of

a British accent, "is that our brain is a sacred trust. Please don't imperil it, any more than you have."

BRISKMAN, MORTON, JERRY, and I were on the train back to New York two hours later.

We got sandwiches and beer, and sat around one of the wide, comfortable tables in the cafe car.

"She's a knockout," Briskman said, in between bites of turkey with mayonnaise.

He was talking, of course, of Jessica, not either of the other two women at the FDA meeting. I hadn't heard the word "knockout" used like that in decades, and even then only in some movie from the forties.

"You sure can pick 'em," Briskman continued, and said to Darius. "Brains-wise, too. We were dead ducks until she started talking."

"Where do you think we are now?" I asked.

"I don't know," Briskman said, and shook his head. "Maybe mallards in a coma? What do you think?"

I didn't know, either. Certainly Andy hadn't been very optimistic. But he was still shaken by Cal Jenkins' Alzheimer's and absence. "I think we have a chance—the big arguments that Jessica, Darius, and you made in the end may have put the right pictures in their minds."

"I hope so," Darius said. "It all hinges on whether they can turn their backs on the picture we painted—whether they'll turn around and look a second, a third time, until they find they just can't leave it behind. They've got us beaten on the details—the numbers—and the logic. There's no denying that. More lives will be saved with Omnin fighting bacterial infections of the brain. We'll prevail only if they're willing to acknowledge what the brain does that cannot be seen under a microscope."

I looked through the window of our speeding train. The

picture outside was a blur. I looked a second, third, a fourth time. It remained the same. . . .

Darius and Briskman went back to their seats to nap. Jerry ordered something harder than beer. I declined, and went to a quieter place to make some phone calls.

WE WERE BACK in New York's Penn Station two hours later. We hailed a cab, and dropped Darius off at his apartment in the Village.

"Kennedy Airport," I then told the cabbie. Jerry and I sat on either side of Briskman. No one said anything. His luggage had been left in a locker near the Amtrak windows during our trip to Washington, and was now in the trunk of the cab.

Traffic was light, and we reached the British Airways terminal in half an hour. I paid the fare—"still on New York," I said to Briskman. Jerry took his luggage.

We stopped at the security gate.

"So, are you going to arrest me now?" Briskman asked. "That's why Jerry is here, isn't it?"

I looked at Briskman a long time. "We're not going to arrest you now," I said. "We don't have evidence."

"Well, thank you so much for the ringing endorsement," he said, unsmiling.

"You're a very bright man," I said. "You were great with the FDA, and very helpful with Rhonda. I owe you a lot on both counts. Even if I didn't, your perversities, your predilections, are your own business. We all have them. Just as long as they don't include homicide."

"Well, thank you again," Briskman said. He took his luggage from Jerry and plopped it on the security conveyor. He took keys and coins from his pockets and put them on the tray and walked through the curtains. No alarm sounded.

He retrieved his change and keys and luggage on the other

side. He turned and gave us a brief, penetrating look. Then he smiled, and strode away.

"You sure?" Jerry asked. I had indeed brought him along because I hadn't yet decided, when we'd left for Washington, what to do about Briskman. Rhonda's story had a ring of truth to it.

"No, I'm, not," I said. "But I checked with Dugan on the train, and there's nothing new in the way of evidence or leads."

"Briskman did come through for us in Washington. I guess he deserves any break we can give him," Jerry said.

"Yeah, but we draw the line at strangulation," I said. "Anyway, we've got Rhonda, she's not going anywhere. We'll look into everything she says about Briskman, and if anything pans out, we'll know where to find him."

Jerry nodded tiredly. We both knew that wasn't completely true, especially with someone on the other side of the Atlantic.

I clapped his shoulder. "It's been a long day. Andy thinks he might get an inkling of the FDA's decision as early as tomorrow. Let's get home and sleep on it."

TWENTY-THREE

 Andy reached me at my office the middle of the next day.

The news was not good.

"Can we contest this anywhere?" I asked, stunned by the news but not really surprised, stunned as by a rock in the teeth that I saw coming a mile away. "What about the courts?"

"Sure, we can take the FDA to court," Andy answered. "But our chances would be nil. No judge or jury would believe us over the FDA. The best chance we had of stopping Omnin was convincing at least some of those people at the Mayflower."

"I thought we made some headway. Some of the faces looked at the end like they might be getting it."

"Obviously not enough," Andy said. "They wanted bacteria in the hand, quasi-organisms they could see."

"How long before they get back to us officially with their decision?" I asked.

"At least a week," Andy said. "They'll want to run it through superiors. But my sources tell me that's just pro forma—no superior is likely to overrule a recommendation not to stop Omnin, not in this climate. People are worried about super-bugs that can stand up to antibiotics."

I sighed.

"Yeah," Andy agreed.

"So I've got a week, at most, to come up with something else," I said.

"Right," Andy said, "though I don't know what that could be, short of inventing some equivalent of a Hubble microscope that might uncover these things."

"Yeah. I'll be back to you."

I REALLY HAD no idea, either, what I could do to change the FDA's mind. But that had never stopped me before.

I called Jenna, Jerry, Briskman, and Morton. Only Morton was in. I was glad I had his number now.

"So I guess that irresistible picture was more in our heads than theirs, after all," he said.

"You did a fine job painting it anyway," I said.

"I've got one other possible avenue to pursue—when you get to my age, you appreciate the value of a backstreet or two in the city of noble ventures."

If only metaphors could carry the day, I thought.

ANDY CALLED AN hour later.

"You're not gonna believe this," he said.

I half laughed.

"I just had a pretty frank follow-up conversation with Rush on the phone," Andy continued. "He said one of our own team called him this morning, and advised him not to stop Omnin!"

"What?"

"Yep. Rush, of course, insists that the call didn't have much influence—that the FDA has its own objective standards. But it had to have hurt whatever chance we had. And Rush wouldn't have mentioned the call to me if it wasn't significant. He brought it up on his own—he wants us to know about it, in case we're considering taking the FDA to court, or bringing this to the media, or whatever other authority."

"Unbelievable," I said.

"Like I said," Andy responded.

"Any indication who it was?" I asked.

"Rush didn't say," Andy replied. "He may tell me later, if it suits his interests. I haven't a clue, except I know it wasn't me, and I'd jump off a bridge if it was you."

I thought I did have a clue.

"I'll be back to you soon—see if you can find out anything more," I told Andy.

I ASKED JERRY to drop by my office.

"It's either Morton, Briskman, or Jessica," Jerry said. "Assuming we both agree it wasn't you or me, and not your friend Andy playing some kind of weird double-agent game."

"Agreed."

"I know Morton the best of the three," Jerry said. "I spent a lot of time with the gent. I suppose he could have some vast reservoir of hatred in his belly—for the NYPD, the CDC in Atlanta, who knows—and he was keeping it down until this morning—Nah, I don't think so. I'd put my money on it not being Morton, either."

"Agreed as well."

"So that leaves Jessica and Briskman," Jerry said. "Obviously we know Briskman better—and what we know, we don't like. But he was great at the meeting yesterday. His line about the brain being a sacred trust was a gem. He obviously feels very strongly about stopping the dissemination of Omnin. He seems to have a lot of loyalty to Morton. Why would he suddenly turn on us—what's his motive?"

"I've been thinking about that," I said. "We may have given him a motive at the airport yesterday."

Jerry looked at me, questioningly.

"He already knew that Rhonda was implicating him in some of the Riverside stranglings," I said. "But he had to have taken at least some comfort in the fact that we hadn't arrested him, and in fact had taken him along with us to Washington. But then we had our little talk at the airport. Clearly that had to puncture whatever bubble of confidence Briskman may have had that I didn't take Rhonda seriously. Sure, we let him go— but my tone and what I said let Briskman know that we'd be keeping a close eye on him." I shook my head in self-reproach. "I always talk too much. What I said made *me* feel good. It had no effect on Briskman except to make things worse."

"But Briskman did feel deeply about Omnin," Jerry countered. "There's no doubt in my mind that he agrees with us that Omnin obliterates memories. So how does the airport scene equate to his suddenly wanting the FDA not to pull Omnin off the market? I still don't see the motive."

"I'd say his agreeing with us about Omnin is exactly the source of his motive," I replied. "(*a*) He believes Omnin mutes organisms in our brains and blots out memories. That's why he comes with us to Washington and testifies so passionately. But (*b*) he believes, after we part company at the airport yesterday, that we're seriously on to him as a co-conspirator in some of the Riverside stranglings. So (*c*) he undermines our attempt to get the FDA to stop Omnin, because the damn drug on the loose can get in the way of any future investigation of the stranglings, can jumble the minds and testimony of any future witnesses we might uncover."

"Jesus," Jerry said. "Just like we were saying to the FDA yesterday. Too bad we can't present *that* to those docs down there."

"It's supposition, still not evidence," I replied. "That's been the problem with our case against Omnin all along. It's convincing to us, because from our personal experience we already believe it. But to others . . . We're not going to be able to get evidence enough to persuade any objective party, until there's a lot more Omnin around, and then, of course, it will be too late, because everyone will be losing memories like pennies out of torn pockets."

"Everyone's goddamn *minds* will be out-of-pocket—including the minds of people like the FDA doctors, who could make a difference," Jerry said hoarsely. "Just like my daughter."

"Yeah."

"Well can we at least get the British to arrest the son of a bitch now?" Jerry asked.

I slowly shook my head no. "I don't see how. We have no evidence of anything, like I said. And even on the level of logical argument: Briskman could just claim that after hearing what the FDA had to say at our meeting, and thinking it over as any reasonable person should, he came to the conclusion he was wrong, and that Omnin should be distributed as far and wide as possible."

Jerry shuddered.

I GOT THROUGH to Jenna a little later, and brought her up-to-speed on the day's depressing developments.

"At least you and I won't take Omnin anymore," she said. "At least we'll have that."

"We'll be the memoried elite in a sea of amnesiacs," I said. "Doesn't sound like all that much fun in the long run."

"We'll have each other," Jenna said.

"I know. That's maybe the most important reason I was calling you. I was thinking we should have a really nice, quiet dinner tonight, just the two of us, soft candlelight, fine wine, cell phones off, at a table in the back of an out-of-the-way restaurant where no one can find us. How does that sound?"

"Sounds wonderful," Jenna said.

I MADE SEVERAL more rounds of calls—to people in California to see if they had found out anything more about Rhonda's alleged calls to Briskman; to Dugan to bring him up to date and see if he had any recent brilliant ideas; to Jessica for the same—all to no avail. I did confirm at Briskman's university that he was back in Scotland, but I didn't get to speak to him. I decided to make another call to Jessica, and told her to be careful.

"Why?" she asked.

I started to explain to her, without mentioning any names, that someone involved in the Riverside stranglings might still be afoot—we had talked a little in the Mayflower cafe about the murders—and since the killings and the amnesia and their investigations were to some extent all intertwined, there was an outside chance that she could be in danger.

"From whom?" she asked.

I realized there was no point in telling her to watch out, unless I told her Briskman was the person to watch out for, so I gave her his name.

Silence, then laughter. "You're joking!"

I assured her I was not, and tried to explain further—

"All right," she interrupted. "I'm going to Japan next week for a conference on bacterial biofilm formation—which may be related to quorum-sensing, come to think of it—and I expect to stay there until Christmas. I'm on sabbatical this fall. So I promise not to tell Terry I'm there if you won't, either."

"Of course, but—"

"No, seriously, I promise I'll be careful."

My only real phone satisfaction came in making a reservation for Jenna and me at a restaurant in Kips Bay, overlooking the East River.

I was packing up to leave, go home and shower, and meet Jenna at the restaurant, when the phone rang.

It was Andy.

"You're not gonna believe this—and this time you really won't," he said.

This time I just laughed, vacantly.

"Our prospects have turned, again—this time for the better," he said.

"Really?"

"I just got off the phone with Rush, and then with Morton—that guy is really something, isn't he?"

I hadn't thought much about Darius since our brief chat earlier. "Yes he is. Was he able to pull something out of a hat for us?"

"To say the least," Andy replied. "He didn't want to say much to me on the phone—I hope he's not angry that you gave me his number along with Briskman's and Jessica's, before Washington. I think I surprised him on the phone. He made it clear he doesn't want to talk about this. But what he told me is amazing."

"He said something to me about using back streets when your main avenues are blocked," I said.

"He used a sewer," Andy said. "But I guess the ends justify the means in this case. You know that one of his students is a millionaire—in the diamond trade?"

"Yeah, I didn't know it was diamonds, but Darius told me in Chicago about his wealthy former student—he flew him in a private plane to and from the funeral."

"Well, Morton spoke to him earlier today about our problem with the FDA. And this guy is apparently a big contributor to congressional campaigns—huge amounts of soft money, or whatever they call it."

"Okay . . ."

"And apparently we lucked out, because one of his beneficiaries sits on that very same House Science Committee that Catherine Shayes works for. So Morton's student puts him, Darius, in touch with this congressman, and they got Shayes on the phone in a conference call, and Darius talked his heart out, as he did at our meeting—except this time, Shayes expressed herself as convinced and called Rush and threatened a major congressional investigation if the FDA didn't at least put a temporary halt on Omnin. Which is what Rush just told me they're doing. And when I asked him why, all he said was, 'Talk to Shayes and Morton.' "

I was practically speechless. "Shayes didn't say a word at our meeting."

"Well, she apparently said plenty today. You understand, of course, that Morton's eloquence was far less likely to be what convinced Shayes and the congressman than the implicit threat that his student would withdraw his millions from the next campaign. That's the way lots of things work in Washington."

"The FDA wouldn't have crumbled so quickly if they didn't think that our arguments had some validity—some merit that a congressional investigation might uncover," I said. "If Rush and company are afraid of being embarrassed, it's because they think there might be something real for them to be embarrassed about. They know the numbers on Alzheimer's—they know there's no way all of our memory-loss cases could be due to that."

"I guess so," Andy said, only partly convinced.

I sighed. "It would be nice if these matters could be decided just by reason and evidence. But as I was saying to Jerry earlier, we were really short on both in this case—or at least, short on any that the FDA seemed willing to entertain, until now."

"The truth is that they're never completely immune from politics and personal factors anyway," Andy said, more supportively. "No person or agency is. It's just a question of which way those factors cut. Cal Jenkins' personal tragedy hurt our cause yesterday."

"That's right."

"And it's not as if the FDA is banning Omnin forever," Andy continued. "All they're doing is revamping and repackaging, so Omnin can be distributed without the Neurolax—which will keep it out of the brain. Rush said they'll be sending out a press release about this early next week."

"Make sure we see a copy first."

"Taken care of already," Andy responded. "Rush said they'll want to keep this low-key—they don't to sour the public on Omnin, just keep it away from the brain."

"It'll probably be front-page news anyway," I said.

"Yeah."

"So that leaves us with just the fatalities from bacterial meningitis on our conscience," I said softly.

"I checked the figures on that," Andy said. "They're around a thousand a year. Very small, statistically. And they're diminishing anyway, with the vaccines. But, right, we can't feel good about those deaths."

"No," I agreed. "But I think we can feel good, on balance, that we stopped the flood of Omnin to the brain. As far as I can tell, I seem to have my full suite of memories back now—I've felt different, revitalized mentally, these past few days—as if the quasi-living colony of whatever it is in my head is now back up to strength. I spoke with Dugan earlier, and he said the same. Jenna too. With our memories intact, we can continue to combat destructive infections of the brain, we can work to improve the vaccines. We can keep searching for the physical substrates of thought, memory. But with our memories under siege, everything's at risk. Darius—and Briskman—were right. When Omnin plays with our minds, it plays with our humanity."

THE SPAGHETTI PIRATA—another version of my favorite shellfish marinara—was superb. Jenna enjoyed hers, too. We sipped pinot grigio, then cappuccino.

"This was a great idea," Jenna said. Her gaze touched mine in the candlelight.

"I thought of it this morning," I said. "It kept me going through the roller coaster."

"At least that's settling down now," she said.

"More like we avoided derailing, or going over a cliff. But

there are lots of bumps ahead. Omnin with Neurolax will be withdrawn and recalled. We'll probably see public-service announcements on TV, telling people to throw it out, or maybe keep it until the new version is available, and trade it in. But some people won't do that. They'll keep the old pills, if they have any left, in the medicine cabinet, just in case. And who knows what danger other drugs now in development might hold. The FDA looks at antibiotics as essential weapons in the war against disease, and they're not wrong. Bacteria make us sick, and their toxins interfere with all kinds of communication in the body. But until the government and the pharmaceuticals understand that cousins to the things that cause disease can help us—do help us, in the case of digestion; maybe help make us human, in the case of what we have in our brains—we won't be out of the woods on this."

Jenna took my hand.

"I know," I said. "This isn't exactly scintillating dinner conversation, and I've been talking about it all evening. Let's talk about something else."

"No, it's important," Jenna said. "We should be talking about it. Maybe the FDA will at least be more careful before they bundle every new antibiotic with Neurolax."

I nodded. "So . . . do you remember what we almost forgot when we first ran into Neurolax and Omnin?"

She smiled. "You didn't forget. I did."

"So, do you want to do it now?"

"Of course I do. You were just so busy with this case—and the Riverside stuff. We still need to decide how big to make the wedding, when in the spring—"

"No, I mean, do you want to do it now?"

"You mean, get married, now?"

I nodded.

Jenna laughed. "*Now?*"

"Now."

"But we won't have time to invite anyone."

"We don't need anyone—other than you and me," I said.

"You're serious," Jenna said.

I nodded again.

She sipped some wine.

"Where would we do it? Who—"

"I know a couple of judges who owe me," I said. "I'm sure one of them would be happy to perform the ceremony."

"What about our blood tests, marriage license—"

"I pulled some strings. I promised that we'd drop by tomorrow, to make this paper that says we passed the blood tests today legal. And I've got our marriage license right here." I patted my vest pocket.

Jenna smiled. "Okay."

"Yeah?"

"Yeah," she said. "But you're still forgetting something."

"Very funny."

She laughed. "No, I mean the rings."

"I didn't forget," I said, and pulled a little box out of my jacket pocket. I opened it.

"When—" Jenna said.

"This morning. I told you I've been thinking about this all day."

"How about your best man? My bridesmaid?"

"We'll have to make do with Mr. and Mrs. Dugan—if you want to go that way," I said.

Jenna considered. "No, you were right—let's go with just you and me."

"Good."

I got the check, and pulled out my cell phone. I got lucky. The first judge I called was in, willing, and just twelve blocks away.

"So let's do this before we both forget," I said, and shut the cell phone off. I left a thirty-percent tip on the credit-card receipt.

"If I never hear another joke about forgetting, it won't be too much," Jenna said, and took my arm.

WE STAYED OUT—dancing, drinking, mostly walking along the East Side by the river—for most of the night after we were married.

I was glad we were on the East Side. I wouldn't have enjoyed walking on the West Side as much, by Riverside Drive.

We were back in our brownstone at five in the morning, the D'Amatos—I could still hear the judge wish us well—though Jenna was going to keep her name.

I took off my jacket, and unzipped Jenna's dress.

Then the phone rang.

"Is that a death do parting us?" Jenna asked, and laughed, a little.

I stroked her face. "The machine can get it. There are some things more important than murder, even to me."

There *were* some things more important than my work.

At least until morning.